THE
BUCKET
LIST

THE
BUCKET
LIST

A NOVEL

GEORGIA CLARK

EMILY BESTLER BOOKS
—
ATRIA
New York   London   Toronto   Sydney   New Delhi

EMILY BESTLER BOOKS

ATRIA

An Imprint of Simon & Schuster, Inc.
1230 Avenue of the Americas
New York, NY 10020

First Emily Bestler Books/Atria Books hardcover edition August 2018

EMILY BESTLER BOOKS / ATRIA BOOKS and colophon are trademarks of Simon & Schuster, Inc.

For information about special discounts for bulk purchases, please contact Simon & Schuster Special Sales at 1-866-506-1949 or business@simonandschuster.com.

The Simon & Schuster Speakers Bureau can bring authors to your live event. For more information or to book an event, contact the Simon & Schuster Speakers Bureau at 1-866-248-3049 or visit our website at www.simonspeakers.com.

Interior design by Silverglass Design

Manufactured in the United States of America

10 9 8 7 6 5 4 3 2

Library of Congress Cataloging-in-Publication Data

Names: Clark, Georgia, author.
Title: The bucket list / by Georgia Clark.

Description: First Emily Bestler Books/Atria Books hardcover edition. | New York : Emily Bestler Books/Atria, 2018.
Identifiers: LCCN 2017053609 (print) | LCCN 2017057310 (ebook) | ISBN 9781501173042 (Ebook) | ISBN 9781501173028 (hardcover) | ISBN 9781501173035 (trade paperback)
Subjects: LCSH: Young women—New York (State)—New York—Fiction. | Self-realization in women—Fiction. | BISAC: FICTION / Contemporary Women. | FICTION / Literary. | FICTION / Coming of Age. | GSAFD: Bildungsromans.
Classification: LCC PS3603.L3636 (ebook) | LCC PS3603.L3636 B83 2018 (print) | DDC 813/.6—dc23
LC record available at https://lccn.loc.gov/2017053609

ISBN 978-1-5011-7302-8
ISBN 978-1-5011-7304-2 (ebook)

For Nicki-Pee
on the m-i-c

Part One

1.

January

'm having a bad nipple day. This morning a new bra smoothed my little rosebuds into nonexistence. But now, midafternoon, they are clearly
visible through my top, as perky as a pair of sitcom stars. I realize this ten
minutes into our weekly all-hands meeting, when it's too late to throw
a scarf around my neck or change clothes. Instead, I slowly and surreptitiously start to hunch forward, trying to get the material of my top to stop
clinging so obviously to my chest. But my nipples refuse to be silenced.

Of course, I am aware the nipple can and should be freed. We all have
them; why deny it? An argument of *distraction* is clearly victim blaming,
while *propriety* feels revoltingly Victorian. But, I am not a ding-dong. I was
alerted as to what was happening with my boobs via a brief but devastating
frown from one of the company's most influential fashion editors, Eloise
Cunningham-Bell. Her look of distaste was all the information I needed:
nipples are not welcome at Hoffman House. Everyone knows I've been
coveting a job on Eloise's team since I was an intern. And so everyone
could guess who is in charge of my nipples. Not I, my friends. Not I.

As a member of senior staff, Eloise has joined those sitting around a
table the size of a beach. The company's quite literal inner circle. I've
joined the ones lining the walls. To an untrained eye, we wall liners
appear impeccably styled and socially relevant. But the truth is, we are
junior sales. Bottom-feeders.

Collectively the inner-circle editors look like a casting call for "diverse Brooklyn fun person." Their expertise ranges from youth culture
to city and lifestyle to menswear to interiors. They're always jetting off to
or coming back from London or Milan, Tokyo or Berlin. I've just gotten

back from the café downstairs, where a rather sad kale salad and I had a brief and underwhelming winter fling.

Senior staff talk. Junior staff listen. I continue to hunch.

The meeting lasts about an hour. When it comes to an end and we all rise to exit, I find myself unexpectedly in step with Eloise herself. Even now, I'm still intimidated. But I force myself to speak. "Hey." I smile, friendly as I can. "I was just wondering if you got the reports I emailed you last week?"

She glances at me, with the chilly impenetrable beauty of a Nordic queen. "I did."

I have no response planned. "Great! I'd love any tips. Or feedback. Feel free to use them—"

"I'm late," she says, striding ahead.

Feel free to use them. What a dumb thing to say. I collapse into my chair at my cubicle, resisting the urge to groan. Eloise doesn't need to use my reports. Her work is perfect. Her taste is perfect. She's probably on her way somewhere unspeakably glamorous: a private showing of a new collection, perhaps, to be viewed with a glass of champagne and inside jokes. Why do I even bother? Oh, that's right: So I can stop scraping by on commission. So I can do something creatively fulfilling, so I can travel. So I can occupy a workspace big enough to merit a door. A door of one's own: this is my Holy Grail.

I duck my head below my cubicle wall to answer my bleating phone. "This is Lacey."

"Lacey Whitman?" The man's voice has a cut of authority.

"Yes."

"This is Dr. Fitzpatrick at Midtown Medical. I'm calling because you missed your last appointment."

My four o'clock pushes open our heavy glass door, brushing snow from her coat collar. She smiles at our receptionist, making a joke I can't hear. "I'm sorry, Doctor"—his name escapes me, so I idiotically repeat— "Doctor; it's been bananas in here. 'Here' being work; I'm at work."

"When can you come in to discuss the samples we took during your Pap smear?" Doctor Doctor is insistent.

"Discuss?" Apprehension, just the suggestion of it, sniffs at my feet. I kick it away. "Can't we speak over the phone?"

"We don't give out test results over the phone, Ms. Whitman. You'll need to make an appointment. When can you come in?"

My four o'clock catches my eye and does an awkward one-finger wave. I point to the phone and mouth, *One second.* "I'm sorry, I really don't have time this week."

Later, I'll remember this afternoon as the Last Day. It wasn't the Last Day where I was free and happy and had the perfect life: show me a contented twenty-five-year-old in New York City and I'll show you a secretly unhappy liar or a deluded happy fool. No, this was the Last Day of feeling like I was in control of my future. It was the Last Day of believing that you only get a set amount of trouble. It was the Last Day of my small life.

Doctor Doctor draws a long breath. "Ms. Whitman, you tested positive for the BRCA1 gene mutation."

The words land with the concise clarity of custard hurled against a wall. I can't stop blinking. "What?"

"I've made an appointment for you with a genetic counselor tomorrow to discuss your options."

"My options? I thought we were talking about my Pap smear."

Papers shuffling. His voice is curt. "You asked about the best time frame to start mammograms. We discussed a test that could help determine that time frame. Do you remember that?"

Blood bubbling into a vial. I made a joke about vampires. "Yes."

"Do you know what this means? Do you understand the ramifications?"

I'm having trouble focusing. "But I came in for a Pap smear . . . Just a routine—a regular . . ." I run out of steam. I stare straight ahead, breathing through my nose.

"Ms. Whitman? Are you still there?"

* * * *

I take my four o'clock: the creative director for Target. There I am, in one of the small, bright conference rooms, presenting next year's fall with lunatic talk-show sincerity. "The trend for the tweed is continuing as an organic-looking base, and the demand for trouser suits isn't going anywhere." My voice sounds unnaturally loud. "Is it lounge-wear? Is it sportswear? Personally, I'm excited about shearling. I think we could see the caplet get reinvented."

I laugh too hard at my client's jokes. Leap too excitedly on her insights. I feel drunk. Drugged, dreaming, split in half. One version of me is saying my lines—or a bizarre, dadaistic performance of my lines—while another version is running around in the wings, unable to find the stage.

When the show's over, I have a missed call from Vivian. Her quick, sardonic voice plays back: "Hey babe, my flight was diverted to Newark because of the weather, so I'll be a little late. New Jersey, yay. Brush up on the latest download numbers, hopefully we can bust them out tonight."

I'd forgotten about the party. I could tell you exactly what I wore to my middle school dance, down to the color of my socks (leopard print, and you better believe they had a lacy frill), but I'd forgotten about Hoffman House's holiday party. Which is, of course, tonight.

I don't think about . . . *it*. It's not a conscious denial, it just feels like something I can outrun, and so I do. I familiarize myself with the fashion editors' new reports, skim *Women's Wear Daily*, and attempt to get on the list for a few Fashion Week parties by sending flirty emails to various publicists. Just before seven, I fish out my day-to-night makeup bag from my bottom drawer.

The gray-tiled bathroom is cool and empty. I lay out my products on the marble counter, a ritual I've always found soothing. Curling mascara, dark pink lip liner, blush . . . my hands are shaking. A wave of nausea sweeps over me. I hold my hair back over the toilet bowl, ready for my sad kale salad to make a surprise comeback. But my body refuses to be sick, settling instead for a slight tremble and overall queasiness.

Ghastly is the word my reflection inspires. My hair, which I've been carefully bleaching a silvery white-blond ever since I moved to New York three years ago, makes me look as sallow as the zombie light of a midnight subway train.

A calendar notification pops up on my phone: *7:00 p.m.: STOP WHATEVER YOU ARE DOING, get ready for party now. Not in five more minutes. NOW.*

I keep a few dresses in the coat closet for events. Tonight, I need bright armor to protect me. Romance Was Born, the electric, extroverted Australian label known for high-flash high fashion. My client at Saks gifted me the dress for Christmas (a sample, not complaining). Chiffon, floor-length, keyhole neck, quarter-length sleeves. The edge of the skirt is red and yellow fire, melting into a print of exotic bird feathers. Iridescent greens and cerulean blues give way to an almost all-white bodice. Paired with my trusty black fedora and a face full of makeup, I'll look like everyone else at a Hoffman House party.

Immortal.

2.

Patricia Hoffman has been throwing Hoffman House's holiday party in mid-January for forty-eight years. The date ensures the guest list isn't distracted by New York's holiday-party circuit in crowded December. As the invite has always read, *No excuses. Anything else goes.* For the company's fortieth anniversary, photographs from four decades of the annual event were compiled in a heavy coffee-table book, something I found in a museum gift shop on a day trip to Chicago when I was a junior in high school. In the 1970s, gap-toothed models the size of pencils ignored fat shrimp cocktails while being hit on by long-haired musicians, dreams of utopia wafting from their unwashed, open-necked shirts. In the eighties, everything got shiny or sharp: safety pins, disco balls, shoulder pads you could cut a finger on. The nineties was bleached teeth, denim everything, big hair, bodysuits. The aughts were flat-out bizarre: high-heeled Timberlands; tight, plush sweat suits, overplucked eyebrows. (The aughts were deeply embarrassing.) Apart from the fact that eyebrows are back to being bushy, this decade feels harder to pinpoint. We're still in it, after all.

It took me weeks to save up for the Hoffman House book, and it was those pictures that made me want—*need*—to land at New York's oldest and most respected trend forecaster. Hoffman House was dead center: of SoHo, of fashion, of everything Buntley, Illinois, wasn't.

As a member of the junior sales staff, I sell two things. The first is an online subscription service to reports created by the various Hoffman House editors, like my best friend Eloise. Most people working in fashion, or any industry that includes style, need to be up-to-date on current trends on a global scale, but they're usually chained to their desks and unable to keep up on their own. The online service is a daily newsletter of inspiration, analysis, and opinion: "the essentials you need to stay on the pulse of your industry." The second thing I sell are trend books. Individual publishers around the world put together seasonal books, two a year—spring/summer and fall/winter.

Big, beautiful books brought me to New York. In their pages, as in most of the city, there is no room for uncertainty.

Trend is retail's dirty little secret. You might think that Victoria's Secret or Apple or L'Oréal are coming up with their new looks and colors and trends on their own. They're not. Every big name in retail buys trend books, and thousands more subscribe to the online service. Each book costs between two and six thousand dollars, while the online service can run you up to $15K a year. I get a 15 percent commission on each book and 5 percent on the online service.

So when I splurge on a cab to take me to the party at the famous Pembly Hotel, it's because I should feel triumphant. I'm on the guest list for the event that means the most to me. But as I slam the cab door shut, I'm fighting the powerful sensation that I'm trapped and water is rushing in, and rising.

We hit gridlock. My driver swears and blasts the horn, again and again and again. We're not moving. Dr. Fitzpatrick's words echo in my head: *I've made an appointment for you with a genetic counselor tomorrow to discuss your options.* A windowless waiting room with bad landscape art and a collective feeling of dread.

Water gurgles up my calves, over the seats, almost to the meter. I'm running out of air.

A hospital bed. Machines that don't stop beeping. The sound of a man crying.

Another horn blast. Another.

"Can you stop that?" I can't help it. "We're not moving."

He mutters something under his breath. When we arrive at the hotel, the ride fifteen minutes longer than it should have taken, I almost forget to pay. I bolt out of the cab in a rush of relief, gasping for air, water spilling like a wave.

"Lacey!" The interns squeal. "You look *amazing*."

"Hi, dolls!" I air-kiss the girls manning the door, all three bursting with celeb-encounter glow. "Love everything about this," I add, circling their outfits with my fingertip: slinky slip dresses, feather crowns, oversize chunky cardigans, and even though I'm keeping a simmering panic at bay, I file away, *Kate Moss. Nineties. Making a comeback?* They giggle and gush as they take my coat, and it's hard to believe that was me, over four years ago, holding the list, intent on being on it, and here I am, and *New York Cancer Care Center*—

"Bar!" I half gasp, half shout to no one in particular. Swimming through the plucked and polished bodies, I smell weed and spicy perfume and wet fur and I'm at the bar, rapping the underlit glass, ordering a white wine in a voice that's too tight, too loud, not mine, when someone taps me on the shoulder and I whirl around. Vivian's sharp eyes are narrowed. "Hey."

The sight of Vivian Lei Chang is instantly calming. Not only because she is, as always, immaculately dressed: silk tunic, leather pants, gold geometric necklace, heeled ankle boots. And not because she is, as always, exuding the eyebrow-arched calm of *I can handle this.* It's because Vivian is part of my regular life—older, wiser, as beautiful and tough as a ninja on the bow of a ship.

"Hey." I hug her in a way that's more like a tackle, getting strands of her black hair in my mouth. *"Hi."*

She extracts herself from me. "What happened?"

The wine appears at my elbow. "Nothing." I start drinking and find myself unable to finish until I've drained the entire glass, all without losing eye contact. Even in my frazzled state, I'm aware this is super creepy. "Nothing's wrong."

"Oh-kay." Vivian's eyes move from the glass to me, to the four square feet around me, searching for clues. "You're acting very strange."

"Am I?" My laughter is maniacal. My hands flap like a loose tarp. "I saw a squirrel . . . eating a piece of pizza . . . in the snow. Snow pizza? I mean, what'll they think of next?" I'm a runaway train, out of control. I laugh some more, then abruptly stop. "How was the West Coast?"

Work is Vivian's catnip. As she recaps the meetings she was taking on our behalf (check-in with our preternaturally talented engineer,

Brock, in Silicon Valley; two investor lunches—one borderline prom-ising, one definitely sleazy), I steer us to a darkened corner, mouthing, *You look amazing* and *I'll come back* to the clients and colleagues we pass. I focus on controlling my breathing and trying to comprehend what Vivian is telling me. "We're on track," she concludes. "I'm confident." She scans the room. I stare into the middle distance with the unfocused eyes of someone receiving a message from the other side.

Is it possible to know and unknow something at the same time? Be-cause when I took the multigene panel test—an all-you-can-test genetic buffet—there was a ladybug-size part of me that knew this outcome was a possibility. Just not a probability. Definitely not a probability. I took the test the way I take an HIV test: to *confirm* a clean bill of health. Not have it blasted apart. I was more than confident. I was blasé.

"Vivian." I turn to her at the same time she says, "Tom Bacon." A man in a light blue suit who looks like a 1960s astronaut, talking to a handful of similarly bespoke dudes. "He's a partner at River Wolf."

"The venture capital fund?"

"But he's also an angel investor. He's the richest guy in this room." Vivian's gaze all but draws a bull's-eye on Tom's blond head. "He could write us a check for a quarter million right now."

"As in dollars, American dollars?"

Vivian doesn't even smile; she's so focused. "He comes on board as lead investor in the seed, River Wolf leads the Series A funding. That's a good story. That's a great story."

This is my story: I'm in this room because I'm both ambitious and careful. I'm the kind of person who gets yearly Pap smears because I thought, like money and respect, good health could be earned.

"Lace?" Viv snaps her fingers in my face. "I said, are you sure it's okay to pitch Tom here?"

I nod, trying to concentrate. "Patricia's supportive. Besides, her flight's been delayed because of the snowstorm."

The company's eponymous Patricia Hoffman—my boss—had traveled to Paris for the Coco Chanel retrospective at the Musée des Arts décoratifs that isn't traveling to the States. It's the first year she'll miss her own party.

Vivian straightens her shoulders. "Excellent."

It's only then that it hits me. We're ten feet away from the app we've been working on for eight months becoming real. I've been hedging my bets: an editor position at Hoffman House or the app. Deep down, I always thought I'd land an editor position first. I'm wrong. This is the moment that Clean Clothes, the app Vivian is certain will buy us both a mansion in the Hamptons, could become a real company.

Shit.

Viv flicks me a smile. "Ready?"

No, no way, not now, please not now. "Born ready."

It feels like agreeing to a round of Russian roulette.

Watching Vivian approach a circle she wants to break into is a master class in networking. It's all about that first smile: confident and warm without being flirtatious or coy. Vivian uses her sex appeal more like a man than a woman. Never a trump card or a desperate bet, rather something coolly innate. Besides the point, yet undeniable. We slip into their circle especially easily, as Tom recognizes Vivian because Vivian knows everyone. "Vivian Chang. When was the last time we—"

"Demo Day at YC, two years ago. You wrote a check for my friend Birdie's black hair care company."

"That's right." Tom nods. "Which was a very wise move."

"And you'll never have to buy your own shea butter ever again."

The men chuckle. Tom addresses them. "Vivian was early at Snapp, that start-up Pinterest acquired a few years back."

Vivian tilts her head, graciously accepting the implicit praise. Being early at a company—part of the team in the first year—gets you almost as much cred as if it was your idea. She gestures at me. "Guys, this is Lacey Whitman, a trend and sales associate here at Hoffman House, and on the founding team of my new company."

"Your first company," Tom clarifies.

"My first company," Vivian says.

Tom turns a piercing gaze onto me. "Fantastic." He pumps my hand, introducing us to the others, the names of whom instantly disappear from my muddy brain. Except for one. The last man. Elan Behzadi. Equally famous for being a talented fashion designer and a moody prick, in the way only men can get away with. He's Iranian, I think, medium build, with light stubble and dark eyes. His gaze is cool, unimpressed, and I'm starstruck and annoyed at the same time. I am out of my depth, and the water is rising.

". . . Millennials and Generation Z are increasingly looking for fair trade when it comes to fashion." How is Vivian a half minute into our pitch? I didn't even hear her start. "Outfits that are on trend and ethically sound. They want personalized attention and authentic advice without leaving the comfort of their smartphone. Clean Clothes is here to solve that problem." Vivian looks to me. My cue to take over.

I have the mutation. I tested positive. My mouth is tacky. I have no idea what I'm meant to say.

Vivian blinks, and continues with my lines. "Consumers create a style profile, similar to Pinterest or Instagram, by snapping or saving pics they like: street style, celeb outfits, their own fresh looks. Our stylists curate a five-piece outfit exclusively from ethical companies that'll look and feel good." Vivian looks to me again, and it's this second look, quizzical, even testy, that inspires a wave of hot emotion to rush inside me.

Vivian keeps talking. "I'm sure you gentlemen know the womens wear industry alone is valued at $621 billion dollars, let alone menswear, kids wear, bridal wear. Clean Clothes is going to be a billion-dollar company by the end of this year."

The circle nods. Even I can tell it's going well. *You can fall apart later; you can fall apart later; get it together; focus.*

When Tom addresses Vivian, it's with the gravity men usually reserve for other men. "You're doing affiliate links?"

She nods. "Consumers get a five-piece outfit, curated for free, every month."

"So, they get sent the physical product?" Tom asks. "Five pieces of clothing?"

"No," Vivian says, "for now, it's just a virtual look. Users don't pay anything unless they decide to buy the pieces we curate for them, which they can do by clicking through to the online retailers we're working with. We're looking at the sort of subscription model you're thinking of after we scale."

"What are your numbers like?"

"Really promising. We've been in stealth mode since last fall and have just under five thousand downloads. Of that, eighty percent of consumers have referred a friend."

The familiar words sound like gibberish. I lock eyes with Elan. His gaze has deepened, suddenly focused entirely on me. As if he recognizes me. We've never met. Heat washes through me, an unpredictable, restless flood. My heart is getting loud in my ears.

Tom's focused on Vivian. "How are you planning to scale? Build an algorithm to match consumers with products they'll like?"

She shakes her head. "It's important we always have a human behind the scenes; that's our special sauce." Vivian turns to me with a breezy smile and *What the hell?* eyes. "Lacey will be training and overseeing the teams of stylists." And even though I can tell she's loath to continue, she says, "She has a pretty impressive superpower. Lacey can tell you exactly what you'll want to wear to any upcoming event, which is why she's such a perfect fit for Clean Clothes. Style plus intuition."

Tom Bacon, the man made of money, faces me. "All right. I'm getting married in the Hamptons in September and I have no idea what to wear. Driving Peter nuts: he's had his tux picked out since high school. Do your worst, Lacey Whitman."

Sweat has broken out over my brow. The room has turned woozy, unstable. I frown and frown again, trying to get a grip on the request, stalling by making a show of carefully scanning his current outfit. "Who . . ." I start to ask. "What kind of designers do you like?"

Tom scratches his chin. "Tom Ford: good strong name. The Brits know what they're doing. Nothing by that talentless hack Elan Behzadi."

Everyone laughs, except Elan and me. Over his shoulder, twenty feet away, I spot Eloise Cunningham-Bell. An unwelcome blast of familiarity.

She hasn't seen me. She can't see me. My heart is slamming my rib cage. I'm losing my grip. The music is too loud; my bra is too tight; my shoes pinch my feet. My hand is on my breast, pressing the soft flesh. I whip it away, alarmed. A hint of a smile tugs at Elan's lips. He knows I am unraveling and he finds it *funny.* "September." I lick my lips. "A

September wedding." A September wedding. That sounds nice. I've never thought a lot about weddings, my wedding, but now I might never get the chance, because my genes have painted a bull's-eye on my forehead. "Fireflies in mason jars, and strings of . . . of little white lights . . ." My diagnosis puts me at an insanely high risk of breast and ovarian cancer, cancers that kill women, that have killed hundreds, thousands, millions of women. Women like my— "Linen . . . Fabrics that . . . breathe . . ." But I can't breathe, because it wasn't supposed to be me, but it is me: it is me; I *will* get cancer; it's in my *goddamned DNA.* The truth seizes my throat, and I almost stumble.

"Lacey?" Vivian's voice is brusque.

"Vivienne Westwood's summer slim fit suit," I reply, a perfect answer but I've lost it. I'm done. "Excuse me." The crowd presses in on me, rendering me airless as I search in vain for the exit.

3.

"Steph's not here." The guy who answered the door gestures inside the loft. "You're welcome to wait."

Ordinarily I'd tell him of course I'm welcome to wait, and do whatever the hell else I want, because I used to live here, I'm OG. But instead I perch stiffly on the end of the old sofa. It's not as comfortable as I remember.

The boy hovers, unsure. "I'm Cooper, by the way."

"Lacey." I don't offer my hand.

The boy—Cooper—is wearing a T-shirt that reads *The Future Is Female Ejaculation*. He's my age, maybe a little older, maybe a little taller, with slightly scruffy sandy-blond hair and rimless glasses. He is the human equivalent of an NPR tote bag, and he is still hovering.

"I like your dress," he offers. "Very . . . modern."

Modern? Is that a veiled way of saying I look ridiculous? Or is Cooper a time traveler from the 1920s and about to ask me to take a turn around the garden? I can't conjure a comeback.

He's keeping a healthy distance from me as he asks, "Are you all right?"

I nod.

"Because you look kind of . . ."

My head snaps at him. "I look kind of what?"

He opens his mouth. I narrow my eyes. He changes tact. "Do you want a drink?"

I fold my arms tight across my chest. "I happen to have received some very upsetting personal news."

"I'm sorry." Cooper settles on the edge of the coffee table. "Do you want to talk about it?"

"No."

"Okay." He sounds so . . . amicable. "So a drink? I have whiskey. In my room."

The loft is the same level of messy since the last girl moved out, but there seem to be more things in frames on the peeling walls. Everything you need to know about it is summed up by the spidery writing above the power switch in the kitchen: *Don't turn me off, I control the fridge.* When the radiator is on, it sounds like someone is trapped in the basement. The loft's comfortable state of disarray feels homey even though Astoria, Queens, hasn't been my home for over a year. When I graduated from entry-level to junior sales last year, I moved into a pea-size studio in Williamsburg (don't worry, nowhere near the waterfront). I could barely afford it but it felt like the adult thing to do. Steph, my old roommate, replaced me with a series of hot, single straight girls whom she fell for one by one and who all broke her big gay heart, one by one. The boy is a smart move. He's got real furniture—a desk, a bookcase. A far cry from the collection of wood pallets and street finds I had to pass off as decor when I first moved to the city. Above his bed, a framed, signed black-and-white photograph. It's a New York City subway car. From the graffiti, I'm guessing 1980s. Four people sit side by side. A drag queen, an older Latina, a black teenage girl with cornrows, and a businessman in a cheap suit. They are all spacing out, bored and relaxed, shoulders comfortably touching. It's intimate and a little funny and incredibly human. His bedroom walls have been painted a crisp light blue. I'd call it a winter pastel: fresh and soothing. This whole room is sooth-ing. I sink onto his neatly made futon. "It's always so weird being back in this room."

"How often are you back in this room?" Cooper scoops up some clothes off the floor.

There's a splayed paperback on his bed, one of those New Agey books written by a monk with a serene smile. *The Art of Being Happy Most of the Time.* "Any good?"

He finds a bottle of Maker's Mark wedged into a very full bookcase and pours two shots, one into a shot glass, one into a Cal Bears mug. "It's interesting."

I slip off my heels and draw my feet to my chest. Yesterday those heels made me happy. Yesterday feels so far away. "Are you unhappy, Cooper-the-new-roommate?"

"No." He hands me the shot glass and settles into one of those absurdly large black office chairs. "Not overall. I just thought it could be useful to hear what the Buddhists had to say."

"To the Buddhists." I raise my glass. "I hope I don't come back as anything icky."

He tips his head to one side, curious. His T-shirt is old, soft, and I wish I was wearing something that cozy. We drink. I close my eyes. Still the taste of pickup trucks and off-brand pop and high school parties around bonfires where everything and nothing happened. As much as I try to retrain my palate, fermented grain mash always tastes like home. Like another life.

Cooper leans forward, hands clasped. "So, what happened to you today?" He sounds genuinely concerned.

I meet his gaze without hiding my fear. It's the first time I've looked him properly in the eye.

Maybe I should tell him. Maybe I want to?

He doesn't look away.

The front door slams. "Lace?" It's Steph.

I blink and call, "In here!"

She appears in the doorway, cheeks flushed from the cold, glancing between me and Cooper in confusion. "I got your text. What's wrong?"

* * * *

We sit cross-legged on her bed, and I tell her about the call from Dr. Fitzpatrick.

Steph Malam is a good listener, maybe from all those kittenish roommates pouring their heterosexual hearts out to her. She's British Indian, which means a *blimey, guvvner!* UK accent and endless patience for ignorant Americans who don't understand history or geography ("Yes, I can be brown and a Brit: there's actually about 1.5 million of us"). Standard outfit: indie-band T-shirts, red lipstick, nose ring. She'd like to be thought of as a bit of a badass but her enormous chocolate-brown eyes fill with tears if she even *thinks* about YouTube videos of soldiers returning home to their pets, or parents accepting their transsexual children. She is bad with money, girls, and being on time, and is so conflict avoidant she will always eat anything mistakenly served in a restaurant rather than send it back ("I don't want the server to feel bad, and honestly, Lace, these braised chicken necks are really yummy"). She makes me laugh and has a heart the size of a solar system. She's my best friend, even if we've never stated that.

I explain what I know, that everybody has BRCA1 and BRCA2 genes. When they work, they stop cancerous cells from forming. The problem is when they're broken; mutated to the point they can't do their job. Then you're screwed. You'd have better odds leaving your keys in your apartment door and hoping thieves ignore you—for the rest of your life. That's what this is: a broken lock against near inevitability of home invasion.

My old roommate takes my hands and squeezes them hard. "It must've been *such* a shock."

"So much so that I ran out of the Hoffman House party like a total lunatic. God, I hope no one saw me."

"That doesn't matter." Steph gazes at me. "How are you feeling?"

"I don't know." I rub my forehead. "I have no idea."

"That's all right." She pats my shoulder. "Just take it a day at a time."

"I have an appointment," I hedge. "Tomorrow. With a genetic counselor, at a cancer care place uptown."

Steph reacts to the word *cancer* as if I just said something unspeakably mean: a shock she's trying to absorb without getting upset in turn. "Wow. Okay. That sounds . . ." I think she wants to say *terrifying*. She settles on "good." She pulls her bob back into a tiny ponytail, something she does when she's nervous. "So, what does all this mean? If you have an elevated risk, then what do—"

"I guess I'll find out tomorrow." I roll off her bed and move to the bookshelf on the other side of her bedroom.

"What's the average risk for most women? Like, five percent?"

Thirteen. "I'm not sure." I unearth a book from the piles on her desk, *Fear of Flying.* "I've always meant to read this. Can I borrow it?"

Steph's silent. When I turn around, she's staring at her phone. "The lifetime risk of breast cancer in BRCA1 carriers can be up to—"

"High, yeah, I know, really fucking high." I sound angry and immediately lighten my tone. "Now is not the time for WebMD-induced hysteria, Stephanie."

"I'm not on WebMD," she says. "I'm on Komen, something Komen."

"Just not now, okay, Steph? Not right now. Don't you have any whiskey? Let's get drunk."

"I'm just trying to understand what this all means." She's almost pleading.

"Well, there'll be plenty of time for that, matey." I glance around, looking for a bottle of something brown. "DNA, you know? Not exactly a cure for it."

"Oh, God." Steph's hands go to her mouth.

"I didn't mean—" I exhale. "I'm fine. Right now, I am totally fine."

"But . . ." Her eyes drift to her phone.

"Steph! Change of subject." I click my fingers fast, searching for anything, literally anything. "Girl barista. One you've got a crush on. Any progress?"

"Barista?" She cannot stop her eyes going to her screen.

"Café on the corner. Tattoo of the horse. She gave you a free latte." Now I'm the one pleading.

"Um . . . yeah, I—went in the other day and . . ." She shakes her head. Her eyes are filling with tears. My stomach crunches. "Lace, I can't. I need to know what this means."

"Jesus, Steph! It's not about you!" Immediately I regret it. "I'm sorry. I'm sorry."

"That's okay. Let it out. Your feelings are valid." She's coming for me, arms outreached for a hug.

I back up, knocking a lamp. Yellow light seesaws across the walls. "Shit. It's late, I should go."

"Lace!"

I hurry back through the loft, stabbing my arms into my coat, circling my scarf too tight around my throat. Steph is behind me, calling for me to *wait, please, wait*. She grabs me as I pull open the front door. "We'll get through this, Lace." Her voice shredded and high. "Whatever happens, we'll get through it."

I pull myself away. The inches between us are a chasm. "This isn't happening to you, Steph."

4.

They say a good night's sleep cures all, and everything feels better in the morning. "They" are filthy liars who should be unmasked and punished. I don't sleep much or well. At about 3:00 a.m. I take a sleeping pill and succumb to a suffocating nightmare about turning into a werewolf that Elan Behzadi keeps trying to put in a runway show. My alarm goes off at six. It's still dark outside when I drag myself into my tiny bathroom. The fact I shower before and after spin class is something only Steph knows about me, and this morning, I am determined to get my butt on that bike. *I* am in control of my body; *I* am its master. I put it through hell four mornings a week, and it rewards me by fitting into size 4 jeans. Hot water blasts my skin. I scoop out some rose-and-bergamot sugar scrub and circle it gently around my breasts. My fingertips swirl over the faint stretch marks and scatter of small freckles. Each breast sits comfortably in my palms, the weight of a small bird.

My boobs made their appearance fashionably late. I was nine before there were any developments worth journaling about, and almost thirteen before a critical mass could justify a real bra. I was dying to ditch the hand-me-down training bra I'd gotten from my sister, but the question was how. By this stage, my dad was more like a special guest star than a cast regular, and my sister spent all her spare time listening to Morrissey and hating everything. I'd started to make money babysitting, which I did in secret because both my family members were not above "borrowing" my savings. I'm the only girl I know who bought her first bra on her own. I told the saleslady my mom was in the bathroom. The lady brought me four soft-cupped sizes, and I tried them all on with the diligence of a scientist. I bought the cheapest, counting out the exact amount on the chipped beige counter. The saleslady, who'd been periodically sweeping the store looking for my absent mother, eyed me as she handed over the plastic bag.

"Is this your first bra?" Her earrings were shaped like little cat faces. I nodded, embarrassed.

She pursed her lips. Frosted mauve lipstick feathered into the cracks. "Sometimes men don't think with their brains. They think with their . . ." She frowned at her crotch. My embarrassment escalated to mortification. "You gotta always use this"—she tapped a temple hidden by a cloud of orange hair—"when it comes to *this*." Her crotch penis.

"Yes, ma'am," I said automatically, while sending a nondenominational prayer for my immediate execution.

She nodded, satisfied, and turned to help the next customer.

My adolescence was full of those moments: well-meaning if disjointed pieces of advice from a loose network of older women that formed an elusive patchwork of womanhood. I needed "sanitary napkins" for when "Aunty Flo arrived"; I might have "urges" but it was best to "let them pass." Rather than being taught to embrace being a woman, the message was ignore it, and maybe it'll go away. All in all, anything to do with sex, my body, or being female was mysterious bordering on shameful, and the less I had to think or do anything about it, the better. You can imagine how grateful I was when my boobs stopped growing at a 32B. The girls are neither pendulous nor bite-size and thus not one of my top five body concerns. (I'm generally okay with what I've got going on, but let's just say my hips don't lie or shut up in any outfit.) Nipples the size of a cranberry, areola the color of a ripe summer peach. I can pull off cleavage in the right push-up bra. My college boyfriend called them "polite." A couple of quiet achievers who have unexpectedly become the stars of the show. For all the wrong reasons.

The sweet smell of rose mixes with the steam. I draw a long breath in and let it out to a count of four, then do it again. For the first time since Dr. Fitzpatrick's phone call, I feel something close to pleasure. Release. Even . . . hope. Perspective. I don't have cancer. I may never get cancer; I'm twenty-five. I'm young, even though it doesn't feel that way. The absurdly high stats Steph found are a lifetime risk: the chances of me getting cancer in my twenties are much, much less. This isn't a death sentence—far from it. Maybe I'll postpone my appointment this afternoon. It's entirely possible my panic is a bit of an overreaction . . .

That's when I feel it. There, on the left side, the underside.

A lump.

Everything stops.

I press into it, around it again and again and again, and it's a lump, I think, I don't know. I do breast checks every now and then, but I'm never sure what I'm supposed to be looking for, and half the time I end up plucking errant hairs or casually masturbating. It could be a lymph node or a cyst or IT COULD BE FUCKING CANCER. I slam off the hot water so hard my hand stings. Rocketing out of the shower, my foot hits the bath mat and keeps zooming forward. I shoot backward on the slippery tiles, landing hard on my butt. Pain shoots up my tailbone. I'm not sure if I'm thankful or sad that there's no one around to witness this.

* * * *

I'm still limping when I get to Midtown Medical, where my impression of a pigeon trapped in an attic convinces a receptionist to squeeze me in to see Dr. Fitzpatrick about my jaunty new bump. To be perfectly frank, I have more loyalty to my hairdresser than my doctor. Fitzpatrick is the kind of white-haired patriarch who probably considers deer heads to be wall art and has a few illegitimate children stashed around the globe, but he takes my insurance and he's close to work.

After feeling my boobs for .2 seconds, he tells me he can't be sure of anything but he'll try to book me in for a diagnostic mammogram and ultrasound after my appointment with the genetic counselor this afternoon. A diagnostic mammogram is different from a screening mammogram; diagnostic means they're looking for something. I have no idea if my insurance covers this, or what it does cover. When I start to cry out of sheer terror, he tells me, "There's no need for that," and that the nurse will handle the scheduling. I had no idea so much empathy could fit in one aging body.

At Hoffman House, my colleagues are all slumped at their desks with breakfast sandwiches and hangovers. With my red eyes and smeared mascara, I fit right in. The interns twitter around me like Sleeping Beauty's forest friends, bearing phone messages and gossip, wanting direction, needing attention. It appears no one noticed my panicked exit out of the party last night. I should feel relieved but I have no room for any emotion or sentiment other than the one blaring in my head, bright red and full caps: CANCER. CANCER. YOU HAVE CANCER. I will myself not to touch *that spot*, which I've done so much it'll either bruise or turn shiny like a brass door handle. The sight of my desk, so neat and cheery, almost reintroduces the water-works. Black-and-white photo-booth snaps of Steph and me pulling goofy faces at a random event, my VIP pass to the Alexander McQueen retrospective at the Met. My copper pencil sharpener in the shape of the Eiffel Tower. My niece's third birthday party invite. Next to my keyboard, a paisley fabric swatch. So small. So innocent. A perfect metaphor for my small, innocent past, back when the goal was just to have fun and get drunk and laugh with Steph, and even though I know I'm rewriting history and it wasn't that easy . . . it was. It really was.

A raspy voice: honey on broken glass. "Lacey?"

Patricia Hoffman is standing at my desk.

Oh no.

Patricia Hoffman is a thousand kinds of fabulous that invokes a heady mix of loyalty, admiration, and fear. I've never worked out ex-actly how old she is, thanks to her devotion to plastic surgery, boy-friends who wouldn't be too old to be dating me, and wigs. She's been married four times, owns *two* town houses in Manhattan, one uptown, one downtown, and rumor has it Paul Simon once wrote a song about her. Classic extrovert with the energy of a freshman, the sophistication of royalty, and the wardrobe of a costume designer. I typically enjoy our brisk bantering. But nothing about today is typical.

"P-Patricia. Hi. How was Paris?"

"The usual." She slips off a pair of gold cat-eye glasses. "Lots of lit-tle boys with silly mustaches foisting cheap champagne on me, trying to get me into their tiny beds."

My cue to offer a peppy reply like "I see you flew Emirates," but I'm trying so hard not to cry in front of my boss that I can't get a single word out.

She pulls off a pair of dusty-pink leather gloves, revealing a manicure the color of plums. "How was the party? I'm so terribly sad to have missed it!"

"It was . . ." I cannot conjure a single decorative adjective or simile. Horrifyingly, I settle on: "Nice."

"Nice?" Patricia peers at me, confused. Which changes to alarm. Which softens to concern. In her nontheatrical voice she asks, "Lacey, are you all right?"

I nod, quick and fast, affecting a smile as convincing as a toupee.

Her brow flicks into a frown. She places a hand on my shoulder. "Come into my office. We'll have the kittens"—the interns, fawning—"pick us up cappuccinos from Le Coucou."

And while the pathetically needy part of me wants to dig my feet into Patricia Hoffman's sheepskin rug and tell her absolutely everything, another, more powerful part of me shuts that down. My boss has already been extraordinarily kind in supporting my working on Clean Clothes after hours, most likely because I've implied that, if we ever got funded, I wouldn't quit my job here. I didn't want to disappoint her or worry her unnecessarily: so many start-ups don't, well, start up. But to be honest, there's something about Patricia's generosity that has always made me feel a bit uncomfortable. I'm not a charity case. I don't want to be anyone's burden or for anyone to feel sorry for me. And I don't want to give Patricia any reason to think I don't belong exactly where I am. I summon the ambitious glint of a thriving New York transplant. "Thanks, but I want to follow up from last night's rampant networking. Strike, iron; you know the drill."

Her smile returns with light relief. "No rest for the wicked."

That was the right move. I smile back. "No rest at all."

5.

I spend the day watching the clock count down to 4:00 p.m. Seasons change more quickly. There's a poster opposite my desk that asks in bold typography, WHO IS AFRAID OF NOW? I'll give you one guess who is afraid of now.

Vivian and Steph call multiple times, and I send each one to the vastness of voice mail. Speaking to either of them about last night feels as tempting as an anal probe.

At exactly 3:30 p.m. I cut out, mumbling something about a *coffee-drinks thing* to our receptionist. Last night's snow is already turning gray and sludgy. I take the subway uptown.

I had assumed the New York Cancer Care Center was a clinic for consultations and sorry-you're-fucked support. I'm unprepared for the fact it's also a treatment center. The woman in the queue in front of me has a completely bald head. My reaction embarrasses me: I find it horrifying. When she finishes at the front desk, I realize I'd been keeping an unnatural distance from her.

I've never liked hospitals. It's fair to say I hate them. For reasons I don't really want to think about.

I'm instructed to wait on one of the immaculate teal-green sofas. Everything looks new and clean and expensive, which makes me worry, again, about my insurance and what exactly it covers. I know I'm putting off calling them, and I know that's cowardly. The prospect just makes everything way too real.

Anxiety itches me. I tell myself it's just a consultation, that nothing bad is going to happen here. But my body won't hear of it, responding instead as if I'm about to give a solo presentation to the entire company. My heartbeat is loud in my ears.

A trashy women's mag is a ghoulish carousel of grinning photoshopped faces. A woman with as much body fat as a rubber band stands over a guy with a waxed chest, tied to a bed. His eyes are slit in a way that indicates either desire, or intent to kill. The headline screams: Unlock Your Fantasies! The Sex You've *Always* Wanted to Have. Rubber Band's breasts spill out of a lacy black bra like a couple of overripe melons intent on escape.

She is textbook sexy.

Breasts are sexy. Everyone likes breasts: ogling them is one of the great American pastimes, like baseball and casual racism. Babies like boobs. Men like knockers. I like mine. But I've definitely never towered over a dude tied to a bed in order to motorboat him with some renegade cantaloupes. Is that what I should be doing, considering one option is . . . well . . .

"Lacey Whitman?"

A woman in an ankle-length skirt, cream turtle neck, and what I strongly suspect is a hand-knitted vest, is holding a clipboard. Demure bob, open face, few extra pounds. Have I tumbled down the rabbit hole back to Illinois? She is bake sales and Tupperware and if she'd ever unlocked *her* sexual fantasies, I'm betting they involved buttered English crumpets and a nice lie-down. She is Judy-Ann McMallow, and she is my genetic counselor.

Judy-Ann's office smells like a hot cinnamon bun as interpreted by a cheap air freshener. Lamps attempt an atmosphere of "cozy," but they don't hide the fact this an office where people get bad news. No fewer than three boxes of tissues are within arm's reach. I perch on the edge of a pillowy love seat as she apologizes about a mess I can't detect. Tea? Sure. She has a pot of chamomile, ready to go. Judy-Ann speaks in a voice I know is designed to soothe me, and while it doesn't do exactly that, it does result in my mimicking her. I've always been something of a chameleon, able to mix it with everyone from billionaire bros to fourth-generation farmers, by almost unconsciously simulating their mannerisms and speech patterns. As Judy-Ann begins in a puddles-of-pity half whisper, I find myself responding in kind.

"So, Lacey, how are you doing?"

"I'm okay, Judy-Ann. I'm okay."

"Good. Now, what do you know so far?"

"I know I've tested positive for the BRCA1 gene mutation, and I understand the risk that puts me at."

"Mmm." Cue look of fervent compassion. "That's tough. I see from your file you didn't see a genetic counselor before taking the test, is that right?"

"Yes," I say. "My doctor didn't mention that as a possibility."

This is, in fact, a lie. The truth is I told my doctor I'd already seen a genetic counselor; that, yes, I understood the risks. I was fundamentally convinced the test would be negative. Seeing a counselor beforehand seemed completely unnecessary; just another way the health-care system was trying to screw me out of my already paltry paycheck. I was more worried about whether my insurance covered the test than the result of it.

"And how are you feeling right now?" Judy-Ann asks.

I pretend to consider the question, and answer in her affected half whisper. "Scared I'm going to die of breast cancer, Judy-Ann."

Her lips move into a sympathetic smile, but her eyes are assessing me, drawing conclusions. "Would you like to talk about it?"

About my fear of dying? With you, a complete stranger? My mirroring trick evaporates. I stare at my feet. "Maybe later."

She scribbles a note. "Let's talk about your family history."

Even though I suspected this was coming, my foot jitters the carpet. "Sure. Won't take long." I explain my grandparents on my dad's side live in Florida, still alive, with no history of cancer. We are not close. "They think abortion is worse than pedophilia, which they know about from the existence of gay men. Last I heard, my dad, Wayne, was working as a pearl diver in Tahiti. He is a free spirit slash terrible father. No aunts, no uncles. My maternal grandparents died in a car accident in Rome in the 1970s while on vacation, but at least they died doing what they loved, which was drunk driving. I have an older sister, Mara, thirty. She lives upstate with her daughter, Storm, who is the most sane member of my family. Storm's best friend is an invisible horse called Bottom, to put that in perspective."

Judy-Ann is unfazed by all of this. "Any history of cancer with your sister?"

I shake my head. "My sister is . . ." How do I put this: a worshipper at the altar of kombucha? "Not exactly a fan of Western medicine. Which includes genetic testing."

"When a sibling tests positive for BRCA1, there's a fifty percent chance the other siblings also carry the gene mutation," Judy-Ann says. "How do you feel about telling your sister about your results?"

"That I won't," I say. "That I can't? That I'm scared?" I wipe my hands on my pants. "My sister is . . . I don't think she would . . ."

"We can come back to Mara some other time," Judy-Ann says. She looks at me pointedly.

"That's all I know," I say. "Like I said, it wouldn't take long."

"What about your mother?"

I stare at Judy-Ann as if she's asked me the most invasively personal question possible, which in some ways, she has. It is surprisingly easy not to talk about your family in a city like New York. Here, everyone is remaking themselves in a model they alone see fit. It only takes a few conversational sleights of hand to plant the message that family is not something you talk about. I feel exposed. I'm squirming in my seat, knowing Judy-Ann is going to jump on this like a drunk girl on a cheeseburger. But this isn't a bad first date. This is serious. I have to face my own stupid fear. I look her square in the eye. "My mother, June Whitman, died of breast cancer when I was five years old. She was thirty-one."

"Thirty-one?" Judy Ann can't hide what appears to be excitement, or possibly relief: *there* is the explanation for my mutation. "That's very young."

I nod, once.

"What was her treatment plan?"

"Two rounds of chemo. She died in the hospital." My voice is robotic. I won't be getting emotional.

"Do you know how old June was when she was diagnosed?"

I shake my head. "I know it was quick. From the beginning to the . . . the end." I remember a dark room, curtains drawn against bright sunlight. The glass of juice I'm holding, so big in my small hands, falls to the floor.

"Do you know what kind of breast cancer it was?"

"I don't. I can try to find out. If it's helpful." I'm worried the juice will stain the hospital room floor and I'll get in trouble. I want to cry, but I'm afraid of waking her. My efforts to help my dying mother, so phenomenally useless.

Judy-Ann underlines something. "It helps to have as full a picture as possible."

"Why?"

The counselor assesses me for a brief, sharp second, her would-you-like-another-cookie? sweetness momentarily flashing away. Evidently, she decides I can handle this. "Hereditary cancer that forms in patients with the BRCA1 mutation tends to be very aggressive. Triple-negative, fast-growing tumors, which means a lower threshold for chemo. I'm just curious if that's the cancer your mother had."

If that's the cancer I will get. If that's the cancer I already have. If that's the cancer that—and surely, I've known this all along—meant my insurance covered the genetic testing in the first place. That made me ask Dr. Fitzpatrick about starting mammograms. The air in the room feels tight. It strikes me as utterly ludicrous that we're sitting here, drinking tea, discussing my possible death as if it's serious, yes, but no more serious than a noisy neighbor ("It's noise pollution. That's what it is: *noise pollution*."). This is my *life*.

"I need a plan," I say. "Tell me a plan."

"We can certainly start to explore your options," Judy-Ann says. "If you're sure you're ready—"

"I'm ready," I say. "I'm ready, let's go."

I have two courses of action. The first is "surveillance." Regular screenings, every three to six months. Mammograms, MRIs, ultra-sounds. Not all of this is necessarily covered by my insurance. I get the impression the screenings are less about making sure I'm cancer-free than waiting for the fucker to show up. The second is . . . it. *Mastectomy*. I still can't form the word without shuddering. In one fell swoop, this reduces my risk from very, very high to very, very low. Real peace of mind. I just have to lose my tits for it.

No. Fucking. Way. "I read online something about BRCA cancers forming earlier in younger generations," I say. "Is that true?"

"Officially, there's no evidence of that," Judy-Ann says. "But I can say personally, yes, I have seen that happen. Often due to lifestyle and environment factors, but we don't know for sure."

"How can I reduce my risk?"

"I'm not a physician," Judy-Ann is quick to say. "I can't officially advise you on that."

"Unofficially?"

"A physician would probably suggest a low-fat, high-fiber diet. Regular exercise."

I'm not naturally thin. I perform the compulsory labor of femininity via spin class and the odd celebrity diet. "I'm pretty healthy."

"Reduced alcohol intake."

"Ouch. Really?"

"A physician might say alcohol increases the risk of breast cancer."

I'm shocked. "Wow, someone should really tell . . . every single person about that."

"How many drinks would you say you have a week?"

"I *say* I have very few, but that's a terrible lie." I laugh weakly. "Me, personally?" I point to myself, as if it might be possible she's asking for, perhaps, the average of everyone in the waiting room. "I have a very social profession. Drinking is really a part of the culture."

"Eight to ten?"

"A day?" I laugh, relieved. "No, no. I mean, sometimes. On weekends. Thursday to Sunday. Including Sunday."

"I meant a week," Judy-Ann says. "How easy would it be for you to eliminate drinking?"

"Very easy." I'm shaking my head, and stop. "How much would that reduce my risk?"

Judy-Ann makes another sympathetic face. "Not very much."

I've never wanted a gin and tonic more badly in all my life.

I'm on birth control for my acne, which Judy-Ann says is good.

The pill is helpful for reducing ovarian cancer risk. "For a lot of women, it's as essential as pills for cholesterol or heart disease," Judy-Ann adds, which surprises me. I'm too young to worry seriously about ovarian, but we run through the signs anyway. Have I noticed bloating, increased abdominal girth, urinal urgency? No, no, no. This is good, good, good. I can keep monitoring myself as I get older. Or there's . . . the other way.

"An oophorectomy." I force myself to say the odd word in a calm, controlled tone.

Judy-Ann nods. "Most women wait until after they've completed their family before they have their ovaries removed. Do you want to have children?"

The huge question is asked in such a low-stakes perfunctory way, I almost laugh. "Kids. Wow. Offspring. Fruit of my loins."

"We don't have to go into it now."

The way I see it, women tend to fall into two camps. There's the always-wanted-kids clucky mom-in-training types, the ones who feel this innate calling; it's like they can see their own future and it involves a family Christmas card and playdates with strangers they met in a park and they're like, Yes. Score. Then there's the women who are like, No freaking way. I'm not destroying my vagina and turning into a milk station for some gremlin to ruin my career, my sex life, and all my best clothes. Fuck you and your biological imperative propaganda, I'm pouring myself another vino and binge-watching *Game of Thrones*, again, because I can.

Me? I'm neither.

I pull at a stray thread on the love seat. "Jury's out on kids."

"Are you currently in a relationship?"

The question every single girl longs to hear! Have you heard that saying "There's a lid for every pot?" These days, thanks to online dating, there are too many lids. New York City is a lid party 24-7 and it is *exhausting*. "No, I am not, Judy-Ann."

Judy-Ann asks, "Do you have any relationship goals?"

"I wouldn't mind being in one," I say. "If only because you're basically a second-class citizen as an unwed woman." Here's something you never hear: *It was a real single-friendly day. There were so many singles there! All different kinds of singles, enjoying some good single fun. I was there myself, as a single.*

"How about a timeline?"

"For . . . ?"

"Marriage, children."

My cheeks and throat tingle with heat. My instinct is to perform indifference, even disgust: *Gross! How bourgeois!* But it's not the truth.

"I don't have a timeline," I mutter.

Judy-Ann makes another note. "For a young woman looking to form a primary relationship, there can be a physical consideration—"

"Let's not beat around the bush, Judy-Ann. You're saying if I get my tits cut off, guys will be less into beating around my bush."

The counselor gives me an almost amused smile. "No, I'm not saying that. It's just something to consider."

A scratch of anger under my collar. "Do you have the mutation?"

"I don't."

"Right. So you and your husband"—probably high school boyfriend, probably married for a billion years—"have never had to deal with something like this."

"That's true. My wife and I have not."

Holy smokes, Judy-Ann's a lesbian? Steph's right, my gaydar is the pits. What else have I gotten wrong about this goddamn shit show? I mumble sorry, feeling about ten inches tall. We're silent a moment. My fingers find my left breast again. "When does this feeling go away?"

"What feeling?"

"This . . . worry." This ever-present, bubbling dread.

Judy-Ann closes her notebook. "It's different for everyone." Which sounds very much like *It never goes away.* "Let's move on to insurance."

* * * *

I'm introduced to Dr. Laura Williams, a breast surgeon. She is six feet and almost disconcertingly beautiful; a tall Kerry Washington, in a white coat. She radiates the calm, efficient kindness that must be in everyone's job description here. A brief breast exam confirms my lump's existence, which leads to a diagnostic mammogram. This takes place on another floor of the rabbit warren treatment center. I change into a white terry cloth robe with an *NY3C* logo embroidered on the pocket in teal green. It's as soft and nice as a hotel robe, which is a surprise. The hazy memories I have of hospitals from early childhood are full of lurid colors, bright lights, and hard smells. The female technician who helps me with the mammogram is polite and polished. The equipment is as shiny as a spaceship.

Did my mother get a mammogram? An ultrasound? How did she find her first lump? It's hard to picture the half-smiling dark-haired woman in the six faded photographs I have getting freaked out and losing control like I did this morning. I can count on one hand the memories I have of my mother, which I know are supposed to be rose-tinted and fuzzy-edged. They're not.

When it comes to my past, there's so much I don't want to remember.

The results of the mammogram are inconclusive, as is the ultrasound that follows. My breast tissue is dense, Dr. Williams tells me. Which is the case with many young women. A biopsy is required to work out if my lump is cancerous. I assume this will be weeks away. No. It'll be now. I am "lucky": yesterday's snowstorm caused a few people to reschedule. I can't help but feel I am already being treated like a cancer patient.

"That's because you are," Dr. Williams says. "We want to give at-risk women the same level of care as women with cancer."

"Suppose it's something." I draw my robe around myself. "What happens then?"

"It's hard to say," the doc replies. "I'd rather not speculate."

Jesus, no one is willing to commit to anything. I just need a god-damn answer. "I'd really rather you did."

"I don't want to panic you—"

"I'm already panicked! Just tell me what happens if this is some-thing . . . cancerish."

"If we caught it early, maybe a lumpectomy. Maybe radiation. Maybe . . . something more radical."

Chemo. The word is such a vicious, nasty slash that neither one of us wants to say it out loud.

"And after all that," I say, "you'd still recommend a mastectomy, right?"

"Theoretically, yes. Probably. But let's see how we go with the biopsy."

Catch-22: all signs point to mastectomy.

No time at all seems to pass before I am lying on a padded hospital bed. Someone in scrubs thinks it's a good idea to show me the needle that'll penetrate my breast to numb the tissue. It is the size of a spear. "Why are you showing me this?" I ask, light-headed and trying not to panic. "I don't understand why you're showing me this." A stranger holds my hand as it skewers my skin. I am a piece of meat. After I'm numb, I feel an awful, unnatural pressure as another long silver needle pierces my flesh on a brutal fact-finding mission. On the ultrasound machine next to my bed is the inside of my breast, looking like a black-and-white moonscape. Everyone searches the screen for the thing that could kill me.

Tears leak down the side of my face. Not because I'm afraid (which I am) or it's uncomfortable (which it is). It's because no one outside this room of polite and friendly medical professionals knows I am on this table.

I am completely and utterly alone.

6.

Vivian calls, again and again and again, until finally, I pick up. She wants to run a postmortem on our pitch, by which she means a debrief of my monumental fuckup.

"I'll start with what I could have done better," she says, her tone bristling with efficiency. "I shouldn't have thrown you in the deep end. It was our first time pitching to an investor for our first round of funding, and I should've been more cognizant of the pressure that put on you. It was a mistake to go for it so quickly, and I'm sorry. Okay, your turn."

I press myself into the far corner of a conference room. Beyond the glass walls, Hoffman House employees sip takeout lattes and send lightning texts. "Something's happened." I tell her everything. She's silent throughout, to the point I'm unsure if she's still on the line. "Hello?"

"I'm here," she says. "Just processing." Another pause. For a wild second, I think she's going to fire me: flush the last eight months down the drain. "I'm sorry this happened to you, Lacey."

Is happening, I want to correct her. "I'm sorry about the party," I say. "I know Tom was a big deal."

I expect her to scoff this off, reiterate that my health is the most important thing, that Tom doesn't matter at all.

"He was," she says. "But there'll be others."

"Sorry," I say again. "I'll catch up on everything by the weekend."

"Okay, good." There's a pause before she adds, a tad hastily, "No rush. Take all the time you need."

Knowing how high her standards are for everyone, from the guy who works at her local bodega to her own parents, I'm sure she doesn't really mean it. And I don't want more time. The ticking clock is already deafening. I find a handful of organizations for women at risk for hereditary cancer. They have strong, sassy names: Bright Pink and FORCE: Facing Our Risk of Cancer Empowered. I become addicted to their website forums, staying up night after night to lurk on the graphic, emotionally raw discussions of our collective fate: *Ovaries out, or just fallopian tubes?* and *Best post-op bra for silicon implant?* and *23 y o BRCA2 + scared.* I feel like a stalker, reading confidential medical files. Threads discuss fertility issues, the pros and cons of "nipple saving surgery," feelings of fear, of isolation. The frankness and the normalizing nature of the discussions are overwhelming. Confronting. They even have a name for women who choose prophylactic (preventative) surgery.

Previvors.

The thread I can relate to most right now: *Anyone else here sick of waiting??* They don't call it being a *patient* for nothing. If you have a mutated gene, you better get ready to wait: for appointments; follow-up appointments; tests; test results; first, second, third opinions. Guess what I'm not? Patient. I am so hysterical with the stress of waiting for my biopsy result that I accidentally spend $200 on shoes, which I definitely cannot afford, as I keep pushing back all my clients. I try to meditate for the first time since . . . for the first time. I breathe in and out. In and out. I try to find inner calm, but all I can think is: *I'm dying. I'm dying. I'm dying.* Burying my mother's death—something I was barely even conscious of—wasn't enough to escape it. I've always wanted life to move faster: to get to the next thing, and the next, and the next. Now I want time to slow down. To stop from delivering me to the future written under my skin.

After forty-eight agonizing hours, Dr. Williams calls while I'm in line at Starbucks. The biopsy is clear. The lump is a benign growth— something common and harmless. To say I am relieved is like calling Charlie Sheen "a bit of a drinker." But all I say to the doc is, "Well, that's good news." I switch the phone to my other ear, conscious of idle eavesdroppers. "And what about my . . . other option? The more permanent one. What are the main benefits?"

"Reducing risk," she says. "Almost to nothing."

The line shuffles forward. "What about the downsides?"

"It's a major surgery," Dr. Williams says. "Anything from two to twelve hours on the operating table. Possibly multiple surgeries . . ."

She continues with a laundry list of nightmare details. I try to keep my face even, as if we're discussing a no-stakes work presentation. "How do you think I should proceed?"

"You are young," she says. "But I have seen breast cancer form in BRCA1 women younger than you. You don't need to rush into a decision, Lacey. But my feeling is, it's always better to be safe than sorry."

Because being sorry might mean being dead. I order a black coffee, then instantly change it to a white chocolate mocha Frappuccino. As I wait for my order, anxiety builds in hot, uncontrolled waves.

What if a tumor starts forming now, right now? Judy-Ann said tumors form like *that*: aggressive ones, triple-negative. That's really, really, *really* bad. I'd need tons of chemo to kill that. *Tons.* But what's the alternative: mastectomy? Breast reconstruction, what, with implants? Fake boobs and scars? That's horrific! Barbaric! That would be *torture*—

"Shut up!" I gasp, inadvertently bolting back a step.

No one in Starbucks even flinches, except one old man who gives me a knowing look and says, "I hear it too, sweetheart." Hashtag New York.

* * * *

I have always been good at making a plan and sticking to it. My college nickname was "Lil' Robot." I know what I'm doing when I wake up because I've thought it through the night before. Which means I'm generally good with decisions. I don't second-guess my lunch order or my life plan. But right now, and quite possibly for the first time, I am ripped down the center. After gorging myself on research and forum threads and what my insurance actually covers, I have information but no direction. Each possible path is frightening and badly lit. I can't make a choice.

Finally, I accept the inevitable.

I need help.

Which is why, come Friday night, I call an emergency meeting of the minds at the loft.

* * * *

Steph hugs me hello as if I just returned from the frontline. Vivian permits a scaled-back version of Steph's signature embrace. (Viv is not a hugger, but this has never deterred Steph from trying.) I don't think they've ever spent time together without me, which suits me just fine. They sit on opposite ends of the loft's old sofa, wineglasses in hand. I've brought all the vino I had at home to stop it from tempting me with its cab sauv and sauv blanc siren song. Steph is comfortably cross-legged in a Blondie T-shirt, purple leggings, and socks patterned with peace symbols. Vivian is trying to find a spot on the sofa that doesn't sag. Her expensive black slacks and a crisp white button-down indicate she came straight from our "office," an overpriced shoe box in a coworking space in Tribeca that has free beer and Ping-Pong.

I am standing in front of a whiteboard. I am ready to begin. "As you know, I have a very important decision to make about my"—I indicate my boobs—"Golden Globes."

Steph raises her hand. "Can we order pizza? Sorry, I know this is important, I just think I'll have a clearer head if we had pizza."

"I'll order it." Vivian is on her phone.

"I can do it." Steph looks around. "Where's my phone? Lace, have you seen my phone?" She runs her fingers between the couch cushions. "I *just* had it—"

"Done." Vivian slips her phone back in her pocket. "Thirty minutes."

"Shit, that was quick." Steph gives Vivian an uneasy smile. "What'd you use, magic?"

"Yelp." Vivian looks back at me. "You were saying?"

On the whiteboard, I write *PRO* and *CON*, and draw a vertical line between them. "Scores out of ten for each pro or con. Six for each column. Got it?"

My friends nod. It's go time.

It takes us over an hour to finish the board. An hour of discussion and debate and wine and more wine. In the end, our pro column looks like this:

Lower lifetime risk of cancer = 10

Surgery / reconstruction covered by current health insurance
    (mostly) = 8

Don't have kids / less responsibility right now = 5

Cheaper and less complicated / horrific than cancer treatment = 9

Time off protected by Family & Medical Leave Act (won't lose
    benefits etc.) = 6

Won't have saggy tits when old = 3

I explain the last one: if I get implants, my breasts stay pert while the rest of me doesn't. It's not a huge bonus, but it won't hurt.

The con column is considerably more grim.

Losing healthy breasts = 10

Recovery could affect career / no income = 6

Won't get to breastfeed = 3

May be for nothing (might not get cancer) = 5

No sensation in new boobs = 9

Guys might find it weird / turnoff =

It's this we can't agree on. "The right guy won't care!" Steph slaps the sofa. Her teeth are slightly purple from the wine. "One. One fookin' point." Her British accent always gets stronger when she's drinking.

"Eight," Vivian counters. "*Eight* points. This is New York. Dating is a blood sport. Guys will use anything to knock you out of the running. Having scarred, fake tits because of *cancer* at *twenty-five* is an instant pass, even if you are hot and smart."

Steph gasps. "That is so mean."

"It's not what *I* think," Vivian exclaims. "I'm just giving you a straight male perspective; you're gay."

"You're a woman!"

"I sleep with men. I have sex with men."

"More than I can say." I take a bite of cold pizza.

"I'm still aware of the existence of men," Steph says. "Who happen to be human, like me. If I really liked someone, I wouldn't care. They won't care."

"Yes, they will."

"Lacey's perfect guy is compassionate and open-minded."

"Lacey's perfect guy is a guy. With eyes and a cock."

"I think my perfect guy would be both," I say. "A compassionate cock."

"What *is* your type?" Vivian turns to me. "I could never figure it out."

"My type?" I shrug. "Shoes and a MetroCard."

"Seriously," Steph says. "What do you want in a guy?"

The Punch-and-Judy show have broken the fourth wall and are staring at me expectantly.

"I don't know . . . Gainfully employed college grad with the wit of Steve Martin, the body of a Montauk surf instructor, and the sexual appeal of a hot cheesy pizza. Ideally done a main-stage TED talk or started a literary salon or something. Funny but not sarcastic. Smart but not a show-off. Financially comfortable but doesn't work *all* the time. I don't mind curly hair but not tight curly: JT solo career not JT *NSYNC . . ." I notice the girls' expressions and cut it short. "But I'm flexible."

Vivian looks skeptical. "On what part?"

I think hard for a long moment. "I'm not flexible."

"Wow." Steph looks worried. "Maybe I'm too open-minded."

"Straight girls could be cut from your list," I offer.

"That *is* my list," Steph says.

The front door opens. Cooper, Steph's new roommate, comes in carrying what looks like a tote bag full of books. "Hello roomie," he says. "Hey Lacey."

I freeze.

To Vivian, "I'm Cooper."

"Vivian Chang." They shake hands. Steph's already on her feet, next to him. "Can we ask Coop about . . ." She gestures unsubtly at the board that, to my alarm, he's examining with interest.

I'm surprised to find myself shrugging. Cooper has the sort of diplomatic open-minded ease borne of well-funded public schooling. Besides, he's already reading it.

The girls tag-team an explanation: "You know, like Angelina Jolie."

"So," Steph says. "What do you think?"

"Be honest," Vivian says. "You're only hurting her if you're not."

Cooper's thinking. We all wait. He is pretty cute, in that scruffy-haired-nerd-who-likes-political-humor sort of way. I actually care what he thinks.

"Assuming that we're not talking about some sort of medical horror show," he says, "I think it depends on if the girl finds them sexy."

Vivian and Steph look taken aback.

"I can't speak for all guys," he continues, "but, generally, guys like it when girls like their bodies. I'm sure there'd be an adjustment period, but if she was into it, I probably would be too. Our bodies are changing all the time. But confidence is what's really attractive."

He gives me a *That okay?* look.

"Wise words." I smile at him. "The Buddhists are rubbing off on you."

"Namaste." He bows jokingly, and heads to his room.

"Maybe you should be rubbing off on him," Vivian murmurs, after he closes his door. "He's cute."

"No," Steph jumps in. "No way. This house is finally a drama-free zone. No one's shagging my roommate." She taps the whiteboard. "One point."

Vivian says, "*Eight.*"

They fold their arms and look at me.

So it's up to me? And my sexual confidence? Fan-fucking-tastic. Silently, and with no small amount of shame, I write . . . 7.

I hate that it matters. But it does.

Final score: Cons 40. Pros 41.

A flutter of relief, even happiness, flickers through me. I have an answer! The indecisive nightmare can stop!

Then it hits me.

I know, intellectually, that it makes sense: a medically sound *127 Hours*. The fact I even have a choice is a privilege: millions of women can't make the decision I can. But it's not a decision I want to make.

I look over at the girls. Whatever they see in my face causes them both to straighten, momentarily sober. They exchange a worried glance. Their open, alarmed need to join forces while I'm right in front of them makes me groan and sink to the sofa, my face in my hands. The urge to curl into a tiny ball is overwhelmingly powerful.

Steph rubs my back. "It's okay. Lace, it's okay."

"But it's not," I say into my hands. "It's kind of not."

A pause. Then Vivian speaks. "How about this." She's using her negotiating-in-meetings voice. "You just commit to thinking about it. That's it. You don't have to make any hard decisions. You just have to think about it."

I look up. I have the distinct impression I look like an orphaned puppy. "For how long?"

Steph uses her soothe-the-baby voice. "However long you like."

I whimper.

"Six months," Viv replies, matter-of-fact.

A deadline. Good. "Six months," I repeat. "I can make a decision in six months." With that airy buffer of time in play, I suddenly feel a little more expansive. I'm up above the whole thing, looking down at landforms, seeing the big picture. The reality is, it's not an emergency. Of course there's the possibility of aggressive cancers forming sooner in younger generations, and I agree that prevention is better than cure. But I still don't need to rush into anything. I want to give myself time to really think about this. And six months feels like a perfect amount of time: luxuriously but not recklessly long. I try something, tentatively. "Say you were gonna do it. In six months. Is there anything you'd, I don't know, want to . . . try or do before then?"

"Do you mean, like, tests and consultations?" Steph says.

"No, I mean the final hurrah. Saying ta-ta to the tatas."

"Oh," the girls say. We all lean back into the sofa, absentmindedly squeezing our boobs.

Steph's gaze goes dreamy. "I'd sunbathe topless in the Greek Isles."

Vivian sips her wine. "I'd titty-fuck a boy band."

I cough laughter, muting it for Cooper's sake. "I've never titty-fucked anyone."

"Oh, Lace." Steph gives me a look of pity. "Even I've titty-fucked someone."

"If we're being honest," I say. "I don't usually 'get there' with a guy. Orgasmically speaking."

The girls pause. Too late I comprehend this is a significant reveal.

"How often do you come?" Vivian asks.

I want to laugh or affect indignation. But they're both looking at me like this is a perfectly legitimate line of questioning. Which of course, it is.

"I'd say eighty-five percent of the time . . ."

"Oh." Steph relaxes.

". . . Is how often I fake it."

Steph spits out her wine. "*What?*"

"I'm a faker," I say. "I know I *need to be more communicative*, but I tried that and it was so awkward. I didn't know what to say. And most of the guys I've hooked up with were basically half-night stands. It's all over so fast."

"You've never had a regular sex friend," Vivian says, like she's just putting this together. "You haven't had a boyfriend in New York."

"Nope," I say. "Just hookups. Hence my salient Meg-Ryan-in-Katz's-Deli impression."

"What about college?" Vivian asks. "You had a boyfriend, right?"

"Ash." I nod. "Total sweetie. But Ash and I were more like best friends than fifty shades of any color palette."

"That was not my college experience." Vivian stretches, her sinewy arms tightening. "I basically didn't wear pants for four years."

"I just had a lot of threesomes," Steph says thoughtfully. "At the time I figured I was really into group sex. With girls."

"What finally clued you in?" Vivian asks.

"First season of *Orange Is the New Black*," Steph says, and we all nod sagely.

I remember the scenes Steph is talking about: full, soapy breasts in a steamy shower. Neck-arching pleasure. Heat radiating from pert nipples. "That could be gone for me," I murmur, glancing at the small dip of my cleavage.

Steph squeezes my hand. "I'd say it doesn't matter, but it really does. To me. I love having my boobs touched."

Vivian nods, like it's a no-brainer. "I can come from just nipple play."

I blink. "Holy polymorphic pleasure zones, Batman." Annoyingly, I'm blushing. I resist the urge to squirm, trying instead to channel my friends' unfazed cool. "Would you guys do it? A mastectomy?"

Vivian answers first. "I would. For sure. Prevention is always better than cure."

I look to Steph. Her face twists into uncertainty. "Maybe, one day? But to be honest, I don't think I could do it now, in my twenties. What if they invent a cure or I changed my mind? It just seems so final."

A cure. What if they invent a cure?

Or what if they don't?

"But wow, I'd miss my breasts," Vivian adds, skimming her fingers over the small mounds under her shirt. She drains her glass. "Lace, you *have* to have the Big O before you even *think* about the Big M."

Steph nods vehemently. "Many O's! You deserve that much."

"But I hate dating," I say. "It's the most unfun fun thing in the world."

"So don't date," Viv says.

"Yeah, just find some bloke to shag," Steph says, then hiccups.

This extensive honesty is not my forte, but if not now, when? If not with the girls, who? "I think my childhood kind of screwed me up. By the time I worked out everything I'd been told was basically BS and my body is, in fact, a pleasure garden, it just seemed too late."

"But it's not too late," Vivian says. "You're twenty-five. Go nuts. Go to a play party or have a threesome."

"I don't like the idea of being one of two girls some guy gets to hook up with," I say. "I don't want to be there for his entertainment."

"But what about *your* entertainment?" Vivian jabs a finger at me.

"Why can't *you* be the center of attention?" Steph says. "Sex happens with other people, but it's really about you, how you feel, yourself."

Sex is about . . . me. I'm responsible for my own pleasure. For working out what turns me on, what I like. And for acting on it. That was not the advice passed down to me by the well-meaning

PTA moms of Buntley, Illinois, in their control-top panty hose and beige grandma bras. Sex wasn't a rollicking adventure park. It was a deserted parking lot you'd best not walk through alone at night. Steph and Vivian are worldly women. I'm a naive child. "I'm a lost cause," I groan. "It's too late for me."

Steph elbows me. "Oh, stop moping. You've got six months."

"A lot can change in six months." Vivian arches an eyebrow.

That's true. A lot can change in six months . . .

Energy swirls inside of me, jettisoning me to my feet. I flip the whiteboard. Uncapping a marker, I write three words in big, bold letters.

BOOB BUCKET LIST

Part Two

7.

My new chapter of sexual exploration starts with snoring. Steph is channeling such serious industrial machinery, I'm surprised the mirror hasn't shattered. I ended up staying over, claiming the car services were surging. Truthfully, I didn't want to face the start of what could be my last six months of IRL boobs alone. It's 7:45 a.m. Not a time I knew existed on Saturdays because I'm usually sleeping off a hangover the size of South America. Welcome to the new me.

In the living room, abused pizza boxes yawn open like cardboard tongues. Red wine turns sticky in the bottom of wineglasses. And there's my list. In the unforgiving light of day, I'm not sure I can go through with it. Or why it seemed like such an essential idea. Maybe it's a sexy distraction from a very unsexy problem. Maybe I needed to make a firm decision about something that wasn't as full-on as yes-I'm-having-a-mastectomy. Maybe it really will help me make that decision. Maybe I was just horny. I take a pic of it on my phone and glance around for something to destroy the evidence.

The toilet flushes.

Steph's asleep.

Cooper.

I rocket to the whiteboard to wipe away the ink with my fingertips. Nothing's coming off. *I used a permanent marker.* Footsteps in the hall. Panicked, I try to flip the board but it's locked into position, and Cooper's padding in with sleep-crazed hair, glasses askew, wearing nothing but Snoopy pajama bottoms, saying, "Oh. Hi."

I stand like a starfish in front of the board, pretending to stretch. "Morning."

"Big night, huh?" He scoops up a few empty wine bottles. His biceps bulge, briefly. For a nerd, they look surprisingly . . . round. A light dusting of hair disappears below the waistband of his pants. His stomach is flat, his collarbone as solid as the handle of a gun. Coop hits the gym. I'm almost leering, but his gaze is polite. "What did you decide?"

I pivot my body to follow with him as he crosses the room. "I'm going to think about getting a mastectomy." I say it like I'm considering switching gyms.

He stops. The courteous host-like facade cracks. "Holy shit. That's intense, right?"

"You could say that."

He straightens his glasses, his face alive with curiosity. "How are you feeling about it?"

"Like I need to do some yoga *on my own*—"

"What's that?" His eyes are on the board.

"Nothing."

"What is that?" He's coming toward me, squinting at the list. "Are you hiding something from me, former roommate?"

He pokes me in the ribs and I gasp, giggling, "No, don't! Don't look!"

I try to yank him into the kitchen, but he easily maneuvers me out of the way with those tight biceps of his. I can't say I don't enjoy this. "Boob Bucket List." His face moves through a series of unusual contortions. "Okay. My morning just got a lot more interesting."

I cross my arms; fine. "Matters of proximity have brought you into this. I will entrust you with this information if you promise to vault it."

"I promise." He zips his lips. "I'm very trustworthy."

This is possibly true. "Sit." I point to the couch. "You're getting the director's commentary so nothing is misconstrued."

"Let me throw a shirt on—"

"Veto." I shake my head. "I'm exposing myself to you. Metaphorically."

"You can do it literally." He settles into the couch, folding his arms. Again, biceps. "If it'll help with your list."

Is he flirting with me? Or is it just banter? Behind his glasses, his eyes are bright. They're not quite green, not quite brown, but it's not the color that's the most striking. It's the intelligence. The corners of his lips tick up in an almost mischievous smile. In high school, I bet he was voted most likely to own a podcast network.

A good comeback escapes me, so I turn to the board, feeling buzzy and a bit goofy, somewhere between *successful presentation* and *day drinker*. "Basically, this is to help me make my decision. Or just help me, period. Okay. Here we go." I point. "Number one: sunbathe topless. Never done it, Steph assures me it's the tits, pun intended. Number two: nude photo shoot." I indicate my breasts. "To immortalize them forever. Number three: wear boobs-on-parade dress to fancy event."

"What's a boobs-on-parade dress?"

"Like the girls on *The Bachelor* wear."

"I don't watch *The Bachelor*."

"Think Tinder meets *The Hunger Games*. With hot tubs."

He shrugs, affecting cluelessness. "Can you describe one to me? Maybe try on something of Steph's?"

"Steph only wears T-shirts."

"There's scissors in the kitchen." He mimes cutting a very deep neckline. He is definitely flirting with me.

I threaten him with a pizza crust. "Don't be cheeky," I say, but another part of me is thinking, *Why shouldn't he be cheeky? We're talking about my boobs.* I spin back to the board. My skin feels warm. "Number four: threesome. Classic for a reason. Number five: role-play. Not sure what that'll entail, but I can do a pretty good French accent: *oui, oui, bonjour Monsieur!* Number six: sex with a woman. That was Steph's idea," I add, turning back.

Cooper has one of the throw pillows in his lap. He has an erection. Obviously. Why else would he do that? The possibility of sex doesn't just enter the room, it barges in with maracas and a flag. The light blush I'm feeling turns into a forest fire, fanning alarm, not lust. My nipples are erect, painfully sensitive. We stare at each other, him "coolly," me "openly panicked." *Sex* doesn't belong here, in the living room, at 8:00 a.m., between a random roommate and me. This whole performance is entirely inappropriate.

Yet I can't stop myself from finishing.

"Number seven: sex in a white limousine. One too many hip-hop videos when I was a teenager, I suppose." I bet he can see my ass hanging out of these boxer shorts. Is he staring at it? "And number eight: sex in a public place." Why am I reading all of these out to him like a perverted schoolteacher? Why did I think this was a reasonable activity to suggest? "Again, something I have . . . not . . . done."

The living room is so quiet I can hear the upstairs neighbors using inside voices. I briefly consider exiting this situation by torpedoing through the front window, Jason Bourne–style.

"So, that's my list." Surely, I'm the color of a stop sign. "I know it's pretty sexcentric, but I figure boobs are related to pleasure, which is related to sex and I'm sort of . . ." *Stop talking, stop talking, stop the words coming out of your mouth.* "I mean, I figured a list would help, y'know . . . *git 'er done.*"

Cooper folds his hands calmly over the throw pillow as if we're both not hyperaware of its function. "I think it's great. Everyone should have a list."

"What's on yours?"

He half laughs, glancing in the direction of the kitchen. He can't leave, not with the huge freaking boner he's hiding under that cushion. He's my prisoner. And that's . . . kind of hot. I sink onto the other end of the couch. "Just tell me one. You know eight of mine."

He exhales noisily, but he's smiling. "Wow. Okay. Let's see." His fingers drum the cushion. "All right. I got one. Promise you'll vault it, okay?"

"Yes, sir," I say, which is not how I usually address guys my own age.

"Sometimes when I'm *romancing the stone*"—he indicates his crotch, which makes me giggle—"I think about this waitress who used to work at a diner my friends and I went to in high school."

"Oooh," I tease. "Blond and buxom?" I do my best Marilyn Monroe purr. "*Little more cream in your coffee, boys?*"

"No." Cooper shakes his head, amused. "She was not sexy. Not in the traditional sense. She was older, like an aunt. Solid. She was actually kind of mean."

"And that turns you on?"

He shrugs, in an adorably helpless sort of way. "I felt like if we did it, she'd . . . take care of me."

"Take care of you?" I'm laughing. "That is terrifying."

"The heart wants what the heart wants," he says. "Emily Dickinson said it first."

"Well, she's been dead for a hundred years," I say. "Maybe she'd do it for you too."

"Oh, *burn*," he says, thwacking me with the boner pillow.

"Ew!" I cry, and we're both grappling like little kids when Steph drags herself in and we spring apart.

"What is going on? I'm *so* hungover." She plops down between us. She smells like a winery.

"Nothing," we say in unison, which sounds far more incriminating than it should.

"I need food," Steph groans, cuddling into me. "I need the home fries at Freddies or I'll die."

Cooper's on his feet, heading for the kitchen. I think about asking him to come with us, but second-guess the best "casual" way to do it, and he's gone. Which is probably for the best.

Steph said he was off-limits, after all.

8.

Freddies has always been our brunch spot. They make Steph's favorite home fries in the whole world: crispy on the outside, creamy in the middle. The servers are uniformly chill and cute in a nonbinary sort of way. And it's got that whole yard-sale-meets-Grandma's-house vibe in the decor: mismatched chairs, framed paintings of big-eyed children, vintage rocking horse in the corner, ferns. For these reasons, it is also half of Astoria's favorite brunch spot. Even though we get there earlier than usual, we still have to wait for a table. "This neighborhood is really changing," Steph says, eyeing the blue-haired couple in front of us. "So many hipsters."

"Steph, we are hipsters," I tell her. "We're the ones changing the neighborhood."

She elbows my ribs, glancing around. "Don't say that."

"Why not? It's the truth."

"I feel bad," Steph says. "Fifty years ago this was all Greek families; it was a community."

"It's still a community now," I say, but I know what she means. And she's right: sometimes it feels like every success in New York happens at someone else's expense.

Steph stuffs her hands in her coat pockets. "My parents had to move out of East London when I was in high school—out of the house I was literally born in—because they couldn't afford the rent anymore. Guess who moved in?"

"Hipsters."

"Punks. Artist punks, a couple." She pauses, remembering. "I had a huge crush on the woman. I made her a mix CD. Sent it anonymously."

"Mix CD." I fan myself. "Be still, my beating labia."

She laughs.

The server threads his way toward us.

"And neighborhoods are always changing," I add. Just like bodies. Just like everything. "Whether you like it or not."

As soon as we order, Steph declares it's time to start on the List.

I almost choke on my coffee. "What, now?"

"Yup," she says, unlocking her phone. "Otherwise you'll chicken out."

A distinct possibility.

Steph frowns at her screen. "Sunbathing topless is going to have to wait. January remains very January-esque. Let's move on to *ménage à trois*." She gives me a wicked grin, her thumbs flying as she scrolls and taps. "Threesomes are bonkers fun, because you're the star of the show. It's honestly the closest I've ever felt to being a celebrity. Ah: here we go. Welcome to your first step of sensual liberation."

Cam and Camila have dark hair, olive skin, and teeth the color of fresh snow. They look like they both enjoy smoothies, a lot.

"They're *YouTubers*," Steph says, making it sound like they're diamond thieves. "I met Camila at Pilates, when I was an undergrad."

"You don't do Pilates."

"But I did frequent the café at Pilates. Amazing vegan cookies, couldn't even tell they were vegan." She taps open their channel. Camila 4 Cam. "Look. Three hundred thousand subscribers."

"That's actually not that many." A video about what they eat in a day starts. Lifestyle-brand stuff.

"Snob." Steph pokes me. "Don't you think they're cute?"

I study their pictures: objectively attractive. "How long were you hooking up with them? How many times?"

"I don't know, a few times. Then a few more."

"Why did you stop?"

"I don't really remember." This could be a lie. Steph flaps her hands about. "It was years ago, but I'll totally text them if you want."

I'm looking for a reason to say no—they're too bland/muscly/earnest. Which Oprah would say is my fear speaking. I hand her phone back. "Sure. If you think they'd be into me. And I wouldn't have to do more than seven push-ups before we do it."

Steph squeals. "Oh, they'll be into you," she says. "You're a hottie with the lottie."

"Just don't tell them about . . ." I indicate my boobs.

"They wouldn't care!"

"Steph, no. It's bad enough your roommate knows everything, but the buck stops there. You, Viv, that's it."

As someone who grew up without a mother, I have zero interest in inviting other people's tactlessness back into my life. Things people have said to my face: "Oh. Oh, God. I don't know how I could've grown up without my mom. She's my best friend. I love her so much. I'm going to call her right now." And "Lucky you, I hate my mother, hopeless bitch. Seriously: you're lucky." And "My friend's mother died when she was young." "My friend's cousin died of cancer." "My friend did the catering for *Fault in Our Stars*. That's about that. Cancer." Or, most common of all, the nonreaction: "Oh. Er . . ." *Cue change of topic.*

When it comes to cancer, I already know that what you so often get is other people's fear.

"Are you sure?" Steph frowns. "It might help to reach out to people. Your community."

"I don't need shitty self-help nonsense, faux empowerment slogans, or ding-dongs judging my choices. This is strictly a need-to-know situation," I say. "As far as the advertisement of my life as experienced through social media, you better believe it's going to be Lacey Whitman's Best Year Ever."

Our food arrives: chia seed breakfast bowl for me, bacon sandwich for Steph. "Didn't you order it with home fries?"

She shushes me. "Salad's great!"

I groan. "Just *tell the waiter.*"

"I need the greens." She takes a huge bite of pork, eyeing the chia bowl. "No egg-white omelet?" My usual order. "Are you trying to make me feel fat?"

"I'm trying to be high-fiber," I say. "I'm trying not to get cancer."

She swallows awkwardly. I shouldn't have said that. Globs of chia seeds slime down my throat.

"Speaking of prevention," she says, which I wasn't aware we were, "I've been researching some things I can do to help."

The idea of Steph helping me with something that is quite literally life-or-death is so ill fitting, it pools around my ankles, ten inches from my toes. I look after Steph. I help her through teary breakups, explain how taxes work, trap spiders, evaluate outfits. When she applied for grad school the year before last, I was the one who put all her schools into a spreadsheet and project-managed her application. The fact she's in her second year of a master's of psychology at NYU is partly due to me. I'm not complaining. I like it. It's our dynamic. But I don't think it works both ways. If she had to, say, pick me up from the hospital, chances are she'd arrive at the wrong one, an hour late. Research plastic surgeons? She'd end up balls-deep in the comments section of a truffle grilled cheese recipe on SmittenKitchen.com. Or worse still, being talked off a ledge over the drama of it all, fainting at the first mention of the word *scalpel*. But beyond her lovable screwball dysfunction and tendency to get a little overinvolved, there's something about Steph's helping me—about anyone helping me—that makes me feel so uncomfortable, I'm almost annoyed. Dealing with the gross aftermath of a mastectomy and breast reconstruction feels like a personal medical issue that I would as likely get my friends to help with as I would a case of diarrhea. The bucket list, they can have. But the surgery and all that goes along with it: that's my business. "Don't sweat it, babe."

"But I want to sweat it. I want to get sweaty."

Teary, more like. Any money Steph is the one who loses it before I do. I spear a slice of strawberry. "I got this, seriously."

From the corner of my eye, I watch her exhale, concerned.

Her phone buzzes. It's Camila and Cam. They're interested.

"Holy smokes, just like that?" I grab Steph's phone. "Camila You-Tube" wants me to call.

"This is New York City," Steph says. "You can get anything in less than forty minutes. Unless it involves fresh air or emotional vulnerability."

Is that a dig at me? I signal for the check. The morning is slouching into the afternoon and I promised Vivian I'd get on top of my Clean Clothes work this weekend. Lil' Robot has never dropped the ball before.

In my best not–that–it–matters voice, I ask, "What's Coop's deal?"

Steph looks up from her hand mirror with half a mouth of red lipstick. "Huh?"

"How did you find him?" I examine the fascination of my cuticles. "What does he do?"

Steph snaps the mirror shut. "No. No way, Lace. Look, I just organized you a threesome, you've got your hands full."

"I only asked—"

"Don't mess up my living sitch, Lace, *please*. He leaves the toilet seat down and makes blueberry pancakes and paid three months' rent in advance. And," she adds, "I might kill myself if you end up dating someone before I do. To be honest, that's why I stopped doing threesomes. I want to be in a *relationship*." She gazes mournfully around the restaurant as if every single bruncher has individually rejected a romantic advance.

"Don't worry, I was just curious." I stroke her hand. "I'm not interested. Frankly I find it offensive that bony hairless nerds have been elevated to Greek god status. I blame Silicon Valley."

I think I fool Steph. But I haven't entirely fooled myself.

9.

My apartment feels cool and deserted, like an empty theater. Signing the lease on my own apartment in New York City had been high on my list of grown-up fantasies ever since I was a kid. Vivian helped me decorate it. I try to think of it as chic and modern. Not stark. Or a little lonely. It just doesn't feel like I thought it would. But it seems like everyone who has roommates longs to live alone, and everyone who does absolutely loves it. Maybe I should get a dog.

My bills from NY3C arrived in a plain white envelope: doom and gloom, oh so discreet. My insurance does cover genetic counseling but it doesn't cover the confirmation test I ordered to double-check my result, and there'll definitely be a copay situation on pretty much everything I do from now on. Let the financial ruin begin.

I pop a sparkling water, put on some languid electronica, and settle in for an afternoon of outfit curation for Clean Clothes. A long list of users requesting outfits greets me; I'm way behind. Usually I knock out a half-dozen outfits a night after work, or first thing in the morning on the days I don't go to the gym. This past week has tossed every part of my schedule out the window. I have to get back on top of things.

The first user's board is SoCal with a twist of boho: crystals, fringed vests, vintage rock tees, hippie headbands. She's sixteen, from California, wanting a new look for school. I put together a loose maxi slip with cute crochet accents, a big chunky cardigan, two-tone Western-inspired cowboy boots, light-reflecting John Lennon sunglasses, and a fun statement necklace heavy with rose quartz and long colorful tassels. Six months ago, I might've thrown in some velvet, but that trend is, thankfully, going the way of all waning trends: into the great recycle basket in the sky.

The looks come in waves: last year there was the prom wave, the Christmas wave, then the New Year's Eve wave. Putting together the outfits feeds my need to be a personal stylist, an online shopper, and busy, period. I believe in ethical clothing, and I genuinely love the brands making it: passionate people using their talent for good. I also love putting looks together. I was the girl who made her own dress for prom, who ruined the bathtub dyeing leather. I love nothing more than digging through a friend's wardrobe, finding things that work, that are a true expression of who they really are. For me, fashion is about more than clothes or runway shows or airbrushed magazines. Coco Chanel said, "Fashion is not something that exists in dresses only. Fashion is in the sky, in the street, fashion has to do with ideas, the way we live, *what is happening.*" This is what interests me. The intersection between culture, identity, politics, and play. I didn't have these words when I first moved to New York, but I knew in my bones what they were about.

Fashion wasn't something that was happening in Buntley, Illinois. It was something that existed over the rainbow, way up high, in the far-off lands of New York and Paris and Milan. The discovery that it was something I had a knack for—not just pulling together an outfit but also understanding the history, seeing the connections between designers, understanding what they were talking about in interviews— that was more than just interesting. It was exhilarating. It was a relief. When I was a kid, designers were my rock stars, the ones whose pictures covered my bedroom walls and school folders. They lived a life where clothes were currency. Where clothes *mattered.* To a kid who had to wear hand-me-downs, whose Barbie was the knockoff "Fashion Doll" from the dollar store, that seemed amazing. Even kind of ridiculous. But dreams are a bit ridiculous. Pursuing something that thousands of other people want to do, and what most of them won't get to do, that is ridiculous. In the best, most exciting kind of way. For me, fashion has always been about so much more than just expensive clothes on skinny models. It's about who I am. And who I'm not.

Usually I find outfit curation for Clean Clothes soothing and enjoyable. It's my meditation, sending brain and body into a placid, comfortable space, a relaxed, even indulgent state of consciousness.

But today, I'm distractible. I can't sink into it like I usually do.

I shuffle through the pamphlets I got from Judy-Ann and Dr. Williams: *Preparing for Mastectomy, BRCA1 and You, Finding Solidarity and Support*. A sea of smiling, concerned women with more racial diversity than the UN. Conspicuously absent: men reeling away in horror, women bursting into tears at the sight of their butchered boobs. My own chest constricts with a small wave of panic. I shove the pamphlets in my desk drawer, telling myself I don't need to rush into anything. Picking up my phone, I find my sister's name. Mara Whitman. My finger hovers over her number.

Hi sis, it's me. Remember how much you didn't want us to take that cancer gene test? Well, surprise, I took it, and, surprise, I have it, and surprise, there's a 50 percent chance you might have it too, byeeee!

Yeah, right. I'll see her in a few weeks. It'll be better face-to-face is the lie I settle on.

I don't even remember opening Camila 4 Cam's YouTube page. It's just on my screen, bleached-white teeth blinding me like a flashlight in a darkened room. One video, I tell myself. I need to know what I'm getting myself into, if I decide to call.

"Hi guys, Camila here." An ethnically diverse Disney princess, flipping a glossy brown mane. I try to imitate her and get hair in my mouth. "Today I'm going to show you three easy workouts that'll give you a bubble butt like mine. Ready? Let's get into it!"

Who doesn't want a bubble butt like Camila's? And who doesn't want to watch Camila showing you how she got hers? I push my chair back, ready to squat till I drop.

Wait: my bucket list isn't about *physical* self-improvement. I might be seeing this girl *naked*, and I best be firing on all four cylinders when I do. It's been a while since I romanced the stone, as Cooper put it. I told Steph and Viv I faked orgasms as a time-saving method. The truth is more complicated. I do it because I don't want to hurt someone's feelings or for the guy to get annoyed. Or really, because I'm not super comfortable coming with someone else. The flow I get into when I'm doing anything from curating outfits or making spreadsheets or even masturbating isn't as flowy when there's other people around. That needs to change. I need to let people in, so to speak. And change, as they say, starts at home.

Feeling very much like I'm dipping my hand into an illicit cookie jar, I slide my fingers under the band of my underpants and focus solely on Camila's perfect ass.

Right about now, my brain usually flips through a series of factory-tested scenarios: lesbian porn clips, past hookups, sexy movie scenes, some standard intern/boss or teacher/student shenanigans. I'm never in my sexual fantasies; I flip perspectives between the characters. But because Camila is someone I might have sex with, I give myself the starring role.

I picture sitting between Camila and Cam. Cam's just wearing jeans and Camila's in black lacy underwear. I imagine making out with Camila. Kissing her in a slow, decadent way, like licking an ice-cream cone on a summer's day. Cam's mouth is on my neck, running his tongue along my jaw until I shiver. In my ear, Camila moans softly and all the little hairs in my eardrum stand to attention. My blood runs hot, and I'm greedy, needing. I run my fingers over her ass, squeezing the plump flesh, and then slide both hands up her body to trace her generous breasts. They're full and soft, spilling out of her bra. Reaching inside, I brush her erect nipples. She gasps, girlish, arching her back. Cam's unbuckling his belt, shucking off his jeans. His stomach is golden, a board of solid flesh. His lips are parted as I slide my fingers slowly, deliberately slowly, into his boxers. I grasp hold of his cock. It's huge and hard as a rock, warm in my palm. He lets out a rough breath, his eyes on my hand. As I start stroking him, Camila's hands circle my tits, squeezing them, cupping them, the tip of her tongue circling my nipple. I am blind with desire. Saliva floods my mouth, the sensitive parts of me throbbing, needing contact. Cam pulls me toward him. I'm straddling him with spread legs. Strong hands grip my thighs and he tips his hips to rub himself against me. My underwear is off. I'm naked, slick with sweat. Cam slides two fingers between my legs. "You're wet," he says wonderingly. Admiringly. "Lacey, you're so wet." I am. I really, really am. Camila's mouth is on mine, our tongues touching, as I lower myself onto Cam. He fills me completely, a slick, hot rush of pleasure. I exhale in release, rocking my hips, and he's bucking up and we're all moving in tandem, thrusting, touching—hands, lips, tongues everywhere—and I'm going to come, holy fuck I'm going to come—

My phone rings. Vivian. I yank my hand from my pants: sprung. It rings out, then starts again, insistent. I answer with my pinkie and scramble to find a washcloth. "Hey babe. What's up?"

In the background, a Katy Perry power anthem. Viv's panting. Treadmill. Gym. "Just checking in. How are you going with the outfits?"

Obviously she's tracking my lack-of-progress. My entire body is thrumming, thrilled, hysterical with stifled laughter. I feel like I just gave sugar to a kid and bore witness to the attendant high. I'm a little guilty, but most of all bewildered, even amused. I try not to sound breathless. "I've been . . . researching plastic surgeons. But I'm getting ready for an all-nighter."

I hear a beep, the sound of the treadmill slowing. Ms. Perry fades. Viv's voice sounds clearer. "Lace . . ."

"Yeah?"

"Is Clean Clothes still something you can commit to?"

I blink once, hard. The sugar high I'd kindled flickers out. "What do you mean, of course I'm committed."

A short pause. "We haven't talked about Hoffman House in a while. Are you still interested in becoming an editor?"

"No. I'm not," I lie. "I'm *fully committed* to the app." Another lie.

"Look, I know you've got a lot on your plate right now. Your diagnosis has already changed your priorities."

"It's affected them," I counter. "But it hasn't changed them entirely. Shit, I've been MIA for only a week."

"I know, I know, and that's understandable," Vivian says. "I'm not mad. I'm just trying to manage the future." She pauses. I wait. "We can at least have a conversation about what it looks like if you were to step out now. Before anything . . . gets affected."

My chest is rising and falling fast. I'm fighting a wave of anger. Step out now? I've been working for free for *eight months*. I own twenty percent of this company. My fingers are clenching the phone. I relax my hand. There's only one way to go head-to-head with Vivian. Match *her* cool head, word for word. "We don't need to have a conversation about it," I say. "I'm one hundred percent committed. I'm seeing this through."

Silence. I imagine us both staring into the middle distance trying to conjure our version of the future into the other's head.

"Great," Vivian says, with the simplicity of a raindrop. "I'm happy to hear it. Also, I might have a plastic surgeon recommendation for you. A friend of mine got her tits done with him last year."

I wouldn't be "getting my tits done." I'd be launching a preemptive strike against my own body. But I make myself sound surprised and thankful when I reply, "That'll cut down on research time." Because that's exactly what she wants to hear. We are self-serving creatures, even if we have the very best of intentions.

"I'll text you," Vivian says. "Have fun with the outfits."

I hang up. It should feel like victory, or relief, but instead I feel like I was fighting someone else's battle, with the outcome undecided.

The outcome that is decided?

Camila 4 Cam 4 Lacey.

10.

February

I've been on hold with my insurance company for thirty-eight ex-cruciating minutes in an attempt to work out various copays when Eloise glides into Hoffman House in a white mink coat and thigh-high boots. Impossibly, she makes eye contact with me. Impossibly, she starts coming my way. *No, not now, please not now*—

"Got a second?" she asks as the on-hold music clicks off and a real, live human says, "Sorry to keep you waiting, how can I help?"

"I'll call you back." I consider swiping my coffee cup and the rem-nants of a bran muffin into the trash, but it's too late. She is here, now, at my desk.

Her gaze flicks over my outfit: plaid wool skirt, sweater embroi-dered with *i miss barack*, slouchy beanie. "What a colorful outfit."

"Thank you," I say, trying not to sound eager or grateful, of which I am both. "How are you?" No, too familiar. "What's up?"

"Fashion Week has been insane this year," she sighs, false lashes fluttering. "I'm a little behind."

"You need me to write a report?" I scramble through my note-books. "I could do something on sculptural silhouettes, or all these remastered reds we're seeing—"

"No, no, no," she cuts me off with an airy laugh. "I just need some-one to fact-check my work and upload a few galleries. Tonight."

She's not the only one behind. I pushed back every client presenta-tion last week. My in-box is as full as a football stadium, and I need to nail down the copays. Find out if I can extend my coverage for more than one night in a hospital, should I end up going through with it. I'm not even sure if getting on Eloise's team is plan A or plan B, now that getting a lead investor for Clean Clothes is something Vivian feels we're ready for. But in the interest of keeping all doors open, I want in on the fashion editor's good graces. Honestly, I'm flattered that she'd ask. Last week in the kitchen, she caught me piling a stack of sandwiches leftover from a meeting into a ziplock bag. They'd only be thrown out; I was planning on having them for dinner. Humiliated, I tried to make a joke. "Free never loses its appeal, does it?"

Beneath the cashmere cardigan knotted around her porcelain décolletage, her shoulders raised in a helpless shrug, as if to say, *I wouldn't know. I've slept on a big pile of money my entire life.* I felt bad about the thought as soon as it came. Neither of us can help where we come from.

Vivian doesn't like Eloise. They met last year at an event at The Wing, an insanely beautiful female coworking space that gives women the right to be free from men while surrounded by lovely things. Vivian thinks Eloise is a snob: *an elitist* were her exact words. I don't agree. Sure, Eloise is no populist, but her taste is impeccable, and she exudes calm, purposeful confidence that is enviably bulletproof. During my first month as an intern, I dropped off her favorite lunch order (sashimi) without having to be asked and she gave me a gold Miu Miu headband encrusted with Swarovski crystals and milky pearls. Yes, she'd been sent the headband for free, but she could have kept it for herself and she didn't: she gave it to me. It was the single most expensive gift I'd ever been given.

So now, all these years later, there's only one answer I can give her. "Sure. I'd be happy to—"

The interns descend. They are explosive with excitement. "Sorry to interrupt—"

"We thought you should know—"

"Omigod, it's so exciting—"

"You're going to die!"

"What?" I ask.

The trio choruses as one. "Elan Behzadi!"

"Invited you—"

"To his show—"

"Tonight!"

I can wrangle invites to the after-parties, but never to the actual shows: those are reserved for people significantly more powerful or beautiful than me—people like Eloise, who is frowning delicately. "Are you sure?"

The interns nod. "His publicist called—"

"You're on the list—"

"*Tonight.*" The interns thrust a phone message at me.

A scribbled address and *7:00 p.m.* underlined three times. My instinct is to squeal. Instead, I channel Eloise's unflappable cool, nodding at the interns as if they'd just handed me some almost-interesting mail. "You're going, aren't you?" I ask Eloise.

"Of course." She's clearly surprised at my invitation, and I don't blame her. I've never been to a main-stage Fashion Week show. And, okay, I know Fashion Week is going the way of Facebook: lame, outdated, a waste of time and resources, but . . . it's *New York Fashion Week*.

"If his publicist called, I better go," I say. "I'm sorry. Hope you can find someone to help you out."

She opens her mouth to reply, pauses, seems to reconsider, then simply says, "Have fun." She turns and walks away.

Why on earth did Elan Behzadi invite me to his show?

11.

"It's obvious why he invited you." The video connection drops out for a second so Vivian's next words come sped-up double-time. "Hewantstoboneyou."

"I don't think *bumbling idiot* is Elan Behzadi's type," I say. "And he's certainly not mine."

"Racist."

"No, dummy. He's old."

"Forties isn't old."

"That is honestly really depressing." I remember when thirty was old. Now it's coming for me while I sleep like Freddy freaking Krueger. "He's probably gay," I add, even though I don't believe this. Elan has been engaged twice, married once, very briefly, to an actress-ish. (According to the rag mags, they are still "great friends," which is obviously "total BS.") "What about this one?" I pirouette in front of the computer. "Too basic?"

Vivian looks unimpressed. She's at the coworking space. Behind her, two guys are having a meeting. Both are holding very small dogs. "You need to make an impression, babe."

"Pass. I've already made one impressive exit around this dude. I'll settle for can't-place-her-face."

"At least show off your legs," Vivian says, matter of fact. "Or your tits. Having any kind of support from Elan would be major."

"You just want free clothes."

"I can afford my own clothes, Lace," she says. "Besides, isn't that on the bucket list: boobs-on-parade dress?"

"What are you, my pimp?" I wriggle out of the dress. "No boobs, no parade, not tonight."

A buzz. "That's Brock on the other line." Clean Clothes's whiz-kid engineer. "Gotta take it. Have fun. Meet Elan!" And she's gone.

When it comes to events, I usually go for hip over sexy. No plunging cleavage or thigh-high skirts: power to the Kardashians but it just isn't me, a.k.a. my authentic personal brand. But the usual ease at which I pull a look together is oddly absent. I yank aside hangers, diving toward the back of a closet stuffed with samples, freebies, and thrift-store finds. It's almost six and I haven't even showered: I'm running out of time.

And that's when I feel it.

The distinctive texture of tulle.

* * * *

I've always liked dressing up. When my middle school put on a performance of *Jack and the Beanstalk*, I begged my teacher to let me be the Goose That Laid the Golden Egg because that was the most fun and outlandish costume in the cast. Being playful with how I look has always made me feel confident. And now, ascending out of the subway into Tribeca, I feel more than confident. I feel like a badass. The long black tulle skirt I'm wearing used to be the underskirt of a terrible bridesmaid dress I was forced to wear at a high school friend's shotgun wedding. I didn't realize how much I needed to rip it from its seams until I started doing it. From there, everything fell into place. I used my trusty hot-glue gun to attach the tulle to a thick black elastic belt, and I'm wearing that over these amazing blue-green sequined boy shorts I nabbed at an Opening Ceremony sample sale. Up top, a tight black turtleneck that scoops in the back and has big cutouts over the shoulders. Secondhand Frye motorcycle boots. Gold jewelry, lots of it, very mismatchy, very Brooklyn. Dark pink lip gloss, a few false lashes, smidge of bronzer. I didn't have time to blow-dry my hair but some sea salt spray makes it look just-got-back-from-the-beach chic. I don't care that my legs are freezing as I join the (massive) line for the show. I look rock-and-roll and, yes, sexy as hell.

I strike up a convo with this gorgeous black dude wearing moon boots and his very short, very funny boyfriend. We share a small joint. We laugh at the ridiculousness of everything.

I'm not precancerous here. I'm just a regular girl. I'm on the list.

All afternoon I'd been fantasizing about finding myself front row, inexplicably rubbing shoulders with Anna Wintour, tossing off a line like, "I'm a friend of Elan's" to explain my caste-hopping. My fantasy evaporates when I'm thrust a paper ticket with an *S*: standing room only. I'm not upset. I'm grateful. This small-town girl is really here, in the center of things, in New York City. I got myself here: not my parents, not a trust fund, not my tits. Me. No matter what the future holds, no one can take this away from me.

I step into preshow chaos.

Like cocktail hour, it's always Fashion Week somewhere. From Sydney to Seoul to Slovenia, Fashion Week rolls around the earth in an unstoppable orgy of hand-stitched hems and hot haute couture. There are only four that really matter: London, Milan, Paris, and New York. Everything else is akin to the regional office throwing a party with paper plates.

Elan's show is at one of the two main venues for this year. Originally a 1930s train terminal, it's a white-walled industrial-looking gallery the size of a high school gymnasium. For past shows, it's been transformed into everything from a fake forest to the palace of Versailles. Tonight, the look is clean, stark, and classic: no shtick, no tricks. A U-shaped runway curves from one set of black curtains to another, lined by four tiers of chairs, with a media rise for a group of noisy photographers at the far end. Beyond the curtains, I imagine backstage chaos: the hive-like buzz of models and makeup artists and assistants, all managing meltdowns by swigging water with electrolytes.

Is Elan calm or stressed out? Does he enjoy this or endure it?

Did my invite mean anything?

No booze or finger food: most of the crowd will be out the door as soon as the lights come back on, zooming to the next show. I jostle into place behind the fourth row and scan the crowd. A costume party with no discernible theme. Sunglasses and wigs and requisite Cool Kid posturing by people trying too hard to look bored (if you're that bored, why are you even here?). Eloise is in the second row on the other side. I try to catch her eye, but she is gazing at the front row with such deeply felt longing, I wonder if it is possible to love a seating arrangement. A-list celebs are present and accounted for in the form of the three Emmas: Watson, Roberts, and Stone. Everyone is pretending like they couldn't care less—*What famous people, who?* I surreptitiously gawk like the Midwesterner that I am and text Steph. No sooner do I hit send than the lights dim. A smash-clash of raucous classical. The show—and subsequent live streaming of the show by every single audience member—has begun.

Elan Behzadi has been a fixture of Fashion Week for as long as I can remember, which admittedly isn't that long. A few tiers below big dogs like Marc Jacobs or Ralph Lauren, he's still one of those younger male designers who seems to always be there: dressing celebs for the Emmys or the Oscars, showing up to parties with a variety of beautiful young sticks, rating occasional who-what-where mentions on Page Six. His line is in Saks and Bergdorf, and a flagship store in the Meatpacking District. His style is sleek and sophisticated, the kind of clothes women like Vivian Chang have hanging in their closets. Tonight's show presents fall's ready-to-wear.

One by one, models pour out from the black velvet curtains like well-dressed lemmings. The mood is luxe, European, classy. Elan uses color sparingly, focusing instead on fine fabrics, perfect fits. Tonight's palette is white, black, cream, and camel, with a single shot of vibrant turquoise blue. Everything is pared back and elegant. Crisp white shirts tucked into hip-slung black pants, cashmere coats cinched at the waist. The evening dresses are gorgeous; it's here Elan really shines. I make notes: *An Elan Behzadi woman is modern, fluent in fashion, effortlessly sexy. I see lunch meetings in lovely hotels, date night at the opera, midnight strolls through secret rooftop gardens.* Even though Elan's official position is he doesn't follow trends, shearling, oversize cuts, and shimmering fringe all make an appearance. Three trends I compiled ignored reports on late last year. Vindicating to see I was right.

The models are otherworldly beautiful; wide-set alien eyes and necks like pieces of pulled taffy.

I'm not a model hater. The world has enough aggression directed at women, I don't need to add to it by putting the boot into young girls born freakishly tall and thin. Honestly, they don't strike me as a happy breed. It's hard to be jealous of girls who seem to be trying very hard not to give in to crippling anxiety. I've heard they're bad in bed, but that could be a sexist rumor.

Does Elan sleep with his models? That would be morally reprehensible: they're younger, more vulnerable, it would be exploitative. How easily it could happen: a private fitting late at night, one finger skimming the side of a small breast, a cocked eyebrow, a silent proposition. Nipple in mouth, guiding him in, coarse pubic hair black through milky fingers, and my head is arching back like the wing of a bird . . . I check myself. My whole body is simmering. I'm turned on. *Focus*, I instruct myself, but I'm biting back a smile. I'm changing. I don't know this new girl, this new energy that she has, but I'm circling her, equally intrigued and in awe.

The final piece is worn by his biggest name walking tonight: Coco Du Bellay, one of the current it girls. French, black, trans, stunning. Her spectacular aquamarine dress is constructed entirely of tiers of fringe. It shimmers against her skin like rolling ocean waves. She struts, lifting her legs like a stallion negotiating sticky mud. Glimpses of rouged red nipples peek through the shifting fringe. I'm conscious of my own nipples, burning bright under my top. My bucket list drifts into my mind's eye: *Sunbathe topless. Role-play. Sex in public.* Everything on my list are things I want to do, theoretically. But for the first time, I feel that yes: I *will* do some of those things.

Or what if I did them all?

We're clapping as Coco leaves, and here comes the full lineup in their last looks, women and men with cheekbones you'd sacrifice your firstborn for. Bringing up the rear is the man himself. Next to his models, he looks positively pint-size, in a fitted gray suit, day-old stubble, and a thin purple tie. He's barely smiling, appearing entirely unfazed as he heads toward the top of the runway. I'm clapping like everyone else as he reaches the end, where he lifts a hand to acknowledge the crowd. I want him to see me. I need him to see me. His gaze barely skates the second row. For reasons I cannot comprehend, I do something very, very embarrassing. Without thinking, I thrust my thumb and pinkie in my mouth and emit a piercing round-'em-up whistle. He turns in search of the sound and I'm so mortified by my childish need to get the Famous Person's attention that I just stand there, stunned. His gaze lands on me, or I think it does, it's hard to tell with the lights.

A flash of recognition in his eyes. The same deep expression from the night we met at the Hoffman House party unfolds on his face.

He sees me.

Everything falls away. A rush of cold. I'm suspended in the vast emptiness of space, cut off from the planet, drifting into blackness. He turns away and I'm back: applause, music, a show, this night. His flock of mannequins begin exiting the runway, smiling and relaxed. The lights brighten, the chatter rises, and I am breathless, thrumming with the memory of Elan Behzadi turning his head in search of me.

12.

I hang out at the after-party for two hours, but he does not come to me. In the dimly lit Chelsea restaurant, I whirl between constellations of fashion editors and buyers, bloggers and hangers-on, fighting the ridiculous feeling that I am waiting for him. He appears every now and then, sliced between slivers of the crowd, but he does not meet my gaze. I laugh like I don't have a care in the world and track him like a spy. Champagne pours from the rafters; I want a drink so badly it hurts, but every time I reach for a glass, a zap of panic: *cancer!* The moon wheels slowly overhead. The night turns as sober as I am. It's not even midnight when I slip away, trying to talk myself out of feeling like a sad, little fangirl.

I've never had real depression. That's my sister's territory. But once I've stepped out of my tulle and motorcycle boots, and washed off my face of makeup, I can't fight the wave of emotion chasing me. Tucked into bed, feeling small and vulnerable, I let it drown me, sinking into all the things I've been trying to avoid.

No man will find me sexy if I go through with it. But I might die if I don't.

I don't want to lose my breasts. I don't want implants inside of me.

I am scared.

I am so, so scared.

* * * *

The next day I don't have any meetings, so I task myself with clicking through hundreds of fall/winter looks from the past few days at Fashion Week, identifying the patterns, looking for trends. Transparent and sheer looks are everywhere. As always, knits dominate, and we're seeing a lot of utilitarian pants and colorful outerwear. Graphic prints. Slouchy suits.

I love looking over the lines. Only after scrolling through dozens of collections do the overarching themes become apparent. It's fascinating to see how the designers interpret the season. Fashion alone can be a bit superficial, but when you connect it to the bigger picture, it really means something. Like the way I see strong reds, pinks, and violets, which reflect the growing feminist movement, or the lack of black and return instead to inky darks and browns, representing the resistance to politics of hate. The political atmosphere as interpreted by fashion is less about literal politics—Right versus Left, Republicans versus Democrats—and more about old versus new values. The twentieth century versus twenty-first. I love seeing how everything fits together; the constant conversation fashion is having with itself.

I finish a report on a trend I'm calling "art gallery nautical" and send it through to Eloise. No reply. I always assume I'm not getting it right or she's busy. But maybe she actually delights in rejecting them, as a way of rejecting everything about me. I know she's proud of her Harvard roots: maybe the fact I've seen a cow tipping firsthand disgusts her.

No. I'm just being paranoid. Alexander McQueen was raised in public housing. Ralph Lauren was a clerk at Brooks Brothers. Coco Chanel grew up in an orphanage. Fashion is not the sole domain of the Rich Kids of Instagram. I'm sure Eloise knows that.

Patricia pings me. *Come into my office.*

I shiver. Later, I'll rake over this reaction.

Somehow, I suspected what the future held.

Somehow, I knew.

Patricia's corner office has views over lower Manhattan: the rooftops and the water towers and the glinting blue pools rich people keep in secret. My boss peers at me over green-edged half specs, eyelashes slick with purple mascara. "You look cute, darling."

"So do you," I reply, "as always."

She smiles. She likes it when anyone flirts with her, even me. "I don't think I saw you yesterday. How was your weekend?"

"Great," I chirrup. "I checked out this hot new cocktail bar in a re-claimed textiles factory in Bed-Stuy. They handmade all their furniture, only play records, and make all their bitters and syrups from scratch."

"Sounds very nostalgic."

I actually went to this bar before Christmas, but I keep a collection of these little performances up my sleeve every time Patricia calls me in. She loves them. I cock my head. "I think it's more a reaction to all the immediacy in our culture. The world feels overwhelming and moves too fast, so we're turning to highly crafted sensory experiences that feel unhurried and real. Old-thentic, if you will."

She nods approval and tents her fingers. "Are you up-to-date on all the new books?"

"Sure."

"We have a prospective new client." She pauses, examining me for a long moment. "Elan Behzadi."

This feels like being handed a plate of spaghetti for no reason at all. I have no idea what to do with it, and yet, my mouth is watering. "But he's a designer. We don't work with designers."

"I know."

"Designers don't buy trend books. Designers make their own trends."

She removes her glasses delicately. "I know. But he said you met at our holiday party, that you were very charming. *Youthful*, I think he said. And didn't he invite you to his show last night? I assumed you'd become friendly."

Why would Elan make it seem like we've become acquainted when we haven't? "Shouldn't someone more senior present to some-one like Elan?"

"Technically. But he asked for you." She pauses, as if about to say something more, before evidently changing her mind. "You'll have to be discreet. He's requesting you come to him. He's in the West Village—"

"I can't present to Elan Behzadi!"

"Why not?"

I can't stay seated; I have to stand. "Because he's . . . Elan Behzadi. He's a *designer*." By which I mean, he's *famous*.

"Oh, Lacey. As my daddy used to say, we all shit in the same toi-let." She chuckles to herself. "He was a little crude, Daddy was. He was a pig farmer, you know. Gave a whole new meaning to bringing home the bacon."

I'm going to present to Elan. He asked for me. Me. I'm having trouble swallowing.

"He's certainly talented," Patricia continues, unperturbed that I've started pacing around her office. "And he knows it. He's aware of the effect he has on people."

"Meaning?"

"He's a flirt." Patricia looks right at me. "Don't fall in love with him."

I laugh, loudly and quickly, although I'm not amused. I'm embarrassed. Exposed. "I don't think so!" I fail to fight a blush. "I don't . . . No."

"Good," she says, as if that settles it. "Start with the Panzetta: you've got that pitch down, and it'll appeal to his sensibilities. Your riff on metallics-as-neutrals is working right now, and that spiel about re-mastered reds. Don't be nervous. He asked for you, remember that." She gazes at me with cool, steady intensity. "You are qualified to have this meeting, Lacey. I mean that. Good luck."

I lick my lips and grip the back of my chair. "When?"

13.

Because I don't know why on earth Elan wants a presentation, I take so many books with me, I can barely get out of the cab. Each one weighs ten pounds and is the size of an atlas. They mostly specialize in color or fashion, i.e., trend, but also interiors and consumer insights. They're beautifully shot and designed, outlining the various trends the publishers see happening in the coming seasons, usually about two years out. The books come complete with USB sticks of all the color palettes, so my clients' in-house designers can start using their chosen palettes straightaway. We buy those books from the publishers, then we sell those books to anyone and everyone working in style: we're the liaison between the publishers and the companies. At any given time, we might have a hundred different seasonally relevant books on offer.

The books are old-school: they're the way forecasting worked before the internet. Even though the future of forecasting will probably all end up online eventually, I love the books. I love their weight. I love turning the thick, glossy pages. I love the way they portray the world: endlessly beautiful, everything in its place. That sort of order is a comfort to me. Perhaps because order felt that way when I was young, or perhaps because the pursuit of perfection is its own satisfying distraction; a catch-22 of unattainable loveliness.

But individual designers like Elan don't buy trend books. It's scandalous for him to even be having this meeting. Designers are not big-box retailers; they're artists. Which is why, as I introduce myself to Elan's doorman, I am nervous and confused and excited, all at once. I'm told to head on up. Elan is expecting me.

In front of the elevator, I get out my phone to call Vivian. I still feel a bit guilty about blowing it in front of Tom Bacon, but now I can turn that screwup into something of a victory. But I find myself pausing, and I'm not sure why. Maybe because Vivian will launch into a prep speech I'm not in the mood for. Maybe because she'll be disappointed if nothing happens.

Or maybe because I just don't want her to know.

* * * *

The door to the penthouse is answered by a stylish young woman in tortoiseshell specs. Mika is Elan's assistant; brusque and intimidatingly cool.

I follow her down a corridor, trying not to bump anything with my two giant bags of books. The apartment (if you can call it that; it's the size of a house) is so beautiful it makes me nervous. Original art on every wall. Sculptures in every corner. The home of a collector. An adult. Every piece of furniture looks like it came straight from those high-end antiques stores where everything has a shocking amount of zeroes on the end of the price tag.

Mika leads me into a room with a polished wooden table and four chairs upholstered with hand-embroidered baroque fabric. The walls are a mossy, silvery green. On the one facing me, a simple black-and-white line drawing of a woman on the edge of a bath, seen from behind. A small buffet holds two solid silver candlesticks, a pale pink ceramic vase, and a stack of photography books. Two of the chairs are slung with a dozen garment bags. A water pitcher sits next to two glasses (hand-blown, naturally—I think anything IKEA would spontaneously combust in here) and a small pile of multicolored pills. Beside them, a plate of Greek pastries: baklava and dense-looking cookies. Sugar scents the air, as subtle as a glance. Mika tells me Elan will be right in, closing the door as she leaves me alone.

I busy myself with finding the book to start with, the Panzetta that Patricia suggested. She's a womens wear expert based in Paris, my favorite of the current batch. The sky, glimpsed through a tall window hung with long patterned curtains, is flat and gray, darkening slowly. There is a hushed, theatrical gravitas to everything around me, a regal sense of style that feels precarious and unhomely. Next to all this, the loft looks like a trash dump. With every passing second, my nerves are less under my control.

There's a collection of small artworks on the wall behind me. The one in the center is a Miró. I recognize the style before the scrawled signature in the bottom corner confirms it. A *Miró*. Deceptively simple: a smiling yellow sun, a crooked blue star, and the profile of a woman in a black and red dress, but it is playful and joyous. Not a major work, perhaps an early one, but a Miró nonetheless.

"It's nice, isn't it?"

I jump and exhale hard.

"Sorry." Elan closes the door behind him. "Didn't mean to scare you." He's in a soft gray T-shirt and jeans, his hair wet, slicked back. Like he just got out of the shower.

I am extraordinarily overdressed. "It's not exactly what I think of as your style," I say.

He looks a little taken aback. A small tuft of chest hair peeks out of the V in his shirt. I want to touch it. "What is my style?"

I'm thinking that it looks happy and carefree, which would imply I don't think he's happy and carefree, which would be rude. "Why don't you center it more? It's such an important piece . . . It's lost, on this wall, with the others."

He looks mildly surprised. "I like it there."

My face is burning. I'm sure he can tell. "I took a class on surrealism."

"At college?" Subtext: *Which you obviously graduated from five seconds ago.* I nod. *Stop trying so hard.*

"I love the surrealists." He comes to stand next to me. I thought he was a few inches taller than me, but we are almost exactly the same height. "Miró said that he conceives his work 'with fire in the soul,' but executes it 'with clinical coolness.' That always resonated with me."

"It sounds like you," I say. "Your work is passionate but very technical, too. All the drama is carefully curated." I stop myself, although I have much more to say.

"Thank you." He says it like he means it, and I relax a tiny bit. "Shall we sit?"

He is far more normal than I expected, pulling out a chair, settling in, and yet there is a palpable energy about him. Something just left of center that marks him as special. Confidence, I suppose. He is both more and less attractive in person. Up close, I see a small scatter of acne scars. His bottom teeth are a little crooked. But his proximity is thrilling, and my body is responding in kind. It's excited; starstruck. The line between this being a meeting and a date feels wafer-thin. It unnerves me further.

"Would you like a drink?" he asks. "Tea, coffee. Or something stronger?"

First rule of fairy tales. Never eat or drink anything.

"No, thanks." I inhale a waft of sweetness from the desserts on the table. I can almost taste the honey-soaked flakes of pastry. "I thought we'd start with Emilea Panzetta. She's one of my favorites."

"Where was college?"

I blink. "Ohio State." I turn the first page. "This spring we're going to see a return to warm neutrals with these gorgeous blush tones—"

"What did you major in?"

"Fashion and business. Our strong blue and green stories will merge into an intense teal that compliments these copper tones so effortlessly. Think sunset over the Mediterranean; bright turquoise offset by eye-catching metallics and—"

"When did you move to New York?"

I give him a tight, confused smile. "Do you want my résumé or the presentation, Mr. Behzadi?"

"*Aziz-am.*" He smiles, his words soft as snow. "I don't want your fucking books."

Anger cracks through me; at him for being a prick, at myself for looking like a fool. Of course he doesn't want trend; he's a designer. I flip the cover shut. "Then you're wasting both our time." My chair shoots back as I get to my feet.

"Wait a second. I didn't say I wouldn't buy them." He counts the stack. "Eight, nine, ten? I'll take them all, Ms. Whitman."

Does he not understand how this works? "Collectively they'd cost forty grand. You can't buy them all."

"Why not?"

"Because . . ." You can't afford it.

Obviously, he can.

"Most people just buy one," I say stupidly.

"Would it be tacky to say I'm not *most people*?"

My commission would be six thousand dollars.

He watches my face change. "Please," he says. "Have a seat."

"Why?"

"Just sit, please." He reaches forward and touches my arm.

I jerk it away, hard.

"Whoa!" He's laughing. "Easy."

"Fuck off."

"Wow," he says. "Is this how you conduct all your meetings?"

Is this how you conduct yours?

Mika breezes in without knocking. "I'm going." She glances at me, curious but nothing more. I don't move. The two talk logistics—flights to London, fittings in the morning, a rescheduled interview. I stand there, burning. Sweat prickles my underarms. Did Elan just . . . buy me? What does he want from me? I can no longer convince myself it's not sexual. I should leave with his assistant: the girl my age, the girl whose world I belong to.

"Anything else?" Mika grabs the pile of garment bags.

I need that money. I just don't know what I'm supposed to do in exchange for it.

"Then I'll see you at the hotel," she says, starting to close the door. "And take those vitamins I left you."

"Leave the door open," he says, and she does.

She's gone.

Silence.

I am still standing.

Elan scoops up the pills. "Vitamin B," he says, "and iron. I always get so run-down doing the season. This time last year I had the flu. Ever since then: pills. So many pills." He swallows them with a glug of water. I'm reminded that he is older: the older man.

Or perhaps, that I am young: the younger woman.

I don't move.

"Please, Ms. Whitman. Sit. You're making me nervous."

"I'm making you nervous?" I almost laugh and cross my arms. "I know karate."

He looks alarmed. And then he starts to laugh. Really laugh.

"What's so funny?" I ask.

"I think . . . me," he says. "I am so out of practice with this."

"With what?"

"Meeting a woman." He leans forward, clasping his hands. His gaze is direct and sincere. "I'm attracted to you. I want to get to know you."

Disbelief battles outrage. Outrage wins. "So you buy my time?"

He lifts his palms, helpless. "A gift? Which I can take back, if you like."

My arms are folded tight across my chest, trying to hold my body together. "I'm twenty-five."

"I'm forty-two." He sounds relieved, pleased; we're making progress. "A Taurus, if you believe in any of that, I have a feeling that you don't. C'mon." He gestures at the open door. "You can leave any time you like. After all, you know karate." He smiles a small smile and tilts his head to one side. "And I think, maybe, you are drawn to me?" He purses his lips and whistles.

I stare at the floor, blushing. He heard me. He saw me. "You . . . You didn't talk to me. At the after-party."

"You were with your friends all night!" he exclaims. "Walled in. I wasn't about to interrupt."

This is true: I suppose I didn't make myself available. I didn't want to look desperate.

He was aware of me. Like I was aware of him. Slowly, inch by inch, I sink back into my chair. "I'll stay. But I'm taking the books when I go."

"Okay," he says. "You were telling me when you moved to New York."

Haltingly, I piece together my timeline, the broad brushstrokes of my movement through the world. I'm a little less guarded than I usually am: perhaps my hometown is as foreign to him as his is to me. He listens, sipping water, as if this is all very normal. I am actively containing whorls of disbelief. I'd like to think I have a pretty healthy ego, an understanding of my own worth, but maybe I don't, because

I cannot believe that Elan Behzadi is courting *me*. Steph is going to flip out. I will, for the first time, shock Vivian.

And yet, I'm doubtful. How many young, impressionable things like me has he charmed with Greek pastries and Spanish surrealism? But even if I'm just one of many, it's still a pretty good story. So enjoy it. I'll be dining out on it all year.

He asks about college, my friends, my life in Brooklyn. The first-date résumé exchange is usually tedious. Today it feels like an important audition. I use all my best lines; jokes so well crafted you can't see their seams. I can't tell if he's actually interested in me. There's a wall between us, a wall I imagine is between him and everyone, which I couldn't begin to dismantle with one conversation. I get the impression he's also trying to scale it, that perhaps he puts everyone at a distance, even those he wants to put at ease. And yet, he does a good impression of genuine. He's insightful. Surprisingly so. "So would you say you use work to prove yourself? I know I do," he adds. "My work life is totally tied to my identity."

"I suppose so," I say. "I've always been a really hard worker. And I've always worked a lot."

"What would happen if you stopped? Who would you be then?"

"I don't know. Someone broke, I guess."

He smiles, and I like this. I like being able to make him smile. "You had to work hard to get out of the Midwest. Like I had to work to get out of Iran."

That he would compare us is flattering. I know about his background as a designer here in the U.S., but not much about when or how he came to America. I give in and take a piece of baklava. Layers of honey and phyllo and walnuts fill my mouth. My eyes flicker shut as I savor the soft, sweet crunch. When I open them, he's watching me, satisfied.

I ask, "What's it like there? Iran."

He gets to his feet, answering me as he disappears through the open door. "The food is really good, and the traffic is really bad." The sticky suction of a fridge door opening. "Have you ever had *fesenjan*?"

"Sounds familiar . . ." It doesn't.

"It's sort of a pomegranate walnut stew. It's amazing. My favorite."

"What was it like growing up there?"

He returns with a half-full bottle of white wine. "It wasn't common to be out in public a lot. We spent a lot of time at home or in people's houses. There was a war on, you know, and the Islamic Revolution made everything sort of . . . stern. There wasn't any privacy. Or freedom. But it's different now. When I go back, I see kids *hitchhiking*. That's wild to me." He pours pale wine into both glasses. "What's your favorite city to visit?"

"New York," I say. "New York City is the center of the world."

He snorts. "No, really."

This is embarrassing. I glance out the window. I know Elan doesn't mean the bright lights of Illinois. But apart from my home state, a few years in Indiana, and of course, college, well . . .

"I . . . haven't traveled much outside the States."

He accepts this with muted surprise. His interest in me is ebbing away. I am uncultured. Inexperienced. He slides the wine my way.

"I can't."

Surprise lifts his dark eyebrows. They're thick and messy. I have the urge to lean over and smooth them down. "Are you sober?"

I know he means *in AA*. "Not exactly."

"I didn't think so." He sips his wine, appraising me. "You're so . . . innocent."

The word mocks me. "I'm not that innocent."

"Innocence isn't bad. You're lucky. Your life is uncomplicated, even though I'm sure it doesn't feel that way."

He's wrong. He's so wrong.

As if reading my mind, he adds, softly, "Or am I mistaken?"

The words catapult out of my mouth in a rush. "I'm not drinking because I'm high-risk for breast cancer and alcohol increases that risk. I'm considering getting a preventative mastectomy."

Silence. I can hear my own quick breath.

His eyes flick to my chest, then back to my face. His expression is changing. Opening. "The night we met, at the Hoffman House party . . ."

"I'd just found out. That afternoon."

"I knew it," he murmurs.

"Knew what?" I'm incredulous: there is no way he could've guessed.

His eyes meet mine. Something strange in them. Something buried. "I just . . . sensed something. In you." I don't know what this means. I want him to tell me, but instead he asks, "When?"

"I'm not sure. Summer, maybe. I haven't decided."

His gaze drifts back to my chest. Almost imperceptibly, his nostrils flare. No doubt he's picturing the full truth of what I've just confessed: a doctor's steel blade, lopsided fake tits. I don't want his imagination there. "But there's something else I'm doing first . . ." My words linger. I smile coyly. It's a display, as unmissable as a neck tattoo.

He bites. "What?"

I demur. "You'll think I'm crazy."

He flicks my arm with his fingertip. It tingles. "Now you have to tell me."

And so I tell him. I want to seduce him, yes, but more so, I want to impress him; prove myself to him. I'm not dull. I'm adventurous. The temperature in the room rises as I say the words *threesome, role-play.*

Sex.

I'm half expecting him to pounce on me when I'm done, an act I don't know if I'll give into or bat back. But instead, he just smiles, as if thoroughly charmed. "What a sweet list."

"Sweet?"

"Yes. You're so vanilla."

"I'm not vanilla." There's an embarrassing hitch of protest in my voice.

He smiles broadly, enough that I can see his back teeth. "I think I did all those things before I was eighteen."

"Well, good for you."

His glass is empty. He takes mine. "Why don't you get out of your comfort zone a little more?"

I'm offended, but not so much that I can't ask, "And do what?"

"What's something you couldn't say in front of your girlfriends? Something less PC?"

I am stripped bare in a dark room, my hands tied above my head. My underwear is stuffed in my mouth. I'm blindfolded. Elan is behind me, stark naked, thrusting into me, again and again and again. Strong hands hold my hips and I moan, groan, scream with pleasure. Shadowed faces watch us. Watch what he does to me, watch how he has me, how he *takes* me— I inhale sharply, and have to look at the table. My pulse has spiked. My nipples are hard. I'm flushed, almost panting.

"What?" His question is urgent. "What did you just think about?"

I stare back at him. In twenty-four short hours he's gone from someone I've never thought about to a keeper of my secrets, a fanner of their flames.

He is not someone I can trust.

The legs of his chair scrape the floor as he half rises out of his seat toward me. I tense, unsure. An electronic trill halts him. His phone. An alarm. He checks it, swearing under his breath. "I lost track of time. I never do that." He slips it back in his pocket. "I have to go." His underarms are damp with sweat.

I got under his skin, too.

He gathers the wine, the pastries, the glasses, heading back toward the kitchen, enough time for me to mouth *What the fuck!?* to myself before he returns. My hands are sweaty, slipping on the books' shiny covers. I almost drop the heavy stack, and he's right next to me, guiding them back to the table. Wine-sweet breath on my neck. "I'll courier them," he says. "Tomorrow."

"You can't keep them." Patricia would kill me.

His voice is gentle and easy. "I promise I'll return your books. Unread."

I don't break his gaze. This is the closest we've ever been to each other. I could kiss him without taking a step. "How do I know you can keep a promise?"

"You'll just have to trust me." He puts his hand on mine. His palm is large and soft. I want those hands on me so badly I almost swoon. I am a half second from grabbing his shirt and pulling him to me. I can practically taste him.

He's behind me as we walk toward the front door, his presence in every pore. In the second we have to decide how to say goodbye,

I thrust my hand at him. He shakes it, nodding with an amused half smile as if this was exactly what he expected of me. "I'm going to London on the weekend, then Milan and Paris."

This man is a different species from me. A species that drinks champagne on airplanes and doesn't check the price tag before buying something. I'm in over my head, which makes me think again of my hands literally tied up over my head, and this strangely sexy man having his way with me.

He leans against his doorframe. "When I get back, let's have dinner."

Given the fashion week circuits, that'll be at least a month away. I hide disappointment. "Sounds dishy." I hit the down button for the elevator.

"I don't have your number."

The elevator doors slide open. "You can get it when you send back my books."

It's early evening when I step onto the timeless tranquility of Greenwich Street. The darkness is young and fresh, not yet sullied by true night. I feel ten feet tall and I'm laughing aloud, drunk with power. I want to keep this feeling as a pet, stroking it whenever I want. I'm so giddy that I skip four twisty-turny blocks before I realize I'm heading in entirely the wrong direction.

* * * *

The next afternoon, I'm thinking about the first time I saw the ocean. The summer between sophomore and junior year. One of the other interns at Hoffman House organized a group trip to the Rockaways. The other girls were from coastal cities and spent the day complaining about the water being gross and dirty, and how crowded it was. But to me, it was incredible. Everything about it was novel: the boardwalk and the salt air and the fact that thirty-four hundred miles east was the coast of Portugal. When I put my toes in the Atlantic I laughed out loud. But quietly. So no one else would hear.

I didn't tell a single person it was my first time at the beach.

I'm thinking about this day when a courier arrives for me. A plain white envelope. From Elan Behzadi. Inside, a small cream notecard with his name at the top in dark blue letterpress. In barely legible scrawled handwriting:

Punish me with karate?

Under it, a cell number.

I unfold a check for forty thousand dollars.

14.

"Wait . . . wait, it's stuck—"

"You're stuck?"

"*It's* stuck— Ow!" Cooper yelps. "My thumb. My beautiful thumb."

"Put it down," I say. "I'm putting it down. One, two . . ."

The brown leather La-Z-Boy thumps into the stairwell, jammed ungracefully in the first-floor landing. Cooper and I exhale, red-faced and sweaty. I'd found him struggling with the chair on the street, on my way to see Steph. There was no way he was getting it inside on his own.

"She's heavier than she looks." He says it almost admiringly, as if the chair has impressed him with its hidden substance.

"The La-Z-Boy's a she?" I ask. "I don't think so."

"Gender's a construct," Cooper says. He readjusts his glasses: black-rimmed today, which make him look like a hipster Clark Kent. Not entirely unappealing. "Wow, you're so close-minded."

"If I recall, I was the one who said we could get it inside, and that sounds like the talk of a revolutionary to me."

"Astoria's answer to Che Guevara?"

"Try Katniss Everdeen." I mime shooting an arrow.

He laughs, once. He is completely engaged, leaning forward on the side of the La-Z-Boy, ready to play along. Someone clears their throat. Mrs. Karpinski, the grouchy upstairs neighbor who never leaves the apartment without a hairnet and a frown, is standing above us on the stairs. We quickly resume our positions.

"One, two, *three*." I haul my end up.

"It's heavy!" Cooper staggers up a step.

"You're such a weakling," I puff.

"No, you're unnaturally strong."

We shove the elephantine chair foot by foot into the loft, until finally, *finally*, it's inside. We are doubled over and panting.

"That was a workout," Cooper says.

I massage my arms. "Who needs the gym when you can haul furniture from the street?"

"Are you sure it's okay?" Cooper rubs his jaw. "It's not going to have bedbugs, is it?"

"Dude. No. No one puts out one piece of furniture if they have bedbugs. And they don't put a 'works fine' sign on it either," I add, pointing to the folded-up piece of paper in his pocket. "People aren't dicks."

"You're right." He inhales, puffing out his chest. "My throne has arrived."

"Technically we are coparents of this throne," I say.

We glance at each other and simultaneously launch ourselves at the chair. I manage to get half my butt in, but so does he. Scrabbling for control, I find the lever and shoot us backward as the footrest jerks up. I end up half on his lap, half on the armrest, one hand around his neck. Which is probably where we both wanted to end up. Steph's not here: she would've come out of her room by now. We're alone in the loft, which makes it feel unfamiliar in an interesting sort of way. I can feel Cooper's chest rising and falling through my thigh. Even when relaxed, neutral, the corners of his mouth lift slightly upward. His glasses are askew. Gold flecks in each iris: I've never been close enough to tell before now. His lashes are surprisingly long, his jaw surprisingly strong—adding to the delicate/manly dichotomy of his face. I realize I'm staring, and he grins, as if to say, *Like what you see, huh?* I make a *Don't flatter yourself* face in return. He says, "I can stay here all night."

"Me too," I counter.

"Great." He shifts. I wobble and have to grab his arm. Muscle beneath my fingers. His hand presses into my back. We're basically holding each other. We're certainly touching each other. He cocks an eyebrow, voice a teasing murmur. "Tell me more about your list."

He says it as if he expects me to leap off him, girlishly offended. What happens if I don't? Watch out, Sheryl Sandberg, your girl's about to *lean in*.

"Tonight," I say, "I'm going on a threesome. Having a threesome?" I straighten his glasses. "I'm having sex with two people from the internet."

His Adam's apple bobs as he swallows. No doubt he's wondering where that boner cushion's at. We are inches from each other's mouths. I could kiss him right now and he'd kiss me back. But then I think about Elan. His apartment and his confidence and the fact he is Elan Behzadi. His six-thousand-dollar commission floating above me like a specter. The way his dark eyes bring me into being, casting me older, mysterious. Even sexy. Suddenly scruffy-haired Cooper in his second-hand chair and shared messy loft doesn't seem as attractive. My body loses interest, wanting instead to replay the way Elan's warm hand felt on mine, the way his closeness picked up my heart rate.

Cooper murmurs, "You are something else."

But really, I am somewhere else.

Cooper is a boy. Elan is a man.

Footsteps coming up the stairs. Steph. I slip out of the La-Z-Boy, and am well on the other side of the room when she comes in.

"Greetings and salutations," I say. "Look what we found."

* * * *

I regale the tale of my six-thousand-dollar commission to Steph with the theatrics of an alien abductee. I'm expecting salacious excitement. But her brow is furrowed, expression doubtful. "He paid you," she clarifies. "Like a prozzie?"

I bristle. "Putting aside that sex work is a legitimate form of employment: he didn't buy me; he bought the books."

"That he won't use."

"I thought you'd be excited," I exclaim. "We were flirting. He was into me. It must be all the bucket-list stuff. It's really upping my game." As I say it, it rings true. I bet my skin is rolling with pheromones. "I'm like catnip right now."

"Sure." Steph is wincing. "It's just . . ."

"What?"

"Isn't he one of those different-girl-for-every-day-of-the-week guys?"

There is some truth to this: Elan's no Leonardo DiCaprio, but he's not a monk. "I didn't realize you were such an expert on him."

"Lace," she sighs. "I just don't want you to get hurt."

"God, I'm not that naive, Steph! I know we're not going to get married and have a bunch of little Persian babies. But don't you think two grown-ass people can enter into something mutually beneficial as long as there's reasonable expectations and clear communication?"

"Did you have that? Clear communication?"

I exhale harshly. "Don't you think I'm hot enough for him?"

"What?"

"You don't think he'd be into me because I'm not, what, worldly enough? Sophisticated enough?"

"Lace, no! No! You're a hottie with the lottie. He'd be lucky to have you, any guy would. I just think you should be careful. Particularly if he's the type to throw around commissions for six bloody grand. That's confusing, especially if you need it. Which you do, right?" Her voice softens a little. "Did you find out how much your copay on the surgery might be?"

Between five and eight thousand dollars. Plus the cost of not working while I recover, and all the stuff I'd have to buy for that. I'm living on my credit card right now, and, oh, did I mention student debt? So, yes. I need the money. But there is a distinct and slightly annoying irony in she-who-falls-for-unavailable-women giving me advice on sexual boundaries. "Fine. I won't cash the check when I get it."

"Don't you get paid automatically?"

I huff out some air. "He made the initial check out to me, not Hoffman House. It's an accounting thing; I'll get a check now. Which I won't cash. Besides he's away for a month. He'll probably screw a million French groupies and forget all about me."

My gaze falls to her nightstand. On top of dog-eared copies of *Tipping the Velvet* and a few awful true-crime things is a brand-new book. *Coping with Cancer: Getting Through Life's Biggest Challenge.* The author, fiftysomething, never met a tea cozy she didn't like, stares from the front cover with a *How are you* really? look of compassion. I click my eyes away. I know it's a just-trying-to-help purchase, but I feel weirdly embarrassed for my ex-roommate, like I'd just caught her doing something odd and private.

Then a flicker of anger. *I don't have cancer, Steph. I might never get it.*

She hasn't noticed. "How's everything else going?" she asks. "Did you make an appointment with the plastic surgeon Vivian suggested?"

"I left a message," I lie. How did Steph know about that?

She regards me with the disappointment of a favored student caught cheating on a test. "You're still doing self checks, right?" She mimes rubbing her breasts in small circles.

"I just got a clear scan. It'd take ages for something to develop to the point that I could feel it." I unearth her only pair of heels: black stiletto Manolos, bought online while very inebriated. "Can I borrow these? For my ménage à trois?"

Steph stares at me, chewing lipstick off her bottom lip in concern. "Lace."

"Steph."

Her tone is as gentle as baby shampoo. "Do you want to talk about it?"

My chest tightens. For a terrifying moment, I think I might cry. I press my lips together until it passes. "What I really need are these shoes." I smile, too big, too breezy. "So can I borrow them or what?"

15.

In the cab to Camila 4 Cam's, Vivian calls. I almost send it to voice mail. "Hey."

"*Bow-chica-bow-bow.*"

I roll my eyes, smiling. "Mature."

"I'm excited for you." She makes a panting noise.

"Shut up." I'm laughing. "Wait, how did you know? Don't tell me I put it into our shared cal."

The pop of a can of something carbonated. Seltzer, for sure. "Steph told me."

I was right. A horrifying vision of the two of them at lunch, exchanging a detailed analysis of everything I say and do. I want to tell Vivian that if she wants to know about my life, ask me, not my best friend. "How's everything going with Clean Clothes?"

Viv starts in on user registration and conversions without drawing a breath.

I'd prefer Vivian didn't know that Elan wants to take me out when he's back in New York. She'd probably give me a series of talking points about the app, or worse still, come along. I need to make sure Steph doesn't say anything to Vivian about Elan and his massive, throbbing commission.

"I wanted to mention," Viv says, "our user ratings for last month's outfits were down. Usually we're averaging 4.3. We're at 3.9."

She says it without accusation. She doesn't need to; it's implicit. "That's less than half a point."

"I know," she says. "Could be seasonal depression, post–Christmas slump. We just can't have it settling below a four. Investors can ask about that sort of stuff."

I have been phoning the outfits in: spending less time per customer, doubling up ideas. I've been distracted. "I'm on it." The cab swings onto Bowery. My stomach swings into my mouth. We're a minute away. "I gotta jump off."

"One more thing." She pauses, which makes me pause.

"Yeah?"

"H&M are developing an ethical line of womens wear starting this spring."

"So? We agreed we wouldn't support any business using slavery in any part of their supply chain."

"I know. But using an H&M line in our outfits might get our sales figures up." She lets out a slightly tense breath. "Girls are using the app, they're just not buying any of the pieces. Let alone an entire outfit. It's getting harder to dance around that. H&M is a brand that our customers can actually afford."

The cab pulls up in front of a sleek apartment complex, all brushed metal and tinted glass. "Sounds like a slippery slope. Our whole sales pitch is ethics. H&M isn't clean fashion, it's fast fashion. Not into it, sorry."

Another pause. "Fine. Let's get those user ratings up this weekend, okay?"

I'm visiting my sister this weekend, but I'm not in the mood to disappoint Vivian further. "Like I said, I'm on it."

Maybe I've been spending too much time with Vivian, but I find it distinctly sharky that she mentioned my user ratings before sending up a let's-sell-out-our-idea test balloon. As if I'd be shamed into submission.

I met Vivian at a women's networking event a few months after I moved to New York. I was the slack-jawed yokel who couldn't contain her excitement at being able to see the Empire State Building. She was charming everyone in the room by being flawlessly relevant: yes, she had read that *New Yorker* profile on the city's new poet laureate; yes, she did have opinions on the future of gerrymandering. I took her out for lunch. She took me on as a pet project.

I already had an entry-level position at Hoffman House, but I didn't know how to behave around rich people, famous people, people with clout. Vivian taught me how to operate in New York, and not just by breaking my tragic vodka-cranberry habit.

Never say you're a fan. Connect over something equalizing. Be genuine. Stay in touch—never ask for favors out of the blue. In fact, never ask for favors. Present opportunities. Think about it from their perspective. Know that everyone in their orbit thinks they're owed something. And never, under any circumstances, post a selfie without explicit permission. Deeply uncool.

The chance to work on Clean Clothes came up late last spring: stars aligning, skill sets locking together like LEGOs. (Also, we'd drunk two bottles of rosé and I'd taken it upon myself to reorganize her wardrobe.) It seemed like I was never going to graduate out of junior sales at Hoffman House: I needed to create my own job. A job in a company that Vivian now seems interested in selling out.

Whatever. I'm off the clock. I straighten the seams of my little black dress (when in doubt, go for classic) and check my reflection in a hand mirror. The photoshopped version of myself bares her teeth at me: all imperfections airbrushed with carefully applied makeup. I don't look like me, and that is good.

Scrawling *threesome* onto Steph's whiteboard was almost in jest, but now that I'm here, I'm 80 percent ready to step over my normcore threshold and into sexual experimentation oblivion. I've spent the past few days googling *How to start a threesome*. I don't have a definitive answer. Half the time it happens in a sexy, spontaneous (re: drunken) way, and the other half, everyone involved practically had lawyers drawing up contracts. I don't want to feel left out. Or for anyone else to feel left out. Am I supposed to stay over? What if I catch chlamydia or, worse still, feelings?

I hope Camila and Cam look as good IRL. But more so, I just hope I can keep up and not freak out like the newb that I am.

I hope I can enjoy sex with two total strangers.

I hope I can enjoy sex, period. Honestly, that's pretty much it.

I'm here. I'm doing this. As if in slow motion, my finger lifts through the crisp winter air and firmly presses the buzzer.

Lights? Camera?

Action.

16.

Camila Hernandez air-kisses both my cheeks in a cloud of jasmine perfume. "Hiiiiiiiiiii!"

"*Hiiiiiiiiii!*" Anxiety pitches my voice an octave above hers. I'm smiling so hard my cheeks hurt. "Shoes off?"

"If you don't mind." She squeezes my forearm, coquettish but friendly. Camila is shorter than she looks on camera, and she's wearing a bit too much makeup, but everything else checks out. And then some. Maybe she's born with it, maybe it's Maybelline, either way the girl is a New York nine, and that's no small feat. (I am a New York six point five, Ohio eight, and Buntley fifty-eight thousand.) She's in a tight black dress too. I congratulate myself on sensing the right thing to wear to a group sex date.

"Great place." Floor-to-ceiling windows, all-new amenities, enough polished concrete to park an SUV. "Holy smokes, did you know you have a view?"

Her perfectly painted brows pincer without creasing her forehead (what's up, Botox?) before it lands that I'm kidding. She laughs, tells me I'm funny. Okay, Camila isn't Amy Schumer. That's cool. I'm not here for a comedy show.

"I didn't know what kind of wine you liked, so I brought both." I hand her the bag of red and white.

"Best of both worlds." She winks. Excitement zips up my back.

My experience of flirting with women is (you'll be shocked to hear) limited. My female friendships are defined by intimacy, but there are clear lines between the affectionate and the erotic. In college, sexuality as a spectrum was a buzz conversation. Discovering yourself wasn't an option: it was mandatory. My friends spent more time discussing their sexuality than enacting it. I kissed a few girls, but it was awkward and tenuous, like trying to find your footing on a slick and unstable bridge. "I'm straight," I concluded sadly at the end of freshman year, adding that I wished so badly that I wasn't but secretly relieved that I was. It was just easier. But now things aren't easy or defined or, as Elan claims, 100 percent vanilla.

Sultry R & B murmurs from unseen speakers. Matching throw pillows line up like Russian nesting dolls. The idea that Camila and Cam have had to do domestic chores like choosing a playlist and tidying up for their threesome is oddly charming.

"Hey there." YouTube's own Cam Velez is coming for me, and, hello, the guy is oven-roasted perfection. He looks like a personal trainer in his tight white tee and artisanal stubble. We hug as if I have zero knowledge of this custom.

"Great place," I tell him, evidently the only thing I've been programmed to say. "How, um, long have you been here?"

"Few years." Cam says. "We both work from home, when we're not traveling." He's got the same vibe as his girlfriend: open and warm with zero sleaze. These guys are clearly pros, which makes me feel even more like a big bumbling baby.

Camila snaps a photo on her phone of her perfectly manicured hand holding a wineglass, before handing it to me. I've given myself a pass to drink tonight, but I'm feeling slightly nauseous with nerves and don't really feel like it: another first.

We settle in the living room, me facing them. "Cheers," Camila says. We clink our glasses. We're all excited, smiling, but I have no idea how to transition from the meeting-new-neighbors vibe to a putting-my-boob-in-your-mouth vibe. When I fantasized about this, there was very little chitchat.

"Steph said you're in trend forecasting?" Cam says, one arm around Camila, the other snaking down the empty couch.

"Three years." I point to Camila's phone. "Apple is coming out with these gorgeous metallic cork cases this summer. Sounds whack, but they're super pretty."

"I love metallics. Oh, you reminded me." She angles the phone at herself. "Hey guys, Camila here. This is my final look for this evening, what do you think? I love it, and I have a feeling our lady friend does too." She shoots me a grin. "She just arrived, and she looks smoking." Cam sticks his head into the camera and gives a thumbs-up. Camila giggles. "Who do you think should make out with her first, me or Cam? Let us know in the comments! Peace!"

My wine clatters onto a coaster. "Are you filming me?" I glance around the room in alarm—*there's a camera there, there, and there!*

"No, no." Camila waves her hands.

"Not if you don't want to," Cam adds.

"I don't," I say.

"Sorry. I should've said something," Camila says. "We share everything with our fans, including our sex life."

Good Lord. Really should've done a deeper dive into their channel.

"But privacy is important," Cam says, "and so are boundaries. Speaking of . . ." He leans forward, hands clasped between his legs. "What do you like in bed?"

Thai food. "Everything, really." Such a lie. "Except, maybe, butt stuff. I'm kind of anal about my, ah, anal."

"Do you prefer vaginal or clitoral orgasms?" Camila asks.

I am trying to be hip and modern, but I'm sorry, this is just so awkward. I can feel myself blushing. "Oh, I don't have one of . . . those."

Cam looks confused. "A . . . vagina?"

"A G-spot," I say. "Vaginal orgasms are just a myth, right? Like honest politicians or sober Australians."

Camila 4 Cam exchange a glance. Camila says, "Every woman has a G-spot. Maybe she doesn't use it, but it's there."

"The clitoris is easier to stimulate, and is quicker to climax," Cam says. "But if you spend a good, say, fifteen minutes working up to it, you can definitely come vaginally." He pauses. "I'm just going to add that." He takes out his phone, hits record, and repeats the same line, all with a customer service smile on his handsome face.

I'm out of my league. My body is a doubtful friend, unsure of the big fun plan I've been talking up all week. Every movement feels dumb and clumsy, like I'm controlled by an amateur puppet master. Without thinking, I reach for my wine and take way too big a sip. It goes down the wrong way and I cough, spluttering, my cheeks now burning, my eyes watering. I wave their concern off—*I'm fine, I'm fine*, but I'm not. I feel vaguely sick, and I know it's because my body is begging to fake sudden intestinal illness and get the hell out of this *Truman Show* porno I've ended up in. But I make it do something harder. I make my body stay, swearing to it that this is in its best interest. Finally, regaining my voice, I say, "Let's just stick with the old faithful: clitty clitty bang bang. It usually takes me a while," I add. "With a new person. It's probably a safer bet."

"Sure," Cam says. "Okay, our rules: we don't maintain contact after tonight except to set up another date. So we don't text; we don't interact on social media. Did you want some more wine? Or something different to drink?"

"I'm fine." I like how taken care of I feel. They're so attentive.

Camila checks her phone and laughs. "Me. They think we should start." Her lips curl into a clear and present invitation. Cam scoots over, making room for me between them.

The fans have spoken. They want this. And so do I.

I position myself next to Camila. Closer than a friend would sit. She reaches up and runs her fingers through my hair. Her liquid brown eyes are focused entirely on me. Her eyeliner is flawless. She says, "You're really pretty."

I tingle all over. "So are you."

She shifts closer. It's going to happen. Her lips part. "Have you ever kissed another girl before?"

"A few times." I'm woozy from her attention. It's pouring over me like honey.

"It's different," she says. Then, a giggly whisper. "I think it's better."

I have zero doubt about that at this moment. "Yeah?" I inch closer. "Mm-hmm."

This is why men are so nuts. This is what's at stake. A girl, this pretty, this sexy, pulling you into her orbit. "Show me," I murmur, and then her mouth is on mine and we are kissing.

The times I've done this, I was so drunk I barely remember it. But now I'm really here. Really feeling how soft her mouth is. How well our lips fit together. I loosen into her, every muscle turning soft as caramel. Her fingers are in my hair, mine are in hers, and I know we look sexy, and I know it feels sexy. It's like I'm looking at us and being us at the same time. But thinking about how I look takes me out of it and I want to be *in* this, experiencing it fully.

Focus. Be here. You're the star of the show.

She breaks away from me, my bottom lip between her teeth until she lets go.

"Wow," she breathes.

"Wow." Cam's voice is low behind me.

"Wosh." Is my sex-dumb attempt of *wow* and *gosh*.

Camila's phone is in her hand like a magician's trick. "Hey guys, Camila here. So, I just made out with our ladyfriend and she is an amazing kisser. Remember, always get consent from your partners, and keep it safe. Peace."

I'm about to suggest we send the phones off to bed to let the grownups have their fun, when Cam's hands find my shoulders and begin massaging them deeply. I groan involuntarily. Warm lips on my neck, stubble brushing my jawline. He finds my mouth, and now Cam and I are kissing, hungrily, passionately. There's something about the switch from a soft mouth to a stubbly one that undoes me completely and it. Is. On.

I'm kissing Cam, and then I'm kissing Camila, and then Cam is kissing Camila, and I'm watching them, and then Cam is kissing my neck and Camila is kissing my mouth and I'm feeling her boobs and we're all writhing and rubbing and letting out little moans. It's not as smooth and porny-perfect as the time I fantasized about this; at one stage I'm sitting on Camila's hair and then Cam and I knock teeth and both say sorry in an oddly formal way. But what's better, what I couldn't properly imagine, is the physicality of three people hooking up. It supersizes all sensation—two mouths instead of one, four hands instead of two, twenty fingers, a million nerve endings. I'm being kissed and stroked and licked all at once. I'm feeling a girl's chest press against me at the same time I'm feeling the hardness of Cam's arousal. I'm not thinking about sexuality—lesbian or straight—it's so beyond that. It's instinctive. It's primal.

Cam pulls off his shirt, revealing a chest that'd give Superman body dysmorphia. I almost double-take: pillows of pecs, buckets of biceps. Dude must work out five times a day. My little black dress is still clinging to my curves. And this feels not just sexy, but also comforting. Usually things move so fast with a guy that I'm out of my clothes before the front door's closed. Which is a bodice-rippingly hot idea, but when we start doing it three seconds later, I'm never as turned on as I am now. And I am definitely turned on: turned out might be a better description. My lady flower has opened and is in full blood-rushing-to-nerve-endings bloom.

In one easy motion, Cam swings me up in his arms and I squeal (I'm not a squealer). He carries me, legs tight around his hips, hands on his hard chest, to a neatly made king-size bed with views of the sparkling city.

Bed.

Sex.

Sex happens in bed.

I'm somewhere between "rock star" and "intruder into rock star's mansion." Familiar anxieties, worn as river stones, jostle into my consciousness: Am I supposed to act like a porn star or an indie movie star? If I'm taking too long, should I just go ahead and fake it?

Breathe, Lace. Stay with the pussy. Stay with what feels good.

Cam drops me onto the bed. Camila is behind us, sipping red wine. Her hair is mussed and sultry. Her makeup is, disconcertingly, still perfect. I almost want more from Camila: a crack in her pristine armor, an indication she's nervous or excited or anything other than business-as-usual. But she's unruffled and completely at ease, as if she's done this one hundred times before. Maybe she has.

In the reflection of the glass, I watch her slowly, expertly, unzip my dress as Cam watches. He steps out of his jeans, revealing black briefs that are the keeper of either a French baguette or an enormous penis. I've never been with someone that big: What if my vagine is too tight? I'm in my sexiest underwear: black silk bra, panties, garters, and sheer stockings. Camila's in her underwear too, a cream bra and panties. Her breasts are a few cup sizes bigger than mine and her stomach softer; rounder. It's so sexy. (Why do I hate my own belly so much?) The idea of all three of us together is ludicrously erotic.

I want this.

"You're so hot," Cam's saying, his gaze switching between Camila and me. "You're both goddesses."

We are all on the bed together, and now I want it: I want them to touch me, to feel me, to put themselves inside me. Someone's fingertips finally press between my legs, hard and deliberate. A shock of energy cracks through me. I gasp. "*Fuck.*" Which is exactly what I want to do.

Cam's behind me. I'm half sitting, half lying between his legs, my head against his chest. His erection pushes into the small of my back. I slide against it until I hear him let out a low groan. Camila snaps off my garter and hooks her fingers around my underwear. The lace scrapes gently against my legs as she pulls them down and away. "*Dios mía,*" she breathes. "You have a beautiful pussy."

Cam reaches under my bra and starts massaging my breasts. I'm not in control of the sounds I'm making: whimpers, groans.

"Can I taste it?" Camila asks, scooting between my thighs on her stomach. Her ass rises behind her like James's giant peach.

"Fuck yes." Cam pinches both nipples and I'm about to come right now. "Please."

I squeeze my eyes shut in anticipation, tensing and untensing. Her warm, wet tongue touches my clit and I cry out. I've never been this turned on; I didn't even realize oral could be like this. Her tongue slides again and again against me. Each time, fast hot waves of pleasure explode down my legs, up my back. Cam squeezes both breasts very hard, which ordinarily would hurt but now just intensifies everything that I'm feeling. He's muttering something in Spanish, humping my back. I'm clutching the sheets because I'm close, I'm so, so close. I look down and see Camila's bobbing head—a girl, licking me—and it's this visual, and Cam's strong hands, and her hot mouth that pushes me over the edge. My pleasure boils over. My body twists like a wild thing; Cam has to hold me down as I start to come in a strangled series of "*yes, yes, fuck, yes*" that get more and more potent as my orgasm intensifies, building on itself, everything spasming, pleasure and pain pushing me to my limit of what feels good. My mouth is dry, my skin is on fire, and for a few long-short moments I am no longer a body but something else entirely: pure sensation, fire and earth, a feeling, a concept.

Wosh.

I am sex.

I am a sex god.

I am an immortal sex god who—

"Hey guys, Camila here."

You've got to be kidding me.

"Wow." She's kneeling on the end of the bed, wiping her mouth, addressing her phone. "I just gave an amazing amount of pleasure to someone and it got me thinking: giving is just as important as receiving. It's seriously so rewarding." She flips her hair and smiles. "We're just getting started, so I'll check back later. Peace."

I pull myself onto my elbows, still vibrating all over. "What do you say we—"

"Hey guys, Cam here."

I jerk around.

He's on his back, speaking into a phone I didn't even see him bring in. "Fellas, number one rule of any threesome: She. Comes. First. I know as a dude it's super tempting to want to get in there straightaway and—"

I clear my throat. "Guys?"

"Get yours," he continues. "But trust me, it's best practices. Let us know thoughts in the comments, peace."

They upload together. Their lips curl with satisfied smiles.

Camila crawls toward me as Cam flips around. I raise both hands. "Hold up. That was incredible but, c'mon." I give them a look. "Enough with the videos."

Camila starts, "You're not *in* them—"

"I can handle a lot of nonsense, but it's just way too millennial for me," I say. "It's me or the phones."

They exchange a very worried glance. Cam rubs his chin. "It's just . . . our fans expect it from us."

"Our fans are very important," Camila says. "They're a *part* of us."

Ho-ly shit. My jaw drops. "You're picking the phones."

"Sex is an authentic part of our channel," Camila says.

"And our authenticity is really important to our community," Cam says, before pausing. "That'd be a pretty cool tweet."

This is why they're so unfazed by group sex. It's not a personal experience for them. It's a performance, conducted by a couple as clean and well lit as the sales floor of an Apple store. What I thought was lack of sleaze and easy confidence is actually just carefully observed brand guidelines.

The sound of their simultaneous orgasm is truly magnificent, or what I hear of it, as I get dressed in the bathroom. I slip out the front door to the sound of dual updates.

The only star of the show here is Camila 4 Cam.

* * * *

The night air is sharp: a shot of espresso after too many cocktails. I swagger, ankles swinging effortlessly into a straight line. Drunk girls get out of *my* way.

My body is glowing and giddy. I feel so happy that I made a difficult choice—to stay, to go through with it, even when I was afraid—and it was the right choice. I hail a taxi like a New Yorker, like I'm summoning my steed.

In the back seat, I type a text.

Baby's first threesome. Curious?

Naturally, I send it to Mr. Behzadi.

17.

After a week of winter sun, the weather turns nasty on the day I drive a shitty rental car upstate. In the fall, the trees lining the highways heading north are showy with color: an impressive parade of red, orange, and yellow (or in trendspeak, scarlet, ochre, and flaxen gold). Now, the landscape is bleached and twisted. I dress down: boyfriend jeans, innocuous black booties, boxy wool sweater. Anything too "New York" invites an eye roll that's more devastating than outright criticism. My anxiety ratchets up with every passing mile. It's not as if I'm scared of my sister. We just . . . set each other off.

I've made up my mind to tell Mara about my diagnosis. I need that to be a mature conversation that doesn't end in her winning the award for Most Passive Aggressive in a Sibling Relationship, an award she has held for a record number of years.

We're supposed to meet at her place but on the way up she messages me to meet at the café: her shift's running late. Mara lives in Boreal Springs, the kind of upstate town that's not cute enough to be a verified tourist trap but not grim enough to drop off the map entirely. When she first moved here, I had fantasies of cozy upstate life: summers spent hiking and wine tasting, winters spent making s'mores and trying to understand poetry. The truth is, people move to economically depressed small towns like Boreal Springs because they're broke AF or they want to be left the hell alone. In my sister's case, both were true.

It was always my dream to spread my wings for New York. Mara told me she was moving there the day before she left, when I was still in college. A naturopathy school she wanted to attend, best of its kind. She lived in a prewar apartment in Crown Heights with four other roommates. It was small. The city was loud and expensive. She didn't even last the year before meeting Storm's father at a dive bar and moving upstate with him two weeks later. (The relationship as a whole was about as fleeting.) By the time I moved to the city, she was already gone.

The bell above the door to the Blue Onion Café dings as I enter. Two groups of customers: day-trippers escaping the weather and locals escaping their own four walls for an hour. You can tell them apart from their shoes.

My niece is sitting in the corner, drawing with crayons. She has smudges of something dark on her face. Her thin blond hair is pulled into uneven pigtails. Her outfit is bizarre: faded Bratz dolls T-shirt, skirt over pants, a zippered hoodie that's way too big. Jesus, Mara, how hard is it to dress your own daughter—I catch myself. No. I'm not doing that.

And there she is. I still get a weird little jolt whenever I see her, half infatuation, half fear. Her shoulder-length hair is growing out from a dark red henna she used a couple of months ago, faded now to a cheap-looking copper. She's in loose Thai fisherman's pants and an old T-shirt. No bra. Tattoos she regrets mark her arms and collarbone. She'd look like a typical backpacker picking up a few shifts before heading off to Machu Picchu, if it wasn't for her face. Even though Mara doesn't wear makeup, my sister is striking. Not exactly beautiful, although she could be if she tried. I'm not sure if it's her personality or her physicality that casts her as bold and unapologetic, but that is what she is. Wild eyebrows she doesn't pluck and icy-clear skin, even though she'd sooner be on reality TV than have a facial. Her pièce de résistance: frighteningly sharp gray eyes that see into your soul and find it lacking.

She acknowledges my presence with a nod, gathering a half-eaten plate of carrot cake and empty coffee cups.

I make myself smile. "Hey, Sis." I kiss her cheek. "Good to see you."

"I'll be done in ten." No *hello*. No *how was the drive?* "Do you want the rest of this?" She offers me the leftover cake.

I wrinkle my nose. "Um, no thanks."

"What's wrong with it?"

"Nothing."

"So try it." She's taunting me.

"I'm not in the mood for other people's garbage, Mar."

She stares at me as if I am flat-out crazy. "It's fine. If it was mine would you eat it?"

"It's not yours. It's a total stranger's."

"What exactly do you think you can catch from leftover cake?"

"I don't want to eat trash!"

She rolls her eyes. "You are *such* a princess—"

"Auntie Lacey!" Storm wraps herself around my legs. "Did you bring me a present?"

I scoop her up. "Hi, *princess*." I nuzzle her neck, and she squeals.

"Ten minutes." Mara turns toward the kitchen.

"Perfect," I singsong, rubbing noses with my niece. "Just enough time to fix your hair. Mommy lets you get so messy, doesn't she?"

And, we're off.

* * * *

Mara lives fifteen minutes out of town, off an overgrown, unpaved back road that feels spooky at night. The house is a decent size for the two of them, with a scrappy backyard that dips down to a creek. Charming when it's warm, but the house is old and the windows are small. It's dim, even in summer, and cluttered. Everything handmade, bought on Craigslist, needs fixing, weird. By the time we get there, the sun has set. I leave my overnight bag in my car. I only end up staying half the time.

Inside, Mara complains about a coworker, her ceramic studio's new opening hours, the cost of gas. I alternate with Vivian's request about H&M, domestic politics, the weather. This is good: the alternative is silence, which means she's really pissed. Low-stakes whining is our girly gossip.

I play with Storm while Mara bubble-wraps a dozen mugs and bowls, readying them to mail. She has an Etsy store selling her ceramics. She's really good, I think, even though she says what she actually likes doesn't sell.

My niece's new obsession is, disturbingly, weddings. All she wants to do is dress up in a white skirt and marry an array of stuffed animals. I play along, but after witnessing the fourth set of largely nonsensical vows, I pull her into my lap. "You know you don't have to get married, darling." I tuck a strand back into the expert French braid I did. "You can be completely happy on your own."

Her head lolls back in my arms. She stares at me with sky-blue eyes. Her father's DNA. Just a little weird. "Are you gonna getted married?"

"*Get* married," I correct her. "Maybe. One day. But I don't need to." How can I explain to a little kid that marriage is not the golden ticket that opens the gateway to lifelong happiness? I have friends younger than me who are getting divorced, or who definitely should be. I'll never admit that I'd like to get married myself. That'd be like announcing I want a housekeeper or monogrammed towels from Barneys: deeply uncool bordering on offensive.

She thinks for a few moments. "Do you have a boyfriend?"

I'm surprised she knows that word. "No."

"Why not?"

The faces that pop into my head: Elan Behzadi and Cooper last-name-unknown: the dude options floating around my universe right now. But Elan never texted me back, and I don't really know Cooper. I draw in a breath. "I haven't met anyone who's right for me."

She scrambles out of my lap, and selects a threadbare teddy with one eye. "You can have Tony." She hands him to me gravely.

"Thank you." I kiss Tony on his red stitch mouth. "I have a feeling this love will be very, very sacred."

She giggles. I kiss her head, inhaling her sweet, little-kid smell.

If I want to have kids who don't inherit my mutation, I have a few options. I can do IVF and only implant an embryo that didn't inherit the mutation. Or I can test a fetus I conceive naturally and terminate it if it inherited the BRCA1 mutated gene.

If my mother had done this, I wouldn't be alive.

I honestly don't know what I should do when it comes to kid stuff.

Storm gallops around the room on Bottom, the horse only she can see. I'm smiling, but a wave of sadness ebbs in my chest.

When I was creating my pro and con list in the loft with the girls, I think I gave not being able to breastfeed a score of three. I'm surprised to realize that was way too low.

* * * *

Dinner is meatless meatloaf that tastes like a lightly broiled boot. Top chef, Mar is not. Considering we grew up in a place where "salad" was canned pineapple, mini-marshmallows, and whipped cream, and every other meal was some version of steak and potatoes, it's no great surprise.

My sister grills me about the app: download numbers, open rates, metrics. I've only explained the behind-the-scenes to her once, and she understands it better than I do. She could've been some kind of genius if she'd gone to college or stayed longer than a year in any job. She's been somewhat supportive of Clean Clothes: "It's not a bad idea," which is her version of "certifiably brilliant." She thinks the outfits are overpriced, but she's in favor of ethical clothing. We agree sweatshops are "shameful and immoral" and most consumers are "selfish b–i–t–c–h–e–s," which feels really nice.

I linger over the mush, not wanting the evening to unfold into the inevitable next step. But, of course, it does.

Today is the day, after all.

On the vegan chocolate cake, five candles and one carob drop. We turn out the lights and huddle around it, singing. Two generations of women, remembering a third.

I have never liked this.

"Happy birthday, dear Mommy. Happy birthday to you."

"Blow out the candles, baby," Mara says to Storm, and she does. "Well done!" Mara kisses her daughter, who beams at me, pleased. I'm not sure how much of this she truly understands. Mara's smile fades. "Grandma June would've been fifty-one today."

We do this every year. I don't know why: it feels morbid, and it makes my sister noticeably depressed in the weeks that follow. But more so, it widens the gap that exists between us, the gap that, in our own dysfunctional way, we do try to bridge.

I never knew my mother. Not like Mara did. I never know who, exactly, I'm supposed to be remembering. We're not on the same page.

Mara gets out the photo album emblazoned with *Memories* in curling pink script. She flicks through the mismatched sun-faded pictures stuck behind crinkly sheets of plastic. "Look, that's me on the tricycle." She shows Storm. "See? That's Grandpa, and Mommy when she was your age."

Dad's the only one looking at the camera, sunburned, holding a tin of Budweiser up to his Tom Selleck mustache. Mara is impossibly small, tongue out, focusing. My mother is clapping, her hands and face slightly blurred.

Storm says, "Can I have a tricycle?"

"One day. There's Grandma holding Auntie Lacey when she was a baby. Isn't she beautiful?"

I know Mara isn't talking about me. In the picture, my mother is unsmiling, holding me as if she's not sure I'm hers, on the junky patio of the house I was born in but don't remember. She's about my age. I cannot comprehend how someone in their midtwenties could already have two children, but of course, that's all of my high school friends now.

"That's Grandma's studio, where she painted." My mother converted the studio herself from a garden shed: in the picture, it's small, crowded with canvas and paint tins. Mara points to the portrait hanging on the wall opposite us: an unidentified woman, green-skinned and ghostly. "Grandma painted that."

It's a good painting, technically, but I wouldn't want it in my own house. It's melancholic, almost eerie. Storm stares at it in silence. Unease feathers in my stomach.

Mara points to another photograph. Her favorite, I think. It's one taken of my mother without her knowing, a slightly unfocused long shot. She's sitting by a large window, staring outside. She has Mara's same fierce features. She looks beautiful, but also, sad.

What is my mother thinking about in this picture? Motherhood? My father?

Cancer?

"You know how Mommy has grump days?" Mara strokes Storm's hair. "So did Grandma. See?"

I think for most women, photographs of their mothers before they were recognizably "Mom" create and complicate the portrait of the woman who raised them. They reveal their mothers were once danger-ously young; hitchhiking or dancing or smoking a joint with a boy who's not their father. This youth is a bridge and it is a chasm; she is Mom and she is a mystery. And holding these two truths in your hands and seeing them, really seeing them, that changes you. It's the kind of epiphany you have in college, when the world seems to be pulling back layers on the daily, and everything is giving off a frequency of light you've only just learned to see. Sometimes I feel like that's where Mara's stuck. Forever sophomoric and serious, offended by everything, outraged at everyone. My sister stares at the photo in front of her. "There's Grandma, doing the dishes. After she was gone, I did that." With the right ears, you can hear the resentment.

I say nothing.

I've always felt like I am nothing like my mother. That was Mara's connection. Moody, artistic, someone who didn't exactly fit into the world, wincing at its brightness, its brashness. But I am connected to my mother. I am genetically programmed to meet her fate.

I want this to be over.

Mara turns the page. "That's Granddad, dressed as Santa."

"I'm pretty sure Dad's d-r-u-n-k in this photo," I mutter.

My sister's gaze shoots to the glass in my hand, because, yes, I've usually polished off half a bottle of wine by now. But I have water. She notices it with a frown. Her eyes flit to mine. I see her conclusion appear, not so much judgmental as darkly matter-of-fact.

She closes the album, and announces it's bath time.

* * * *

An hour later, we sit on the lumpy orange lounge chairs near the fire, which has reduced to a handful of glowing embers. My foot bounces into the old rug. I am nervous.

My sister thrusts a mug of ginger tea at me. "You're getting an abortion, I assume."

"I'm not pregnant." The ceramic mug is too hot to hold comfort-ably. I close my fingers around it.

"Oh. What, did Dad call you?"

"No." This catches me off guard. "Does he call you?"

She shrugs, pulling her cardigan around herself. "Sometimes he sends money. For Storm."

I am shocked. Then angry. My father doesn't send *me* money. Shit, he only sends Christmas cards every other year: the cheap kind you buy at the post office: *Hey, kiddo! Happy Christmas, and all that jazz.* I don't even have a current address. Does Mara? She hates him as much as I do; why does she still stay in contact?

I can't get sidetracked. Focus on the facts, Lace. Every individual has two copies of the BRCA1 gene, passed down from their parents. If I have the mutation, that meant Mom had it (no cancer on Dad's side), which means Mara has a 50 percent chance of having it and if she does, then Storm has a 50 percent chance of having it too. My mouth is tacky. Tension cuts each breath short, slicing at my chest. "Do you remember that article I sent you at the beginning of last year? The one about the . . . test?"

"The test for cancer," Mara says. "Of course I do." An irritated huff. "I don't think that's a very good idea, Lace."

"Why not?"

"I told you why not."

"I want to talk about it again," I mumble.

"Why?" Her back straightens. "You didn't take it did you?" Her gaze whips to me like a spear, banging through me.

The hot, quick fear of my sister's impending wrath trumps everything. I'm shoved back into our family home, reacting in the way I know best. I lie. "No! No, I was just thinking about it." Fuck. Exactly the kind of lie Dad would tell: a stupid one.

Mara relaxes a little, her posture softening. She likes when I beg her opinion. "Think about it, Lace. You find out you have this mutation— if this test is even reliable, which I doubt—and then you're thrown into an underfunded, unreliable medical system that has a history of misdiagnosing and mistreating everyone, especially women. Biopsies and mammograms and MRIs every month. Jesus, the stress of that alone would cause cancer, whether you have the mutation or not."

I can't bring myself to say I don't think this is how cancer works. "Or there's . . . the other option."

"Oh what, a mastectomy?" She rolls her eyes. "That is truly the height of privileged hysteria. The article said there'd been an increase in them ever since what's her name—Jolie—took hers off. I mean, can you imagine?" She tosses me a disgusted look.

I can imagine.

My sister can tell. Once again, I try to summon the courage to tell her the truth, but before I can, she puts down her tea. "Lacey. You are twenty-five years old. Your brain isn't even fully formed yet. You are not old enough to make a decision like this: permanent, life-changing. It's not like dying your hair pink or wearing a tutu to prom."

It *wasn't* a tutu. For some reason, my sister has never gotten over that. I bite my cheek.

She presses her fingers into her forehead. "Look. I love my daughter. She is the best thing that ever happened to me, she is. But if I could have my time again, would I get pregnant by a bipolar drug-addict who disappeared the second my water broke? Uh, no. That was a stupid decision, and it's one she and I have to pay for the rest of our lives." She's welling up. Her chin trembles. "Look, maybe when you're settled. You have two jobs, you don't want to fuck that up." She leans toward me. "You're doing good, Lace. You know? You're doing good down there."

My sister has never said this to me. I start tearing up too. "Thank you, Mar."

Mara threads her fingers into mine. The feeling of her calloused fingers undoes me. I have to close my eyes. My sister's voice is soft and compassionate. "If you find out, you live life by its rules, its values," she says. "Not yours. You're not in charge. It is."

I freeze. Can this be true?

Mara pulls her hand away and shifts back toward the fire. "Besides: you can't stop fate. If either of us are destined to get it, it'll happen." We stare at the dying embers, one by one turning to ash. "It'll just happen, and we won't be able to stop it."

18.

---

make an appointment with Vivian's plastic surgeon.

It's not as if my sister's warning didn't land with me: it did. There is considerable truth to the fact my diagnosis is directing my life right now. I should've been more informed about the consequences before I got the test: it was stupid not to be. But this is where I am. And by the end of the drive back to Brooklyn, I've settled on the two key reasons why I disagree with Mara. First, I *am* old enough to make important decisions for myself, about my future. And second, I don't believe in fate in the way she imagines it, as something that happens to you, regardless of your involvement. I have free will, and I use it.

Knowing my sister is wrong and acting in direct opposition to her advice feels both freeing and frightening. It's the feeling of looking around for an adult and realizing I am the adult. I am my best option.

* * * *

Dr. Dan Murphman's offices are as sleek and impersonal as a Midtown cocktail bar. Black leather sofas, bright track lighting, shiny new issues of *Cosmopolitan* and *Vanity Fair*. On the walls, framed articles of Murphman in various Top Doctor and I'm So Great lists. A bit arrogant, but I suppose that's to be expected. He was one of the first names that came up when I googled *New York plastic surgeon*.

The bottle-blond receptionist has jugs the size of basketballs. I've always been a bit judgy about women with implants. Now I might be the one getting fake tits.

I see you, karma. I see you.

It's 12:58 p.m. I text Steph.

Here. This place is terrifying. Where you at?

It was her idea to come. I told her she didn't have to but she was surprisingly insistent.

Even though this is just a consultation, tension tightens my muscles. I tell myself to relax but I rarely take my own advice.

Trying to busy myself with Clean Clothes outfits proves fruitless. I'm distracted with thoughts of boobs. I found an article online about women who "go flat" after mastectomies: no reconstruction at all. I thought about this, because I want to consider all my options, but it's not for me. I can't imagine not having breasts, to the point that it's worrying. I mean, they won't function as breasts from a biological standpoint. I'll have minimal, if any, sensation. So who am I getting reconstruction for? Me? Or the way I appear to others? As a woman, the question of appearance is complicated enough. If I wear a short skirt, am I celebrating my sexuality or succumbing to a sexist stereotype? Let's say celebrating: but what if I wear that skirt to a meeting with a male client because I know it'll give me some kind of advantage? And is it actually an advantage? I could ponder this endlessly: one thing I know for sure is that my client is not questioning what _he_ wears when he meets with me and neither is anyone else.

The receptionist calls my name: Dr. Murphman is ready for me. I gather my purse, annoyed and yet oddly satisfied that Steph didn't make it.

I knew it. I can't rely on her.

* * * *

Dr. Murphman has a framed portrait of himself above his desk. It looks like an actor's headshot, the kind a casting agent might consider for LA Gym Owner or Sleazy Investment Banker. Slicked hair, every tooth capped, and I strongly suspect chin implants. Flanking his picture are very boobalicious photographs of Kourtney Kardashian and Salma Hayek. Did Murphman do their boobs or are the pictures supposed to make you assume that?

"Hi. Dr. Dan Murphman—you can call me Dan." He extends his hand. Manicured fingernails. Firm shake.

I take a seat. "Lacey Whitman, you can call me Lacey Whitman."

"Great," he says, glancing at my file. "BRCA, right. Honestly, you're making the right choice."

"Honestly, I haven't totally decided yet," I say, crossing my arms over my chest. "I might end up sticking with surveillance. Mastectomy's just so . . . final."

His face flickers, and I wonder if he meant I was making the right choice coming to see *him*. "Well, as you can see, I'm best in class. Even though the circumstances might not be ideal, I promise you'll walk away with a beautiful set of breasts, covered by insurance. That's a home run."

Home run? Seriously? I'm so miffed by this I can't think of what to say.

"Now, some breast surgeons take too much tissue to be able to deliver a good result," Dr. Dan continues. "Who's on your team?"

I thought the point of mastectomy was to remove *all* the breast tissue. "I haven't decided yet."

"I can make some recommendations of some surgeons who are excellent, best in class." He reaches for a clicker. "Let's take a look at—"

The door flies opens. It's Steph, flustered, in her leopard-print puffy jacket and bright orange beanie. "Sorry I'm late. Subway drama. Hi." She waves at Murphman. "Steph. Friend of Lacey's."

He indicates Steph should sit. "As I was saying, let's take a look at some of my work."

Steph sinks into an empty chair. I give her a smile. I'm a little relieved that I was wrong about her. She came.

Murphman hits the lights. A projected image of two sets of boobs lights up the opposite wall. Steph jumps. "Cripes! Wasn't expecting that." Then, "Ooh. The ones on the right are rather nice." The pictures are cropped from the bottom of someone's chin to the top of her stomach. The breasts on the left, the "before," are small, the size of apples. The second pair are at least a cup size larger: full and lovely. Pale pink scars circle under both breasts like silvery snail trails.

Murphman speaks without looking at them. "Example of smooth, round silicone-gel breast implants—270 cc, subpectoral. A 32A/B to a 32 C/D."

I have to admit: they look good. "Is that a BRCA reconstruction?" I ask.

"No, just regular augmentation." He clicks the remote. Another four more boobs appear. Again, the after looks fuller than the before. "Saline breast implants—"

"Can we go back to that last one, please?" Steph is sifting through a loose pile of notes. "I'm curious if you think, um, wait a second . . ." Half her notes slide to the floor.

"Let's do questions at the end of the presentation," Murphman says without looking at her.

Steph stiffens.

He gestures to the wall. "—placed under the muscle through an areolar incision."

The next set of boobs appears, and the next and the next, a never-ending series of nipples from more breasts than world cultures in the It's a Small World ride. It has the effect of completely desexualizing boobs, making them seem almost alien. I'm unsure how many of these women are previvors, like me. Next to me, Steph's foot is jiggling the carpet.

The presentation ends. The lights flick on. Dr. Dan Murphman smiles with all his teeth. "Thoughts?"

Steph looks like she's just eaten something bad. She hates him.

I ask, "What kind of reconstruction would you recommend for me?"

The doc says, "Let's take a look," and hands me a paper gown to change into.

Steph hovers, unsure. We're not the kind of friends who swim naked together. "Should I wait outside?"

"If you want to be involved, you're probably going to see them eventually." I steel myself, and start unbuttoning my shirt. In less than a minute, I'm sitting half-naked on an examination table, tits out. Steph gives me a brave smile. There's an almost imperceptible blush coloring her cheeks.

The doctor glances at my tatas with quick dispassion. "Implants," he replies. "You don't have enough fat for flap."

This is what I'd already assumed: "Flap" surgery rebuilds your breasts using fat from your thighs, your tummy, your butt, wherever you can spare it. It's the most natural-looking reconstruction, and it leaves you with breasts that are soft and warm, aging as you age. But it also takes the longest to recover from because you need two surgeries, and it's complicated keeping the flap of skin and fat alive. Regardless, it sounds like having a couple of butt-boobs is off the table for me.

Murphman recommends expander-implant reconstruction. "Temporary implants called expanders are placed in pockets formed under the chest muscles. Over several months, the expanders are gradually inflated with saline to stretch the skin and muscles, each time requiring an in-person appointment." He sounds like he's reciting information from a textbook. "During a second, shorter surgery, the expanders are replaced with implants."

"And how many of those have you done?" I ask.

"Plenty," he says. "Like I said, the key to a good outcome is leaving me tissue to work with."

"Isn't the key making sure she doesn't get breast cancer?" Steph asks.

Murphman grins at her as if she's just made a joke, and indicates my left breast. "I'll be able to fix this asymmetry." I didn't even realize the girls were asymmetrical. "Give you more of a lift here, and here . . . You're a, what, 32B?" He guesses correctly. "We could easily take you up to a C cup." He points to the picture of Kourtney. "Or a D cup." Salma.

"I don't think I want to go bigger," I say.

"I can make you any size you want," he says.

"Yes I know," I say, "but I think I'm happy being part of the Itty-Bitty Titty Committee."

Steph snorts.

"To be perfectly honest, most women want to go bigger," he says. "Big breasts are beautiful."

Steph rolls her eyes.

"Right," I say, "I'm just not sure if they're for me."

"If you're on the fence, go bigger. Trust me. Breasts are what makes a woman a woman," Murphman says. "They're the most fundamental part of a woman's anatomy."

I know this isn't right. But I remember the way Elan's face started to change in his apartment, before I told him about the bucket list. The burgeoning sense of what had to be disgust, as the truth of my plan played out in his mind. Maybe going bigger is an option. The upside for having two massive scars for the rest of my life—

"That's total bullshit." Steph's voice surprises us both. "I'm sorry, but that's just not true. Being a woman has nothing to do with how big your tits are. And let me tell you, as a woman who has been blessed with a couple of boulders, it's not all fun and games." She ticks off her fingers. "I always have to wear a bra, even though I hate them, I get chronic back pain if I'm on my feet all day, and I get catcalled a million more times than girls with small tits."

Dr. Murphman holds up a hand. "Young lady—"

"Fuck you," she says, and turns to me. "Lace, you don't know how lucky you are, having small tits. You choose when you want the world to see them, respond to them. I don't get that choice. Guys think big boobs is a constant invitation, like, if I'm born a double D, I'm obviously a fuck machine. Why do you think I wear T-shirts all the time?"

Murphman opens his mouth.

Steph holds her hand up. "Take your big-boob wankfest and shove it up your tight bleached arsehole." She gets up, opens a door to the walk-in bathroom, closes it, opens the actual door, and hurries out.

* * * *

"Steph! Wait!" I catch up with her in the elevator bank.

She spins round. Her face is the color of a tomato. She looks dazed. "I'm so sorry. I don't know what came over me."

I'm dumbfounded. "What just happened?"

"I just couldn't stand him talking to you like that." She peeks back in the direction of the office, wild-eyed. "Did I just tell a surgeon to shove something up his arsehole?"

"Yes." The elevator dings open. I pull her in, grinning. "And it was brilliant. Thank you. You're right: fuck Barbie boobs. Fuck that guy."

The elevator doors close. I flush, angry and confident and grateful for my friend.

19.

March

It's generally understood that every Hoffman House employee, even the interns, are well-rounded in the vocabulary of New York. We can rave about our favorite dishes at the hottest new restaurants (toasted kasha salad! cavatelli with 'nduja!); we've seen the Francis Bacon retrospective at the Guggenheim ("Often conceived as a visceral, instinctive painter, he's a much more considered artist than once believed"); we're excited about DVF's S/S collab with RiRi, and if you don't know the abbreviations, don't even bother. The prohibitive cost of this knowledge is never discussed. It takes an incredible amount of cunning to appear casually connected. To this end, I spend Saturday at the Met. But I can't focus on the paintings. I can't shake the thought that all these timeless, priceless works of art are all just dots and swirls. That when you break it down and look up close, everything is just . . . a mess.

Every time I call Mara, she screens. I know I have to tell her—for her sake and for Storm's—but I'm terrified she'll be angry with me for getting tested without her permission. She doesn't want to know. Even if I do tell her, she probably won't get tested, so all this information will accomplish is her being mad at me and ensuring I see even less of my niece. I'm at a loss.

I refocus on the outfits and get the user ratings back up to a four, just barely. Vivian's satisfied. It feels like a chore. I remind myself that hundreds of ambitious young women want to be in my position, working on a hot new start-up with Vivian Chang. Women like Olivia, Jordan, and Calley, college pals who visit for a weekend, all four of us jammed into my tiny studio. They are in awe of my life, which Olivia decrees "perfect" and Jordan declares "even better than it looks on Instagram."

I step out of the way of their jealousy and let it dress me, secretly ashamed. Only I know this designer outfit is actually a knockoff.

After my disastrous meeting with Dr. Murphman I put researching the Big M on the back burner. My considerably more successful threesome with Camila 4 Cam has me keen to keep on with my bucket list, but with whom? How? Elan never wrote back after my text about the threesome, and Cooper is inexplicably in Berlin for a few weeks. Do I cast a net out via online dating, which I and everyone I know hates with a fiery passion? Hang around bars and wait to be bought a drink—"Dirty martini, *extra* dirty"? Drive up and down Fifth Avenue screaming, "*Does anyone want to engage in mutually respectful carnal pleasure?*"

This is what I'm turning over in my mind, takeout lunch special in hand, when I hear someone call my name. In the middle of the faces streaming across Mott Street in SoHo on a sunny Tuesday, I am suddenly face to face with Ash Wilson. My college boyfriend.

"Ash!" I gape at him. "What—? Where—? Ash!"

He laughs and gives me a hug. I'm rocketed back five years, to skinny dorm rooms and bad cafeteria food and being the old married couple everyone made fun of but secretly wanted to be. He smells the same: pine soap and trustworthiness.

"Holy shit." I squeeze his arms. "You're jacked."

"I started working out." He gives me that goofy modest Ash smile, and I melt a little, just on instinct. He was always so cute: face like a teddy bear, blond flop of hair. Stocky but not fat. And now, fit.

I pull us out of the way of another wave of hungry office workers: me, the New Yorker, him, the tourist. "What are you doing here? Are you visiting?"

"No. I live here."

"*What?*" I slap his very solid arm. "Since when? Why didn't you email me?"

"Since ten days ago," he says. "I have a sublet in Bushwick while I find something."

"That's awesome," I say. "Not the part about Bushwick—bit too rustic for me—but it's awesome you're here. Is Michelle with you?"

His face shifts. "Michelle and I—we called it off."

"Oh. Wow, I'm so sorry," I say automatically. This stuns me. Ash has always been my go-to example of a Nice Guy. Nice Guys don't call off engagements. Or leave their very needy extended family behind in Ohio to move to New York City. "We should get a drink. Catch up."

"I'd like that," he says, and I can tell he means it. "I'll text you."

"Do." I'm squeezing his arm, again. "It's really good to see you." I let our gaze linger for a few seconds longer than necessary before I turn away, a long and lazy lasso tossed around his torso.

And just like that, the bucket list is back in play.

* * * *

We arrange to meet the following Friday. I actually get a few butterflies as we shore up our plan.

I know *exactly* what I'm going to get him to do with me.

Ash and I were not what you'd define as a passionate couple. Stable, yes. Sweet, for sure. But save for a few hot, gropey, very tipsy make-out sessions when we were first getting together, backstage after rehearsals (we met in drama club), Ash and I bypassed the honeymoon phase in favor of the domestic-bliss stage. And that's because we were mind-blowingly inexperienced when it came to any and all parts of a sexual relationship. We didn't know how to talk about our relationship, and by that I mean we never talked about it, not objectively. Ash's family members are strict Lutherans. They were technically okay with sex before marriage but not at all practically. We weren't even allowed to be in a room by ourselves with the door shut, even in the middle of the day during a hot and heavy game of Risk or Settlers of Catan. We ended up doing it, but it was furtive and awkward and 100 percent missionary 100 percent of the time.

Honestly, I didn't even really mind. In a way, I was grateful. We were always super careful. I was on the pill and we used condoms, so I was never worried about STDs or getting pregnant. And I got to sidestep the awful sex-in-college phase. One by one, my smart, kind girlfriends were falling for absolute dingbats who couldn't give less of a shit about them. The girl in the dorm next to me lost her virginity to someone dressed as the Joker at a Halloween frat party. She was blackout drunk and never even found out, exactly, who it was. We all knew it was rape, really, but she never wanted to do anything about it. Watching her try to laugh it off as if it was funny and wild was the most depressing thing I've ever seen. That was sex in college, in a nutshell. Hooking up was supposed to be fun, but it just made most—not all, but most—of my friends sad and anxious. I'd cuddle into Ash with a bowl of microwave mac-and-cheese, streaming old episodes of *Sex and the City* on my laptop, and thank my lucky stars.

But that was years ago, and I'm different now. My body and I are slightly better acquainted, and I'm (slightly) less embarrassed talking about it.

I suggest we meet at my place. I'd love to "show it to him," dot dot dot.

* * * *

On Friday night, my ex arrives right on time, in a pressed collared shirt and dark jeans. The old Ash wore baggy sweatshirts and faded chinos. I answer the door in a drapey chiffon robe dress, and yes, you can see my bra. His eyes go to it immediately. He looks startled.

I've changed too.

"Come in," I coo. "*Entré.*"

"Cute place." He slips off his shoes. "Very . . . contained."

"We're not in Ohio anymore, Toto." When I accept the bottle of wine he hands me, I let our fingers graze. "It's *so good* to see you, Ash." I give him a Very Meaningful smile.

Dinner is roast veggies and a quinoa salad: nothing too heavy, the boy's bench-pressing. I dim the lights when he's in the bathroom. We curl into my love seat, my legs hooked over his. "Michelle was a great girl, but when I thought about spending the rest of my life with her . . ." He lets out a breath. "I couldn't do it. I kept thinking it was cold feet, that I'd get used to the idea. But it just got worse. I felt paralyzed."

"You poor thing." I stroke his arm. "Poor Masher." His pet name.

"She didn't take it well," he says, draining his wineglass. "Tried to run over me with the car. She says it was a visibility issue but . . . she did."

"Awful." I shake my head. "Just awful." I'm channeling every seductress I've ever seen on TV. Every word is as slippery as silk.

"I wanted it to work, Lace." His gaze is intense. "You don't know how much I really, really wanted it to work." We're staring at each other. His eyes flick to my lips, back up to my face, and at the exact same moment, we close in on each other. His lips feel soft and familiar, like a comfy pair of slippers. He opens his mouth. I pull back.

"Hold up," I say. "I want to try something."

"Lights on?" He looks nervous.

I tell him about my bucket list. Not the reason for it, just its existence. "And so, because we're friends, because we know each other, I was wondering . . ." I can feel my face going red. "How do you feel about . . . role-play?"

He sits back. "Role-play?"

"It's basically the same as drama club, except we're acting out sexy scenarios instead of *Guys and Dolls*."

"What kind of scenarios?"

I unhook my feet and tuck them underneath myself. I'm more tongue-tied than I want to be. "Basic scenarios. Standard scenarios. Boss and, um, intern."

"I'm the boss?"

"Actually, I'm the boss." My gaze pinballs around the room. "I have this fantasy that I'm a power bitch, and a sexy intern—you—seduces me. I try to resist, but you're just too hot and I give in and we do it on my desk."

"I haven't done any acting since college," Ash muses. "What's my backstory?"

I'd laugh if I didn't feel so awkward. "It's not really about the acting, Ash, it's about . . . creating a rich fantasy world where we can play out different power dynamics. It'll be fun."

Ash frowns at me, thinking it over. If it's not an immediate yes, it's obviously a no. Vague discomfort deepens into real humiliation.

"Forget it," I say. "Dumb idea—"

"I'm in," he says. "I want to."

"Are you sure?"

"Yes. This is my new life. I want to try new things." He gets to his feet purposefully. "Let's go."

I slip into black pants, heels, and a white button-down, unbuttoned to expose a peek of my bra: power-bitch chic. Already I'm simmering: equal parts nerves and something else. I position myself at the desk, flip open my computer and adopt Patricia's excellent posture. Everyone wants to be my boss, and channeling her is surprisingly sexy. The idea that I can fuck and fire someone makes me feel expansive. Already I've summoned my ex from the New York chaos and made him appear here in my apartment. This small but powerful act makes me sit even taller. I'd chosen this bucket list item because I figured it'd be easier to get out of my comfort zone with someone I'm comfortable with. But as I pretend to study a spreadsheet, I realize I'm not that comfortable with Ash anymore. He's grown up, and so have I. And that's a good thing. That makes all this even more exciting. I'm not exactly turned on, but I'm alert. My heart's beating a little faster.

If I play my carnal cards right, maybe tonight's the night Ash and I don't just have very quick, slightly shameful sex.

Maybe tonight's the night we *fuck*.

Ash knocks on my wall.

I bark, "Enter!"

He's adopting a nervous posture, blinking shyly. "Ms. . . . Whitman?"

I break character. "Babe, no, it's not really me. Make up a name."

"Oh," he says. "Okay."

We reset.

He knocks again. "Ms. . . . Huffington?"

Sure, whatever. "Yes?"

"I have those reports you were after." He hands me my electric bill.

I peer at it. "This is very poor work. Very poor. I'm sorry, I don't think this is a good position for you." I recross my legs and arch an eyebrow. His cue to seduce me.

Ash clasps his hands together. "Please, Ms. Huffington. Please don't fire me. My family's relying on this paycheck. I'll have to go on food stamps." He's doing some sort of Southern accent. "Ma's got dysentery of the bowel; Pa's in jail for killing a man over rat meat—"

"Cut, cut." I wave my hands at him. "This isn't *Oliver Twist*. It's meant to be sexy."

"I was going to do a whole 'if there's any way I can change your mind' thing," Ash says. "*I'll do anything, anything at all—*"

"But my fantasy isn't sexual assault, it's that you're seducing me. Me, overcome by lust, not you crying through a blow job."

We reset.

Ash knocks again. "Ms. . . . Huffington?" He sounds like Marilyn Monroe, each syllable a puff of cotton wool.

"Yes?"

He slinks in the room. I have flashbacks to the year we did *Chicago*. "I have those"—the word's a naughty whisper—"*reports* you were looking for." He hands me the bill, leaning over in a way that suggests he's showing me his cleavage.

This is certainly not what I was expecting, but I find myself oddly intrigued. If Ash is playing a woman, am I playing a man? The thought of fucking Ash-the-girl is . . . interesting. "Thank you." I lower my voice. "Remind me of your name?"

"Real name's Cindy, but the boys call me Sugar." He hops up on my desk neatly. "On account of the fact I taste so sweet."

I get up, so I'm looking down at him. If I had a dick, it might be getting hard. "I'm surprised we've never met. You're very, very fetching, Miss Sugar."

He bats his eyelids. "It's a hard business to get ahead in. So I make it my business to give head *and* get hard."

"*Get* hard?" I say. "Oh, I thought you were a . . . lady."

Ash blinks. "Yes. I am a lady. A lady man."

"You're transsexual?" I'm not keeping up. "Pre-op or post-op? Wait, I don't think I'm supposed to ask that—"

Ash calls cut in exasperation. "I got confused. Sorry, Lace. I'm no good at this."

"You know what might be easier?" I put my hands on his shoulders.

"If we just played ourselves. I'm me. You're you. We just haven't met be-fore." I do up a few of my buttons and extend my hand. "Hi. I'm Lacey."

He smiles at me, getting it. "Ash."

We talk. It's not exactly role-play, but it's working. As we pretend to be two strangers meeting in a Brooklyn bar, I find I'm presenting the very best version of myself to my ex-boyfriend. The me that's funny and warm and witty and interested. I've always told myself I'm a bad flirt. "I just don't get it," I'd whine to Vivian and Steph. "What even *is* it? Double entendres? Drunk giggling?" But as we sit here and pretend to be ourselves, I realize not only am I flirting . . . but I like it. I'm energized and present. It's just being playful. That's all flirting is: play. I can play. I can flirt.

Our conversation deepens. I tell Ash about the difficulty in balanc-ing my sales job and the app, and how neither is like what I expected. He tells me about the finance job he just quit, the lease he just broke. The way New York is stripping away old skin, helping him reinvent himself. He is more self-assured, but there is a sensitivity to Ash that I've always found very attractive. When I make him laugh, he touches my arm and I shiver. The air crackles with sex-and-the-city possibility. I can't help but wonder: Am I actually into my ex? Can you ever get over an old love if love hasn't gotten over you?

Meanwhile, at the other end of the sofa, Ash refills his wineglass and faces me in full. "If you could change anything about your life, what would it be?"

To not be BRCA positive. "I'd like to be closer to Mara." The answer catches me off guard. It takes me a moment to recognize it as truth. "I'd like for us to love each other more."

His gaze traces the contours of my face. "That's beautiful."

You're beautiful, Ash. Heat rises inside me. I want to kiss him. But not like in college.

A real kiss.

A New York kiss.

I edge toward him. "Tell me a secret." I run my thumb up and down the edge of his hand. I feel each stroke in my own body. "Tell me something no one else knows about you."

His lips part. I imagine swinging my legs over him, his hands on my bra, and will we do it on my bed or the love seat, and maybe I still love Ash and maybe I always have . . .

"I'm gay."

"Mmm." I lean toward him. "Hot."

He stops me. He looks terrified. "No, I am. I'm gay."

"Let's do it on the kitchen floor!" I grab his shirt.

"Lace, I'm gay. I'm gay. I'm a gay man. I think about gay things, all the time." He lets out a sound that's partway between a moan and scream. "God, I said it. I said it out loud."

Something very weird is happening. The air in the room ripples. "Are we still . . . Sorry, I'm a bit confused—"

Ash is on his feet. "I'm gay. I like cock. I love it. Oh my God. Oh my God."

"Are you serious?" Emotion, crazy emotion that I can't even begin to identify is rocketing through me. "Are you being serious right now?"

Ash is nodding very, very fast. "I can't believe I said it. I can't believe it."

"That's great," I say in a dazed whisper, because I know that's what I'm supposed to say, but I don't really mean it, what I mean is, "Wait, what? Since when?"

Ash looks at me as if for the first time. His face crumples into something strange and new. Pity. "Oh, sweetheart."

"Since when?" I shriek.

He sits back down next to me. "Well, always, babe."

"But we were together for three years!"

"I know. Oh, I know."

"You told me you loved me. I lost my virginity to you." My head is whirring like a piece of broken machinery. "Sorry, I know this is good for you, I know it is, but I'm just . . . having a little trouble . . . Who else knows?"

He shakes his head. "No one. You're the first."

Fuck it. I need a drink and I don't even care if it gives me cancer. I run to the kitchen and unearth a dusty bottle of whiskey from under the sink. I slam a shot, straight from the bottle. Ash does the same. The booze hits me like a truck, a wonderful, wonderful truck. I immediately do a second. "Fuck," I say. "*Fuck*."

Ash is looking at me with big, wild eyes. He's breathless. "Do you hate me?"

My gay ex-boyfriend is vibrating like a spinning top. He looks like he's just been rescued from some lunatic's basement, stunned to be in the outside world. I could tell him to get back down there: that it would be a terrible idea to come out, that he'd destroy his family. But I can't do that. My future isn't getting back with my ex. It's hours of him deciding whether he's a twink or just into them, Chris Pratt versus Chris Pine. "Of course I don't hate you," I say. "I'm just . . . surprised."

"I'm so sorry, Lace. I really am."

I'm not okay with this. Not yet. But I hand him the bottle and make myself sound blithe. "So which of my friends' boyfriends did you jerk it to when we were together?"

He laughs, grateful. I smile back and pretend that my bewilderment isn't already becoming pain.

20.

For me, fashion is something that helps me understand and express myself. But honestly, it's also a form of armor. Sometimes I dress to impress, and sometimes I dress to deflect or even intimidate (who's going to assume a girl in bright red six-inch stilettos is nervous about saying something dumb?). What truly scares me about a mastectomy, and medical stuff in general, is how much it exposes me. There's nowhere to hide. It's about me, just as I am.

Me, just as I am, is not an easy thing to think about this week. I've always accepted I am a little behind the eight ball when it comes to the boudoir. But discovering that my ex-boyfriend, my *only* ex-boyfriend, never found me truly desirable—that he was essentially *lying* to me for *three years*—hits me very hard. It's that big twist moment in a movie that rewrites the whole script, beginning to end. Ash's sexuality is the Keyser Söze of my life. All the good times—the kisses, the cuddles, even our pretty bad sex—he wasn't feeling it like I was, to the limited extent that I felt much at all. Ash just wasn't that into me.

What else have I invented? What else isn't really there?

After the dust settles and I've indulged in a few weepy shower moments, I make two very firm decisions. First, I'm going to tell Steph that I like Cooper. Then, I'm going to ask him out. I am. I'm going to ask a guy out, and not some wimpy-ass "we should get beers sometime": the invite that could be a hang or a date or nothing at all. I am going to declare my intentions, unequivocally and in a way that leaves no room for misinterpretation.

* * * *

I'm outside Steph's building when my phone rings. The name stops me in my tracks.

Elan Behzadi.

At first I'd been obsessively counting the days he'd been away, ticking off a month in my mind, but after I never heard back from him, I'd stopped. Hard to believe it's been a whole month since I sunk my teeth into a piece of baklava in his West Village pad and all but bragged to him about my health, or lack thereof.

It's a rainy Saturday evening, and Steph and I have big plans to make Alfredo pasta and watch *Postcards from the Edge*. I'm not just excited about carbs or the wit and wisdom of Carrie Fisher (bow down slash RIP). Some light social media stalking of Steph's Instagram comments has confirmed Cooper is en route back to Brooklyn.

Elan was only ever going to be trouble; everyone in the world could see that. The sensation that he could see through me, like my skin was made of cellophane, has faded. I remember it, but no longer feel it in my bones. And I am distinctly pissed he hasn't contacted me until it served him: his needs, his schedule. Who's too busy to send a lousy text? Honestly, I would've settled for emojis. *Emojis.*

Feeling like a straight-up boss, I send his call to voice mail and hit the buzzer.

* * * *

"I'm being so bad." I help myself to a second serving of delicious cheesy pasta. "This is so bad."

"No, this is Saturday night." Steph tucks her feet underneath her, cozying into the couch. Outside, rain rattles the window.

"I remember." I lick my fork. "Living with you was terrible for my beach bod."

"Lace, every bod is a beach bod."

"I know, I know. I just want mine to resemble an ironing board with a nice pair of tits." I say it without thinking. Then I remember.

No tits for me. If I go through with it.

Steph touches my shoulder. "You'd still have a nice pair of tits. You'll always be a hottie with the lottie, Lace. Always."

I put my fork down. "I wanted to talk to you about . . . something."

"Oh?" She sits up, alert. "Yeah?"

I brace myself. The prospect of honesty, and it being something someone doesn't want to hear, makes my heart thud and my palms sweat. Maybe she'll storm out, slam the door. Leave me alone in the loft. But I want to be honest. In the way Ash finally was with me. "I like your roommate," I say. "I want to ask him out. Sexually speaking."

"Oh." She deflates. Of course: she was expecting cancer stuff. Inwardly, I slap my forehead with my palm. I get ready for her to whine something about what a good roommate Cooper is and not to complicate things with shagging. "Fine," she says. "Whatever."

"Really? I had this whole speech about being respectful and putting our friendship first but needing to go after what I wanted—"

"I said, 'Fine.'"

I push my luck. "Is he dating anyone?"

"Don't know. Don't think so. He's never brought anyone back here, thank God."

I bite back a smile. Perfecto.

She slides her big brown eyes at me. "There isn't anything else . . . on your mind?"

"Like what?" I twist pasta around my fork. "You want me to beg you to accept my heirloom jewels if I get cancer and die?"

Steph tuts. "I've just been thinking a lot about what you can do. They say it's important to connect with the community. Do you want to do a fun run?"

Part of me knows I'm not handling this like the Good Cancer Patient: socially minded and proactive, beautifully brave, admirably strong. But another part wants to tell everyone to fuck off. No one knows what I'm going through, and even if I was the best orator in the world I wouldn't be able to communicate how it feels to know that your own body is a ticking time bomb. The pasta sits sludgy in my stomach: I ate too much. Great, now I feel sick. I can't quite look at her. "I know you're just trying to be a good friend. But I have to do this my way."

She opens her mouth.

I glance around for the remote. "It's getting late. We should start the movie."

* * * *

Hours later, Steph's snoring at the other end of the couch when I hear the front door open. The sound of a suitcase being wheeled in. A zingy swirl of excitement pulses my eyes open. Cooper comes into the living room quietly. I pretend to wake, rubbing my eyes.

"Oh, hey," he whispers, his voice hitching up in surprise.

I blink groggily and look around as if I have absolutely no idea how I've ended up here. "What time is it?"

"Just after two."

I switch off the TV, which has been playing the DVD menu on a loop. The room flips into darkness. "Guess we fell asleep watching the film."

Cooper pulls his suitcase toward his bedroom, not breaking my gaze. "You didn't wait up for me?"

"No," I say, defensive. Oh, wait, I *like* this guy. I reconsider. "Maybe."

He grins, and my stomach does a fun little flippy thing. "See you in the morning," he whispers.

"It is the morning," I whisper back.

"Then see you soon."

You betcha.

21.

I wake to Steph pulling on jeans and sneakers. "Leaving so soon?"

"Sunday study group," she says. "Christ, I'm so late."

"Bummertown." I prop my head up. "I thought we'd do brunch."

She gives me a look. "You're such a shit liar. Have fun hitting on my roomie."

I give her a wan smile, thinking that, actually, I'm a pretty good liar. Because when Cooper emerges, yawning, semi-naked and in search of coffee, our plan to go get ingredients for his World-Famous Blueberry Pancakes feels both effortless and entirely spontaneous. "I'll just shower," I say, giving him the chance to admire my ass cheeks in strategically chosen boy shorts as I head to the bathroom. It's only after I'm in the shower that I realize (a) I just displayed my buttocks as part of a mating ritual, like a brazen chimpanzee, and (b) I've never done that before in my life.

* * * *

It's a gorgeous March morning. The snap in the air feels fresh and vibrant, no longer brutally cold. Last night's rain scrubbed the streets clean, and the promise of spring hides in every unfurled bud and patch of pale sunlight. With our canvas bags in tow, we pass young families with red-cheeked kids on wobbly scooters and groups of friends hoping to beat the brunch rush, daring to do so without a thousand winter layers. Cooper looks real cute in a forest-green parka. His dark blond hair peeks out from a plaid red lumberjack hat. He dresses well, even for a boy. I am slightly nervous, in a good way. I feel alive. Ready. "How was Berlin?" I ask. "What brought you there?"

"Meetings," he replies. "But I just love it there." His eyes are shining, even though he looks a bit jet-lagged. "It's gritty and romantic and modern and historical. It's everything."

"Do you speak German?"

"*Ja.* I'm a quarter German."

I smile up at him, charmed and intrigued. "What's your story, Coop?"

"My story?" He smiles back, playful. He likes me. For sure. "Which version: white kid from San Francisco overcomes the burden of middle-class privilege, or liberal tech geek rethinks life plan after getting exactly what he wants?"

All of you. I want all of you. "I'll take the lot."

Cooper's last name is Cooper. His first name is Noam. After Chomsky. His dads—yes, Cooper is a gayby—are both socialist academic types, one professionally (Moritz, assistant professor of religion and human rights, half-German), one personally (Alan, radio journalist reporting out of NPR West). He speaks of them fondly and with respect, as if they are friends. I can picture his adolescence: grass-fed beef burgers sizzling on a solar-powered electric grill, eaten with accomplished adults at a long table, where he's encouraged to speak up, share an opinion that's thoughtfully received. Coop and his dads and the crème of the Bay Area intellectual crop kicking back, enjoying being multiculturally cool and radically open-minded.

College in Berkeley; Cooper, nerd genius, gets a full freaking ride. Majored in computer science. Dormed with Liam Ryder, a name that is instantly familiar but I can't think why. Liam was charismatic, hungry, and from real wealth: Father-buys-yachts-and-senators kind of wealth. They became best friends and talked about starting a company, like all boys of a certain age did. After a few failed starts, something took off, midway through senior year.

"Wait," I interrupt. "You had a start-up too? I didn't know that."

"Buckle your seat belt, sister," Cooper says. "It's going to be a bumpy ride."

Cooper created See365, an educational platform that used virtual reality to train people in hands-on topics. He was excited for how it could be used to train doctors and surgeons in rural or developing areas, where they didn't have access to universities and proper hospitals. The technology seemed like it had a lot of promise, and Liam wanted to go all in, fast. Cooper didn't really think they needed to raise a bunch of money and hire a big staff, but Liam convinced him this was the best and only path. They raised a huge seed round of $10 million at a $35 million post-money valuation, solely from one investor Liam brought in, a family friend, a Rockefeller. They hired forty staff members—engineers, designers, marketing, and salespeople. They dropped out of school to work ninety-hour weeks. No days off. No social life. They slept in their office. It felt like weeks went by in between seeing the sun. But the buzz was huge. Liam was telling everyone they'd be a billion-dollar company in twelve months' time.

But he was lying.

The technology was cool, but it wasn't selling the way they thought it would. Their business-development team started signing bad deals just to keep the lights on. They weren't bringing in real revenue, and now they were burning a ton of money every month on employees. Liam and Cooper started getting nervous they were going to run out of cash and wouldn't be able to raise more because, ultimately, the business was failing.

That's when SynCorp International came knocking and offered to buy them out.

They were offering $40 million.

I stop in my tracks and gasp, a real movie gasp. "You're fucking kidding."

"Nope."

I stare at him, frantically recasting him in my mind as a multimillionaire. It's like finding out he's part alien.

Cooper holds up a hand. "Wait," he says.

Even though this was less than the mega millions they wanted the company to be worth someday, it was better than their valuation, and could be a good way out. But Cooper didn't want to do the deal. SynCorp International was a billion-dollar engineering company whose biggest client happened to be the US military. They were responsible for training and simulation services. Not rocket science to work out that See365 would be used to train US soldiers. Things were already strained between the cofounders. Both felt the other was getting more than his fair share. It was Liam who had the connections to the Rockefeller investment money, but Cooper who created the software in the first place. Starting at a fifty-fifty split, both their equity was chipped away as they brought on new employees, and was now at 33 percent a piece.

They argued. Viciously. Creating technology for warfare was a major ethical disaster for Cooper. But it seemed like the only way out, and it was a huge carrot being dangled in front of them: $40 million. In the end, Liam wore Cooper down. He agreed to the deal.

"Holy smokes," I say. "Payday, times forty million."

"Not exactly," Cooper says.

What Cooper didn't know was that Liam did the deal with the Rockefeller at a three-times liquidation preference. That meant the Rockefeller got his money back times three before anyone else got paid out, in the event of a deal. Liam was desperate to get a big, fat deal done to look good in front of Father. It was the only way he could get the Rockefeller over the line in the first place. Now, of the $40 million the company was bought for, $30 million went to the Rockefeller, leaving $10 million to divide among the other shareholders.

Cooper should've ended up with close to $13.2 million. In the end, he walked away with just over $3 million and never spoke to Liam again. He was twenty-four years old.

It takes me a long time to gather a response. "Why are you living in a shared loft if you're a millionaire?"

"Because I'm not a millionaire." Taxes ate up a chunk. Then Cooper's dad Moritz was hit by an Uber. He was on an informal sabbatical from his untenured university position. After fighting with the insurance company and Uber for six months, both refused to pay the hospital bill, which was fast approaching seven figures. Cooper footed the bill. He says it like he was picking up the check. "Then I bought the dads a big fancy house. It'll be my house eventually, so it wasn't totally a martyr move. I have some stocks and bonds and shit, nothing too crazy. I'm not scraping by but I'm not superrich."

"But you could afford to get your own place. You don't need a roommate."

"True," he says. "But I wanted some company. After everything went to shit in San Francisco, I moved to LA, got an overpriced one-bedroom, and ended up spending a lot of time talking to my cactus. When it started talking back, I figured I needed a change. I like Steph; I like Astoria. It's a good place for me to figure out what I actually want to do. What makes me happy. And that," he says, "is what I'm assuming you meant by my story."

I'm experiencing that distinct sensation of arriving at an online date and realizing that the guy is . . . amazing. And cute. And clever, and has a cool job, and appears interested in me. Ladies of the world know how rare and thrilling and off-putting this is. I liked Cooper, but I didn't really *like* like him. Now that is becoming a distinct possibility. I feel underdressed, underprepared.

Coop isn't an easy get. He's a catch.

Be. Cool.

The grocery store doors slide open. He smiles at me. "We're here."

We go in search of blueberries, eggs, maple syrup. Everything organic, farm-fresh, local. It's easy. Fun. I tease him; he teases me back. I'm getting groceries with my boyfriend, and after we go home and make pancakes, we'll have lazy Sunday-morning sex, then see a movie, then get dumplings. By the time we leave the store, my interest in Cooper has reached DEFCON 1. I am actively containing an adrenaline spike.

When he asks me about *my* story, I don't give him my usual set of half-truths and sleight of hand.

"My mom died when I was five," I say. "Breast cancer."

He doesn't look at me like I'm someone who needs saving. He doesn't appear mortified or unsure. He doesn't say, "I'm sorry," prompting an equally generic and thus meaningless response. He just listens. And that lets me talk. Openly, without pretense or sarcasm.

I tell him about growing up without a mother, raised by an odd confluence of Mara, my dad, PTA mom–types, and the internet. How my sister was the one who made my middle school lunches and did the laundry and helped me with my homework but how much she openly resented that, how much she hated my father. I adored my dad, idolized him, even. When I was a preteen his constant new business ventures—importer of Balinese furniture, real estate agent, manager of a Beatles cover band—were exciting and cool. They meant we moved around Illinois a lot, and I got good at moving. Sometimes I just lived out of boxes, and there wasn't anyone around to tell me not to. There wasn't anyone around to tell me not to do anything: I never had a curfew; I could watch as much television as I wanted. My memories of those years are happy. Piling into our beat-up yellow Kombi van, singing along to Paul Simon cassettes, Dad grinning down at me, one hand on the steering wheel, the other flicking a cigarette out the car window, on the road, yet again. When I started high school in the small town of Buntley (home of a turkey farm he'd invested in), things changed. I didn't want to move anymore. I'd made friends, real ones, ones I didn't want to discard. My sister had a boyfriend whose house she basically lived at. Or, could have lived at, if it wasn't for me. When Dad's next great big thing arrived, Mara and I put our foot down. I remember that day clearly: my father was furious, yelling at us to start packing. Mara yelled back. She was nineteen years old and fierce as a tiger. We weren't going. Not again. We were done.

She won. We stayed. Then the disappearing years started. He'd just leave, middle of the night, usually with a note and a few bills for food. He'd come back, eventually, maybe after a few days, a few weeks. One time it was months. And, like my sister, I started hating my father too. He wasn't an adventurer. He was a loser. A vagrant.

I put myself through high school. I worked part-time jobs, saving what I could and studying the rest of the time. Education was my ticket out. I knew this, and everyone kept telling me I was smart, I could make it. Got into Ohio State with financial aid. Interned at Hoffman House like my life depended on it. Landed an entry-level sales job. And here we are.

"Wow," Cooper says. "That's quite a tale."

I can tell I've rattled him. We walk in silence for a few moments. I said too much. I sound like the kid of a hobo and the sister of a rage monster, which in some ways I am. He sold a company for $40 million, and I worked a summer job at Fudgy Wudgy Ice Cream. He loves Berlin. I've never even been to Boston.

Good one, Whitman.

"You're really impressive." He sounds embarrassed. "I obviously had a pretty sheltered upbringing."

"I think you're really impressive," I say. "Not just selling a company, which is obviously pretty baller. Taking real time to work out what your deal is: it's very . . . evolved."

"Thanks," he says. "Can I ask a big question?"

We're back at the loft, outside the front steps. I remember when these steps seemed novel. My childhood was entirely flat. "Sure."

He looks me right in the face. I take the chance to stare back. It's not that he has male-model cheekbones. But I really like where his cheekbones are. "What makes you happy?" he asks. "What's worth doing?"

I don't want to say, "I don't know," but they are the first three words to come to me. I can't say "pancakes" (too glib) or "talking to you" (too honest). What makes me happy? Who asks questions like that? Noam Cooper, emotionally evolved egghead and far too attractive for my own good. "I'm still figuring that out," I say. "But when I do, you'll be the first to know."

"Excellent," he says, "and for the record, you're impressive, Lacey Whitman."

We climb the stairs to the first floor, and I'm buzzing, buzzing, buzzing.

He takes the lead with breakfast, and is there anything more attractive than a dude who knows his way around a cast iron? I make coffee, subtly admiring the way he can crack an egg with one hand. Technically, I only allow myself pancakes on Sundays. But if Cooper was my boyfriend, I'd eat them every single day. We chat about trend forecasting. He knows the basics. I fill in his gaps, like how powerful celebrities are these days. Kim Kardashian wears a trucker hat and cutoffs on Monday, and Forever 21 has a new line of trucker hats and cutoffs in just two weeks. "It's all about having your finger on as many pulses as possible," I say. "In order to stay ahead of the curve."

"And you're ahead of the curve, now." He flips a pancake. "Thinking about getting a mastectomy."

The word invades the kitchen. I'm aware we haven't discussed my bucket list or my health, and it felt deliberate, the cozy construction of a fantasy where we're just two regular twentysomethings, maybe, kind of, crushing on each other. The morning splits a little. I mumble affirmation, hoping we can skate past it.

He puts a plate of pancakes in front of me. They smell like butter, sugar, heaven on earth. "How's everything going with that?" he asks, taking a seat opposite me.

I promptly lose my appetite. "Fine."

He forks pancake into his mouth, watching me as he chews and swallows. "You don't like talking about it?"

"I don't talk about it."

"Forgive me for sounding like a touchy-feely liberal, but I am a touchy-feely liberal, so: it's probably a good idea to talk about it." He shoves more pancake into his mouth and smiles idiotically, which makes me laugh a little.

I carve off a tiny piece of pancake and swirl it into some syrup. "I'm not big on emotional theatrics."

He shrugs. "Okay."

His acceptance feels unusual. I take a little bite. Delicious. "Well . . . it's . . . a nightmare."

Cooper keeps eating but he's listening closely.

The tight ball of apprehension in my chest loosens a tiny bit. That little drip of honesty felt . . . good. "Feels like I have to plan my own funeral but I can't tell anyone I'm going to die." I take a deep, cautious breath. I can hear my heart in my chest. "I just feel . . . very alone and very scared. I've worked really hard to create a life for myself here, but this makes me feel that it's not a solid life. I get this surgery, something goes wrong, I'm sick, in pain, I can't go back to work, I can't pay rent, I end up where? With my sister?" I let out a hard laugh.

"How common is that?" Cooper asks. "Complications, things going wrong?"

"I don't know. The forums are full of horror stories."

"Forums?"

"Online cancer clubs. Real cheery places," I say, even though my sarcasm is a little unfair: some of the women who post seem perfectly cool.

"They could be a good way to meet people," he says, "who are going through the same thing you are."

"Maybe." I take another bite, then another.

"You got dealt a shit hand, Lacey. There's no denying it. But the more you can open up to people, let them help you and support you, the easier it's going to be."

We gaze at each other, a deep, raw space opening between us.

It's not sexy.

It's intimate.

Cooper pushes his plate aside, scraped clean. "And how about the other thing?"

"The bucket list?" I smile. The mood in the room lightens. "Not bad, actually. Kicking ass, taking names."

"I was thinking about that list," he says.

"Oh, really," I tease. "What were you thinking about?"

"Do you feel like you won't be able to do those things afterward?"

I think on this. "No. I guess I'd be able to. But some of them wouldn't be the same, and some of them I just want to do now." I eat a big mouthful of pancake, suddenly hungry. "What about you: made any moves on that diner waitress yet?"

He grins and takes his plate to the sink. "Not exactly." He checks the time. "But I do have a date this afternoon."

The word ricochets through me. I keep my voice indifferent. "Oh yeah?"

"Yeah, we're seeing a movie at BAM." I can't tell if he sounds apologetic or not: there's something definitely off in his tone.

I keep chewing, casually. "First date?"

He pauses. He's counting. "Sixth, I think."

"*Sixth?*" The word shoots out of me like a flare. "You like her." It sounds like an accusation, and why did I believe Steph when she said he was single, why, why, why?

"I don't know. I guess." He definitely sounds uncomfortable, and of course he fucking should, we've basically been on a date all morning. Haven't we? "She, ah, started an organic tampon company."

I bet I know who it is. Elsa, a ridiculously beautiful Swede who doesn't shave her armpits and smells like essential oils. A wifey. They'd make a great couple.

"Fun." I want to stab something. "I should get going."

I gather up my purse and coat. The waves of humiliation I'm radiating could fill an ocean. I stayed over for him, opened up to him, orchestrated this entire morning for someone who has a girlfriend, and of course he does, and of course it's not me, with my dud DNA and potential breast removal. I zip up my coat so fast I catch the skin on my stomach. I don't even flinch at the pain. "Bye!" I zoom toward the front door.

"Lacey," he calls after me.

I don't want to turn around, but I do. My smile is so frozen it could cut glass.

He's rubbing the back of his neck, awkward, unsure. Poor baby: must be so hard when all the girls you're stringing along catch up with one another. But even as I'm resisting the urge to scratch out his eyes, I want him to want me. To choose me. Because don't we have something?

Finally he looks up. "I'm sorry," he says quietly. "Just bad timing."

I cock my head, smiling; *Whatever do you mean?* "Thanks for the chat," I say. "See you later."

I'm not going to feel it: the hard wallop of rejection, the slow crush of disappointment. This is the time girls like me call their mothers. I hear them, walking from the subway or curled into coffee shop corners, *I don't know what went wrong. I really cared about him, Mom.* And in the silence when they're listening, faces a crunch of sadness, I imagine what they're hearing. *He doesn't deserve you, darling. It'll be okay. I love you so, so much.*

I, on the other hand, make escape plans.

He picks up on the second ring. *"Aziz-am,"* Elan says, "I'm so glad you called."

22.

I don't tell Steph or Vivian about my pending dinner date with Elan. I want to, but I want them to be excited for me more, and I have a feeling what I'll get is a warning and even the possibility of this irritates me, so I keep my mouth shut. Funnily enough, the person I do end up telling is a complete stranger. Beatrice "Bee" Weiner, the "crown jewel of Staten Island" (her words) is forty-six, a divorced New York native, and active on the BRCA forums. While most forum regulars are fond of using abbreviations like DH ("dear husband"; gag) and signing off their polite, hopeful posts with smiley emojis and hearts, Bee is as frank and funny as a well-timed fart. Her first post: *All right bitches, I'm getting my titties cut off this summer. Gotta couple of beaver tails strapped to my chest: size 40D squared. How soon till I can motorboat my ex?* We've started emailing, and it's her I confide in. *Nice one, Whitman*, she writes me back. *Let's hope Persia knows how to speak pussy.*

I work some contacts and borrow an Opening Ceremony dress for our date. It's a sample from the upcoming spring collection: pleated black silk with a subtle gold-metallic shimmer that falls an inch above the knee. Tie-up spaghetti straps, scoop neck. It's a loose A-line so I wear it belted, no necklace, and after much consideration, pair it with fierce orange stilettos (Louboutins, eBay) and a dark green clutch, which sounds totally bonkers but looks wild in a let's-party-like-it's-1999 way. I blow-out my hair and am in the process of finishing big smoky eyes when my doorbell rings. It's UPS. A package for me: a large cream envelope and a short note in scratchy, messy handwriting on Elan's custom stationery.

Wear this.

A red lace bra and matching panties fall into my hand.

I stare at them, confused. *Does he think I don't have my own underwear?* Then it lands.

Oh.

Oh.

I toss it all on my bed, panicked. I can't wear underwear that a man—essentially, a *stranger*—couriered me before a date. I don't even know how he got my address. Called Hoffman House? Bribed an intern?

It's obviously a power play. Wearing the underwear indicates that I'm submissive, that I can be controlled.

Or does it? Are we playing a game; is this an offering?

Am I supposed to play hard to get? Should I be indignant; is that the good-girl thing to do?

Would it be boring to ignore lingerie? Would it be rude to say no?

I exhale harshly: it doesn't matter if I'm rude, and I don't need to be a mythical "good girl": what matters is what *I* want.

Do I want to wear the lingerie?

Cautiously, I scoop it off my bed. The bra is my size, and the idea he was able to appraise me so accurately is equally disconcerting and erotic. It has a small gold clasp in the front between the two cups, which I've always thought appeals more to men than women: easy access. They're a beautiful, well-made set, even if the color evokes a certain trashy, red-light district feel . . . which is not entirely unsexy. Imagining Elan's own arousal in selecting them, writing the note, licking the envelope, makes everything in me thicken.

It's 7:40 p.m. I need to call a car if I'm going to make my carefully planned lateness of exactly ten minutes (fifteen is insolent, five is too eager). In the mirror, a girl with glossy orange lips and mussy-sexy hair stares back at me. I don't recognize her: we are older, independent, going on a date with a famous-in-some-circles man who feels complicated and intimidating. It's difficult to tell if this new girl I see is a me I am discovering or a me I am moving further away from, like the fairy-tale heroine unwisely venturing deeper into the shadows of a dark, enchanted forest.

* * * *

The restaurant is buzzy when I arrive. Every table is full of attractive, overpaid people gesticulating above plates of handcrafted pasta and grilled swordfish. I'll be getting the famed mafaldini with pink peppercorns and parmigiana Reggiano: naturally I'd researched the restaurant the moment it was confirmed. Noemi opened seven years ago on the Upper East in the shell of an old garage; all bleached wood, white furniture, and floor-to-ceiling windows. It would almost feel Brooklynesque, but for the starched tablecloths and overly rehearsed quality of the staff. The hostess—no doubt an aspiring actress with those cheekbones—checks my name on a glowing screen. I trail her through the low light of glinting chandeliers, into a smaller backroom with just a few tables. There, in the far corner, scrolling through his phone, is Elan.

My heart doesn't leap into my throat: it's already there; it's been there for hours. He's wearing a slim-cut gray oxford, rolled at the sleeves to reveal the sort of watch that's advertised not as a timepiece, but a family heirloom. His dark hair is in place with the right amount of product, and he's shaved; no more stubble. He looks handsome, a word I don't think I've automatically conjured for a date before. When he sees me, his eyes pulse open a tiny bit, which makes the two hours of preening entirely worth it. As he stands, his eyes travel across my collarbone.

He can see I'm not wearing the red bra.

His lips touch my cheek, one hand on my waist. I smell aftershave; warm leather and spice. I'd swoon if I wasn't so tightly wound, so hyper-aware of every little thing happening. "You look different," he says, in a voice that doesn't need to be raised to be heard. "You're less nervous."

He's wrong about that. I take a seat—very comfortable—and place the pressed white napkin on my lap. "How was Paris? Where should I go for croissants?"

"*Sucre Et Épice*," he says, in what sounds to me like a perfect French accent. "Without a doubt. It's this little place in the Fifth. The head baker there, Christelle, makes everything according to her grand-mother's recipes. *Pain au chocolat*, éclair, tarte tatin—"

"Don't," I groan. "You're going to make me book a flight right now."

"What's stopping you?"

I can't afford it. I might be getting a mastectomy. I'm scared to go overseas on my own. "Nothing," I say. "You've inspired me. I'm going next summer."

"Summer in Paris." He leans closer, his voice a murmur. "Can I come?"

I'm smiling. "Okay."

"Excellent. We'll get a cheese plate in Le Marais—do you like cheese?"

"It's only my reason for existence."

He chuckles. "So we'll go out for *fromage*, and— Oh. Hello."

A tall man in a very nice suit is at our table, shaking Elan's hand. Silver hair, black-rimmed glasses, broad smile. It's Jeff Goldblum. The actor. I saw *Jurassic Park* a hundred thousand times. I am starstruck.

". . . own a little restaurant downtown called Whitewood," Jeff's saying. "Just checking out the competition." He twinkles at me. "You must try the mafaldini. It's what angels would taste like if we were able to harvest them like farm animals. Wouldn't that be amazing?"

"That's what I'm getting," I say, mildly horrified to find myself gushing. "I'd already decided."

Elan gestures at me. "This is Lacey Whitman. She's at Hoffman House."

"Oh." Jeff's eyes illuminate. "How is Patricia?"

Of course Patricia knows Jeff. "Wonderful," I say. "She just got back from Paris."

"I love Paris," says Jeff.

"I love Paris," says Elan.

"I love Paris, too," I say, slipping a glance at Elan. "We were just planning a trip."

Elan smiles back at me. It's more than merely interested. He looks utterly fascinated. I almost lose control of my bowels.

Jeff half bows. "Lacey Whitman, an honor and a pleasure. And Mr.

Behzadi"—he turns back to my date—"you have to come to the summer house again. I will beat you at table tennis."

Elan laughs. "No, you won't."

"Yes, I will." Jeff addresses me again. "Did you know this man is very good at table tennis?"

"I'm not," Elan says. "You're just very bad at it."

Jeff chuckles, and I decide right then and there that this is the absolute coolest moment of my life. After he leaves, I can't help asking Elan how he knows Jeff Goldblum.

Elan frowns. "I think I met him at a party. Kevin Bacon's place in Malibu. No, no, sorry. At Jess and Justin's. The Timberlakes."

Jess for Jessica Biel. A nickname. Kevin Bacon's house in Malibu? I can't help it. I start laughing.

He cocks his head. "What?"

Your life is crazy! But if you act like it's no big deal, so will I! "Nothing," I say, and pull myself together. Remember when Jeff Goldblum was at my table? I do.

The waiter arrives for our drink orders. I ask for a glass of white, something light and acidic. Elan orders a red. "I thought you weren't drinking," he says.

I'm flattered. He remembered. "Calculated risk."

He nods, but my reply glances off him. I'm almost disappointed he doesn't push it. I like the idea he'd be worried about my health. Instead, his eyes are on my shoulders. "Did you get my package?"

A warm flush rolls over me. "I did."

"And?"

I'm still conflicted. It annoys me that I can't decipher my own desire. I don't want to be used or taken advantage of. But I can't deny the whole thing turns me on. Snapping open my clutch, I show him the inside. Red lace.

A slow, curling smile. "You brought it."

I nod.

His voice is a murmur. "So go change."

I hesitate, squirming. "I'm not sure who I'm doing it for. You or me."

"What if it's for both of us?"

"But it's not my fantasy. I didn't initiate it."

He props up the side of his face with one hand, as if he could stare at me for hours. "I think you want to. I think it excites you."

"It does," I admit. "But I don't know if I can trust you."

"To do or not do what?"

I'm not sure how to put this. "Is this your signature move?"

He furrows his brow.

"Do you send underwear sets to all your dates?" I try to make my question light, but it sounds laden.

"Some," he says. "But only the ones I end up getting engaged to."

No . . . he didn't just . . . say that . . .

"I'm kidding," he says. "That was a joke. A bad one." He leans toward me. His gaze is so intimate it's as if we are already in bed. "I'm here. You're here. I like you. You're still doing your list, yes? I want to be on it."

More than one item on my bucket list could be accomplished in red lace . . . The waiter reappears with our wine. We shift apart. The tension eases without dissipating completely. Elan lifts his glass. "To new horizons."

I touch my glass to his. "Or, the gift to see the same ones with different eyes."

He inclines his head, and I wonder where the hell that came from, congratulating and questioning myself at the same time. As we order, and the talk recedes into less risqué territory, I try to untangle the twin threads of discomfort and arousal that are twisting around me.

In order to protect myself from hurt, humiliation, or the somewhat darker possibilities of young sex, I opted out. Here in New York, I use ambition and romantic fatigue to avoid it. And even after having another girl's tongue kiss all my lips and some gender-ambiguous role-playing with my gay ex-boyfriend, I find it so hard to honestly answer the question: What's your fantasy?

What do you want?

I've always wanted to feel in control, but a part of me wonders if my fantasy is *not* being in control. The power-bitch fantasy I chose to try with Ash-the-quivering-intern passed the feminist smell test.

Consciously so. It's light-years harder for me to admit that the idea of being the one who quivers, the one taken advantage of, also appeals. The image I conjured the first afternoon I spent with Elan comes back (and has it ever left?). I'm tied up, my hands above my head, my body stretched long like a piece of tanned leather. I'm blindfolded, gagged: entirely powerless. And he's behind me, jack hammering into me in a way I don't usually like but I know men do, his gaze heavy with raw, open lust. It's dark and unsoft, unromantic, and yet, it has control over me. It is addictive. The more I let it in, the hungrier I become.

Desire floods me like a rash.

This is why Elan sending me underwear makes my nipples hard as rock candy. And yes, this is all for my little nips. Because one day soon, they might not feel the way they feel now. I can't sidestep this any longer.

I push back my chair and pick up my clutch. "Excuse me," I say. "I'm just going to slip into something less comfortable."

* * * *

The white-tiled bathroom smells like gardenias and is an aggressive level of clean. I unbelt, undress, stuffing my strapless bralette and cotton underwear into my clutch. The red lace is scratchy against my skin. I try to dress calmly but my heart is pounding, sending thick waves of heat. I press my fingers between my legs and cautiously lift my fingers to my nose. I'd always accepted the idea that vaginas smell bad: not a rotten-sturgeon level of gross, just a smell you'd rather not have in a scented candle. But I like how I smell: warm and a little salty, like fresh baked bread and melting butter. I like that I'm wet. My body is a purring sports car tonight, eager to be taken for a spin.

I slip back into my heels and take a moment to admire my curves and soft lines, skin pale against the red. The bra is a push-up. The top of my breasts have heaved up an inch, two pillows of white-peach flesh glowing in the discreet bathroom light.

Is there cancer in them?

As I stand here, half-naked and turned on, midway through a date with one of the city's most eligible bachelors: Am I dying?

23.

Our food has arrived. I take a seat, smiling a deliberately demure smile at the man across from me. His eyes graze my shoulders. Next to the tie-up spaghetti straps of my dress, the red straps are bold, even brazen. Not hiding them works. The intentionality is sexy.

"How does it feel?" he murmurs. "How does the lace feel against your pussy?"

"All right, take it down a notch, Persia." I wave my butter knife at him. "Let's not get creepy."

He grins and slices his veal. I withhold my opinion on the ethics of eating baby animals and instead fork ripple-edged pasta into my mouth, suddenly ravenous. It's coated in butter and cheese with a sweet, spicy hit of peppercorns.

Jeff Goldblum was right. Angels to the slaughter.

We chew in silence, observing each other. He looks like he'd rather be eating me.

"Ask me something," I say, "that's not about what I'm wearing."

He swallows a mouthful of meat. "How's work?"

I skim over a basic update. "And things are ramping up with Clean Clothes."

"Clean Clothes?"

"The app I'm working on. With my friend, Vivian Chang."

"Ah, yes," he says. "She was pitching it to Tom."

The night I ran out like a lunatic, literally fearing for my life. I keep my face even. "Vivian thinks she's found a lead investor in China, Mr. Zhu. Which is a huge relief."

"Because you've been working on it for . . ."

"Ten months. A long time to raise the seed . . ." I sigh, toying with my fork.

"What's wrong?"

I don't think vulnerability is a good look on a first date. But I'm surprised by how much I want to open up to him. I can't stop myself. "Maybe I'm losing interest. I don't know. It always felt like something I should be doing—starting a company with a smart friend. But now, I'm not so sure." I can't help but think about Cooper, and his post-start-up soul-searching mission. I'd never really thought about what would happen if I got what I wanted: my comfort zone is the pursuit, not the spoils. "How do you know when you really want to do something, as opposed to what you *think* you should be doing?"

Elan's eyebrows prick. Not in discomfort. In interest. "If it feels right, I suppose. In your gut and your heart." He forks potato gratin into his mouth. "It's a problem more specific to women than men. Women are much more concerned with appearance."

I temper a small flurry of rage with a large sip of wine. "Well, we live in a society that values us for the way we look," I say. "That actively prejudices against women who don't fit an impossible ideal. It's no wonder it's a point of concern."

He's surprised by my response, most likely at the implicit anger lining its edge. "I just meant that generally women are more preoccupied with how their actions look to others. Like you say, they're more concerned with behaving how others think they should behave. I think women should just do whatever they want."

So condescending, even though I don't think he means it that way. "It's a bit more complicated than that. Women are expected to be likable and kind and totally selfless. We can't just do whatever we want: What if it's to stop shaving our legs, or be rude, or get fat?"

"I think that'd be great."

"No, you wouldn't," I say. "You didn't have one model over a hundred pounds in your show who wasn't drop-dead gorgeous. The parameters of choice are different for women and men. There are different consequences for behavior. I'm not worried about how things look because I'm neurotic or vain or weak. It's because I'm trying to survive in a patriarchal society."

"How was everything?" The waiter is back at our table, scooping up empty plates.

My face is flushed. I've never said something like that on a date before. I don't even feel particularly comfortable expressing myself like that on social media. It's strictly the territory of a booze-fueled girls' night, Steph and I one-upping each other in theatrical outrage. But I don't feel bad about it. I'm not even embarrassed. In fact, I feel confident. The flush in my cheeks is already cooling.

Perhaps I needed to say that. To even out the fact I'm wearing the red lace bra.

"Dessert?" The waiter offers two small menus.

I don't wait for Elan. "Thank you," I say. "I'm still a little hungry."

Elan's gaze is bright, and maybe even impressed, as if I've just called an unexpected checkmate. "So am I."

* * * *

He pays for dinner. I offer to split it, but he dismisses the thought as if it irritates him. As he extracts a black Amex (the kind used by people for whom the subway is a distant memory), I glimpse the total. Two hundred and sixteen dollars—I'm thankful he pays. While I look moneyed in my fancy dress and shiny heels, truthfully I'm broke AF. Besides, I get the impression that $216 is chump change to Elan Behzadi, a thought that is both disconcerting and strangely delicious.

Outside, I pull my coat around myself, waiting while Elan makes a quick phone call. I'm not sure who he has to call at ten at night, but I try not to worry. I have no idea what's next; come home with me or goodbye forever. I could be anxious, but I decide to feel liberated. There's something exhilarating about not knowing where I'll end up. There's a tease of true spring in the late March air.

He exits, trailed by two fashion-student types: lots of layers and thick-rimmed glasses, giggly drunk and wanting a selfie. He obliges, intense and unsmiling. As he nods goodbye, their gaze finds me. I draw myself taller, and yes, I can see what I want in their eyes. Not envy, although it's certainly a secondary characteristic.

Acceptance.

I'm the kind of woman they expect to see Elan Behzadi walking toward. I'm not a star fucker, but I can't deny the sweet jolt to my ego. This whole thing is so exciting and special, and maybe I think this because I've had three glasses of wine, or maybe I'm just soaking in the sensation of an attractive, semi-famous man putting his hand on the small of my back and politely asking me if he can give me a ride home.

We walk down a quiet cross street, away from the bright lights of the avenue.

"Does it bother you," I ask, "that I'm taller than you in these heels?"

He chuckles, and I love that I can make him smile when the fashion students could not. "No," he says. "You look very sexy in those heels. I'm not intimidated by tall women." He stops in front of me so quickly I almost run into him. His brows rise deliberately. "Or strong women." He moves closer, to kiss me.

I take half a step back.

He tips his head, surprised.

I'm a little surprised too. "I . . . want you. I just . . ."

A car pulls up behind us. "What?"

"Is this a bad idea?"

"No. It's a fantastic idea." He moves toward me.

Again, I hesitate. What I want to say, what I can't say is this: *Will you hurt me?*

I hear someone get out of the car behind us and open a door.

He threads his fingers in mine and slowly turns me around. Behind us, taking up three car spaces, is a white limousine.

"No!" I can't believe it. "You didn't . . . That's not . . ."

It is. Number seven on my bucket list: sex in a white limousine, my tawdry teenage fantasy.

Elan grimaces at the open door, where a uniformed driver stands, waiting. "Let me go on the record as saying this is the most tacky car I have ever seen in my life. I hate it, I hate everything about it."

"Oh my *God*." I beeline for it, gliding my hands over the glossy ivory exterior. It is beautiful and silly and entirely over the top. I love it. "You're *insane*." I whack him with my clutch.

He grins, enjoying my reaction.

A limousine. He hired a limousine, for me. I wonder if this was the plan all along or, more likely, if this was the phone call.

I passed a test.

Elan gestures at the car. "Shall we?"

Through the open door, a minibar with champagne flutes, and leather, so much leather. Getting inside is a double-edged sword; I feel it, I know it. Because once we kiss—once we fuck—I'm not sure if I can stop myself falling—into like, or love, or lust, or obsession, or all four. But I can't not do it. I have to get into the white limousine. I owe it to my sixteen-year-old self, bored out of her brain in Buntley, longing for a New York life. The life I now have.

I climb into the belly of the beast.

Here.

We.

Go.

24.

I wake to the sound of a shower. Soft sheets that smell clean, a tidal wave of morning light.

I'm in Elan's king-size bed.

I stayed over.

My tongue has the texture and taste of shag carpet. Before my muddled brain can formulate its need, I see the elegant glass of water on the bedside table. I gulp the whole thing, wiping my chin as it spills down my bare chest.

Oh, hello boobs.

Apparently, I slept naked.

My dress, shoes, bra, and underwear are on the floor in a careless tableau: *Still life, West Village, morning after.*

I remember taking them off. Thank God I didn't drink too much, because yes, I remember all of last night.

We hadn't even opened the champagne before we started making out in a hungry, desperate way, as if we'd been waiting for this for years, not weeks. A new mouth on mine: demanding, experienced. Almost immediately, he pulled me onto his lap to straddle him, his legs spread wide across the black leather. He ground me against him slowly, his hips tilting up so we slid against each other. Heat through his hands as he clutched my thighs. I could feel his hardness through my slippery red underwear. His eyes were dark with desire as he yanked my left spaghetti strap undone. I gasped. My left breast exposed in bold red lace. The sight of it—or perhaps my willingness to be undressed— made him release a rough breath and a quick, pleased smile. I felt exposed, even submissive, on display for this man I barely knew. It turned me on. I was aching so much it almost hurt. I leaned forward to kiss

him again, but he ducked his head, moving me back. Without breaking eye contact, he untied the other spaghetti strap. The black-and-
gold material pooled at my waist. I was only in my bra. The good-girl
cop in me knew I should protest or at least slow things down, but I
couldn't. I didn't want to. I wanted him to strip me bare. To take me,
in the back of this limo. In one swift movement, Elan expertly undid
the clasp in the front of my bra. The cups sprang aside. My breasts
were completely exposed. My nipples were hard as diamonds. I was
breathless. He leaned back against the leather for a long moment,
appraising me. Then one hand found the small of my back and he
almost shoved me to him. He consumed my left breast, putting the
whole thing in his mouth. He rolled his tongue around it, sucking,
greedy. I groaned. Not a stage groan. Not a groan for effect. A real,
deep growl of pleasure. Then the right breast, his thumb pinching my
other nipple. He played; he squeezed; he licked and bit as hungrily as
if I was made of sugar. I saw stars. I was so aroused I couldn't speak.
His fingertips grazed the outside of my underwear. The sensation
cracked through me like a gunshot. I bit back a yell. My teeth were
clenched as he pulled my panties aside.

I realize now that my fantasy was never sex in a limo. It was being
desired, in a way that was overwhelming and all-encompassing. Elan's
desire was confident and entirely unashamed. It was adult; it could
teach me a thing or two. Waking up here in a man's apartment in the
middle of the West Village, I feel older. No one except Elan knows I
am here. The possibilities of my life are as expansive as outer space.

The steam pouring from the bathroom smells like a fancy spa: mas-
culine, musky, the smell of a $37 bar of men's soap. The shower turns
off. I quickly arrange the sheets around myself in the most flattering
way, propping my head onto my hand. He walks out of the en suite
bathroom, toweling his hair.

He's naked.

I'm not one of those girls who hands-down loves the peen. I feel
about penises the way I think I feel about children: not that into other
people's, possibly into what's mine. To me, the penis is never going
to win second prize in a beauty contest. It has the same sort of ugly

charm as a Christmas sweater or a French character actor. But I've always felt quite affectionate about my bedmates' appendages (we called Masher's Captain Fantastico, which, looking back on it, does seem a little camp), and already, I feel a connection with Elan's private eye. In its state of rest, decidedly midsize. But once the engine gets hot, his small, soft sword becomes a luxury SUV, sustainable by design with an intelligent start/stop system.

"Hey there," he says.

"Hey yourself."

I admire his taut little coconut butt as he strides over to a low black dresser. Underwear from one drawer, dark jeans from another. He pulls them on, smirking at me. "You talk in your sleep."

"I do not."

"Yeah, you do." He disappears into a walk-in closet full of color-coordinated shirts on silver hangers.

I sit up, alarmed. "What did I say?"

He comes back out, holding two button-downs, one lavender, one white, both freshly laundered. "Which one?"

I point to the white. "What did I say?"

He heads back into the closet. "Something about . . . Barack Obama."

I laugh, confused. Relieved. Then it hits me. I bet it wasn't Barack Obama. I bet it was BRCA. The way I say it, all one word: *Brack-uh.*

There is nothing sexy about that.

My lover comes out in the white shirt. His eyes trace my limbs, under his sheet. "There's more to you than meets the eye."

I can see him picturing me in the back of the limo, thrusting, groaning, sticky with sweat. I let go last night, in a way I don't think I have before. "I was pretty drunk."

"Hey, own it. I feel honored." He slips on his watch. "I made the bucket list."

Is that it? Are we over? I'm okay with that, or, I can pretend to be. One crazy night, one more item off my list. And yet, everything in me wants to see him again. Do all that again. I want him to keep looking at me, the way he did in the back of the white limousine. Like I'm the only woman in the world.

"In a rush?" I ask, trying for "lightly."

"I have a meeting."

I pull the sheets tighter around myself. "It's Sunday."

He pauses, midway through running some product through his damp hair. His smile is patient. "I have a brunch meeting with Tim George, my business manager. I'd invite you to come but it'll be boring, trust me."

I relax a little and glance around the room. "Should I . . ."

"Take your time. Have a shower; hang out if you want. There's pastries, and an overly complicated cold-press juicer."

"Actually, I have to catch up with my ex."

Not entirely true: Ash and I have plans to get coffee later this week, but I'm seeing my sister this afternoon. I say it because I want a reaction: intrigue, or better yet, jealousy.

"Okay. Sorry, I'm already so late." He's back at the bed, leaning over. I want him to kiss me slowly, passionately, but he does it quick, like I'm a friend. No more *aziz-am*s for me. "Last night was great. You're great."

"*Great* is a really boring adjective," I say, disappointment and pleasure crashing inside of me.

He laughs. "Last night was . . . magnificent." He's left the room, calling from the hallway. "You're splendiferous!"

The front door slams. I'm alone.

How should I feel about all this? Blissed out? Pissed off?

I settle on really fucking . . . *great*.

For now.

25.

My sister's house is a circus. The front door is unlocked, and when I push it open, two children scamper past me, dressed as Ninja Turtles. "Siouxsie, Sal!" a female voice yells after them. "Don't run on the road!"

There are more hyperactive children in the backyard, knees damp with mud stains. Storm, dressed in a makeshift fairy-princess outfit, chases two smaller boys, then spins around as they chase her, all of them squealing. In the living room, half a dozen chattering women are knee-deep in bubble wrap, boxes, mailing labels, and stamps. They are Boreal Springs locals, evidenced by their collective look of "I pickle my own vegetables." Hippies, basically; harmless. One has a baby on the boob; several have unshaven armpits. I didn't dress down today: I wore what I wanted. It was meant to be defiant. But in my black shiny leggings, purple lipstick, and cropped leather jacket, I am at best an overdressed city slicker, at worst, a clown. When I lift a tentative hand in greeting, they all stare a second longer than necessary.

"Lace." My sister gets up, unthreading her fingers from a half-dozen mugs. "This is my sister," she says to the women, crossing to give me a quick peck.

"Did you forget about our lunch?" I murmur.

"No." This annoys her. "I figured you could help. I had a big order come in, last-minute." You'd be forgiven for thinking this boon is a massive inconvenience. "This is Kathy from next door, Pam from my yoga class, Sue from the studio—"

They all smile somewhat quizzically at me, as if I am a bizarre piece of furniture Mara's dragged home from a flea market.

"Lacey lives in Brooklyn," Mara finishes.

"Ah," the women say. This explains everything.

I touch Mara's arm. "I was hoping we could talk."

Studio Sue asks, "Mara, do you want the plates and mugs bubble-wrapped separately or together?"

Yoga Pam points to a plate of brownies. "Do these have nuts in them?"

"Mom, I'm thirsty!" a Ninja Turtle wails.

"We'll talk later." Mara ushers me to a spare spot. "Stick these labels onto those boxes."

"Sugar cookie?" Kathy-from-next-door offers me a plate. Sensible ash-brown bob and a gold cross over her terrible turtleneck. Unlike the crunchy granola types, Kathy-from-next-door has a distinct Kathy Bates in *Misery* vibe.

I take a cookie, even though I don't want to. My hangover is demanding something fried. My conscience is demanding an honest talk with Mara about the test. My ego wants to announce last night's sexploitations to everyone. My cynicism knows no one in this room has heard of Elan Behzadi.

Storm hurricanes in with a gaggle of friends. They grab sugar cookies and thunder into her room as mothers call various reprimands and reminders. I stare after her.

I have to tell Mara, and it doesn't matter if she doesn't want to know. Storm has a right to know. My sister will be thirty-one next year. The same age my mom was when she died. I might not be around in ten years time to tell my niece about her own risk if Mara doesn't.

"And what do you do, Lacey?" Kathy Bates turns to me.

Unwillingly: "I work in trend forecasting."

A round of wrinkled noses. "What's trend forecasting?"

Mara pulls her faded red hair back into a messy ponytail. The same ponytail my mother had in Mara's favorite photo of her, sitting by the window, staring outside as if she's unhappy but resigned to her fate. I'd never realized it was the same length, and almost the exact same cut. Has she done that deliberately? "It's a way of telling the future," I reply faintly, and then I ask Mara if we can talk in her bedroom.

* * * *

Mara stands in her doorway. "Can this wait? I don't want everyone down there doing my work while I'm not helping."

"Can you shut the door?" I slip off my jacket, overheated.

Mara raises her eyebrows high. She turns around to quietly close the door. When she turns back, her face has changed. "You got the test." Her ability to jump to accurate conclusions when it comes to me has always been disturbingly Olympic.

I can't speak. I nod.

She folds her arms. "And?"

The words seize in my throat. I stare at the balding carpet.

"Fuck." My sister presses one hand to her mouth.

I step toward her, but she holds up a hand. The warning strikes me in the chest. My need to have her hold me flares painfully.

An exhausted worry washes over her. She raises her eyes to the ceiling. When she speaks, it's more to herself than me. "And I just— Christ, everything at the worst possible time."

"What?"

She sighs, and presses her fingertips to her eyes. I'm eight years old again and asking for help with my homework. "Nothing."

But I'm not eight. "I'm not saying you have to fix this, Mar. I'm not saying you have to do anything, I'm not saying you have to be involved."

Her palms turn skyward. "But who else is?"

I start to babble. "I didn't plan it; it just came up, as an option, in the moment, and I thought it'd be a good idea to rule it out. I didn't think I'd have it, I really didn't think it would happen."

"Why not?" Mara hisses. "You know our history."

"I don't know," I say, and now I'm crying. "I'm an idiot, what do you want me to say?"

Mara flicks her hands at me. Her eyes are icy. "So, what? You've started getting the screenings? Have you had a mammogram? You know those things can give you cancer."

I inhale hard through my nose and shut my eyes, willing them to stop filling with tears. *I can do this.* I meet my sister's gaze. "Mara, I'm thinking about getting a mastectomy."

Her expression lands somewhere between disbelief and disgust. "Don't be ridiculous, Lacey."

"Spending my life getting screenings, waiting for cancer to happen, is not a path I want to go down. A mastectomy reduces my risk to pretty much nothing." My heart is speeding. I'm trying to sound calm and reasonable, but the truth of what I'm saying is making me panic. "You don't know what it's like, waking up every day wondering if today's the day I find something, if today's the day I start to . . . to *die*—"

"Lacey," she interrupts. "Stop. Just stop." For the first time in a very long time, she looks at me in the way she looks at Storm. She opens her arms.

I fall into her. She wraps me up and I let myself melt, burying my head into her chest like I used to do when we were children. She's never worn deodorant but I love her smell: spicy, fruity, undeniably my sister. I close my eyes. She strokes my hair. "Poor baby," she murmurs. "Don't worry. I can help."

I nod into her chest.

"We'll put you on a clean diet," Mara says. "Vegan; no fats or animal protein. You'll need to start taking vitamin D."

"I've already cut back on booze," I tell her, wiping my nose.

"Good girl."

"It's so hard," I say with a wry smile. "But if I go through with it, I'll be able to—"

"No, sweetie." She tucks a lock of white-blond behind my ear. "You don't have to go through with anything."

I stiffen. "But I might. I'm still thinking about it."

She stiffens. "No. You're not."

I pull back. "Mara, I'm really thinking about this. It's really an option for me."

"No," she tells me. "It's not."

"It is."

"No, it's *not*." She says it as if we've already had this irritating conversation a thousand times before. Her face becomes hard. "Are you crazy? Or just stupid?" She forms her words as if I'm a child. "You're not having a mastectomy, Lacey. You are twenty-five years old. You don't have cancer. I can help make sure you never get it."

"No, you can't, Mar. You can't. We can't stop what's in our DNA. I have it. You—you might have it too."

Mara stares at me, her gaze flickering fast between my eyes.

"You might have given it to Storm," I croak. "You understand that, right? You need to get tested, Mar. You need to know."

"No!" She thumps the wall with her fist. "Goddamn you, Lacey."

"Mar," I whimper.

"You're so selfish! You've always been so fucking selfish." Her cheeks are blotchy red. "I was the one doing the housework, keeping the lights on, while you're off, wearing a tutu to prom!"

"What is it with you and that fucking tutu?" I groan. "Why do you care what I wore to prom?"

"Because I never went to prom!" she shouts back.

"Yes, you did!" I'm amazed she'd even attempt this. "I remember the dress you wore: black, a black slip."

"No, I didn't." Her words are acidic. "Remember? I was all set to go, and then you threw up, and then you threw up again, and Dad was who-the-fuck-knows and I had to stay home and look after you."

"No," I say, uncertain.

"Yes," she says. "*Yes.*"

A new memory: Mara in a black slip and smudgy eye makeup, holding a cold compress against my head, hissing into a landline: *Can't go anymore—my stupid sister.*

Is that right? Did she miss prom for me?

"It's always been about you," she says. "Your future, your dreams. Dad left it all to *me*. He didn't even *ask.*"

"I know," I say helplessly. "I'm sorry—"

"You had no right to make a decision like this without me," she shouts. "It affects me, and it affects my daughter, and you made it without me because you're selfish and you're stupid."

"Hey," I snap. "Back off. I did ask you about the test. I can't live my life based on your needs. I have a right to take control of my health, which is what I'm doing, with or without your help. I'm not stupid, and

I'm not selfish, and if you call me those things again, we're through." I snatch up my jacket. "You know what's interesting, Mar? If Mom had gotten this test, she might not be dead. She could've done what I'm going to do, and we'd still have a mother. Storm would have a grandma. But if it was solely up to you, you'd have told her not to do it and she'd have gotten cancer and died. Think about that when you make a decision that could save your daughter's life."

I tear out of the house, a hurricane of dark feeling. I drive less than a mile before I have to pull over on a quiet back road dappled with sunshine. I switch off the engine, put my head against the steering wheel, and start weeping. I cry as a release. I cry because I love and hate my sister. I cry because I feel exhausted and alone. After ten or so minutes, I switch the engine back on, and I drive myself home to Brooklyn.

26.

April

New York is a town of many unspoken rules, and most of them revolve around the subway. Never get on an empty subway car: it's empty for a reason. Always have your MetroCard in hand when approaching the turnstile. Never eat on the subway, or worse yet, make eye contact with anyone eating on the subway. When it comes to fashion, things are less rigid, but for one rule: don't try too hard. When I moved to the city, I figured everyone stepped out in fashion-blogger-worthy outfits every single day, perfect down to the last statement pinkie ring. But in reality, New York is less about over-the-top splash and more about low-key style.

Except for one day of the year.

And that day is the first real day of spring. On that day, when it's above seventy before 9:00 a.m. and your weather app assures you it's only going to get better: embrace it.

That day is today. The city is a palette of pretty dresses the color of Easter eggs. Strappy sandals show off brand-new pedicures and just-shaved legs. Dudes wear T-shirts. Babies emerge from their strollers' miniature sleeping bags. Strangers smile at one another. We made it.

My friend from the BRCA forums, Bee, sends me a picture captioned *Good morning, New York!* She's on the Staten Island Ferry, flashing lower Manhattan. I laugh out loud. Without overthinking it, I ask her out for a drink: the first rosé of spring? A rooftop with water views? She texts me back two words.

FUCK. YES.

It's official: my first meet-up with a fellow BRCA babe.

I arrive early at work, determined to allow the new season's energy to jettison me out of my lazy winter rut. There are conferences to attend, travel to book. I'm excited to dive back into what New York has to offer now that the spring sunshine is finally warming the cold concrete. No sooner have I slipped into my chair, first iced coffee of the year in hand, than my phone lights up with texts. Vivian. I didn't work the weekend like I'd promised. Our approval rating has fallen. From a four to a 3.2. The lowest it's ever been.

My early-morning enthusiasm nose-dives. I didn't work the weekend because I was fucking and fighting, and even the latter sounded better than putting together outfits. My weekend felt like real life, like things that matter, and the app . . . does it matter? Is it what I want to do? I care about Vivian, and I don't want to walk away from all the work I've already put in, but I can't deny the fact that creating outfits for teenagers who don't even buy them has become very low on my list of priorities.

My fingers hover over the keyboard. I try to think of a response that isn't an excuse, a promise, or a lie.

I can't.

Patricia pings me. Gratefully, I leave my phone behind as I head to her office.

* * * *

"Can you believe it's already April?" Patricia swings around in her chair, dressed head to toe in florals: a breezy pink-and-green pantsuit complete with an elegant fascinator that only she could pull off. Even her nails are painted with petals. "What do you think?" She gestures to her outfit. "Too much?"

"Oh no, I love it." I take my usual seat across from her. "Derby Day meets tea with the Queen."

"That's exactly what I was going for!" she says, and beams.

I love my boss. "How was London?"

"Fabulous, fabulous!" she trills. "Except for the weather, the food, and the architecture."

I roll my eyes. "You're such a snob."

"That's why everyone keeps listening to me," she says, and winks. "Now, we have a lot to catch up on." She slips on her reading glasses to glance at a page of notes. "Ah, yes: Elan Behzadi. Ten books. One heck of a commission. What was all that about?"

I shrug, maintaining eye contact. "To be honest, I'm not sure. I started with the Panzetta, like you suggested, and before I could get any further, he said he'd take the lot. I think you were right. I think he was just curious."

"Money and an inquisitive mind," Patricia muses. "A dangerous combination." Then, with a delicacy I don't miss, "What did you make of him?"

I pretend to consider this as if it's never once crossed my mind. "He's very impressive. Charismatic. Intelligent. But he has an over-blown sense of his own worth. And I didn't get the impression he was particularly happy."

"All that in, what, five minutes?" Patricia asks, almost sharply.

I will myself not to blush. "I'm a very perceptive person, Ms. Hoff-man. Just like you."

She smiles, flattered. "Indeed. Well, we shall see. He's your client, but let me know if he buys anything else."

This seems unlikely. Even though I'm broke, I kept my promise to Steph: I haven't cashed Elan's commission check. The prospect feels gross. The last thing I want is for whatever's happening between us to have anything to do with money. "Will do."

"There's something else we need to talk about. Your sales for the past three months show a downward trend." Patricia pushes a spreadsheet of numbers at me. "And you've been seeing far fewer clients than usual."

I steady myself, readying the words I've been practicing. "I know I've been underperforming this winter. And I could blame seasonal affective disorder or lack of interest from clients, but I won't. The truth is . . ."

"Yes?"

"Patricia, the truth is . . ." For a wild moment, I consider telling my boss about my diagnosis and the mastectomy and even the bucket list and how my whole life feels like it's been sliced up and rearranged into a shape I barely recognize. But it would completely change the way she sees me. I'm the sales gal who's tough as nails, who (up until now) works all day, drinks with the clients till dawn, then is back at my desk at 8:00 a.m. to do it all again, in a brand-new outfit, having somehow fit in a spin class and blowout. I'm not the employee who is sick and vulnerable, who needs special treatment. Who needs help.

Plus, I don't have the energy to manage Patricia's judgment of me. What if she thinks I'm too young to make this decision, like Mara does? Or what if I don't end up going through with it—will she think me weak? A coward? I can't tell her. Not now. Not ever. "The truth is I wasn't sure about my future. I've been here for three years, and while I'm enjoying it, I'm not really moving forward."

"You want more responsibilities," Patricia says. "And a pay increase to match?"

I nod, masking surprise.

She smiles, pleased. "I'm so glad you said something, Lacey."

Did I?

"It's time we start thinking about what's next for you," she says. "A position on the fashion editorial team will become available around October. Eloise is leaving us."

"Really?" I'm obviously thrilled, so I temper it with, "How sad."

"I know how much you want this job, Lacey," Patricia says. "It's okay to be excited."

A salaried position. The chance to write and travel and be in the inner circle. No more commission or uncertainty. No more sales.

"Of course you won't be replacing Eloise," Patricia says. "There'll be a little internal shuffle and you'd be coming on as the most junior member of the team. But it's still an editor position."

"Of course, yes. Can I ask if Eloise is staying in the industry?"

"She's pursuing a family-related opportunity."

No way. I drop my voice to whisper, "She's pregnant?"

"You sound surprised."

"She doesn't strike me as someone who'd . . ." I trail off, stopping short of making a joke about a hostile womb.

Patricia gives me a twinkly little smile: she gets it. "If you want to commit to me, I want to commit to you. Expectations for your level of professionalism and quality of work would be very high. But, I really do see a future for you here. You don't have to decide anything right now," she adds, "but is this something you'd like to think about?"

"Yes," I say. "Of course it is."

She folds her hands in front of her. "It behooves me to ask about your start-up. A position like this doesn't allow for side projects. Is it something you're still committed to?"

When I started working with Vivian, Hoffman House had become my dull day job and Clean Clothes was the shiny new toy. But things have changed. Quitting a sales job for a start-up was fine in theory, and when I didn't care about benefits. How could I take time off from Clean Clothes? We don't have policies in place for sick leave. Even with Zhu's promised money, there's no security at Clean Clothes. Everyone loves telling you 90 percent of start-ups fail in the first year. After Vivian gets her money from Zhu, she won't need me; she can hire someone else. I can walk away and maintain our friendship. It's the only path.

"I've enjoyed working on that project," I say. "But if this position is open, I'd look to transition out of the Clean Clothes team immediately and refocus my efforts here."

Patricia extends her hand. "I'm so pleased, Lacey. I really am so very pleased."

We shake hands. I'm grinning, giddy, like the surprise winner on a game show.

27.

Vivian has no idea that I'm still interested in moving up the rungs at Hoffman House. But now, I have to tell her. Dreading this, I text, suggesting dinner at her place. She messages back:

Let's just meet at Steph's.

The separate corners of my world fold around to meet each other in an entirely new configuration: one that leaves me on the outside. Before I can try to find a way in, my work phone rings, my email pings, and a coworker swoops by needing advice. The day dashes ahead of me, daring me to chase it.

* * * *

With the position of fashion editor as the carrot dangling over my desk, I double down. I want that job, even if I have no idea how I'll manage it and take time off for a surgery. Later, as I ride the crowded N train to Astoria, finally able to space out, I think idly about doing it over summer, while I'm still in sales. Take the hit, somehow, recover early fall, and be ready to transition in October, as Patricia suggested. I could just tell everyone it's a root canal. Or maybe the job's a sign that I should wait: bank experience and money at Hoffman House and do it down the line when it's less of a rush. I've always liked crossing things off my to-do list—the bigger the better—but perhaps I'm giving way too much energy to worrying about all this right now.

I believe what Steph said to Dr. Murphman, the world's worst plastic surgeon, that big boobs don't define a woman. Some women don't have any reconstruction at all. Transwomen might not have "real" boobs and they're still women. Androgyny persists as a trend: I did a report on it last year. *The line between what it means to be a man and what it means to be a woman has blurred. We're seeing this on the runway and in the street.* At the time it was interesting, even empowering. Now it feels way too close to home. I don't want to *become* a trend against my will.

The train empties out the closer we get to Astoria–Ditmars Boulevard, last stop on the line. I finally get a seat.

It's easier for me to think about the practical aspects of all this—timing, choosing doctors, health insurance, research—than it is about the emotional, the psychosexual. How I'll feel if my breast tissue is replaced by silicone implants. If two long scars define the look of my chest. When I allow myself to feel it, I am terrified of what my mutation could rob me of: my breasts, and later, my ovaries.

The woman sitting next to me is reading something on her phone that's making her smile a secret smile, absentmindedly tracing a fingertip along the tops of her breasts, barely aware of her own light touch. I feel a surge of guilt at the attack I'm considering on my own body: heaping sensual pleasure with one hand, while in the other, I'm hiding a knife.

* * * *

When I open the loft door, I hear Cooper speaking in a low, serious voice. "What about a convertible loan?"

"It's still a loan." Vivian. She sounds congested, like she has the flu. "If we have to liquidate, it's senior. They'd probably take everything. At this stage . . . that's likely."

Steph is on the couch, a look of uncut empathy on her face, holding a box of tissues. Cooper is at the other end, hands clasped between his legs. His expression is stern, dadlike. Between them is Vivian Chang. Her eyes are red and puffy. Ice queen Vivian Chang, a regular of thirty-under-thirty lists everywhere from *Forbes* to *Elle*, is crying.

My purse slips from my fingers. "What's going on?"

"Zhu fell through." Vivian blows her nose without looking at me. "Brock quit today. We don't have a developer. We're out of money. It's over."

The words don't quite land. I can't make sense of what I'm seeing: Vivian Chang falling apart.

"So, you have your developer's equity back, right?" Cooper says. "He hasn't even been with you for a year."

Vivian shakes her head. "He negotiated an accelerated vesting schedule."

Cooper asks, "Which was?"

Vivian's eyes are on the floor. "Six months. He's fully vested as of last week."

Cooper lets out a whistle. "That's low."

I knew Brock owned 30 percent of the company, ten points more than me. But I didn't know he could leave and keep it. I keep waiting for Vivian to look at me and acknowledge the fact that her head stylist, and currently the only other member of the team, is standing right in front of her. She doesn't.

Cooper asks, "Have you looked on AngelList?"

"Of course I have!" Vivian wails.

"What about crowdfunding?" he asks.

"We don't have a physical product." Vivian pulls more tissues from Steph's box. "The app is already free. I don't have money for perks: that's the whole problem." She blows her nose again. "Do you know what percentage of VC funding goes to women? It's like, two percent. Two fucking percent." Her voice is shaking. "I'm in so much debt: I borrowed so much money. I'll never start another business again. I'm a f-failure." She starts crying in earnest, shoulder-shaking, heart-wrenching sobs.

Steph's next to her, taking Viv's head to lay it on her shoulder, holding her as she cries. "Shhh," she murmurs, rocking her gently. "You'll be okay. It'll be okay." She gives me a look: *Do something.*

A strange, ugly horror has wrapped around my bones, as if I'm witnessing something deeply humiliating and fundamentally wrong. I can't move. I know I should comfort Vivian, but I can't.

Does she blame me for part of this? I am a part of the company, after all.

I stare at Cooper. He gets to his feet, gesturing for me to follow him into his room, closing the door behind him.

Ordinarily I'd be excited to be in Cooper's bedroom, one step closer to the inner workings of his brain. But now I'm just numb. Confused. "I thought Zhu was a sure thing."

Cooper leans back against his door. "Nothing's a sure thing until the contracts are signed."

"But Vivian said he was so keen—what happened?"

"He took a hard look at some of the KPIs: conversion rate, MAUs, LTV. And," Cooper says, "the outfit ratings."

Me. That's my responsibility. "It's my fault," I say. "I did this."

"It's not your fault," Cooper says. "Look, this happens. The low point. They call it the 'trough of sorrow.' The moment where everything feels like it's not working, that you're a failure, a fraud."

"Right."

"You doubt yourself," he continues. "You're wondering, what am I doing? Am I screwing everything up?"

"Yeah," I say. "I understand."

"You feel like an idiot." Cooper's pacing. "That you've wasted everyone's time; that nothing you do will be good. You're a loser, and you always will be—"

"Coop," I cut him off. "I got it."

"Right, sorry." He fingers his collar. "A little start-up PTSD."

Behind Cooper's door, Vivian's still crying. I'm afraid to go back out there. "I've just never seen her like this. I don't even know what to do."

Cooper rubs his eyes under his glasses. "Start-ups are intense: the highs and the lows. And she's right: there's an insane gender bias when it comes to who gets funded. It's criminal." He takes a deep breath. "You're not a cofounder; you're not responsible for investors. The best thing you can do is get your ratings up. Viv will probably do one more round of investor meetings, and then . . ." He shrugs.

That's it.

Clean Clothes is over.

Vivian doesn't wear her heart on her sleeve: like me, it's hidden in an inside pocket. So it's been easy for me to think that failure, in the unlikely occurrence it could happen, is something she could handle—effortlessly, and without breaking stride. Yet another thing I was wrong about.

The first few months I was working for Clean Clothes, I couldn't
believe that one day I could get paid to do it. It was easy and fun, planning a look for another girl in a faraway town who I always imagined
would be so pleased to get my ideas. But they're just strangers wanting
free advice. The fact I feel this way is part of the problem. If I was still
firing on all four cylinders, maybe we wouldn't be in this position. I
wish I could feel the way I used to. I wish I could fix all this for Vivian.

"I'll get the ratings up," I say, more to myself than Cooper. "I'll
do it for her."

His eyes are soft with concern. In a way that isn't awkward or lusty,
he steps forward and gives me a hug. We hold each other. He feels
strong and solid and like he really cares that I'm in this mess and he
really hopes it works out okay. Before it lingers into something soft and
uncertain, he lets me go.

I keep my face neutral, but his absence hollows my chest, leaving
me cold.

28.

create outfits until 8:00 a.m., fueled by guilt and love and cold determination. Then I drink two espressos and go into work, where I see seven clients back-to-back. By the end of the day I'm making as much sense as the Mad Hatter. I crash by 9:00 p.m., but set my alarm for 3:30 a.m., and am back at it when it's still dark outside. This becomes my routine. Everything else is back-burnered. I cancel my drink with Bee.

Rather than phoning the outfits in like I have been, I take more risks and am more diligent in putting together the selections. I work faster, figuring the longer the delay in getting the outfit after requesting it, the more ambivalent the user might feel, and thus a lower rating. I revisit some of my favorite blogs: *Sustainably Chic*, *Leotie Lovely*, *My Green Closet*. I trawl the spring looks of sustainable designers, making new folders of influences. For the art director's assistant from Seattle, a collarless silk shirt, wide-leg pant, linen scarf, gold bar earrings, leather penny loafers. For the free spirit from Portland, floral-print maxi skirt, loose-fit V-neck cotton tee, denim d'orsay flats, hippie beads, canvas satchel. I try to stay on autopilot. But as soon as I let my mind off its leash, it jumps all over Cooper, and Mara, and being BRCA1. It gnaws at the knowledge that the fashion editor position is a better path than this. But its favorite toy of all is Elan.

Elan does not call. Or text. I'm surprised. Dinner, and what happened after dinner, went well. Didn't it? The weekend comes and goes. I stalk his Instagram. I don't think he manages it himself; it's more publicity than personal. On Monday night, a photo appears: Elan in a tux at a charity event for children's cancer. On his arm, Coco Du Bellay, the it girl who walked his New York show. The caption simply reads: *My muse* 👑. They are both glowering, haughty, carved from ice. They are untouchable.

Perhaps I never had dinner with Elan, never had sex with him in the back of a white limousine. Perhaps it was all part of a particularly detailed stress-induced hallucination. Because the idea that one day, I might appear on Elan's Instagram, dressed in couture, eyes low and lidded, seems as likely as my falling down a rabbit hole and ending up in Wonderland.

* * * *

Because I am weak, I leave my phone ringer on, even after I go to bed. I have just started dropping off into peaceful oblivion on Wednesday night when it pierces me awake.

Elan Behzadi calling.

I whip out my retainer and hurl it across the room. "Hi."

The tinkle of ice cubes in a glass. His voice, a low growl. "Come over."

My pulse spikes. I consider throwing off my blankets, zooming into a cab. But I'm exhausted. My head's stuffy with sleep. "I'm in bed."

"It's nine."

"I've been busy."

"With what?"

I elbow my way up, and switch on my bedside light. "Clean Clothes."

A blink-long pause. "Chinese investor?"

"Fell through."

"Pity." I picture him at home in the West Village, spread out on a sofa. Glass of whiskey in one hand, his cock in the other. "Dinner. Tomorrow."

Yes. But: "I can't."

"If you don't want to see me, why'd you pick up the phone?"

"I do." I rub my face. "It's complicated."

"Friday, then. C'mon. You can't work all the time. I need to see you."

I smile, pressing the phone to my cheek. "You do?"

"You're in my head." I hear him sip and swallow. Now his voice is raspy, close. "I want to fuck you in an alleyway. Your legs around my waist."

I'm right. He's horny. "That's really romantic, Elan," I say sarcastically, but the image floods me with heat. My body, while currently exhausted, is interested in this. After being so hard on it all week, I feel bad denying it what it so clearly wants.

"I don't do romance, darling. I'm sending a car. Friday at eight."

"Seven," I say. "I swear, I'll be asleep by nine."

"Seven thirty," he says. "And you won't sleep all night."

"But I'm not—"

He's already hung up.

* * * *

On Friday, a black town car pulls up outside my apartment at 7:45 p.m. I'm expecting it to take me over the Williamsburg Bridge, into downtown Manhattan, but we head north, through Greenpoint, into Queens.

I'm too zonked to guess where we're going or plan my opening lines. I managed to sneak a catnap this afternoon in an empty conference room: being able to sleep rough has always been a gift of mine. I'm wearing a long floaty skirt in a pretty rose pink and a soft white button-down, rolled at the sleeves, open at the neck. Striped black-and-white flats; hair in a loose ballerina bun; simple, glowy makeup. It's casual, but you can make out the shape of my legs through the skirt.

I've never had sex in public, which is why it was on my bucket list. This is my fantasy, but tonight it might also be Elan's.

I don't do romance, darling.

My generation isn't romantic, not in my experience. Red roses, grand gestures, and candlelit dinners are clichés and bourgeois, as relevant to romance as high interest accounts are to happiness. Everything our parents told us was good is bad: marrying young, the penal system, Woody Allen, almond milk.

But isn't hiring a limo romantic? Isn't ferrying me to an unknown location for dinner romantic? It is to me.

We're in Flushing, referred to by some as "the Chinese Manhattan." It has the look and feel of what I assume an Asian city is like. In the three or so years I've lived in New York, I've only been a handful of times: a birthday dinner, a bad date. The car stops in front of a busy Chinese restaurant called Golden Century.

Inside, a crowd of people are waiting for tables—locals, students, hipsters, tourists. Low ceilings, shouted conversations, sizzling pork, chili oil. Unlike most of the old-school places on this block, the interiors are modern. Banksy-style graffiti on fresh white walls, comfortable booths. Framed *New York Times* and *Wall Street Journal* reviews hang next to a signed picture of Lady Gaga, standing where I am now. I recognize the restaurant name: it's a chainlet in the city. This is the original outpost.

But Elan isn't here.

He's sent me here as a joke; a lesson? He thinks I'm sheltered, vanilla, too white—

There he is. By the kitchen, talking animatedly with a Chinese man in a Bart Simpson T-shirt. He's in a loose black linen button-down, faded black jeans, white slip-on sneakers.

I relax and tense at the same time, the push-pull of relief and anticipation.

I am hungry.

He catches my eye and waves me over.

Bart Simpson disappears out the back. I follow Elan to an empty booth in the far-right corner, the only free table in the joint. Padded vinyl seats and a variety of dangerous-looking chilis in squat metal pots. We slide in together. Our knees bump under the tabletop. I feel it like static shock. I am the most alert I've been, perhaps ever.

He says, "You made it."

"I'm very good at getting into cars."

A flicker of a smile. We're warming up.

His eyes move unabashedly around my face and dip into my shirt, unbuttoned enough to allow a peek of black lace bra. The sight of it seems to relax him. He props his chin onto the heel of his hand. "I'm happy to see you. There's something about you that's very comforting."

The fact I let you see my underwear. That's gotta be pretty comforting.

"You feel familiar to me," he continues. "Why is that?"

Because you date women in their twenties? But even as insecurity arises, I admit there's something in this man that feels familiar to me, too. Even if he doesn't mean it, or is just projecting something else entirely, there is something in Elan Behzadi that I am drawn to in a subconscious, bone-deep way. I just don't know what exactly that is. Yet. "I don't know," I reply, toying with the chili pot. "But you should be careful."

"Why?"

"We're two minutes in and you're already sounding dangerously romantic."

He snorts. I can't tell if he's acknowledging or dismissing this. Two Tsingtao beers appear on our table.

Elan lifts his. "TGIF, eh?"

I laugh, and tap my bottle to his. The beer is cold and hoppy, conjuring BBQs, rooftops, flip-flops on hot concrete.

Summer is coming.

I say the first thing that comes into my head. "What are we doing here?"

"This," Elan says, "is the best Chinese food in New York City. Northwestern Chinese, different from what you're used to. Assuming you had ethnic food in Buntley, Illinois."

"We didn't," I say. "But I never told you my hometown."

His face cracks. He glances away, embarrassed.

I almost gasp. "Have you been *googling me*?"

"Have you googled me?" he shoots back, defensive.

"Of course," I exclaim. "Of course I have."

He takes a long sip of beer, and then another. "So much information these days," he mutters. "It's hard to resist."

I am thrilled. The image of him scrolling through my Instagram, my Hoffman House bio, even the silly articles I'd written for various pop culture sites that paid a total of zilch, is the single most encouraging development of whatever-this-is, and that includes the fact he's seen me naked. I don't even list my hometown in most of what's online, starting my origin story closer to college. He would've had to work to find that out.

He's curious about me.

I'm on his mind.

Something anxious inside me releases. I sit back and take a long, satisfied pull of my beer.

"You look like the cat that swallowed the canary," he says.

Resisting the instinct to make a crude comment about *swallowing*, I ask, "How did you find this place?"

"I used to live around here. It was my local."

"You used to live in Flushing?"

He nods. "When I first moved to New York, a million years ago. The owner—Robbie, the guy I was talking to—he opened this place the same year I started my own label. We were dead broke together. I ate here every other night and paid him in clothes."

So cool. "How old were you when you moved here?"

He arches an eyebrow. "I thought you googled me."

"I was mostly looking at pictures," I half lie. There's not a lot of information available about Elan's past prior to coming to America.

He chuckles. "Twenty-two."

That's how old I was. It's strange to think about someone's younger self, the many paper dolls layered over an individual that make them complete. I want to pluck out Elan at twenty-two, see how we measure up.

"What were you doing before you came here?" How much of our journeys overlap?

He glances around the restaurant. "I, ah, played football. Well, soccer to you."

"Right, of course." I assume he's joking. He's not. "Do you mean, professionally?"

After a moment, he nods. A suggestion of tension in his shoulders. "Yeah."

"A national team?"

He rubs the day-old stubble on his jaw. "Yeah, U–Twenty-Three. The national under-twenty-three football team, in Iran."

Elan as former professional athlete is not something I (a) expected or (b) found anywhere online. How does a young Middle Eastern soccer player become a leading US fashion designer? Or more to the point, why?

Before I decide which thread to pull, Robbie arrives with our food.

Hand-ripped *biang biang* noodles seared in hot oil topped with stewed pork, cumin-spiked lamb burgers stuffed with hot peppers and pickled jalapeño, generously filled spicy-sour lamb dumplings topped with cilantro, crunchy cucumber tossed in black vinegar and garlic. Food from the city of Xi'an, known as the first capital of China, starting point of the famous Silk Road, hence the emphasis on Middle Eastern spices. Robbie grins at me. "I hope you like spicy."

"I like everything." Not entirely true. I don't generally eat lamb, or any baby animal. It feels cruel, but it seems rude not to try the food the owner, Elan's old friend, hand-delivered to us.

We gorge. It's nothing like the Americanized Chinese food I'm used to. Everything is fiery, aromatic, rich with spice, slick with chili oil. The noodles are the best: wide and soft and chewy. I can't stop putting them in my mouth. It's a decadent theatrical degustation. We moan and roll our eyes back: *Try this. This is so good.* Our lips stain crimson with chili oil.

When we can't eat any more, we slump back, comatose. My mouth burns. My blood sings.

Unlikely we'll be fucking in an alleyway now.

Robbie appears back at our table, smiling. "Well?"

"*Xièxiè nǐ, wǒ de lǎo péngyǒu,*" Elan says. "*Měi yīcì dōu měiwèi.*"

Robbie's smile broadens and breaks into laughter. "Sorry, man." He giggles. "Your Mandarin is still shit."

"Hey, shut up." Elan swats at him. "I'm trying to impress the girl."

I press my lips together to keep from grinning like a carnival clown.

There's no check. Elan tells Robbie to expect something in the mail. By the still-crowded doorway, the two men pound each other on the back. A table of kids my age nudge each other. "Who?" one of the guys asks.

"*Elan Behzadi,*" the girls whisper in unison.

Pride inflates me like a balloon. He holds the door open for me. I feel the girls' gaze on my back as we leave together.

Elan knows a bar a short walk away. Am I up for a drink?

I'm up for anything.

We walk side by side, past fruit and vegetable stalls, and vendors selling Chinese-language newspapers. The air is a mix of diesel fuel and sizzling duck. I ask him about living in Flushing, what it was like twenty years ago. He tells me about his first roommates, a vegan nudist from California, two students from Beijing obsessed with *Baywatch*. His first studio above a laundromat that was too humid and smelled like detergent. Days spent studying, nights spent cutting cloth, dreaming, creating. He packed his only suitcase full of samples and took it on the subway to show buyers. I'm a quiet detective, gathering each piece to complete a picture. The specific nature of fortune seeking fascinates me. I can relate. The more I uncover, the more I have to learn. But I have staying power. I'm committed.

Black Cake is a small, cozy bar that looks old but is new. Edison light bulbs, no TVs. A girl with a cloud of seventies frizz plays dominoes with a lanky boy sporting a curled mustache. We take two stools at the end of the bar and order whiskies.

He asks, "So what happened with the Chinese investor?"

"Zhu?" I'm surprised he brought it up. "He took a look under the hood, didn't like what he saw."

"Which was?"

I smile, charmed by his interest. "We have good user acquisition but bad sales conversions."

"Why?"

"Truthfully, most teenage girls can't afford fifty-dollar T-shirts. Even if they want to buy ethical, they can't."

"Interesting." He swirls his whiskey.

"Why do you find that interesting?" I ask teasingly.

"It might be something I'd like to get involved in." He says this casually, like he's talking about checking out a restaurant I recommended.

In the far reaches of my brain, a soft alarm sounds. I ignore it. "What do you mean?"

In a quiet, unhurried way, he tells me how he looked up Vivian Chang: quite a résumé, knows what she's doing. He read the articles in *Fast Company* and *Forbes* when she first launched the app last year. He thinks it has potential. Do I have it, on my phone?

It's a little buggy, because we no longer have a developer, but it works. He asks where I source the clothes from, questions user base, popularity. Before I know what's happening, I'm pitching, using all Vivian's best lines: *Disrupting a multibillion-dollar industry. Fashion that doesn't cost the earth.*

"Do you like it?" he asks. "Do you believe in it?"

I imagine Vivian sitting behind him, mouthing what she says about all investors: *Tell him what he wants to hear.* "I do," I say, and it's not a lie. The enormity of what is happening right now comes into full focus like a tsunami on the horizon. "What kind of involvement are we talking about?" I ask. "Investment?"

"Maybe," he says. "Or maybe as an adviser on your board of directors."

Elan Behzadi, familiar to every industry insider and fashion fan, as influencer. That changes everything. That's even better than money.

"Why?" I exhale. "For me?"

His lips twitch into a smile, not unkindly. "I'm a businessman, Lacey. It sounds like a good idea." He edges closer. "And you're someone I want to get into bed with."

I'm staring. I can't look away. "Metaphorically or literally?"

He traces a finger down my forearm, summoning a trail of goose bumps. "Both."

I shiver. "Is it ethical?" I ask. "For us to be . . . involved."

"I can keep a secret," Elan says. "If you can."

I can. I can keep a secret. Lust and fear and power churn inside me.

His eyes pool dark.

He tugs me from my stool.

I go willingly.

In the alleyway behind the bar, under the roaring freeway overhead, he pushes me against a cold brick wall. His mouth on mine, and I can't get enough, I need more, want more, need him in a way that overtakes everything. I am untamed, wild, an addict. A clink as he undoes his belt, pulls down his jeans. In the yellow light of a streetlamp, his cock. Stiff and warm. I need it inside me.

In my ear: "You're on the pill, right?"

I nod.

My skirt is too much material. It feels like years before he finds my underwear, pulls it down, off, away. He positions my back against the wall, my legs around him, holding me under my thighs. His cock finds its way past the trimmed hair of my pussy. One push and he's inside me. We both groan, hard. I've been dreaming about the wet, hot feeling of this. Our bodies joined, messy and panting and unrestrained. He moves again and again, his teeth on my neck, his biceps pulsing. My shirt is ripped open, and he stares down at my breasts, hypnotized, thrusting, getting faster. He's about to come, I know, I can tell. "Fuck me," I moan, "fuck me, fuck me, fuck me—"

And it's this image I can't get out of my head as Vivian, Elan, Tim George, and I are all shaking hands in a cool, bright conference room, one week later.

29.

I don't want to lie to Vivian. But saving her company is more important than the truth.

That is what I tell myself: that I'm doing this for Vivian. For us. But if I'm honest with myself: painfully, brutally honest, I want to go into business with Elan because we'll spend time together—as entrepreneurs, as equals. And against his "I don't do romance" of it all . . . he'll fall in love with me.

I know how this sounds. Oh, do I know. But the heart wants what the heart wants, and if there isn't a clear and easy path, the heart becomes a master manipulator.

A crook.

Casually, I ask Steph not to say anything to Viv about what really happened at Elan's trend-book presentation all those months ago: my huge (*uncashed*) commission check, our hot flirtation. It's irrelevant, because I'm definitely *not* interested in anything beyond Elan saving our company. Steph, trusting to a fault, accepts this. She's distracted, crushing hard on a new transfer in her course, a pretty tattooed blonde who seems dangerously heteroflexible and thus entirely on-brand.

I tell Vivian that Elan reached out to me about the app after coming across the articles in *Fast Company* and *Forbes*. Vivian's initial suspicion gives way to enthusiasm easily. She wants to believe. "That'd change everything," she says. "His network, his *net* worth."

"Almost a million followers on Instagram," I say. "Double that on Twitter."

"We can do exclusives with his new seasons." Vivian's practically babbling. "We'd be written up in every blog in the country. Elan on the board means investors, for sure—" She stops. "Wait. We don't know what he wants yet, right?"

"No," I say honestly. "We'll find out at the meeting."

Which is now. Vivian and I sit across from Elan and Tim George, a polished and most likely gay African-American asking smart questions that Vivian is fielding like a pro. Elan is silent, his gaze shifting between us. On the surface, professional. But every time we lock eyes, I feel cold brick on my back. Hard heat between my legs. I'm certainly blushing.

Tim is outlining the scope of Elan's potential involvement: one tweet a quarter, one Instagram post every six months. Introductions, mentions. Elan knows editors at *Vogue*, *InStyle*, *GQ*. He plays golf with the editor of *TechCrunch*, is on a charity board with two of the founders of SXSW. Vivian is practically quivering. But we're both waiting for the hammer to fall.

In exchange for what?

Tim and Elan take a moment to confer in private. Vivian and I sit without speaking. Even though the air is cool, sweat snails down my back.

They return after a few minutes.

"Mr. Behzadi is interested in joining the board of directors of Clean Clothes," Tim says. "In exchange for thirty percent equity."

Vivian exhales a soft breath of disbelief.

My mouth falls open. The men stare back, impassive as concrete. A flash of fury tightens my muscles. Before I can snap a response, Vivian says, "That's very high. Most advisers come on at less than one percent."

Elan speaks for the first time. "But you don't have any other advisers, do you?"

The room is so quiet I can hear Vivian swallow. "Not officially."

"Not at all," he says. "Or investors, or even a developer. It's just you two, right?"

Vivian doesn't say anything. I can feel her wondering how he knows that.

"Your problem is your customer base," Elan says. "Teenage girls can't afford fifty-dollar T-shirts. The people who follow me can."

I am throbbing with anger. The tension between us is so thick, I can barely see. My own words, used against me. And yet, I want him.

I'm getting turned on, quickly and against my own will. My body is betraying me: willfully, recklessly.

Vivian asks if we can have the room. The men step out.

"Thirty percent is too high," I hiss. "Way too high, that's crazy, right? I was thinking three, maybe five. But thirty? Thirty percent? That's fucked, right?"

Vivian's voice is spookily soft. "It's unusual," she says. "But so is this situation."

"Meaning?"

"Meaning without Elan, we don't have a company."

"But I only have twenty percent. *Twenty.* And I've been working for free for ten months."

Viv shrugs. She looks exhausted. "I don't know what to tell you. He's a name. He has influence. Twenty percent of zero is still zero, Lace."

"Where does his share come from? Not Brock's, obviously."

"We eat it," Vivian says. "It comes from us."

I can't believe this. I brought Elan in because we're fucking and now I'm the one getting fucked. Or am I? Viv's right: my equity is only worth something if the company becomes profitable. Without Elan, it probably won't.

"It's so unfair," I say. "He'll own double what I will for a few fuck-ing tweets."

Vivian nods and glances at the closed door. We can see both men through the soundproof glass windows, avoiding our eye contact. Viv-ian's expression belies none of our desperation. "Look, it's up to you. I don't want to bring on someone who'll piss you off. You know him better than I do. What do you think? Do we go for it?"

Deep down, I know I don't want to continue working on the app, despite my effort so far. This is the perfect out: No, I'm not comfortable with Elan coming on. Yes, it's over.

Elan's head is bent toward his phone. A text? To whom? Jealousy, an unfamiliar, intoxicating monster, rears inside me with such force I forget to breathe. Holding on to Elan isn't a hazy desire. It's a painful, desperate need.

I know it's the wrong thing to do. I do it anyway.

"Yes," I say. "I want him."

30.

May

I fall for him like a winter sunset: a startling, sudden betrayal.

Everything theoretical—I *could* love you, I *think* I'm falling for you—becomes absolute. The way he takes his coffee fascinates me— black espresso, so European, so chic. His choice of laundry detergent, a delight: French organic lavender, shipped all the way from Aix-en-Provence! His opinions on film, politics, art, and, of course, fashion all feel like important lessons. Obsession overtakes me like a disease, dividing and multiplying at a rate I can't control.

I understand the irony.

I know from every bad-boyfriend article in *Cosmo* that the fact we have to keep it secret should worry me.

It thrills me.

Even though it's not technically an affair—we are both single, as far as I know—it takes on the trappings of one. Furtive messages, illicit rendezvous. Elan is not so famous that paparazzi are a problem for him, and this is Manhattan, not LA; there's simply less interest in celebrities here. But without explicitly saying anything, it's clear he's not ready to go public, and I don't want Vivian finding out. So, we're a secret. We define nothing. I never know when I'm going to see him. We won't speak for a few days, and then he'll text me out of the blue: *It strikes me that I have no idea what you're currently wearing. Please remedy asap.* I respond as if I don't know exactly where he is—the Frick, the Upper East—all tracked through social media. I want so badly to be there with him, his hand on the small of my back, claiming me, forsaking all others. But I'll settle for being the one he's texting. For now.

With Ash, my desire was a cozy blanket, always where I left it. With Elan, my desire is a snapping, sparking live wire, whipping around like a mad snake. Uncontrollable and uncontrolled. I am constantly hungry, but I can't eat. I lose weight; as obsession expands me, I exist less in the world. Some days, I am so overwhelmed by the way he is constantly, unbearably, on my mind and in my body, that I'm reduced to tears. It baffles me. I claim allergies.

I understand love songs and greeting card clichés. Love: a drug, a puppet master, a devil.

For me, the love I seek takes the form of sex.

We have a lot of sex.

That is what we do most.

One of the first times I catch the subway to his apartment after work, lust builds in my body to such a degree that I do not feel in control of myself. My insides roil, my breath shortens. I sit, eyes out the window on clumps of commuters, trying to contain myself. I can't. My underwear is soaked. I'm anxious, even afraid. When he answers the door, I can't speak. I want to consume him like a cannibal, suck flesh from his bones, snap femurs with my fangs. We fuck on the hallway floor, only half-undressed. "Harder," I groan, my eyes rolling back in my head. "*Harder.*"

I cannot get enough of him. Not because it feels good, which it does, or because he's showing me new things, which he is.

It's because when his body is on top of mine, my fingers digging into the back of his neck, his breath hot on my collarbone, I feel completely certain of my body. Its soft, mysterious power. Its wild, unstoppable force. Its insatiable, bottomless hunger.

Sex with Elan is gluttonous dessert. I feed my body in huge, sticky handfuls, unconcerned with calories, oblivious to consequences.

* * * *

Spring grows more confident. New York sheds the last of its winter fur in favor of supple new skin. Elan attends a conference in LA, then a speaking engagement in Kuala Lumpur. In his absence, I go through the motions of my life. I work. I work out. I go to rallies in Union Square and then to Central Park to see the fragile new buds on winter-dead trees and try to feel hopeful. I maintain a perfect social media presence. I do outfits for Clean Clothes, but I don't have to work as hard anymore.

Within a week of Elan taking ownership of 30 percent of Clean Clothes, we sew up the seed. Tom Bacon, the venture capitalist I fell apart in front of at the Hoffman House party back in January, comes in for $250K. An angel investment; his own money. It's a bro deal, albeit a small one. He doesn't believe in us: he has a crush on Elan. "Men use money to suck each other's dicks when they can't actually suck each other's dicks," Vivian slurs, drunk on prosecco to celebrate the deal.

I laugh. "Elan is one hundred percent gay." I'm wearing a silk scarf to hide a hickey he gave me, blood vessels burst and broken under my skin.

Tom's money keeps the lights on, but only just. Vivian and I both get a small wage. I use mine to start paying off the credit card debt I incurred earlier in the year, when my diagnosis knocked me off the commission game. True to his word, Elan tweets about us and we get a modest uptick of new users. We hire a second outfit curator, Suzy-from-Texas, a first-year fashion student. I train her over Skype. "Thank you so much for the opportunity," Suzy-from-Texas keeps telling me, all corn-fed enthusiasm and big-sky optimism. "Y'all are making my dreams come true!"

We still don't have a full-time developer. What's left of Tom's money gets us a freelancer in Estonia, but Vivian is waiting for Elan to connect her to his contact at *TechCrunch*. She's hoping for an article that'll attract another high-level developer like Brock. Elan is dragging his feet on the intro. I offer support, but no one expects me to be twisting Elan's arm.

Officially, we barely know each other.

He doesn't mind if I'm between waxes or on my period. Somehow, I'd always imagined this would be an important compromise or milestone. But all he says is, "I don't care," and it's not an issue. Theoretically. My body still has the power to embarrass me with its rampant hairiness and indicators of (useless) fertility. I try not to let it. As time passes, something changes. It's not a growth. It's an absence. Of worry, of concern. I trust that Elan loves my body.

I don't trust that he loves me. But, he's changing, too. Softening. Letting go. He doesn't say "I love you." But this is what he does say, in a moment of shared breath, sweat-slick skin. "I like you. Too much."

I replay this until it wears thin.

I like you—dark eyes drilling mine—*too much*.

I know I feel this more than he does. I'm waiting patiently. I don't know what I'm waiting for until it happens.

We're in bed, late on a Wednesday. He's scrolling through his in-box. My head is on his chest, my fingers tracing his skin in soft, aimless circles.

I feel something. Through his chest hair.

Scar tissue.

My fingers run the length of it, but there's not much to feel, barely an inch. I sit up, wanting to see better. Beneath me, he tenses. His face complicates.

"You found it."

I can't not touch it, the bump of raised, hardened skin. "What happened?"

He takes off his reading glasses. "I was in an accident. When I was younger."

"What kind of accident?"

"A bad one."

I am aware this is a moment: a moment of adulthood. I have to have the right reaction. *I'm someone you can trust.* The empathy I'm already flooded with infuses my words as I ask, again, "What happened?"

"Remember how I told you I used to play football?"

I nod, containing excitement.

He switches his phone off. "Do you really want to hear this?"

I have never wanted anything more badly in my life. I slip my hand in his, and squeeze. "I do," I say in my best future-fiancée voice. "I really do."

Over twenty years ago. Ko Samet, Thailand. The U23 team was on tour, playing a friendly game with a young Thai team. "It was a pretty wild time," Elan says. "We took the official season very seriously, but the off-season matches were times to let loose." A group of young men from a country where drinking is illegal, on tour in permissive, reckless Thailand. Not hard to imagine how wild it could get.

They play the match, resoundingly beating the Thai team. Celebrate at a barefoot beachside bar. "The whole team was partying: drugs, alcohol, girls. A crazy night. And then, out of nowhere, Sofia shows up."

"Sofia?"

"My fiancée." Sofia Marino, daughter of the Italian ambassador to Iran: beautiful and rebellious, unlike any girl he'd ever met. She'd flown all the way from Iran to Thailand to find him. "She was . . . apoplectic." He says the word as if it could still hurt him. "I was so drunk when she walked into the bar, I thought I was hallucinating. We had an epic fight. Very dramatic. She broke up with me. I begged her not to. I convinced her to come back to the hotel. Figured we could work it out there."

I picture a young drunk Elan pleading with his firebrand fiancée, the Italian who speaks to him like no other woman ever has. I like her, and I am afraid of her.

"It takes an hour, but I get her on the back of my motorbike. It's one or two in the morning, I don't remember . . ." He trails off, his eyes looking into the past. I wait. When he speaks, it's in a low, calm voice, almost unemotional. "I don't know what happened. Maybe I hit a ditch, or missed a turn. But the next thing I know, I'm waking up in hospital. Sofia's in the next bed, hooked up to a ventilator. Covered in bruises. Barely recognizable. I was conscious for a minute or two, passed out again. The next time I woke up, she was dead."

"Oh my God," I breathe. "I'm so sorry."

"Don't be sorry for me," he says. "It's my fault she died."

I swallow. I can't deny this is true. "So, what happened? I mean, were you charged . . . ?"

"The football federation covered it up," Elan says. "Two of my friends went on the record saying we took separate bikes. We were all twenty, twenty-one. We didn't know any better. We wanted to save our own skin, and the federation didn't want controversy."

"Holy shit." I'm being entrusted with what, manslaughter? Worse? It's in the past, almost before I was born, yet still, I feel I've been handed something fragile and asked to keep it safe.

I will.

"So, this." Elan points to his scar. "Draining a collapsed lung. I have more." His knee, his jaw; I see them, now that I'm looking. "I broke my pelvis, busted my right leg. Four surgeries. I didn't want to live, but my body was in such good shape. Of course, I couldn't play anymore. Spent a year watching American soaps on my parents' sofa in Tehran. And then, something snapped. I didn't want to be an invalid for the rest of my life. As part of physical therapy, I started sketching. I drew the dresses and suits I saw on television. I was good at it; it was easy. It was fun. A friend's sister told me about fashion school in New York. She brought me brochures. It wasn't just that everyone looked young and happy. They looked purposeful, like the world was waiting to open up to them." His gaze grows wistful. "Their lives looked perfect in those pictures: not a hair out of place. It made me feel hopeful."

I know this feeling. The recognition of it floods through me like acceptance. I curl even closer, pressing my body to his.

He continues, "I decided: that was it. I'd do whatever it took to have that life."

This is why Elan's past starts at his American education. This is what is missing. I have it. I know.

Something else: our connection. The way he first noticed me at the Hoffman House party. That was what he recognized. We've both come face-to-face with death. He was spared. My fate is still being decided.

Elan shifts so he can see me. "Do you think I'm a monster?"

"No," I say. "Of course not. You were young and stupid, but it was an accident."

His breath leaves his body. He draws me into his arms. "Thank you," he says, his voice closed and thick. "Thank you for saying that."

I hold him. I've never felt as close to another human being.

He's entrusted me with his scars. I only hope I can trust him with mine.

31.

I will go to my sister's for Mother's Day, just like last year and the year before that and the year before that. "To celebrate your mother?" Elan pauses by the open fridge door, bottle of cold brew coffee in hand.

I nod, reaching past him for a yogurt. "Yup."

"You don't find that . . . a little morbid?"

"I find it a lot morbid."

Elan opens the bottle and takes a swig. "You don't really get along with your sister, do you?"

"Not really. We had a huge fight last time I was up there."

"So don't go. Why would you go?"

I give him a bemused look as I peel back the foil. It's odd: now that I know about his scars, they're all that I can see. "Of course I'm going. She's my sister."

* * * *

Mother's Day. A cheesy but nevertheless touching time to celebrate your mom and reflect on all she's done for you. Except, of course, if you don't have a mom. Then it is an uncut, unequivocal nightmare. And it lasts *forever*. Somehow, everyone with a loving, living mother finds this "holiday" sneaking up on them every single year—"*This* weekend? Are you sure?" The maternally orphaned see an Easter egg and know, like winter, *it's coming*. For me, the relentless onslaught of reminders and gift ideas and greeting cards all form a giant billboard that screams: YOU DON'T HAVE A MOTHER BECAUSE SHE'S DEAD. Never thought about it that way? That's because you have a mom. Everyone else—I see you. Oh boy, do I see you.

When I get to Mara's, Kathy-from-next-door is sitting in the dim living room, flicking through a gossip magazine. The hairs on the back of my neck straighten. We greet each other with forced cheer. "Mara's just taken Storm down to the creek," she says. "She wanted to catch some tadpoles, bless her precious heart."

"Yes, bless it." This doesn't explain what she's doing here, as comfortable as if it was her own home.

I put the apple pie I brought on the kitchen bench.

"Did you make that?" Kathy asks.

"No," I say.

"Oh." Her fingers find the small gold cross on her necklace: *Jesus, give me the strength to deal with someone who doesn't bake.* Her turtleneck is so high it's taken half her chin hostage. "I have a wonderful apple pie recipe," she says. "I'll have to give it to you."

"No, thank you," I say, very politely. It's so awkward I'm almost enjoying it.

We both glance in the direction of the backyard. Empty.

I perch on the edge of a lounge chair opposite her and we trade fake little smiles. She taps the magazine cover reverently. "Can you believe it? Jen and Brad back together. *And* she's pregnant. I always knew. I never gave up hope."

I laugh. "You know those things are completely fictional. They probably haven't spoken in years."

Kathy's eyes grow dark. Uh-oh, I've popped a Brad-and-Jen bubble. "I heard you're getting a mastectomy."

All the air is sucked out of the room.

Kathy folds her hands. "A woman in my church group had one of those, for the same reason you are." She cocks her head at me, her voice soft. "They butchered her. Eight surgeries, and counting. First the implant burst, then an infection. Every time, she said, 'I wish I hadn't, I just wish I hadn't.' Her beautiful breasts—gone."

I struggle to find my voice. "It's none of your business."

"I'm just telling you what I know."

"No, you're trying to scare me. What, you think I'm not scared enough?" I'm on my feet, backing away. "Mara had no right to tell you—"

"Lacey, dear, I don't want you to make the wrong decision—"

"It's nothing to do with you!" I say. "My body has *nothing* to do with you!"

"God has a plan for all of us," Kathy says loudly. "You're safe in the shadow of the Lord."

I'm furious. "Jesus *Christ*."

Her eyes go black. "Don't you *dare* take the—"

"What's going on?" It's Mara, at the back door, boots muddy.

"You told her?" I point at Kathy. "You told *her*?"

Storm is galloping around the backyard. Mara steps inside and slides the glass door shut.

Kathy gets to her feet, simpering. "I heard y'all arguing last time she was here. I was just telling little Lacey about my friend, who—"

"Did you tell her?" I ask Mara.

"No." Mara folds her arms.

"Well, she sure has some pretty fucked-up opinions about my situation," I say.

"Lacey," Kathy tuts. "Language."

"Oh, fuck off Kathy." Mara strides through the house to stand next to me. "How dare you talk to my sister about her health after eavesdropping on us. What are you still doing here? We went out twenty minutes ago."

Kathy tugs at her turtleneck. "I was just being neighborly—"

"You can stop." Mara points to the front door. "Get out. And don't say another word to my sister about her choices ever again."

Kathy glances between us, her color fading. She clutches her cross. Opens her mouth.

Mara steps forward.

Kathy flinches. She scoops up her ridiculous magazine and hurries for the front door.

My sister, the tiger.

* * * *

After lunch, we slice up the apple pie, to have it cold with vanilla ice cream. Just like how my mother used to eat it. As we wait for the ice cream to defrost, we watch Storm drawing on her belly on the living room floor.

"New dress?" Mara nods at the red silk shift Elan gifted me from his new collection. Currently my most treasured possession.

I half shrug. Nothing gets by this woman. I brace myself for a comment about my atrocious spending habits, readying an elusive "I got it for free" response.

"Pretty."

I'm so surprised it takes me a full five seconds to manage a simple, "Thanks."

Mara pulls her hair back, her eyes on Storm. "The strangest thing happened to me this morning. When we were down at the creek. These two people walked by; a couple, a man and a woman. The woman looked *exactly* like Mom. For a split second, I saw her, in the face of this stranger. I actually gasped. And then it was gone. I saw the person for who she was, a little shorter, different nose, different everything." Mara turns to me. "Has that ever happened to you?"

I rake through past experience. "No. But I wish it had. I wish I knew her that well."

Mara nods, thinking about this. "It must be hard," she says. "For you."

"What do you mean?"

"I remember Mom," Mara says. "Even though it hurts. Even though it's really, really sad. Who do you remember?"

A ghost? An idea? Illness, pain? This is the hardest thing about Mother's Day for me. I don't, for a second, wish any more sadness on myself, but the people I know who lost their moms last year or five years ago or ten years ago, got so much more time with them. I only have a handful of memories. None of them much more than flashes, impressions. Who do I remember? "I don't know," I say. "But I don't think it's the same person."

Mara grips my shoulder and squeezes it hard. I drop my lips to her fingers and kiss the back of her hand.

"Mo-om," Storm singsongs. "Is the ice cream ready yet?"

"Yes, darling," she calls back. "It's ready."

We eat on the living room floor. When our bowls are scraped clean, Mara leans over to get the photo albums. I put my hand on her leg—*wait*.

"Storm, honey," I say. "Where do you think Grandma is?"

"Dead," Storm says solemnly. "In the ground."

"Yes," I say, pressing back a smile. "Where else?"

"In the photo books that Mommy has," she says, pointing.

"That's right," I say. "Where else?"

"Ummm." She thinks. "I dunno."

"What about in the apple pie and ice cream?" I ask. "That was her favorite dessert."

Storm's face twists. It's too complex a concept for her.

"Or your pictures," I try, pointing to her crayons and paper. "Grandma liked to draw, too."

Storm's eyes are wide, trying to take this all in.

Mara says, "I see Grandma in the bookshelf. Some of those are her books. All the ones about art."

"I see Grandma," I say, "in my bed. Because most of the memories I have of her are when she was lying down."

"She used to lie on her back," Mara says. "And Grandpa used to feed her chicken soup."

The memory comes back to me, faded but perfectly whole. "I remember that." I'm standing in a doorway, watching, they don't know I'm there. My father, gently spoon-feeding my mother broth from a white bowl with a green leaf print around the edge. Afternoon light filters through patterned curtains, moving in a soft breeze. It's not the sterile hospital room. It's a bedroom: it must be our old house. As I stand there, small in the doorway, I realize that she isn't just sick and she isn't getting better. In that moment, I understand that my mother is dying.

I have no memories from that house: this is new. This is the only one.

People talk about cancer as a ruthless, clever foe: something to fight, to outwit. But in my hazy, imperfect recollection, cancer was less like a cunning killer and more like a quiet, relentless rain, slowly drowning the ones it had chosen while leaving you, perfectly dry, to watch.

"Do you know where I see Grandma the most?" I say to my niece. "In your mommy." I smile at Mara. "Your mommy has the same gray eyes and the same strong spirit."

Mara strokes Storm's soft, corn-silk hair and smiles back at me. A little sad, a little serious, but a smile nonetheless. "So you see, darling, Grandma might be gone, but if we look carefully, she's still all around us."

For better or for worse. My mother is still inside of me, in the complex blueprint that makes up my physical body. For better, or for worse, she is still with me.

32.

June

I get my father's current address off Mara. Florida, where he grew up. I heard once that most people die within a fifty-mile radius of where they were born. I write a letter. My first correspondence in years. "Don't expect too much," Mara warns me, over the phone. "He's still Dad."

"I know," I say. "I just figure he should know what I'm thinking of doing." What I don't admit to Mara or even barely to myself is: I'm curious what he'll say. Hell yes or hell no. If he has any advice. Bizarrely, I think I'd listen to it. My letter isn't long, just one page, outlining the facts and a few details of my life. Enough to say, *I'm okay, I don't need you.* Enough to say: *But if you get this: reach out.*

* * * *

"Mmm," I groan. "So good. *Sooo good.*"

Steph gives me a funny look, winding pasta around her fork. "You're very . . . vocal these days."

I lick Alfredo sauce off my finger. "Carbs and dairy. Must express appreciation." My entire body vibrates with pleasure. It needed pampering of the pasta kind tonight, and now it's purring like a fat happy cat.

"There's nothing specific that's inspired this orgasmic gastro gratitude?"

It's pointed.

I pause. Unsure.

Steph sighs and hands me her phone.

A photograph of Elan and I.

A tiny part of me is relieved: *this* is why she's been acting so strange all night, atypically evasive, decidedly awkward. In a post-BRCA world, bad news is no longer limited to celebrity breakups and what wasn't available at the bodega. But the larger part is horrified.

Sprung.

In the picture, Elan and I are at his local coffee shop, a cute French place on the corner of his block, waiting for our morning order. He's got one hand on the back of my neck, the other in his pants pocket. He's smiling at me and I'm staring up at him. An annoyingly obsequious look on my face, but I do look pretty, and you can see my whole outfit, which is on point: black silk jumpsuit, blush-pink bomber jacket, black nails, pale-pink lip gloss. Behind us, baskets of baguettes and buckets of peonies. The morning light makes my skin look flawless, my hair like spun gold. Objectively, it's an extremely cute picture of two attractive New Yorkers who look very much in love.

I love this photo as much as I feel invaded by it.

My heart is smacking my ribs. The caption reads: *Spotted at my local! NY-designer Elan Behzadi + his beautiful ladyfriend #streetstyle #newyorkmoment*

It's a British girl's account, someone Steph follows called SJ. *London gal taking on the Big Apple!* her bio reads. *I love fashion, pugs & Keanu Reeves.* She only has three thousand followers. This picture already has more than a thousand likes. Because she's tagged Elan. That means it's on his Instagram, too.

"Do you know her?" I ask.

"Not personally," Steph says.

"I can explain. I just need to message her."

Identifying myself as "the girl in the picture," I ask SJ in a nice but urgent way to take the post down: *It's a little complicated*, I type, *but we're not a public couple.*

Now, all I can do is wait. And face Steph, who is looking at me with puppy-dog eyes and a brave little smile. I'd almost prefer it if she was furious: that, I'm familiar with. "Do you want to talk about it?" she asks, in a soft no-judgment voice.

I don't. But now I have to. I explain how, after her initial reaction, I didn't feel comfortable telling her that Elan asked me out. And then about the limo, and dinner at Golden Century, and staying over on weekends, and then weeknights, and how even though he's a genius, he still feels misunderstood, and how he feels sad, and how much I want to cure him of that sadness, and how brilliant he is, and how being around him is like having backstage tickets to my favorite band every night of the week, and I can't believe this is my life and basically, for the past month or so, I've fallen head over patent-leather heels in love with Elan Behzadi.

"You obviously really care about him," Steph says.

"That's an understatement. I'm basically president of his fan club." I catch myself gushing. "As well as being his equal in all matters of love and, um, life."

"That's great, Lace." Steph touches my hand. "I'm happy for you."

I don't quite believe her. "Are you?"

"What do you think Vivian will say," Steph asks, "when she finds out?"

"She won't find out. But even if she does, it's none of her business."

"But it is her business," Steph says, "Clean Clothes is literally her business."

Ouch. "If it was only up to me, I'd probably tell her," I say. "But Elan thinks it's better to keep our business and personal lives separate, and so do I."

"So it's Elan's idea," Steph says. "To be secret."

"His life is very complicated." Even to my ears, it's an excuse. But I can't stop myself explaining that if we were to go public, then it's on the record, permanently. "It's only been a month."

"Or so," Steph says. "A month or so. Two months?"

I'm starting to get annoyed. "We're still working out how we feel."

"But you know how you feel," Steph says. "You just said you're in love with him."

My restraint snaps like a cheap chopstick. "Steph, why don't you just tell me what's on your mind? You've obviously got some therapy thoughts about this. What, is he stringing me along? Am I being naive?"

Steph bites her bottom lip. "Are you still doing the bucket list?"

"I'm having a lot of sex, if that's what you're asking."

"But 'a lot of sex' wasn't on the bucket list."

"That was the point," I say. "The outcome."

"So you're not doing the bucket list," Steph clarifies. "What about your BRCA stuff? Have you seen another plastic surgeon? Talked to Patricia? What about rescheduling with that woman from the forums you were supposed to meet up with—Bee?"

"I'm still only twenty-five, Steph," I say. "It's not like I'm forty-five: I've got time."

"It's one hundred percent your choice," Steph says, hands up in placation. "I'm just wondering . . ."

"What?"

She levels her gaze at me. I brace myself. "Are you putting his needs over yours?"

This is not what I expected. I pivot, trying to find the best way to disarm this.

Steph continues, "Sometimes in a relationship where there is a built-in power imbalance, like there is with you and Elan, it can be easy to prioritize the needs of the more powerful person. I'm your friend, not your therapist. I'm always going to support you, no matter what. But my advice is: don't get too disconnected from your own agenda."

"I haven't." Even I can hear how defensive I sound. Upsettingly, there is more than a grain of truth to what Steph is saying. If I'm honest, I do want Elan and I to be a public couple. I want to meet his friends, go to events together, for him to stay at my house, for us to talk about the decision I have to make. But as each week goes by, it feels more and more like we're living in a separate reality, as connected to my real life as the residents of a snow globe. I can't look at her when I say, in not much more than a whisper, "But I can't be totally honest with him about my needs."

"Why not?"

"Because he'd probably end it."

"Well, that's not a very good relationship," Steph says. "Is it?"

No. Probably not. But the idea of not seeing Elan, not having him in my life, is more than foreign. It's distressing. I'm not just close to him. I'm trapped.

The front door unlocks. "Hello?"

It's Cooper.

What perfect timing.

"In here," Steph calls, giving my arm a pat.

I arrange my face into neutrality. His lights up when he sees me. "Hey, Lacey! Long time." He sinks down next to me, eyes sparkling. "Wow, it's such a beautiful night. T-shirt weather! I walked by the river and there were all these people dancing, and I ended up doing a tango with this total stranger. I love New York! This city is the best!"

Is it?

Steph grabs our empty pasta plates. "More rosé?"

"I'll have some rosé." Cooper looks at me hopefully.

"I should get going," I say. "Long subway home."

"I can drive you," Cooper says.

"You have a car?" I'm shocked.

"Uh, yeah," he says. "I know, it's ridiculous. I pay more to park it than to drive it." His eyes haven't left mine. Enough unspoken words jostling behind them to require crowd control. "Let me give you a lift."

I can't. I can't split myself between two men, even if one of them probably wouldn't care less. I need perspective, not Cooper's warm body inches from mine. "Thanks," I say. "But the subway is a good place to think."

I gather my things and hug Steph goodbye. I understand this was needed and that now we should feel closer. But our hug is awkward. The urge to flee takes hold, and I resist the impulse to run out the door. "Are you all right?" Steph asks.

I nod, instinctively, and then shrug, honestly. "I'll talk to Elan," I say. "And, Steph?"

"Yeah?" She's so open it makes me nervous.

Fighting the urge to mumble at my feet like a teenager, I look her in the eye. "Thanks for being such a good friend when I'm such a bad one."

She looks like she wants to say more but she knows I want to go. "You're not a bad friend, Lace," she says. "We've all got flaws."

Mine just happen to be family-size.

Cooper's in the bathroom. I linger in his bedroom doorway for a moment. It feels like standing on the edge of someone's soul, peeking in. Light blue walls, stacks of books, a closed silver laptop. On his desk, a harmonica. Is he learning to play? A gift that's gone unused? A piece of his past he's carried with him? I want to curl up on his futon and wrap his blankets around me, inhaling the smell of his sheets.

I leave without saying goodbye.

* * * *

I'm almost at the subway when I hear a male voice calling my name. It's Coop, running to catch up with me.

"Did I forget something?"

He runs both hands through his hair, panting a little. "I'm . . . not . . ."

"Finishing your sentences?"

He laughs and adjusts his glasses. He meets my gaze squarely. "Can I take you out for dinner?"

I blink. "A date?"

"A date."

"A date date."

"A date date date." He grimaces. "Oh boy."

I shift my purse onto my other shoulder. "What happened with Miss Organic Tampon?"

"Truthfully," Cooper says. "She wasn't very funny."

The revelation gushes into me, filling me from top to tail. There is something about Cooper that sates me completely, in the way of a bowl of hot soup on a snowy night. Part of me wants to say yes, heck yes, let's go right now! But that would be more about punishing Elan than connecting with Coop. "I can't. I'm . . . seeing someone."

"Oh." He's surprised. "Cool."

"I'm sorry," I say, meaning it. "Just bad timing, I guess."

He lets out a wounded breath. "I deserve that."

I touch his arm, and yes, I do want it around me. I feel like a fool for getting caught up in Elan when this boy, this smart, kind, cute-as-hell boy, is right here in front of me. I want to say I'm sorry, and that he deserves the best, the very best, but everything that flashes into my head sounds like a bad breakup song.

And so I just squeeze his arm, give him a small smile, and continue down into the cold subway.

33.

Elan is in his study, hunched over his computer, face bathed in blue light. Beyond the open windows, the city honks and shouts and bristles with unspent energy.

"Let's have dinner tomorrow." I circle my arms around his neck. "At Noemi."

He doesn't look up. "Sure."

It's so easy, I'm momentarily speechless. "Great. I'll make a reservation. Let's invite some of your friends," I add, trying to sound impulsive.

"I don't have any friends."

"Yes, you do," I say. "Everyone has friends, even you. I'd like you to meet Steph. She's my friend."

He takes off his glasses and looks at me with the perfect poise of a marble statue. "I don't want to meet your friends."

"What?"

"I don't want to meet your friends."

"Why not?"

"I just don't."

I contain my emotion: a rising punch of anger. Of fear. "Okay," I say, trying for calm, failing. "No. Not okay. I want you to meet my friends. I want to go out. I want to be part of your life."

"You are part of my life. You're here every other night," and there's something about the way he says it—placating but edged with irritation—that makes me realize mostly, I invite myself here.

"Stay at my place this weekend."

"I thought you said it was a shoe box without a view."

"It *is* a shoe box without a view."

He gestures around him: the beautiful apartment, the beautiful view. Why would we want to leave all this?

"I want . . . more," I say.

"What about Vivian?" He says it as if he's laying down a trump.

"I don't care about Vivian. This is more important. We're more important."

"We?"

"You and me. I care about you."

"I care about you."

We're dancing around what matters, making it murky with careful word choices, sleight of hand. "I *really* care about you. I think—" Horrifyingly, my throat closes up. I'm barely able to squeak, "I'm falling in love with you." Tears fill my eyes. I turn away, ashamed.

"*Aziz-am.*" He's behind me, turning me into his arms, kissing my forehead. "You are so sweet. I like you so much." He moves back, speaking gently. "But I don't feel the same way."

Everything stops.

He continues calmly. "I can't be anybody's boyfriend right now. There's so much going on. The Clean Clothes thing is so much more work than I thought, and I'm already behind with the pre-fall collection. Mika gave her notice last week, and finding a new assistant is really going to be—"

"Oh my God." I push him away. "You're such a prick."

"Excuse me?"

"I told you I loved you, and you're worried about finding a fucking assistant?"

"Hey, I don't owe you anything. I never lied to you."

"No, you've just been fucking me in secret: your terms, your agenda, your needs."

"What?" He looks disgusted. "This is a two-way street, honey."

"Ugh, don't call me honey. Don't call me anything at all." I stomp out of the office, into the bedroom.

"Lacey. Lacey, c'mon." He follows me. "Where did this come from? I thought we were happy."

"We were." I snatch my sweater, my toothbrush, shoving them back into my overnight bag. "But there's a path, you know, there's forward momentum."

"But don't you think it's easier to keep it simple? Especially if it has an end date?"

"Who says it has to have an end date? God, you're such a pessimist."

"No, I mean . . ." He pauses, pained.

"What?" I ask. "Not all relationships have to end, you know." In his face, I see sadness. I've touched a nerve. Sofia. The dead ex-fiancée. Is that why he's not married? Is there something in him hard-wired to think that everything good has to come to an inevitable, tragic end? I drop my bag. "I get it, Elan. What you're going through. But the past is the past."

"It's funny you say that," he says. "Because I'm thinking more about the future."

"Me too." I take a step toward him. "I make you happy. You make me happy. We can do this. I know it's scary; commitment—"

"That's not what I mean." He looks uncomfortable. "Your . . . operation."

A rill of ice. "What about it?"

"You're still thinking about it?"

I can't move.

He inclines his head, as if it's all very unfortunate. "An end."

"There is life after mastectomy, Elan," I say, my voice five times louder than I intend.

His brows draw together, his face turning almost comically unsure. Not for him, there's not.

"I'm sorry, love," he says. "But I can't go on that journey with you."

Journey? It's a preventive surgery. I'll be fine in six weeks.

And yet, I know this. I've known this from the moment I told him about it. I know this because of what we do talk about and what we don't. I know this because of the way he looks at my breasts when we make love: as if they are a rare collector's item, about to be sold at auction. To him, I'm a novelty, erotic because my body has an expiration date. Because it will change. Because it will be taken away from him.

"I'm going." I pick up my bag. "And I'm never coming back."

I wait for him to stop me.

He doesn't.

* * * *

When I get home, there's a letter waiting for me. The one I sent to my father, not even a week ago. It is unopened. On the front, a scrawl in blue pen: *No longer at this address.*

I can't tell if it's his handwriting or not.

34.

I delete Elan's number and all his texts. I throw away my ticket to his Fashion Week show, the champagne cork from the limo. I leave my Elan Behzadi red silk dress outside a Goodwill store. It's so beautiful, and definitely one of the nicest pieces in my closet, but I can't imagine wearing it and not wishing it was Elan who was zipping it up. I want to purge myself of everything, even if it hurts. I linger on his check: six thousand dollars, my commission from the sale of all the trend books he bought. It's just money, and I need money. But then I remember the look on his face when he said the word *operation*, as if it was a dirty thing done by dirty people, and a wave of hatred overcomes me. I tear the check into tiny pieces. The loss of so much cash feels as perfect as punching a brick wall, even if it's stupid and hurts like hell.

I consider getting in touch with Cooper, but first I feel too fucked-up, then the internet tells me he is back in his second home: Berlin. I'm not sure what I'm supposed to do with that. Pine? Be strong? Be friends? In the end, I do nothing.

No more boys.

No more distractions from what I'd promised myself to do in the first place: serious thinking about the lifesaving surgery that Elan finds so distasteful. So I'm going to look at breasts. Not a slideshow. Or a sideshow. I'm going to what we in the preventive cancer community call a show-and-tell. It's almost July: my six-month deadline to make a final decision about my mutated gene.

A show-and-tell is an event where women who've had breast reconstruction gather in a room, take their tops off, and allow other women who are in the market for the same kind of thing to prod, poke, ask questions, and essentially see their future in the flesh. This is my Friday night.

It's Bee, my friend from the forums, who strong-arms me into going. She doesn't seem at all fazed that I blew her off a few months ago with all the willful negligence of a member of Congress. We plan to meet for a drink beforehand.

The Midtown bar Bee picks feels oddly familiar, although I've never stepped foot inside it before. Sports on multiple screens, a sea of business dudes sweating in bad suits with hairlines that have long since sounded the retreat. A guy who looks like he'd send a dick pic to himself tries to buy me a drink. I feign illness and scan the room. I don't know what Bee looks like. Her profile pic is a rather graphic picture of two horses having sex. Just as I think she's not going to show, the crowd parts. Like a lighthouse glimpsed through stormy seas, I spot the woman who must be Bee. She is unmissable. Not because she is a five-foot-nine blonde who's close to two hundred pounds. Because she is wearing a plunging sequined top that exposes the center halves of her extraordinarily generous breasts. No bra. They'd be visible from space. "Whitman! Oh my God, look at you. You're gorgeous, you know that? You're fucking gorgeous; I knew you would be. Get your ass in that chair. Sit. I ordered us whiskies, I hope you're a drinker. I am." She fluffs out her hair, grinning. "Like my mama said, always have two bottles in case you knock one down."

A waiter swings by, setting down two glasses of whiskey and a plate of cheesy tater tots. I haven't eaten tater tots in years. Bee waves him back. "Sweetheart, hold up, come back here."

He does. A hundred pounds wet and pale as skim milk.

"Baby doll, what's this?" Bee holds up the whiskey. Barely a shot in a tumbler.

"The, um, Jack you ordered."

"Boo, this isn't enough to buzz a baby. You see these?" She points to her tits.

He looks panicked. "Yeah."

"I have to cut these puppies off. I'm getting a fucking mastectomy because I have the cancer gene. You know Angelina Jolie? You whack off to her? I have to do what Angie did, but do you think I'll look as good in a red-carpet dress afterward? I don't know, probably. Anyway:

be a doll and see about getting me a drink to match my tits, can you? You're an angel, I bet you have a big dick." She hands the drinks back to him. He's hiding a grin. Bee is *that* friend: crude but harmless and kind of hilarious. She turns her attention to me, smiling. "How *are* you?"

I love her.

I thought it might be weird meeting a stranger from the internet without the built-in structure of an online date, but it absolutely is not. Bee is no-bullshit, funny as hell, and a genuinely warm person. The first sip of whiskey transports me back to the Midwest. That's why this bar is familiar. It's the bad sports bar in every small town. Awful but known, to the point it's almost comforting. The blaring baseball and blasting AC and complete lack of pretension. The cheesy, salty tater tots: I'd forgotten how much I love tater tots. We eat them with our fingers, sip our whiskey, and talk about what we have in common.

"Mama died of breast cancer when she was seventy," Bee says. "Her sister when she was sixty-eight; ovarian. My big sister, Maureen, at fifty. On her fucking birthday, no less. Two months ago my little sister, Audrey, found a lump. Stage three. Going through chemo. She's thirty-nine. Thirty fucking nine."

"God, how awful."

"It got all the Weiner women," Bee continues. "We are riddled with that fucking disease. I was always too chickenshit to get the test. I figured I couldn't go through with it, even if I knew. But after Audrey, I thought, 'No. You are done taking my family. It stops here, fucker.' So I got tested. Positive, of course. And here we are." She shakes her breasts. They wobble like custard in a bowl. "Sayonara, suckers. Your time is fucking nigh."

Bee is getting flap surgery, rebuilding her breasts using the fat from her tummy. Both the alcohol and the conversation are wrapping me in a cozy comfort. I'm sure Bee is the kind of person who could maintain a spirited conversation with a potato, but our online rapport easily translates in person. But mostly, it's just a relief to be talking about cancer stuff without having to manage other people's reactions.

I ask her the date of her first surgery.

"About a month. I'm also going through a divorce—"

"Oh no—"

"My third." Bee sighs. "Winner of the JLo Taste in Men Award, right here. My last husband was more mutt than man. Everything made him want to hump me or take a shit. My brother's going to help me, afterward. And by help me, I mean smoke all my weed and complain about my *Downton Abbey* addiction."

"I love *Downton Abbey*."

"Me too! I'm planning to rewatch the whole series." She squints at me. "You're a Mary, right? Perfect skin, taste for foreign cock."

I laugh and pop another tater tot in my mouth. "Nailed it. You?"

She gestures to herself. "Mrs. Patmore, baby! Girl's my soul *sister!*" She sings the last word, her voice rich, almost operatic.

"You have a good voice," I say. "Do you sing?"

"When I was younger. Cabaret. Silly stuff."

"I'd love to hear you sing," I say. "You'd be dope." *Dope.* I haven't said that since high school.

"I think that ship has sailed," she says. "But you're sweet for saying. What about you? What's happening with Persia?"

"We broke up." I think about the photo the British girl, SJ, posted: our sweet coffee shop scene. She took it down, just like I asked. I'll never get that moment back.

"Oh, darlin', your face went all sad. You really liked him, huh?"

"I guess I did."

"People will tell you, 'You're young, you'll meet someone, don't worry, get over it.' But fuck them. I remember getting dumped at twenty-five. It hurt then, and it hurts now. It always fucking hurts because we're women and we give a shit."

"Cheers to that." We tap our glasses and finish our drinks.

She burps. "Another?"

"If I do, I'll have five more and bail on this thing." I check the time. "It's about to start."

"You're right. Gonna powder my nose." She gets up, then leans next to me. Her breasts are the size of volleyballs. "Do you think the waiter was into me? Scale of one to ten, how close to child molestation would that be?"

She's forty-six. He looks twenty. "If you were a guy, seven. But you're not so, three?"

"I like those odds." She pats my back and heads for the ladies'.

My phone rings. As always, I hope for *Unknown Number*, i.e., Elan. As always, it's Vivian. Elan is an hour late for a meeting they've had set up for a month. And he's not picking up. "Have you spoken to him?"

I tense. "Why would I have spoken to him?"

"Can you email him?"

"Haven't you done that?"

"Yes." Testy. "Multiple times."

"Why would he respond to me if he hasn't responded to you?"

"You guys seem to have a bond."

It's an accusation. My voice is ice. "We don't."

Vivian exhales. "I knew this would happen. I knew it. First Brock, now Elan. *Jesus.*"

"Calm down. He's a busy guy. He's on a crazy deadline for the pre-fall collection."

"What does that even mean? And how do you know that?"

Bee reappears with a fresh coat of lipstick. She points at our waiter and does a very lifelike imitation of a blow job.

I'd laugh if Vivian wasn't stressing me out so much. "Email Tim George," I tell her. "Make it clear Elan only benefits from a company that's worth something. I'm at a cancer thing, I have to go."

I hang up without waiting for her response, and join Bee by the door. She shows me a piece of paper with a cell number on it. The waiter's. Unbelievable. She tucks it under her left boob. "Let's check out some titties."

35.

Our tickets direct us to a conference room deep in the bowels of a Marriott hotel. Outside it, a long line of women wait to have their names checked off a clipboard. On the forums, hundreds of women post and comment, but it's another thing to see them in the flesh. All these women, dealing with the same shit hand I got dealt.

Bee taps the woman in front of us. "You here for the titty show?"

"I am." She has gray hair and fine lines, but a clear youthful energy. She's the same age as my mom would be. "You're in the right place."

A volunteer marks off our names. "You're both BRCA1?" She hands us a string of purple Mardi Gras beads. "The beads match your mutation, so you can find other women like you," she says. "Yellow is BRCA2, pink is CHEK2, green is PALB2, and so on."

"All the colors of the mutation rainbow." Bee slips the beads around her neck. We exchange a *Here goes nothing* look and pull open the heavy conference room door.

I haven't really known what to expect. I assumed the atmosphere would be either somber and respectful, like a wake, or terrifyingly grotesque, like the scene in *The Witches* when they pull off their wigs. The atmosphere feels closer to a family reunion, with all the attendant emotions. Two hundred women have beads around their necks and plastic glasses of wine in hand. Some are talking and laughing. Some are shedding a tear. About a quarter of them are topless.

"Alrighty then." Bee whips open her top like Magic Mike. Her areolae are the size of dinner plates. "Gonna find me some big girls to talk to. Good luck, kiddo." She's gone before I can tell her that I think only women with reconstruction are going topless.

I grab a cup of almost-cold white wine and wander through the festival of breasticles.

According to Hollywood and porn, most breasts resemble modest basketballs located somewhere above a ski slope stomach. Not here. Flesh is abundant: round bellies, wobbly arms. All shapes and sizes are on display: breasts that hang, breasts that bounce, uneven breasts, barely there breasts. Breasts of all skin tones, from coal black to alabaster white. And, of course, these breasts have scars. Some are almost invisible, running along the fold where the bottom of the breast meets the chest. But some are long and bold, running across the breast, taking the nipple. Some are perfect case studies. And some are warnings.

I'm reminded, again, of how strong women are: to be here, showing up, giving back. To have taken their health into their hands in the first place. The women who have had mastectomies, whether they're preventative or in response to cancer, are quite literally opening themselves up to other women to answer their questions and quell their fears. Elan's reaction to my surgery—that it's an end point—seems ridiculous, childishly squeamish, and pathetically hypocritical. He's hardly an Adonis; he's hardly a man. A good man would not be freaked out by the women in this room. But my anger at him doesn't cloud my vision. I feel more clearheaded than I have in months. I am exactly where I am supposed to be.

I'm not the youngest person here, but most of the boobs on display belong to older women. My eyes rove pendulous breasts, child-rearing breasts, large and luscious, fantastically fleshy breasts . . . until they land on the Holy Grail.

A modest 32B, perky and taut. Nipples intact. The scars run along the fold under the breast, so neat they're almost invisible. I can tell they're implants. No reconstruction looks 100 percent natural. But overall, these breasts are beautiful.

And so is the girl they belong to. The side of her head is shaved, grown out half an inch. The rest is a tumble of black, woven with small plaits and tiny speckled feathers. A sprinkle of fine tattoos dot toned arms: the arms of a dancer or an athlete. Her eyes are almond-shaped and ice blue. Ethnically ambiguous: Japanese Nordic. She is startling.

"Sorry." I back up. "Didn't mean to stare."

"Isn't that the point of all this?" Her lazy, easy smile reveals small, precise teeth.

Just like that, I'm on the Kinsey scale.

"Where did you get them done?" I ask, taking the opportunity to stare, again, at her perfect breasts.

"Here in the city. New York Cancer Care Center."

"That's where I had my genetic counseling!" I'm thrilled. "You liked it? Your doctor, the team?"

"Oh yeah," she says, and I can't ever imagine her being stressed about anything, ever. "They were great. I completely healed in a few months." She moves toward me, her breath tickling my ear. She smells like hippie deodorant: sage and rosemary. "That's the thing about getting them done when you're young. You heal so much faster. It's almost unfair." She smiles at me, again.

Would we adopt children, or have them naturally?

"Who was your doctor?"

"Eric Ho," she replies. "He's an expert in DTI: direct-to-implant. One and done."

"I read about that!" I say. "Just one surgery."

"That's right. I think expanders are a scam by the hospitals and insurance companies to get more money out of you. Why would I want to keep going back every few weeks, you know? Why prolong it?"

Why indeed? "Do you mind seeing the scars every day? Honestly, is it weird?"

"I studied in Japan for a few years," the girl says, her eyes resting on me with the weight of a sunbeam. "They have this tradition there, where they repair anything broken with gold. So the flaw is seen as something that's just part of the object's history. It's seen as something beautiful."

It's been a while since I've had this kind of New York moment: crossing paths with someone extraordinary. "It's so weird I didn't think of NY3C as an option," I say. "But everyone there was pretty cool."

She twists her fingers through her hair. "It worked for me."

I am flush with elation. This feels so *right*. "Did you meet with any other doctors? What shape did you choose? Do they feel cold? What about—"

"Why don't I give you my number?" The girl nods past my shoulder. There's a crowd of women behind me, subtly rubbernecking the world's best reconstruction. I've been monopolizing the most popular rack in the room. I hand her my phone.

"I'm Luna," she says, and of course she has a cool name, she is the coolest person I have ever met. "Text me."

"I will," I say, backing up. "Roger."

"Your name is Roger?"

"No, no, Lacey," I say. "Lacey Whitman. I meant 'Roger that. Roger to texting.'"

"Okay," she says, before turning her attention to the woman behind me.

Awkward ending, promising connection. I walk back into the boobfest, smiling. Not just because I'd secured a good plastic surgeon recommendation, here in New York, at a center my insurance covers.

Steph was right. I do need to start putting my needs first. Number six on my bucket list.

Sex with a woman.

36.

July

I book a consultation with Dr. Eric Ho. Immediately, I see the appeal. The director of integrated plastic surgery services is polite, warm, and professional, and he's wearing a nifty purple bow tie. He's fantastic; Luna was right. We've been texting. Or, I've been texting incessantly, and she's been responding periodically. It's like she doesn't realize we should be Brooklyn's answer to Ellen and Portia, which is totally bonkers. Or my gaydar is still reliably terrible and she's not even gay. Or she's not interested.

In his very tidy office, Dr. Ho walks me through a one-step bilateral nipple-sparing mastectomy. He establishes that I've met Dr. Laura Williams, when I first had my screenings. She's the breast surgeon Dr. Ho works with. "As the breast surgeon, Dr. Williams makes an incision underneath the breast, in the inframammary fold," he says, "finding the plane between the fat layer and the breast layer. She carves the breast tissue away from the overlying skin and nipple, then removes the whole breast in its entirety in one fell swoop through that incision. The tissue is turned inside out so she can immediately send it to a pathologist who can evaluate the tissue behind the nipple. Once it comes back negative—no indication of cancer—I proceed with the reconstruction."

His tone is so soothing he makes the surgery sound like something I might want to do to relax.

Dr. Ho asks, "What size do you want to be at the end of the procedure?"

I tell him I want to stay the same. "Small boobs. Big dreams."

He smiles. "That shouldn't be a problem."

He uses a 3-D photographic imager to calculate the volume of my breasts: he'd plan to replicate the same volume using the implants. On the computer screen, I can see what my new breasts will look like. Quite similar to my real breasts, except they won't sag beyond the inframammary fold. The implant will keep me extraordinarily perky till the day I die. I won't even need to wear a bra.

"Ninety-nine percent of women choose silicone implants," he says. "Saline tends to be more like a water balloon. The silicone will ripple and wrinkle less. It'll look and feel very natural." He hands me an anatomic-looking implant about the size and shape of a small mango. It's clear but has a textured surface, soft and squishy. The good doctor explains how it all goes down: the lifting of muscles, attaching of donor skin tissue, placing of implants, securing of drains, closing of skin. I understand 75 percent of what he says, but I'm recording our meeting and can listen back again later. "All that's left is one simple scar," he concludes. "It'll all take between two and a half to three hours."

"Will I have to have follow-up surgeries? I read online I have to swap out an implant every ten years."

"No," says the doc, explaining how the incorrect but widely held assumption arose as a result of the mean time women have implants in, including those who voluntarily swap them for (often) bigger implants after six months or so. "Assuming there's no problems, you may have the same implants the rest of your life."

"How many of these surgeries have you done?"

He doesn't even sound braggy when he replies. "One thousand seven hundred and sixty nine."

Impressive. "Not your first time at the rodeo, huh?"

He shakes his head with a smile. "No, ma'am."

"And did any of those women contract breast cancer after the procedure?"

"Of those patients, we've had two," he says. "Which means your lifetime risk of developing a breast cancer, as a BRCA carrier, goes from seventy, eighty percent, to less than one percent."

I can't help it. I'm sold. I've known this is the right thing for me to do ever since the pros outweighed the cons, back in the loft when the girls were helping me decide what to do. Now, I'm ready to commit. "I'm in. I want to do this." I rise to my feet and shake the doctor's hand.

"Excellent," he says. "You're making the right choice."

A rush of relief: *yes*. This *is* right.

"Have you given any thought as to when you'd like to schedule your surgery?" Dr. Ho asks.

There are still so many factors I have to work out. I need to plan recovery time. The end of the summer is always slow for Hoffman House, and it'd mean I get it all over and done with before Eloise quits. But the most time I have off is over Christmas. "I'm not sure."

He gives me a tactful smile. "Don't wait too long."

"I'm only twenty-five," I say.

"I had a BRCA1 patient who wanted to wait until she was closer to your age," he says. "She was diagnosed with a stage three last month. She's twenty-two."

Twenty-two? I snap into focus.

"There's no need to rush into anything," he says. "But better to be safe than sorry. Every month you wait increases your risk."

Mom was thirty-one when she died. That's not far off. I need to do this. Now.

I schedule my mastectomy with Dr. Eric Ho and Dr. Laura Williams for the end of August.

I am stunned to realize this is only a month and a half away.

I have six weeks to finish my bucket list, before my boobs-as-I-know-them are gone forever.

37.

Steph squints at the invite on my phone. "What is it?"

I thrust the screen closer to her face. "Night of Yes: Dance Party and Sensual Experience."

She swats the phone away and flips a page of a very dull-looking textbook: *Theories of Developmental Psychology.* "Are you stroking out? On what planet would we want to pay to have a sensual experience with a bunch of strangers in Bushwick? It's actually a reoccurring nightmare of mine and I'm not even kidding."

"This planet," I say. "Luna invited me. She's performing."

"Who"—page flip—"is Luna?"

Oh. Right. "I didn't tell you about her?"

"I think I'd remember the name Luna. It has a certain hipster ridiculousness that tends to make an impression."

"I met her at a cancer thing. She's had reconstruction, with the same plastic surgeon I'm thinking of using. Actually, the same plastic surgeon I *am* using." I bite my bottom lip. "I, ah, booked my mastectomy."

Steph's mouth falls open. "When?"

"When's the surgery or when did I book it?"

Steph bolts upright. "Both!"

"Booked it a few days ago for the end of August." I roll off her bed, studying the ceiling. "It all happened so quickly, I haven't had time to tell you."

"Well, that's great." Steph shakes her head, confused. "Sorry, I wasn't expecting you to . . ."

"Listen to you? I did. You were right. I was putting Elan's needs first, and I did need to get back on track. So that's why we have to go

tonight. I've only got six weeks left to spoil these amazing lady cakes."
I grab Steph's hands and shove them onto my chest.

She squeals. "Stop, sexual assault! My body, my choice!"

I let her go, giggling. "I met this girl. Luna. You'll love her; she's
amazing. She can put us on the list, so it won't even cost anything. Please."

Steph sighs and takes my phone, reading the invite. "'A celebration
of love and sexuality, discovery, and acceptance.' So, what: an orgy?
Like *Eyes Wide Shut*?"

"I think it's more like a BK costume party where it's okay to get a
little nasty."

Steph wrinkles her nose. "That's disgusting." She gives me a funny
look. "You're surprisingly chill about all this. Who are you and what
have you done with Lacey Whitman?"

I take this as a compliment. "I'm an open-minded human, Steph.
Look, you don't have to do anything you don't want to. They go on
and on about consent, they'd probably kick you out for an unwanted
high five. There'll be performances and cheap drinks and everyone
will be dressed up. What else are we doing tonight?"

"Studying. My thesis adviser wants to see three new chapters by the
end of summer; cruel and unusual punishment."

"What about later?"

She shrugs. "I might google my crush's boyfriend and then you can
watch me cry for a bit."

"Exactly. We're going out. Who knows? Maybe tonight's the night
I cross number six off the bucket list."

Steph flips her textbook shut and heads for her closet. "Will there
be white limousines at this party? They won't last long in Bushwick."

A roll of tingles sashays up my spine. "No. I mean . . . sex with a
woman."

Steph spins round. "Hang on. This girl Luna . . . Is this a date?"

"Maybe. She's superhot, in a Eurasian Ruby Rose sort of way. I
can't stop thinking about her."

"You," Steph says, "and a girl?"

"You're being surprisingly judgy for a lez."

"I'm not being judgy," Steph says. "I just didn't think you'd actually go through with that one."

"Why not?"

"I love you, darling," Steph says, turning back to her closet. "But you're a boring heterosexual, and you always will be."

I can't conjure a retort. As much as Steph covets an all-access pass to my brain, she doesn't know everything about me. I like Luna. And not in a let's-do-spin-class-then-get-smoothies kind of way. In a put-your-mouth-on-my-mouth-and-let's-get-freaky kind of way.

Steph holds up a short blue tent dress. "What about this? It's so short you can see pubes."

I pretend to consider it. "No. You're a boring T-shirt and jeans girl, and you always will be."

"*Lace.*"

I grab Steph's towel from the back of her door. "You're just jealous. That I've got a date with a girl and you don't."

Steph's face flickers. I'm right. I'm vindicated and ashamed at the same time.

* * * *

I try to relax under blasting hot water. I shouldn't have said the thing about Steph not having a date. That was childish: I'll apologize. But, I'm also annoyed. Of all the people who should understand sexual fluidity, Steph should be number one. Isn't that some sort of cornerstone of psychology school: anyone can be anything because it's the fucking twenty-first century?

Elan still hasn't called. Or texted, or anything. I can't believe that one day, I'm privy to what he sounds like when he comes, and the next, we're not speaking to each other. It's more than sad. It's scary. This factor of dating, the anyone-can-leave-at-anytime clause, shakes me to my core. It's enough for me not to get into something to begin with. If I can't be sure someone's not going to fuck off with all of my feelings, what is the point of giving them away in the first place?

Is that why I like this Luna girl? Because ultimately I am a boring heterosexual, and so ultimately she can never really hurt me?

This is what is on my mind as I barrel out of the bathroom and straight into Noam Cooper. Also in just a towel.

We both say, "Oof," and stumble back.

"Coop." I pull the towel as tight as I can. "I—thought you were still in Germany."

"Got back last night." His eyes dart above my head, as if trying to find a nonsleazy place to land.

"Good trip?"

"*Tolle reise!* Sorry, that's German for, 'I'm a pretentious ass.'"

I giggle. His chest looks like it's been carved from marble. A bit like a Montauk surfing instructor's chest. "How long are you back?"

He leans against the hallway. Warmth from his body rolls off in waves. "How long do you want me back?"

My smile widens. I love the way he flirts with me. I want to run my fingertips down his chest. Feel the hard heat of his stomach muscles under my hand.

His towel twitches.

Steph sticks her head out of her door. "Oh, hey, Coop."

We both stiffen.

She strolls out of her room. "How was Berlin?"

"Reliably Berlinesque," Cooper says, his voice shifting into something more assertive and this-isn't-weird.

Steph stands between us, forming the world's most awkward triangle in the narrow hallway. "We're going out tonight. Lacey has a date. With a girl."

I shoot her a look—*What the fuck?*

She looks back evenly, calling my bluff—*You do, don't you?*

"Wow." Tired defeat edges into Cooper's gaze. "Good for you."

"Yes, it's very exciting," Steph says. "Lace is being quite the Don Juanita these days."

"Excuse me," I mutter, resisting the urge to run back into Steph's bedroom and burn it to the ground.

38.

It's a sweltering night, the kind where the heat feels like a giant tongue. Sweat trickles down my back, into my underwear. Our costumes—mandatory, apparently—are a little last-minute, but I think we'll get a pass. Steph's gone for sexy librarian: black-rimmed glasses; a white button-down, open to reveal generous cleavage; and tight black pants that show off her amazing ass. A *Reading Is Sexy* pin and a bold red lip completes the look. My look is a little more out there. Ripped fishnets, big hair, stripy bodysuit, cropped jacket. Black lipstick. Heels. Blade runner meets circus freak.

I know I look good. But underneath all this armor is an unlocked door in the form of a microscopic gene. Maybe I'll come home and everything will be as I left it. But my body is twitchy. Despite the pleasure I have been spoiling it with, it suspects an attack.

The venue's a few minutes from the subway. The neighborhood is industrial and devoid of greenery. We walk past shuttered metal doorways. In winter, it'd be spooky, but it's high summer and a Saturday and people are everywhere, roaming and reveling. Things between Steph and I, however, are tense. We haven't said much to each other since the spat at the loft, and the fact I'm wheeling between guilt, fear, and anger is not putting me in the mood for a dance party and sensual experience. We're almost there when Steph stops short. "Should we talk about it?"

I play dumb, like a total monster. "Talk about what?"

Both eyebrows raise to her hairline. "Our fight."

My insides seize up, every organ on guard. "It wasn't a fight."

A slow, irritated breath out. "If you say so."

"Let's just go," I say, taking a step and then stopping again. "What do you want to talk about?"

"It's fine," she mutters, walking ahead of me.

"No, *what?*"

"It's just—holy guacamole, is that the line?"

A colorful queue of people, fifty deep, are waiting to get into the world's most unassuming building. From inside, muted music throbs, spiking louder whenever someone enters or exits. "We're on the guest list," I say. "C'mon."

I stride to the front. A woman with painted flowers over her boobs and cheeks swirled with silver glitter is holding a clipboard. "No photographing nudity," she says, in a way that sounds very rehearsed. "Always ask before touching someone for the first time. Don't assume consent for one activity means consent for all others—"

"Excuse me." I elbow forward. "Excuse me, we're on the list. Guests of Luna: Lacey Whitman and Steph Malam."

"Guest list still has to wait." Glitter Face gestures to the end of the line.

"But we're on the list," I repeat. "We're VIPs."

Glitter Face looks at me as if trying to ascertain if I'm high or just a bitch. "Guest list has to wait."

"But—"

"Lace." Steph puts a firm hand on my arm. "Let's get in line."

I twitch out from her grasp. "Can you stop managing me for one second?"

She looks stunned. She backs up, hands raised, then turns and walks to the end of the line.

Glitter Face narrows her eyes.

I join the end of the queue behind two guys dressed as sailors and two girls dressed as drag kings. Steph has her phone out, scrolling.

"What," I ask, "are you doing?"

"Checking," she says, "Twitter."

"We're supposed to be hanging out," I snap. "Socially interacting."

"Oh-kay." She switches off her phone. "Let's socially interact."

We stare at each other in hot silence for a second before we both open our mouths.

"I'm not sure what you expect from me when—"

"The thing about you is—"

"Lacey." Spoken coolly, cutting through the noise. It's Luna. Black hot pants, white crewneck muscle tank, neon-yellow bra. Her dark hair is swept back in a messy side braid.

"Hey." We hug, brief but exhilarating. "This is"—momentary lapse—"Steph, this is my friend Steph."

Steph is staring at Luna as if she is a rare exotic animal. Her phone falls from her fingers. We all hear it hit the concrete.

Luna picks it up. The screen has shattered. "How annoying."

"No, it's fine," Steph says. "Who cares? Just a phone, just a thing."

"Very Zen," Luna says.

"That's me, Zen Steph. That's what everyone calls me. Right, Lace? Doesn't everyone call me Zen Steph?"

"No. No one calls you that." Great. Now Steph likes Luna too, that's perfect. I wish I'd invited Bee instead. "Can we go in?"

Luna makes a face. "Guest list has to wait. It's an anti-hierarchy thing."

"Yeah, we were just at the front, and this one here was making *such* a scene," Steph says. *"Let us in; we're VIP!* Like we're bloody rock stars or something!"

Luna chuckles.

I pretend to smile. "See you in there."

"I'll wait with you guys," Luna says. "My show isn't for another half hour."

"That's so nice," Steph says. "You're so sweet. You're nice and you're sweet, and okay I'll marry you! Twist my arm!"

Luna laughs. Steph laughs. I fold my arms because if I don't, I think I'll actually shove Steph.

The line shuffles forward.

Luna points at Steph's pin. "I have that badge. I got it at the library at NYU."

"Bobst? That's where I got it! I'm doing a master's in Psychology, second year."

"No way. I did my undergrad in psych. Did you ever have Professor Lancaster?"

"She's only my thesis adviser!" Steph screeches. "Oh my God, she is so brilliant; I'd be totally in love with her if I wasn't so intimidated!"

"That's *exactly* how I felt."

I yank out my phone to check how much a car home will cost, putting the spending cap on escaping this awful bizarro world at approximately $1 billion, when I see a text.

From an unknown number.

Hi.

I know the number. Even though I've deleted it, I know it by heart.

My entire body lights up. Luna and Steph are midway through realizing they once lived with the same awful roommate—*he was always painting portraits of himself! Yes, and giving them away as gifts! The worst!*

Oblivious.

I shouldn't text back. It took so much just to get through the past month. But this is the most alive I've felt in weeks. My blood's running hot. Neglected body parts blaze alive with the enthusiasm of a pep squad.

I text, *Hi.*

Nothing. My mouth is dry. I am staring so hard at my phone, I could drill right through it.

Undulating gray dots appear. He's typing. I'm dizzy.

Come over?

My breath comes out of me in a rush. Fuck you. Fuck you for thinking after all this time, I'd drop everything and come crawling back. I'm not your fucking servant and I'm certainly not your girl-friend, you made that abundantly clear when you broke my heart. Answering his text was another mistake in the series of mistakes that make up my so-called life, and the fact Elan Behzadi is my Jordan Catalano is so profoundly depressing, I might kill myself.

What should I write?

So you can break up with me again? Pass.

In your dreams.

lol

We're two drag kings away from getting inside.

I'm not going to get dragged back into this sick spider's web, I'm not. I type, *At a sex party in Bushwick. Don't text me again.* I switch off my phone, determined not to check it for the rest of the night.

Glitter Face looks up from her clipboard. "There," she says to me. "That wasn't so hard, was it?"

It wasn't hard at all.

Our wrists are stamped YES, in black block letters.

Glitter Face unhooks a short velvet rope. "Welcome to the Night of Yes."

39.

I've been mentally preparing myself for more nudity than an average episode of *Girls*, but when we walk in, nothing of the sort. Relief, and disappointment. But it's early, relatively speaking, so who knows what this night will descend into. The first room is already crowded. A long mirrored bar is clogged with partygoers. Above it, male and female go-go dancers gyrate in human-size birdcages. A DJ is lofted in a balcony above us, playing upbeat electronica. To our immediate left, a silver pole extends to the ceiling. A Zendaya look-alike twists around it in a gold bikini to a bopping crowd of focused onlookers, including a handful of people in tight black T-shirts that have *VOLUNTEER* on the back and *YES* on the front.

"Coat check's to your left; dungeon's to your right!" a bearded man in a tutu calls, pointing.

"Dungeon?" Steph looks scandalized. "What happens in there?"

"S and M stuff," Luna says.

Steph and I exchange a giggly glance, the novelty of raunch putting our tension on hold. Everyone is in costume, but the theme is disparate. A guy dressed as Waldo, a seventies disco couple in plunging bodysuits and skates, a gaggle of 1920s flappers, dapper gents in suits. A lot of light-up flower headbands and obvious fishnets. Romantic fairyland meets jazz baby meets leather kink. A fun, weird mix: Burning Man in Brooklyn?

Steph raises her voice over the music. "I'm going to the loo."

"I'll be at the bar," I say, and she disappears. Luna's gone too.

A short man dressed like a drug kingpin sidles up to me. "You're beautiful, baby."

I look away. He melts off. Interesting that it's easier to deflect un-wanted attention at a sex party than a standard bar.

"Hey." Luna reappears by my side, holding two pale pink cocktails.

"That was quick." I accept a drink.

"Performer perks. Where's Steph?"

"Bathroom."

"Alone at last," Luna says, with a distinctly flirty smile.

A little bubble of excitement. I haven't forgotten how much I liked kissing Camila. Luna takes my hand and leads me to an area filled with soft cushions and potted plants—very *Arabian Nights*. We settle on a beanbag, looking out over the crowd. We smile at each other, and then, smile at each other again. I can't land on something to open with, not wanting to sound pedestrian or predictable. I have to say something. Anything, I have to say literally anything at all or this becomes officially awkward in five, four, three, two—"What's in this?" I hold up the drink.

"Not sure. I think gin?"

"Long as you're not trying to roofie me," I joke.

She leans closer. "What?"

I raise my voice. "I said I hope you're not trying to roofie me."

She knows I'm joking, but she doesn't find it very funny. "Nope."

Fail. Reset. I clear my throat. "I met with Dr. Ho," I say. "He was fantastic. I'm all set." I point to my chest and make a scissor-snip motion.

"Great," she says. "If you have any questions or anything, let me know."

I have a million questions, but a Brooklyn sex party doesn't seem like the right time and place. "So when does all this turn into an orgy?"

She laughs. "Things get looser the later it gets. It's not that wild up here. People go for it more in the dungeon."

I'm not sure if it's an explanation or an invitation. "The dungeon" is not somewhere that screams romance to me. "Cool," I say, a response that is both pedestrian and predictable.

"There you are!" Steph, navigating the unstable floor of cushions, loses her balance and tumbles into Luna's lap. "Sorry!" She giggles, taking her time to extract herself.

Luna grins and gestures to Steph's shirt. One dark brown nipple has escaped her bra. I'm expecting Steph to be mortified. Instead, she giggles. "I'm really getting into the spirit of things, aren't I? Rogue nipple spotted at table seven!" She shakes her chest.

Luna laughs like it's the funniest thing in the world.

It is not.

Steph sips Luna's drink. "What are we drinking? Mmm, gin?"

"Good guess," Luna says, bizarrely impressed.

"Yummy," Steph says. "So, what kind of performance are you doing tonight?"

"Aerial silks. It's like aerial gymnastics—"

"I know what it is, it's brilliant! How long have you been doing that?"

"About four years." Luna settles back into the cushions. "I started taking classes before my surgery to get fit, but I liked it so much I stayed with it."

"Is that your full-time job?" Steph is practically panting.

"Not full-time. I'm a part-time social worker and I teach yoga and pick up a few cater-waiter gigs here and there. Sort of a jane-of-all-trades."

"Jane-of-all-trades!" Steph throws her head back and howls. "That is *hysterical*!"

Luna laughs too. Did they both manage to get high behind my back? Because all this is about as funny as a funeral.

"Okay, I should head backstage and start warming up." Luna squeezes my arm. "When we start, try to get close to the stage." She gestures to a raised stage currently filled with people drinking and dancing. "That's the best view." She hands Steph her drink. "Keep this."

"Thank you so much," Steph simpers. I roll my eyes, and she catches me.

Luna gives a little wave and threads off through the crowd.

"What?" Steph asks.

"There's something particularly gross about watching you flirt," I mutter. I regret it as soon as I say it, but our dynamic feels oddly permissive right now, even if it's unprecedented. We always squabbled as roommates—whose turn it was to take the trash out or pay for takeout—and while we don't have those little domestic disputes anymore, if there's anyone I'll pick at, it's Steph. Usually, that's okay. But tonight, things are shifting.

Steph's face hardens. "That's mean."

"Is it? I thought flirting with your friend's date was meaner."

"I'm not flirting," Steph says. "I'm being friendly."

"Being friendly with an exposed nipple is flirting," I tell her. "I read it in *Cosmo*."

"Well, maybe we have more chemistry than you," Steph says, taking a fussy sip of her newly procured cocktail.

I almost spit mine out. "That doesn't give you permission to make a play for her. She's my date. She's *mine*. Okay?"

Steph stares at me. "You're touchy. Did something happen? Something with Elan?"

"Elan?" I shout, startled. "God, *no*. I haven't talked to him in weeks."

"Breakups are hard. I get it," Steph says, in a way that's flat-out condescending. "It's normal to rebound with someone unavailable—"

"It's *not* about Elan. I will *never* see him again." Even as I say it, I feel a humiliating gush of sadness. "I like Luna. She's not a rebound, and she's not unavailable. If you're worried she'll choose me over you . . . you should be. She will."

Steph blinks at me; once, twice. "Ouch."

That was cruel; that crossed a line. I prickle with shame, and pretend that I'm not. "I'm going to get a better view. Come with?"

She shakes her head. She's turning red.

Fuck.

I get to the front of the stage and stake out a position dead center.

Steph and I have never liked the same person, for obvious reasons. Luna probably won't choose me: in the collective ten minutes they've spent together, she and Steph probably do have more of a connection. But watching them flirt, right in front of me: that's hard. Am I really that unlovable?

And how, exactly, will a goddamn mastectomy make me more lovable?

The organizers are clearing partygoers from the stage.

The show is about to begin.

Lights dim.

Music fades.

The crowd quiets, turning its collective attention to the empty stage.

Movement from above.

Two swathes of red silk tumble from the ceiling. Wrapped into them, spinning around in a perfect circle, is Luna. Half-naked, now only in hot pants. Her skin is lightly painted in gold glitter. Her long dark hair whips around her like a serpent. The crowd *oohs*. Using only the red silk twisted around her body, she forms fluid, lithe shapes, spinning and twisting. So light. So effortless. Everyone in the room is mesmerized. She looks beautiful; vital. Most beautiful of all, her breasts. She hasn't hidden the scars. They are what make her look strong.

She lands soundlessly on the stage and meets my gaze. She smiles and extends a hand, gesturing for me to join her. I shrink back, shaking my head.

The crowd pushes me from behind—*go on, go up.*

To a small swell of applause, I join her. A black harness appears beside the red silk. I'm being strapped into it by two assistants, and Luna. "You're not afraid of heights are you?"

I can do this. I can do what she did, because she did it. "No."

Straps and buckles tighten around me securely. The faces of the crowd are turned up at me, a sea of lights and fake flowers and burlesque masks. "I got you," she says. There's a *whoosh*. My feet leave the ground.

I'm flying. Luna twirls my arm, twisting me around. The party swirls below me and I'm laughing and squealing, weightless and free. The red silk spirals around me, Luna, a smear of gold next to me. We whizz back and forth, through color and light. I am birdlike with bones made of air.

And then I'm descending, lowered back toward the earth. I could've been up there for five seconds or five minutes, I have no idea. The assistants are unbuckling me, and Luna is beside me, smiling, her eyes bright. She holds my hand up and the crowd cheers, again. I am filled with love: for her, her courage and beauty. I pull her close, and put my hand on her cheek. We kiss. I know the crowd is cheering even louder, but I'm barely conscious of it. All I feel is her: warm breath, soft lips, new and powerful. I pull her closer still, my hands twisting into her hair, tasting sweat and gin. Her body feels lean and muscular under my fingers. I feel her smiling, her mouth on mine. We break away and I'm liquid fizz, silly and high.

I meet the gaze of the crowd for the first time, laughing.

And I freeze.

Everything around me tightens.

Through the blinding lights, I can just make out Steph, still on the cushions, watching me with an odd sort of blankness. But she's not who I see first. That would be the person standing a few feet away from her.

Elan.

40.

Even though Elan is wearing a simple black mask, I can tell it's him: his posture, his hair, the way he's looking at me. Intense and wolfish. My blood curdles. Steph turns her head to follow my gaze. When she realizes who the man in the mask is, her head snaps back to me. I see her form the words: *What the fuck?*

I scramble off the stage. The show's over, a DJ's playing, and the crush of people around me are now dancing. I push through naughty nurses and dudes in Mexican wrestling masks, desperate to find him, get him out of here. I'm furious and panicked, but a part of me is thrilled, even flattered.

His dark head, six feet away. I prepare to pounce. Steph materializes in front of me. Behind her eyes, a war. "Outside. Right now."

With a grip that'll leave a bruise, she drags me out of the party. She lets me go around the corner from the line that has gotten even longer since we arrived.

"That's him, isn't it?" she spits. "The guy you allegedly broke up with."

"Not that it's any of your business, but I have broken up with him. I haven't seen him in weeks."

"This is the kind of place forty-five-year-old fashion designers like to hang out, is it?" Steph scoffs. "Just a coincidence?"

"He's forty-two," I say. "Jesus, are we really fighting about a guy? I thought we were feminists."

"We're not fighting about a guy! We're fighting about the fact you just lied to me. Again."

"I didn't lie," I say. "Look . . . I guess I told him where I was. But I also told him to leave me alone."

"You told him where you were? How is that anything other than an invitation?"

"What does it even matter to you? My life isn't your business! It's nothing to do with you!"

"Wrong," Steph says. "It does matter to me. It matters to me to see straight girls leading on gay girls. I know what that's like, Lace. It fucking hurts and it's also manipulative and selfish—"

"Jesus, Steph, stop calling me straight! I'm not straight, okay? I might not be a full-on lez, but there's a spectrum and I'm on it."

"No, you're not. You're obviously way more interested in my roommate and the fuck buddy you invited than that girl in there, who, trust me, you'd be all over like a rash if you were, in any way, shape, or form, into girls."

"*God.*" I feel like pulling my hair out. "I didn't invite Elan. I don't even understand why we're arguing. None of this is happening to you. This is *my life.*"

"Well, I'm sorry, but I'm not going to stand by anymore and watch you turn into a selfish bitch."

I gasp. "Excuse me? What did you call me?"

Steph looks at me without blinking. "I called you a selfish bitch."

I'm floored. "I was diagnosed with BRCA1 this year. I'm getting a fucking mastectomy. I could get cancer, Steph, fucking *cancer.*"

"I know. I know all about your life, Lace. Even though you like to shut me out and occasionally lie to me, we only ever talk about you. How's my thesis going? What about my family? Did you know my dad's in hospital right now? No, you wouldn't. Because in the past six months you've never once asked me about me."

The ground is unstable beneath me. I open and close my mouth, unable to locate a thread of anything.

Steph's eyes flash at me. Every word is intent and deliberate. "You got a bad diagnosis, Lace, really bad. But you're not actually sick right now: you're still a human being. You're still accountable. You still have to play by the same rules as everyone else. You don't get a pass to be a bitch for the rest of your life. So stop juggling dates and be a fucking grown-up. And try to think about other people's feelings for a change."

With that hanging in the air, she heads back into the party.

I am blind with rage. My fist slams the brick wall. I don't even feel it. How *dare* she. How dare she accuse me of all those things, all those *lies*. My *best friend*, what a joke, what a sick joke. No one cares about me. No one understands me. I am alone, and I always will be because I have to be. I know what's best for me.

Be a grown-up?

Okay. I'll be a grown-up. I will go after what I want, and if that makes me a selfish bitch, then I am a fucking selfish bitch.

Like a hurricane, I obliterate my way back into the party.

I find him by the bar. "Hey," he says. "There you—"

I grab his wrist.

"Whoa." Elan almost trips. "Where are we going?"

We are going to the dungeon.

41.

The light in the dungeon is a dim, dark red. I descend the stone steps—yes, stone, like a real dungeon—with sudden trepidation. My blood is still coursing through me like a wildfire, but I'm nervous now. There's no music down here. It's not a party like upstairs. It's serious. The space is cool and labyrinthine, with a low ceiling. Probably an old cellar. *Thwack, thwack.* In one corner, a man in leather pants is whipping a very large woman's back and ass. Her skin is covered in welts. I blanch.

"She's loving it," Elan says in my ear. "Look."

And yes, she has a strange half smile on her face, even as the whip comes down hard again and again and again, hurting her. A completely naked guy is masturbating, watching them. This, too, is permitted. There's something slightly camp about the whole scene; I almost feel like laughing. I want to make a joke. But it's not a joke. I'm on the brink of losing my nerve.

Elan takes my hand. "C'mon." I let him lead me forward.

We pass a foursome fucking, three guys and one girl. A woman with a shaved head leads a man on his hands and knees by a dog leash. Another woman is pinned to a wall, legs splayed. I keep telling myself it's all consensual; we are all adults. I am unnerved, out of my depth. But the strange dark sex of this place is also arousing. It's just not arousing anything in me I am familiar with.

That's what I want. That's what I'm here for.

We get to an empty room. Stone walls, dull light. A metal hook in the low ceiling, a long piece of leather hanging from it.

My vision wasn't a fantasy. It was a premonition.

I tell Elan about it. The image that came to me the first time we met. My hands above my head. Blindfolded. Gagged. People watching us, in the shadows.

His jaw is loose. "Are you sure?"

I nod. "I am."

He steps away from me. Shadows pool around his eyes, turning them black. "Wait here." He returns with a piece of satin and a ball gag attached to a leather strap. For my eyes and mouth. "It's clean," he tells me, rubbing it with the satin. "Okay?"

"Yes." My voice is a whisper. I clear my throat, and try to say it louder. "Yes."

He steps close and places his lips on mine. I'm so wound up, I can barely kiss him back. He moves away. "Take your clothes off." His voice is dispassionate. A quiet order.

I obey.

I slip off my heels, and roll down my stockings. Finally, I'm just in my bra and underwear.

"All of it," Elan says.

A few people have gathered to watch. An audience. I don't think Luna will come down here, but I can't be entirely sure.

"Don't look at them," Elan says. "Look at me."

I train my gaze back at him. Beneath the black mask, he is a stranger and strangely familiar, a combination of my lived experience and the image I know from glowing screens. Real and unreal. My bra and underwear fall away. I close my eyes and raise my hands above my head.

Surrender.

My pulse is slamming, a runaway train. I am blackness and sensation, a hot freeze of anticipation, of wild electricity, of sweat.

My hands, looped in leather. My eyes, shut with satin. My mouth, filled with plastic. Everything tight. A prisoner secured.

Warm fingers on my side. I jump.

"It's me." His voice, soothing, behind me. "Are you ready?"

I nod. But I am unsure. This doesn't feel how it did in my mind.

I'm not turned on. At all. My body has left me. It has disappeared.

He grasps my waist. I hear him breathing, feel him steadying him-self. Even though I'm blindfolded, I shut my eyes. He inhales and slams into me. Air comes out of me in a choked grunt, the plastic gag ball pressing hard against my tongue. He feels huge, splitting me open like a ripe piece of fruit. And then again, and again, and he is fucking me hard and fast in a way he never has before. The way I asked for. The way I imagined. And it is nothing like how I imagined. My body is a thing, a piece of meat, hung up on a hook like a pig in an abattoir. I am a batting cage, a beat-up old sofa. I am entertainment. I float away from the party, up, over Bushwick, over Manhattan, which is just a diorama, just a cartoon skyline. I am at sea, a piece of wood tossed around in a storm, splintering and breaking apart as monster waves smash and crash and pummel me. Through the choppy gray-green water, I see a dark shape. Thrashing the water, more powerful than the storm.

Something is out there. Something is waiting.

He comes inside me, a strangled groan on the nape of my neck. "Fuck," he pants. "Fuck, that was hot. Holy fuck."

I just hang there, waiting.

He kisses the back of my head.

I twist away. "Untie me." It comes out a mumble.

He slips the ball gag out of my mouth, still breathing heavily. "What, babe?"

"Get me down."

I face the stone wall and pull my clothes back on with numb fingers. My costume is tight and ridiculous and I just want to be at home, in sweats, forgetting this.

I've never felt more raw. More exposed.

I turn back around, expecting to find Elan behind me, hands clasped, suspecting my unease. But he's on his phone. The sight of him more interested in whatever the fuck is on that screen and not me, says everything. I leave without waiting for him. He catches up to me at the bottom of the stairs, telling me to wait up. A stream of people separate us, everyone jubilant, excited. With every passing second, I feel worse about what just happened.

He follows me out of the party, back onto the street. It's so humid, I'm sweating, parched. I need to find Steph. I need to get out of here. "Lacey," he's saying, "Lacey, what's wrong?"

"Nothing."

"Clearly, something's wrong."

"It's just . . ." I can't look at him. "I didn't like that."

"Oh."

"I mean, I really didn't like it." I want him to hold me. To comfort me. I can't keep the need out of my face as I look right at him.

"Oh," he repeats. He blinks. He glances past me.

"Oh?" I mock. "That all?"

He shakes his head and shrugs. Not annoyed, exactly. Just uncommitted. Uninterested. "What do you want me to say?"

This was a huge mistake. Letting him back in, letting him fuck me. He doesn't care about me: he told me as such, and I ignored him. "Why am I surprised?" I take a step closer and let my voice drop low. "Your ability to hurt women has always been criminal."

He says nothing.

Does he get I'm talking about Sofia? The woman he basically murdered, all those years ago? I have no idea. His face is completely blank.

He turns toward the street and hails a passing cab. He doesn't even look back at me once as the taxi begins to take him away.

42.

The safety of flannel, of pink skin warm from a shower. The mattress sags underneath me, marshmallow-soft, taking my weight. I know it can hold me. My body tentatively tries relaxing. There is order, here, faint but very real. I am grateful for piles of textbooks, dog-eared and ruffled with Post-its. I am grateful for damp towels left on bedroom floors: we can hang them up in the morning. Not everything needs to be perfect.

"Here." Steph hands me a mug. "I know you don't like green tea but it's all we have."

"Thank you." A breathy female voice warbles from her laptop. I'm not usually a fan of the "I am beautiful but sad" singer-songwriter genre. But at 3:00 a.m. on a sad Sunday, it feels appropriate.

Steph gets into bed beside me. She's angry. "I still can't believe him," she says. "Total fucking sociopath, leaving you like that."

But Steph's eyes are lowered. She's still pissed with me, too.

I don't blame her.

The tea is scalding, burning the soft flesh of my mouth. "Tastes like dirt."

"What?"

"The tea. Tastes like grass. Or the earth."

"It's all we have."

"No, I'm . . . I'm not complaining."

She's mad at me but she's also protective, maternal. She doesn't know where to look. We sit in silence for a moment. A new song starts on the laptop. The lyrics rhyme *new dawn* with *forlorn*. "What happened to your dad?"

She sighs and maybe she's relieved I asked a question she could answer. "Cycling accident. But he'll be fine."

"I'm so sorry. That sucks."

"It's hard. Being so far away. I guess he's lucky this is his first really bad accident. He's on that bike every day. Maybe it was only a matter of time."

And maybe it was naive to think I could go on a sexual odyssey without something like this happening to me. "I'll send him some Sudoku books. He likes those, right?"

"Yeah," she says, sounding surprised I remembered.

I shift to face her more fully. "Sorry I got so mad at you." I wince, remembering the white-hot fury I felt. How it burned through me, obliterating logic, driving my hand to hit a brick wall. The skin is broken on my knuckles. When I press it, it sounds in my body like an alarm. That's what rage feels like. A screeching hot alarm that I'll do anything to shut off. "I always thought Mara was the angry one," I say, more to myself than Steph.

"It's funny you say that," Steph murmurs.

"Why?"

She hesitates.

I put my tea down and touch her hand. "Why?"

Steph's big brown eyes are the size of the Pacific. "I know we're, like, each other's chosen family," she says, "but lately you treat me like your actual sister. And I'm not. I'm not your sister, Lacey. I'm your friend."

She's right, of course. But that line is hard for me to see. Hard for me to obey. And part of me doesn't want to. Maybe because I don't have family here in the city. But it is different. I can't take Steph for granted. I mean, I can't take Mara for granted either, but I really can't take Steph for granted. "I understand," I say. "I hear you."

"I'm sorry for calling you a selfish bitch," Steph says.

"You weren't exactly wrong."

"But it wasn't kind," she says. "And I'm sorry I said you were a boring heterosexual. I think I was just jealous." She pulls at a stray thread in the duvet. "Do you think you'll see Luna again?"

"Oh." I sit up. "Did you see her, or—"

"I told her you were feeling sick and we had to bail," Steph says. "She was cool."

"Good. And to answer your question, I don't think so," I say. "I was thinking about what you said, about stopping juggling dates. It's pretty clear who's best for me."

Steph nods sagely. "Justin Trudeau."

I exhale soft laughter. "Exactly. The Justin Trudeau of this loft."

"That seems inevitable," Steph says. "Just don't have sex in this room, okay?"

The thought is bewildering, but Steph's looking at me with a smile and so I smile back. I can't believe we're talking about a boy, a crush, after what happened, but we are and it's okay. I'll be okay.

"You deserve love, Lace," Steph says. "Everyone does."

This makes me feel like I am made of pure gold. We snuggle under the covers and switch off the bedside light. It takes my eyes a second to adjust to the darkness.

"I know you won't," I say, "but please don't say anything to anyone about any of this."

"Lace." Steph rolls over and gives me a look. "I wouldn't be a very good best friend if I did that, would I?"

I replay the words in my head: *best friend*. I suddenly feel very shy. "We've never said that," I whisper. "Out loud."

"I know," Steph says. "I was waiting for you."

We smile at each other. "Why'd you stop waiting?" I ask.

"Because a girl needs a best friend," Steph says, "after her biggest sexual fantasy turns out to be a massive dud."

I smile and feel sad and angry but somehow also strong. My voice is quiet in the dark. "It is actually really hard," I say. "Being twenty-five."

"Yeah," Steph says. "It really is."

43.

Later that day, I have a meeting with Vivian. It does not go well. Elan has gone completely MIA on Clean Clothes. Tom Bacon wants to see evidence of the support we'd assured him Elan's involvement would bring—the good press, the celeb endorsements. None of this we have. But there's no legal way we can make Elan do anything. "I just don't understand," Vivian keeps saying. "Why'd he come on board if he's not really committed?"

I can't tell her. Not only because I can't bring myself to admit that I lied to her. I can't tell her because I don't really know. Maybe it was about me, maybe it wasn't. Clearly, I've never been able to read Elan. Or trust him. I hate him, but I don't want Vivian to clock the depth of my feelings for him. She keeps pushing for me to check in with him: plan a lunch, or at least call until I get through. I'm vague, citing my work commitments, his busy schedule. She gets snappy; I get defensive. This was all a huge mistake that I orchestrated.

Bee calls me on my way home. "You are such an angel," she says. "Seriously, you're too much."

I'd sent a small bunch of flowers and a big bottle of whiskey. Bee's surgery is tomorrow.

"How are you feeling?" I ask.

"I have a week's worth of lasagna in the fridge and six seasons of *Downton Abbey* ready to stream," she says. "Good to go."

"Call me," I say. "Any time. I'll come visit when you're up for it."

It's a gorgeous summer afternoon in Williamsburg. The hipsters and their iced bulletproof coffees are out in full force. Summer turns the city friendly: we won the battle with winter, the sun is the spoils. It's bizarre to think the dungeon in Bushwick is only three miles away.

One of the things I loved about moving to New York was the clean slate: I had no past here, no Brooklyn backstory. Now the city is starting to form layers, my life here a messy papier-mâché.

Walking along the East River, I allow myself to feel the memory of last night. The unbearable disappointment of a man I gave a little piece of my heart to. My fantasy was about a loss of control and, no, I don't have control over what's under my skin. But I can control who gets there. I must control that. I am the one in charge of my body, and I need to make choices that are always, without fail, in its best interest. My body wanted to try the scene in the dungeon, right up until the very last second. It was the wrong decision to indulge that desire, with Elan, at that party. Now, my body needs comfort. Sunshine. A slow, gentle walk along a body of water in order to regroup and heal.

Ahead of me, an older couple are strolling, eating ice cream cones. As we pass, the woman looks right at me and smiles. It lights up her whole face. I don't see wrinkles and lines. I see joy. I'm reminded of something Patricia said to me in her office last week, as we shared a plate of French macarons. "Life is long."

"Really?" I frowned at her, suspicious. "I always thought the opposite."

"Darling," she said. "I've been a Republican, an Independent, and a Democrat. A blonde, a brunette, and a redhead. Straight, gay, questioning. Life is *long*."

There's always something new to learn. Something new to try.

On a park bench overlooking the river, I snap a picture of the water and send it to Steph: *Wish you were here & not studying.* I've been making more of an effort with her after our fight. A standing weekly dinner date where we alternate picking a new (cheap) restaurant. Calling her before I go to bed for an end-of-day catch-up, like we used to when we lived together. It reminds me how nice it is to be a good friend to someone as nice as Steph. How far away I've gotten from that this year, a year in which I've needed her more than ever.

I put the work in, but I'm not truly afraid she'll ghost me. Maybe that's why we're such good friends. Deep down, I trust that Steph won't leave.

I make a call. Cooper picks up on the second ring.

"You always answer unknown numbers?" I ask.

"I live on the edge," he replies.

In the background, an uneven symphony of metallic clangs. "Where are you?"

"I'm about to do a fencing class."

"Fencing, like the sport?"

"Yeah," he says. "My first one."

"Curious," I say. "I might need a debrief of that."

"I'd love to." He doesn't downplay his eagerness. I like this. "How's Thursday?"

* * * *

It takes two days to narrow down a list of eleven possible restaurants to just one. I choose Glasserie for its collective score in the categories of ambience (low-key romance), food (Mediterranean with an Israeli twist), location (a yet-to-be-gentrified strip of Greenpoint, a.k.a. desolate, a.k.a. hip), and X factor (the restaurant was a nineteenth-century glass factory—the prints throughout are from original glass fixture catalogs).

I'm planning on wearing a high-waisted floral-print skirt and matching halter-neck crop top. Messy pony, big hoop earrings, summer sandals: classic first-date look. But the night before, I change my mind. It feels wrong. It takes me all day to work out why: that outfit feels too young. I don't want to look like a girl. I want to look like a woman: someone quietly in control, not someone taking a million selfies and drinking a bit too much. And even though, objectively, I know all my clothes are entirely age appropriate and really, there's nothing wrong with the occasional tipsy self-portrait, the feeling sticks, morphing eventually into a general sense of unease. As I swipe a coat of clear gloss over my lips at 6:45 p.m. on Thursday evening, I'm trying to ignore the voice in my ear that keeps insisting that no one can be this nice, this good.

That everyone, like it or not, has scars.

* * * *

He's sitting at the bar when I arrive. Dark slim-cut jeans, short-sleeved collared shirt, very nice leather lace-ups. A Warby Parker model on his day off. His eyes widen when he sees me. "Wow, Lace. You look . . ." He is satisfyingly lost for words.

My grown-ass lady look translated into a black pencil skirt, silk cream tank, and nude heels. Minimal makeup, gold stud earrings, and a low sleek pony curling around my shoulder. It's not until this very moment that I realize I look like Vivian Chang.

". . . fantastic." He finishes a full fifteen seconds after he started. Our gaze tangles, catching, dangerously intense for so early in the evening. I think, *You want me.* I think, *I want you too.* My insides twist, but then someone wanders between us, and the tension breaks. He runs his hand through his hair and grins.

The restaurant is full and lively. Decor is that playful brand of rustic industrial modernism that is specifically "Brooklyn." Light thoughtfully appointed by amber fluorescents, quilted-glass bulbs, and twinkling candles in jars. Our table is by the window, set with a tiny vase of flowers and antique cutlery.

Apart from the trip to the grocery store, Cooper and I have never spent time together outside the loft. He's already seen me in my pajamas; he knows about my bucket list; he's even gotten me to open up to him. It's dating in reverse.

"So, fencing." I settle into my chair. "Gonna go pro?"

"I wish," Cooper says. "It's actually really complicated and cerebral. Like high-stakes chess."

"I haven't played chess in ages. My sister and I used to, when I was a kid. She always beat me."

"I play with the dads sometimes. What's your weakness?"

"I'm too aggressive. I don't protect my king. Yours?"

"The opposite. I take too long to make a move." He takes a sip of water. "We should play sometime."

I arch an eyebrow. "I thought we already were."

He laughs. We order some wine; check out the menu. Cooper is vegetarian. I had no idea, and yet, of course he is. We decide on Bulgarian feta and horseradish pickled beets, zucchini pastry with ricotta and spearmint, foraged mushrooms and snap peas. When the waiter leaves, I rest my chin on folded fingers. "So," I begin, "you're a vegetarian and a fencer—"

"Amateur fencer—"

"Amateur fencer." I cock my head at him. "What else don't I know about you?"

"Lots of things."

"Like what?"

He puts his water glass down somberly. "You're going to find this out eventually."

Oh shit. The motorcycle-accident-in-Thailand moment.

He sucks in a breath. "Back when I was in high school, and the beginning of college, I was a . . . Potterhead."

I wait for clarification.

"Harry Potter," he says.

"The movies?"

"Obviously they were books first, but yes."

Maybe I'm not getting this. "You were a Harry Potter fan."

"A pretty big fan."

"How big?"

"Well, it started with the books, then fan fiction, then posting on forums, then moderating forums, and then I created a fan website, Why So Sirius. We were one of the highest-ranked fan sites in the world. I met J. K. Rowling a few times." He says it like he met God.

"How many times have you read the series?"

Cooper sits back, puffing his cheeks out. "Fans tend to exaggerate, so I try not to, but I'd say, fifty? Fifty times?"

"Fifty times?" I almost choke. "The same books, fifty times?"

"I get it: you probably read them once."

I stare back at him blankly. "I never read Harry Potter."

Cooper's glass hits the table so fast it sloshes. "*What?*"

"Shhh. You're yelling. Look, I know the basics: Daniel Radcliffe's a wizard, and he's trying to stop everyone turning into a Muggle."

"That's not—" His eyes roll back in his head. "You must've seen the movies." Not a question.

"I think I saw one: *The Chamber of Fire?*"

Now he looks ready to pass out. "It's *Chamber of Secrets* and *Goblet of Fire*. Oh my God. You're a Potter virgin. I almost feel jealous of you. You get to experience it for the first time."

I laugh. I'm finding all this pretty fucking cute. "That's assuming I want to read it."

"Lacey," Cooper says. "I don't want to sound too dramatic, but I can't be with anyone who hasn't read Harry Potter."

Be with anyone. He wants to be with me. The concept is so exciting, and I want it so embarrassingly badly, it clams me up. I stare at the table.

He mistakes it as apprehension. "I mean . . . I didn't really mean that. I'm getting ahead of myself." He shakes his head and meets my gaze. "I like you. You know that, right?"

I feel fizzy, giggly. "I don't imagine you'd be here if you didn't."

"I'm an entrepreneur," he says, "which means I've been at many, many dinners I didn't want to be at. This is definitely not one of those." He reaches forward to take my hand, folding his fingers into mine. His thumb strokes the inside of my palm. The slow, languid movement turns every bone in my body molten. I might explode.

In a low, sexy voice he says, "I know I said I didn't want to get ahead of myself, but I really want to kiss you right now."

I'm strongly considering hurling the table out the window so I can suction my mouth onto his, when our wine arrives. He squeezes my hand and slowly pulls his away. I feel shimmery, light-headed. He lifts his glass. "To summer."

But I can't hear the word without silently adding *surgery*. The shimmer dulls. "May it never end."

44.

We linger over soft, sweet mouthfuls of *panna cotta* with rose-water syrup. When the check comes, Cooper reaches for his wallet.

"Let's split it," I say.

"Oh, no," he says. "My treat."

"Really," I say. "I'd be more comfortable if we did."

"Can I ask why?"

I shrug. "I don't see why you would automatically pay because you're a guy. I earn money too."

"Of course you do. But it feels good to be able to treat someone."

"Sure. But being paid for is its own kind of pressure."

"Meaning?"

I lean forward on my elbows. "Meaning that when I kiss you later, I want it to be because I want to. Not because I owe you."

We split the check.

* * * *

The night air is velvety warm and full of potential. Where will we kiss for the first time? On my love seat? By the river? In another bar? There is another bar around here, an intimate little speakeasy. It's romantic with dark, hidden corners—Ella Fitzgerald and prohibition cocktails. That works. I can't remember which street it's on, so I break the cardinal rule of a good date and pull out my phone.

Three messages and one missed call.

From Bee.

Sorry to do this, but are you around?

Babe, something's wrong.
Lacey, I need help. In pain. SOS.

My heart starts pounding. Something went wrong.
"Where to?" Cooper asks, his voice playful.
I look up in a panic. "Staten Island."

* * * *

Cooper drove, thank God, but it'll take us an hour to get to Bee's. My anxiety is building, clenching my chest like a giant fist. "She's not picking up. Why isn't she picking up?"

"Who's there with her?" Cooper asks.

"Her brother. I don't even know his name. I figured she wouldn't actually need me. I'm so irresponsible." I resist the urge to hit the window. "Can't you go any faster?"

"I'm going the speed limit."

The city is a streak of bad billboards and endless freeway. "Pass this car, he's going so fucking slow."

"Lacey, I'm going as fast I can." His voice is tight. He sounds annoyed, which makes me annoyed.

I try Bee again. Again it rings out. A flash flood of worst-case scenarios: pain, infection, death, disaster. Something on the stove catches fire, a room full of smoke, she can't move to get out. "Fuck," I mutter. "*Fuck*."

"Calm down."

"Don't fucking tell me to calm down." I regret it as soon as it leaves my mouth, and yet, I can't help it. He has no idea about any of this: how scared I am. For Bee. For me. This is my future.

In pain. SOS.

We drive the rest of the way in silence.

* * * *

"That's it!" A narrow single-story house with an overgrown front yard behind a chain-link fence. "Four Five Two Wentworth." I'm out of the car before he's even fully stopped, pounding on the front door. "Bee? Bee, it's Lacey!"

Nothing, even though there are lights on inside. The front windows are locked. So is the door.

"Bee!" I cry. "Bee, it's me!"

"Side gate." Cooper points. "I'll give you a boost."

I take off my heels and hitch up my skirt. Jumping over, I land amid soggy garbage bags and old bike parts. This neighborhood is so quiet; it's spooky. I unlock the gate, and we run down the side of the house to a concrete patio. A sliding glass door. I peer inside.

Bee is lying on an old brown sofa, eyes closed. Her chest and stomach are both bandaged, the two sites of her surgeries: her stomach where they removed tissue, and her breasts where they inserted it. Through the white gauze, yellow and brown stains. A bottle of pills lies scattered on the mottled beige carpet, amid empty take-out containers and plastic bags of trash.

"Bee!" I try the door. It jerks open. Inside smells like cigarettes and something sweet: flowers. A colorful bunch on the kitchen counter, absurdly cheerful in the messy kitchen. The ones I sent. What a stupid gesture. "Bee!" I lightly slap her face. "Bee, it's Lace. Wake up, babe, it's Lacey Whitman."

She comes to, eyes fluttering. Immediately, she winces, exhaling harshly. "Pills." She tries to swallow. "I knocked them . . ."

"Down? Or back? Bee, how many of these have you had?"

She shakes her head. "No—none."

Thank God she's not OD'ing. "Water, get a glass of water," I snap at Cooper. The bottle reads, *Two every four hours, as needed.* I lift the glass to her lips, help her swallow two pills. Every movement is causing her pain, spasming across her face. "What happened?" I ask, staring at her chest, the bandages. Two plastic drains the size of grenades are fixed to the left and right side of her body. The drains collect postsurgery fluid. I know from the forums it should be pale pink. Bee's is dark red. The insertion site is swollen with puss.

She speaks with her eyes closed, breathing shallowly. "Think I— have an infection—can't move—passed out from the pain."

I smooth the hair away from her eyes. "Where's your brother?"

"Had to work. Been gone—a few days."

"You've been here on your own?"

"Thought I could . . . take care of myself . . . but something . . . went wrong." She flutters her eyes open. "Need to . . . empty the drains."

I look around for my purse. "I'm going to call an ambulance."

"No," she says immediately. "Copay's . . . fucked. Please—Please don't. I can— We don't need—"

"Okay, no ambulance. What about your doctor?"

"In my . . . phone."

I find the number she was given for an on-call doctor when she was dispatched from the hospital. A nurse puts me through, but the number rings out and it transfers back to her. "He must've stepped away," she says. "He'll call back."

I explain the situation and convince the nurse to talk me through emptying the drains and changing the bandage. In a kitchen sink piled with dirty dishes, I wash my hands and take off my jewelry. Cooper hovers behind me, pale, unsure. "Can I do anything to help?"

This question has always annoyed me: routinely offered by men apparently incapable of starting to help of their own accord. I hate that he's here, seeing Bee in pain and me unhinged and panicky. I hate that our lovely night has ended here, and I hate that I'm having all these feelings in the first place. I make myself smile at him. "Help me with the drains."

Kneeling next to Bee, I take hold of the plastic drain and unplug the small stopper on top, like the nurse explained. Bee winces: it's definitely infected. With as little movement as I can, I empty the contents of the drain into a measuring cup to record the amount.

"Oh." Cooper covers his mouth. "Shit."

He disappears down the hall.

"Hope he . . . finds a bathroom," Bee says.

I'm embarrassed for him; it's bad, but it's not that bad. I pour out the second drain, and knowing this is a house with only one bathroom, head in his direction.

He's kneeling over a toilet, glasses in one hand. "Sorry," he pants. "I'm so sorry, Lacey."

I tip everything down the sink and rinse it away. Splash back from the tap splatters my tank top and a stupid part of my brain tells me I'll have to get it dry-cleaned. I need to change. Back in the living room, I refit the drains and crouch next to Bee. "Do you have hydrogen peroxide?"

She waves a hand, eyes still closed. "Bathroom . . . cabinet."

Cooper is wiping the toilet seat down. He looks how I feel, which is completely mortified. "Lacey, I'm so sorry. I'm not usually like this."

"It's fine," I say, even though it's not, exactly. I find some Neosporin and Walgreens antiseptic skin cleanser. "I'm going to change her dressing and make sure those painkillers kick in. When the doctor calls back, we can make an appointment for tomorrow." Fresh water, pillows, soothing music, a damp washcloth: there's a million tiny things I can do. None of them essential. All better than nothing. "We could probably knock over the kitchen tonight."

"You're going to stay?"

"You're going to leave?" I can't keep the surprise out of my voice; he hasn't helped at all.

"No," he says, quickly changing tack. "No, I was just— I'll help. What can I do?"

I know this isn't an easy situation, but c'mon, dude. Step up. "Nothing. You should go, it's an hour back to Brooklyn."

"No," he says. "No way. I'll start on dishes. Then I can . . . do a grocery run. Pick up supplies—"

"Cooper, it's fine," I say. "Seriously, you should go."

"But—"

"I want you to go. I'm asking you to leave. Please." Because if he stays a second longer, he'll see just how much I wanted this. Just how much I needed him. And just how much he disappointed me. "Seriously. It'll be easier if I'm on my own."

45.

August

stay with Bee for a week. She's in so much pain, she can barely move, even doped up. After a lot of wrangling and red tape, I set up a video call with a doctor, who diagnoses inflammation, not infection, related to dead fat cells because of a blood-supply problem. It may mean more surgeries. Bee breaks down when she hears this. I hold her hand as she cries. She's only embarrassed about this later, as we sit side by side, watching the upstairs-downstairs adventures of the Crawley family.

"Sorry," she says. "About all the"—she mimes crying—"boo-hoo, earlier."

I pause the show. "You don't have to apologize for that. You don't have to apologize for anything."

Her face is flushing pink. She looks atypically uncomfortable. "God, you don't even really know me . . ." She can't finish.

"I know that you need my help," I say. "I'm happy to be helpful. Honestly."

"You're a saint," she says. "You're a goddamn angel."

"I'm just doing what anyone would do." Or, remembering Cooper, ought to do.

At first, it's hard for me to see the brutal distortion of her splendid chest. Bee did not have nipple-saving surgery because she's going to a smaller cup size and losing too much skin (if she kept them, her nipples would've ended up somewhere under her armpits). Red, angry scars run horizontally across where her nipples used to be, and lower across her stomach. She's planning to have nipple reconstruction—tattooing and a skin graft—but she'll never get sensation back in the reconstructed area. It won't pass as "normal" ever again.

At times, she is lucid and funny. But more often, she is tired and sad, crying even though she can't say why. This doesn't make me uncomfortable. In a way, it reminds me of being with my sister and her mercurial mood swings. I make the connection as I shop for groceries in old denim shorts, with greasy hair and no makeup. Just like I used to shop for groceries back in Buntley, when no one gave a crap how I looked and the chances of running into anyone from Fashion Land were approximately zero.

The store is the exact opposite of the well-lit everything-organic shops in my neighborhood in Brooklyn. There are bins of knock-off DVDs next to the plastic-wrapped asparagus, the tips turning mushy. The shelves are narrow and crowded. The radio plays one song for every nine ads. The air smells vaguely like someone's lunch. My fingers graze the candy selection, selecting a Snickers. Mara and I used to shoplift chocolate bars, slipping them up our sleeves or in the waistband of our pants. It was the only time we ate name-brand chocolate. I wonder . . . I glance around "casually." Immediately, I lock eyes with the hardy-looking shopkeeper, who is watching me as if she knows exactly what's on my mind. I smile blithely, drop the bar in my basket, and ask where the Velveeta is.

She bags my groceries into plastic because I forgot to ask Bee about a tote. I have the feeling this is the kind of place where they'd find totes a little . . . precious. We make stilted small talk, but the second I mention Bee's name, her face lights up. How is she, how was the surgery, who am I, how do I know Bee?

"I'm Lacey," I say. "I met her through a cancer-support group."

The shopkeeper's face softens. Her eyes are a lovely periwinkle blue. "Beatrice is a good girl, a real good girl. She feeds my cats when I go visit my son."

When I try to hand over my credit card, she waves it away.

"No, no, no. You tell her Irene said to get well soon. We're all thinking of her. We're all sending our love."

I walk home along sidewalks that are cracked, past houses with sparse flower beds and sun-faded American flags in the window. Some people would see this and think "poor." But to me, it looks like a community, the kind of place where you get your groceries for free when you've been in the hospital. Where it's in your best interest to get along with everyone because everyone knows your business and you're better off being friends than enemies.

This was not an insight my father took to heart. His businesses—and his family—failed because he was a flake. When I was a kid I believed him when he said he'd be home for dinner, just like all his business partners believed him when he said a check was in the mail: he was too magnetic, too sincere to be a phony. I think he really thought he could make his promises happen, through spontaneous good fortune or the way the universe seems to work things out for a kid. There's only so many times you wait for hours after soccer practice for a lift home before you just stop asking. At about the same time, he and I realized that everything coming out of his mouth was untrue. He gave up on me and Mara, and we gave up on him. And every time he made less effort to even pretend to parent us, Mara's resentment for being the one left in charge grew.

I was in high school. The idea of trend forecasting in New York City felt like the most perfect sort of future one could imagine. New York: a city framed through television shows and breathless anecdotes of star spotting and skyscrapers. Trend forecasting: predicting the future, understanding how it works. And all approximately one thousand miles away from my disappointing hometown; a sister simmering with bitter rage, a father who'd failed us both and never even apologized for it. But in a way, that was the fuel I needed to rocket myself out of there, to land my ass where I wanted it to be. As I round the corner to Bee's house, my feet slapping the hot concrete in a pair of old flip-flops, I feel a sudden gush of pride at how far I've come. And yet, how close to home I am here, with my friend who needs me.

"Did you get my Velveeta?" is the first thing Bee calls when I walk through the door.

I laugh and fish out a packet of individually wrapped neon-orange slices. "You know it's not even cheese. It's *pasteurized prepared cheese product.*"

"Who cares?" Bee says. "It's delicious." She sings, perfectly in tune, *"Make it with Velveeta, it cooks better."*

"You really need to cut an album."

"Right. *Commercials from the Eighties*: my big break."

"I'd buy that." I hand her a slice, making a show of wrinkling my nose.

"You want one," she says, eyeing me.

"I don't."

"You want that sweet cheese product in your mouth, girl. Stop fighting it." She starts chanting. "Eat the cheese. Eat the cheese. Eat the—"

"All right, fine! I'll eat the cheese." I plop down on the carpet and peel the sticky plastic away from a slice. It's salty and smooth and reminds me of going to friends' houses after school, where they had big decadent fridges full of junk food and five kinds of pop. My mouth is watering. "Okay, it's pretty good."

We giggle. For a moment, I wonder if I'm pulling my mirroring trick with Bee: turning chameleon in order to fit in and make her comfortable. No. I'm not. I can be myself around Bee. The self that's a little different from the Lacey who Steph and Vivian know. The Lacey who's a tad less concerned with maintaining the persona I've made for myself in this city.

I don't need to be anybody but myself around Bee.

* * * *

Cooper sends a gift basket of fruit, a huge delivery that barely fits in Bee's small kitchen. I text him a sincere thank-you. He calls. I screen. I still feel confused about what happened. Who acted worse: me, him, or both of us? I'm so inexperienced when it comes to a real relationship. I know it's not all hot sex and great dinner dates, but I have so little practical experience of navigating romantic disappointment and human vulnerability.

I cook and I clean. I do laundry, monitor Bee's meds, empty her drains. I buy a detachable showerhead so I can wash her hair. We watch all of *Downton Abbey* and a lot of very bad reality television. Neighbors drop by; one with a homemade casserole, another with a bag of apples and tomatoes from the garden. They are chatty and comfortable around Bee, even as she's swaddled in bandages. I say I'm from Illinois. Not Williamsburg. Certainly not that I work at Hoffman House.

I miss a showcase for new Scandinavian designers and the opening of a Fashion Week photography exhibit that everyone is talking about. "Sorry," I say to Patricia, when I run into her in the kitchen one morning. "I had something I couldn't get out of."

"Your loss, darling," she says, extracting a bottle of pomegranate juice from the fridge. "But I'd be lying if I said it wasn't fabulous."

It doesn't bother me as much as I expect. The brief expansion of my life into the fifth borough has given me perspective. Plus, I get to enjoy my Melanie-Griffith-in-*Working-Girl* "Let the River Run" moment every morning on the Staten Island Ferry into Manhattan. One morning as we're about to dock, I get a call from the New York Cancer Care Center to schedule some presurgery appointments for my mastectomy. Which is, impossibly, in a few weeks' time. The days are falling away. I can't keep up.

At the end of the week, Bee's brother, Frankie, returns. He is quiet, unsure how to behave around me and unable to grasp the severity of his sister's condition. Not because he doesn't care. Because he is exhausted. I was expecting someone charismatic and careless, blowing back in with a crappy present and overblown on-the-road stories designed to hide the fact he just fucking left. It's only as I head back to Williamsburg the next day that I realize I was expecting my father.

46.

Cooper and I arrange to meet by the East River on Sunday afternoon. It's sunny in the morning, but rain clouds gather over the city as the day wears on. You can smell the storm that's coming.

After my week with Bee, I'm not sure what I'll feel when I see him. Cooper seems a part of my life that's a little foreign to me right now. But when he appears, in a faded red hoodie and Converse sneakers, my heart contracts. We hug hello. It's a real hug: he holds me, and I let him.

"It's going to rain," he says.

"Let's walk until it does," I say. "We can always run for cover."

Cold sweeps along the waterfront, whipping my hair across my cheeks.

"I want to say again how sorry I am," he says. "I handled it all so badly. I should've stayed."

"Thanks for saying that," I say. "But it was my fault too. I shouldn't have pushed you away so quickly. I should have let you help."

It feels good to be honest and direct. We're realigning so quickly. As always, I feel safe with Cooper. There's a solidity to him that has nothing to do with size. We fall in step. The cool air feels fresh against my skin, alive in a way the sluggish summer heat is not.

He asks how Bee is doing, and I give him a rundown of our week together.

"She was really lucky you could be there," he says.

"I know. It shouldn't be this hard to recover. But it is. I'm not really prepared for it." I pull my cardigan around myself, unable to look at him. "I haven't told my boss yet. Every time I think about it my throat seizes up."

"You have to get time off work," Cooper says. "You have to talk to your boss. She'll understand. What about your friends?"

"Bee won't be well enough, Vivian's consumed with the app, Steph's got her thesis. Mara has Storm, and hates the whole idea on principle."

"But haven't you been planning this with them?" Cooper asks. "Surely your recovery is a priority."

"We haven't . . . locked anything in. I haven't . . . I just find it hard to . . ."

I replay something Bee said to me, late one night just before I went to bed. I'd said something about not wanting to bother Mara with playing nurse for me and that I didn't feel comfortable asking my friends to step up, really step up. She looked at me. Curious, and a little sad. "If you think asking for help makes you weak," she'd said, "am I weak to you?"

"No," I'd said, "of course not." But the point hung in the air like lead.

Why can't I get past this? Why can't I just change the way my mind works?

"Well, I'd be happy to help," Cooper says. "If you need an extra pair of hands. I'm obviously not Doogie Howser, MD," he adds, "but I'll be there for you. If you want."

I replay the words in slow disbelief, as if hearing them too quickly will make them pop like a balloon. *I'd be happy to help.* As if it was a given. *I'll be there for you.* The backs of our hands brush and then with no effort, we are holding hands. We are holding hands like a couple.

"When?" he asks.

I'm breathless. "End of this month."

"Oh." Cooper stops walking. His forehead twists into uncertainty. Our fingers unthread. "I have a trip coming up. Back to Germany. I'm actually going for a job there."

"What?"

"Chief technology officer for a VR company in the social-good space. Way out of my league. It's crazy I'm even being considered—" He catches sight of my face. "I'm sorry. I didn't know how to tell you."

My chest feels numb. "You're moving to Germany?"

"Only if I get this job, which is a long shot. Chances are I'm staying right here."

"But maybe not."

Cooper looks pained. "No. Maybe not. I applied for this thing months ago. Before you and I . . ."

I nod. I can't look at him. I stare at the water, where the wind is making rough little whitecaps.

"Lace." He runs both hands through his hair. "I like you, you know that. But talking about my helping you after a mastectomy and we haven't even"—an uncomfortable laugh—"kissed. It feels like it's moving so fast. Like I'm already your boyfriend."

But you're not. And you don't want to be. A hot tear spills down my cheek. I turn away so he can't see.

Behind me, Cooper makes a strangled noise. "I don't want you to think I don't care. That I won't be there. If I can be, I will, I promise."

"Right," I say, "you'll be the one vomiting in the bathroom at the first sight of anything unsexy."

He's silent. Raindrops spatter the concrete like bullets. Something's wrong with me. Everyone I care about leaves. No one sticks around. A safety net I imagined was underneath me has revealed itself to be nothing more than a trick of the light. I start walking away.

"Lacey!" He calls after me. But he does not follow me. He lets me leave.

I hold myself in until I get to my apartment. Then I fall apart. I cry because I am scared and disappointed and alone, and so is Bee, and so are so many women in this fucked-up world. I cry because I messed this up and it's my neck on the line.

I cry because I don't want to lose my breasts.

I can't do it. I know I should, but I can't.

I call the New York Cancer Care Center, and I cancel my surgery.

47.

In lieu of the surgery, I book a screening at NY3C, the alternate path for a high-risk cancer patient. I am increasingly distraught as the date arrives, certain something will be found, a punishment for my cowardice. Nothing. I'm perfectly healthy, which is its own complicated diagnosis. If I'm in such good health, why consider a life-changing procedure? A hard, angry part of me is almost disappointed. My worst self wants to get sick, just so everyone can feel really fucking bad about not coming through for me.

I go through the motions with Clean Clothes, giving the lion's share of the work to Suzy-from-Texas, our other outfit curator. Vivian's in San Francisco for a conference and investor meetings; we haven't talked face-to-face in weeks. The next time Steph and I have one of our cheap-and-cheerful dinners, I tell her about Cooper but play down how much it crushed me. "Probably for the best" and "easy come, easy go" are both phrases that come out of my mouth. When Steph tries to dig deeper, I change the topic.

I throw myself into work, keeping my sales numbers high even through the dog days of summer. I do what I should've been doing this whole time: refocus on the fashion editor position, bombarding Eloise with textbook-perfect reports, being sure to CC Patricia. My one on fashion influencers in the Middle East is so good, I'm asked to present it in-house. It goes well, and Patricia decides to put it on the site, for paying customers.

"You look surprised," Patricia says.

"Well, yeah," I manage. "The standards for editorial are as high as Miley Cyrus on any given day."

Patricia chuckles. I trust she knows I'm actually quite fond of the wily Ms. Miley. My boss has a laser-sharp ability to know when to laugh at a joke and when to hook the dreaded eyebrow of disapproval. It's part of what makes her such a successful member of the upper echelon: Patricia has taste, in people, as well as in things.

* * * *

One day later, Eloise's assistant sends me a meeting invite. Just me and Eloise, in her office. It has to be about the job. One step closer. I dress as carefully as one defuses a bomb. At the last second, I add the gold Miu Miu headband that Eloise gifted me when I first started. Full circle.

I haven't been in her office since I was an intern. As I take a seat opposite her, I try not to stare at the gorgeous black-and-white photographs of Paris street scenes, the 1920s silk nightgown hanging on a satin coat hanger, the tall bunch of white roses. Every detail, perfect.

Behind her desk, her stomach blooms like an overripe heirloom underneath a tight white bodysuit. She looks fantastic. Naturally, Eloise understands all the implicit rules of modern pregnancy: be beautiful, not sexy. Talk of cravings is okay; talk of placenta and shitting yourself on the delivery table is not. Love every single second of it and never, ever complain. She caresses her belly gently as she gazes at me from behind her desk. "Patricia thinks you're the right fit for my job."

Patricia has talked to Eloise about me. I try to make my rehearsed words sound natural and genuine. "I am so excited about this opportunity and I really feel that—"

She cuts me off with a little wave of her hand. "I don't agree. I don't think you're a fit."

I'm thrown. I wait for clarification or an amendment. Nothing. Unease seeps into my stomach. "Well, I've . . . I've been here for three years."

"I know. I checked your file. Patricia does like an underdog." Her gaze is curious. Cold. "I just had no idea how much that would blind her."

I'm taking small, shallow breaths. "What?"

"I'm going to be frank. You don't have the pedigree, taste, or composure to be a fashion editor at Hoffman House. Your taste is colorful but parochial. You've shown no real commitment to this place." She taps a piece of paper on her desk: my résumé. "You never did an MBA.

You've never even attended a conference or a course outside the city. For you, fashion is a foreign language. You speak it conversationally. But you'll never be a native like me and the members of my team."

My jaw works, opening and shutting. My vision swims. I can't conjure a response.

"I really believe in this place," she continues, her gaze fixed on me. "I respect it, as much as I respect my own reputation. And I'm telling you: you will buckle. You probably think I'm being mean, but honestly, Lucy, I'm doing you a favor. You don't have what it takes."

She called me Lucy. She doesn't even know my name. I make myself respond. "I . . . I . . ."

"Yes? What?"

"I'm right for this job. I believe I'm qualified."

She shrugs simply. "I don't. I know it's ultimately Patricia's call, but when we talk, I'll have to be honest. The members of my team know how I feel."

I stare at her. Frozen.

She looks pointedly at the door, then back at me. This is over.

With limbs that feel waterlogged and a rapidly pin-holing vision, I make it back to my cubicle. I'm panting. My hands leave sweat marks on my desk. I rip the headband off so fast I pull strands of hair from my head. I walk to the nearest window and in one easy motion, toss the headband onto the street below. It arcs gracefully, like a glittering, falling star.

48.

It's a hot, sunny afternoon when I visit Bee. We lay out on the back patio on old towels to sunbathe. Topless. Number one on my bucket list. When I scribbled it on Steph's whiteboard back in January, I assumed this would take place on a remote beach boasting sand as white as the GOP and drinks with tiny umbrellas in them. A concrete patio in Staten Island was not what I had in mind.

But it's better.

Bee's breasts are healing, slowly. She has more freedom of movement, able to reach for a coffee cup without wincing, but she's scheduled for more surgeries later this year.

"All good," she says. "Weiner women are tough as balls. Besides, I'm psyched for all those sponge baths." She pretends to address someone between her legs. "Higher. *Higher.* Don't hold out on me, Doc: Little Bee needs some loving."

I laugh. "I'm just glad you're okay." We sip cold lemonade with just a tiny splash of whiskey (Bee's still healing) and I tell her about what happened at work, with Eloise.

"What a fucking bitch," Bee says. "I'd slap her if I didn't have a pair of butchered tits. So, what, no promotion?"

I shrug. "I've decided I'm still going for it." What I don't know is how much sway Eloise has with Patricia: if her disapproval cuts me out, period. Work has been horrible. The fashion team is nice enough to my face, but I have no idea how they really feel. It's draining and depressing: feeling like I'm constantly having to prove myself around them all. "Fuck her. Fuck Eloise."

"Right on, sister. Stick it to the wo-man." Bee lowers her sunglasses and looks at me. "So you know what that means."

"What?"

"You have to come clean with Vivian. About everything."

I cringe. "I can tell Viv about the job. But I can't tell her about Elan."

"Why not?"

"Are you kidding me? She'd lose her mind. I lied to her."

Bee gives me a funny look. "Who taught you to do that?"

"Do what?"

"*Lie.* You have a little problem with lying, Whitman." She ticks off her fingers. "You didn't tell Steph about Elan until she caught you; you haven't told your boss about the surgery or that you were dating a client; you haven't told Vivian about this job you're going for while still working for her, or that you were fucking the sole member of your board of directors. Did someone in your family lie a lot? Is that where this comes from?"

I close my eyes. The sun turns the back of my eyelids red. Bee's not like Steph—already with an opinion. She's waiting for my answer.

It's not as if I lie to make myself more powerful, like a politician or a crook. It's more a way to stay afloat: as an employee, or a friend, or a girlfriend, or even a cancer patient. And I guess, thinking about it, that's the way my father lied too. It was almost as if he lied because he didn't want to let us down or lose us. Fat lot of good it did him.

I squint up at the sky, at the vague thumbprint of the moon, milky-white on the horizon, and murmur. "It's just easier than telling the truth."

Bee purses her lips at me and shakes her head. "That's where you're wrong, chicken. It's really not."

* * * *

I meet Vivian in a café in South Williamsburg, just before it's about to close. Blank-faced, she listens to me bumble through an apology-strewn explanation of my job prospect. "I was okay compromising a junior sales gig, but I can't compromise the fashion editor position. I can't work a sixty-hour week for Hoffman House and then do the same for Clean Clothes. And that's what you need."

"But you told me you weren't going for that job," Vivian says. "You told me you were committed to the app."

I can't meet her laser-beam eyes. "I'd started to think the fashion editor position was out of reach. That's why I got involved with Clean Clothes."

"But it's in reach now." Her voice is as hard as a fact.

"Yes," I whisper. "I'm sorry. I wasn't . . . entirely truthful about that. I didn't want to let you down. I need options, Viv. I don't have a safety net."

Vivian's voice is flat. "It just looks so shit: a member of the founding team quitting, so soon after the lead developer left. So much of all this is perception."

I shift in my too-hard chair. "But we're not really . . . progressing, are we? Even with Tom's money, we're not growing like we should be, right?" Because Elan Behzadi fucked us both over.

Vivian stares out the window, her stony expression reflected in the glass. If she was any tougher, she'd rust. "The company is facing some challenges, none of which are entirely unprecedented."

"Viv," I say. "It's me. You can be honest with me."

She laughs, once, I assume at the irony of my plea. Her eyes swing to mine. "Did something happen with you and Elan?"

"What?" I cough and clear my throat. "What do you mean?"

"You were so keen for him to be involved, even though it diluted your equity."

I should tell her the truth. It's the right moment; she's already upset with me. But Bee is wrong—I can't. I can't handle the disappointment Viv would feel: in me for being unprofessional and a liar, and in the future of the company, doomed over a lover's spat. I can't bear the burden of any more disappointment. Distressingly, and in a way that feels almost beyond my control, I feel myself channeling my father. His bravado. His deception. "Babe, nothing happened with Behzadi," I say. "Maybe, there was a time when I wanted it to. But nothing did."

She stays staring at me, neither accepting nor denying this. After an excruciatingly long moment, she looks back out the window. "Then I just have one favor to ask."

"Anything."

"I need you to come to a wedding with me."

* * * *

Tom Bacon invited Vivian and me to his wedding out in the Hamptons after coming on board as lead investor. Vivian never gave me my invite, claiming to have forgotten in the madness of getting the seed round closed. She wants us to go together, as the team we're not. The plan is to provide a united front for the three seconds we'll get with Tom, with a secondary aim of networking with influencers who might prove more useful than Elan. I don't want to go, but I owe it to Viv.

The invitation came on a bed of silk in a vintage wooden cigar box.

> *Tom Bacon and Peter Lennox request the honor*
> *of your and your guest's attendance at the Bacon family*
> *estate in East Hampton, New York.*

I trace the lettering: real gold leaf. "I can't believe we both got a plus one."

"I can," Vivian says. "They're rich, gay, and interracial. Half of New York will be at this wedding."

I bet that half includes Elan. The prospect fills me with prickling, hungry dread. He's sent me a few text messages, even an unchecked voice mail, wanting me to call. I haven't responded. I just don't have the bandwidth for it.

At my weekly dinner date with Steph (a buzzy new Ethiopian restaurant in Clinton Hill), I beg her to come as my date. She refuses, citing her thesis and some snark about gay weddings being a bourgeois construct.

But when I come by the loft the following weekend, she accepts. Enthusiastically.

"I thought you were busy with your thesis," I say. "You said all of September was completely out of the question."

"It's only a weekend."

"But aren't gay weddings 'bourgeois constructs steeped in middle-class morality and neo-capitalistic values'?"

She laughs as if I'm not quoting her exact words back to her. "I heard Betty Who is playing. She's awesome."

"How did you hear that?"

A micro pause. "Vivian told me."

"Oh." So they're still in regular contact. Whatever. I lay back on her bed, listening for door creaks or water running: anything to indicate there's someone else home. But the loft is silent. "Okay. Well, I'm happy you're coming. Someone to endure this with."

Steph clucks. "Don't be such a spoilsport. It's going to be the fanciest wedding you or I have ever or will ever attend. Can you blag me some nice flats from one of your designer mates?"

Steph has never asked for a designer hookup in her life. I elbow up to frown at her. "Why the sudden interest in fashion, Stephanie?"

"Or don't," she says, "I can always rock some flip-flops."

I gasp in faux horror. "No! God, no. What are you going to wear?"

"T-shirt and jeans? But like, a really nice T-shirt. Minimal stains."

We both laugh. I jump to my feet. "Stand aside, Steph. Your personal stylist is in the building."

I spend the next hour doing a major cleanout of her closet. It's fun and we laugh a lot and we don't talk about Cooper. Which feels very deliberate. I assume Steph would tell me if he moved out, but maybe she's trying to be less up in my business, and is waiting for me to ask. When she's in the bathroom, I sneak a peek in Coop's room. Blue walls and books. He still lives here. I tiptoe in, feeling illicit. It's such a calm, interesting space. I want to open every drawer, flip through every notebook, try on every shirt. The harmonica is still on his desk. I put my mouth on it, where his mouth would have been, and blow gently. The sound is much louder than I expected: high and thin, five notes in one. I put it down quickly, my heart jumping. I want him to find me in here. For both of us to bumble through a conversation to find a way to say, "I'm sorry. Can we try again?"

The toilet flushes, and I slip out, closing the door behind me. As I put my final touches on Steph's outfit, I can't help but wish I was adjusting the bow tie of a Harry Potter–loving nerd with surfer pecs. I throw my arm around her shoulder and squeeze. "You look amazing."

Steph squeals, preening. "I love it! Oh, we're going to have so much fun."

I smile back, hopeful. Maybe she's right. Maybe we will actually have fun.

Of course, I had no idea we'd have nothing of the sort.

49.

September

The weekend before the wedding, I drive up to Mara's. She makes iced tea and tofu burgers with the taste and texture of old carpet. We sit on the back patio in wide-brimmed hats and sunglasses, watching Storm bolt around the backyard. The house is a maelstrom of toys and princess costumes and strewn DVDs.

"You have no idea how often I've had to watch *Moana*," Mara says. "Do you want to know how far *I'll* go? Back in time so I can murder everyone who made that fucking movie."

Watching my niece do just about anything these days is enough to make me spontaneously ovulate. "What a nightmare."

"You have no idea," Mara says again.

"Look, Mommy!" Storm runs up with a stick. "Look! It's a stick!"

"That's great, baby," Mara calls back. "Stay where I can see you, please." She pours herself some more iced tea. Instead of drinking it, she turns the cup in a restless circle. "Have you rescheduled the surgery?"

"No." I let out a heavy sigh. "Maybe you were right. Maybe I am too young to make a decision like this. I've royally fucked up a lot of other things this year."

My sister half shrugs without looking at me. As if unconvinced.

I stare at her. "You still think I shouldn't do it, right?"

She purses her lips, avoiding my gaze. "I don't know. I—I don't know."

My sister never, ever changes her mind about anything. She still maintains Hanson is a good band because she believed that when she was nine.

This is different. I wait.

She picks up an orange and peels the skin with her fingers. It takes her a long time to speak. "There was a really long period when I thought I'd never get over Mom dying. I'd live with it, I'd get used to it, but I'd never truly move past it. It was in me, like . . . well, like a cancer. But lately I've started thinking that being a mom is my way to get past it. To heal myself. Being a mom makes me understand Mom, and it makes me feel closer to her, even though she's gone." The orange is unpeeled. She slices it in half with a paring knife, perfuming the air with a spray of citrus. "Storm is my life. I don't want to be one of those annoying parents who says, 'You'll understand when you have kids,' but you will understand if you have kids, Lace."

I smile a small smile.

She cuts the orange into quarters. "And maybe I owe it to her. To Mom. To find out. If I . . . if Storm . . ." Her jaw tightens.

She's considering it. I can't believe it . . . but then again, I can.

Finally, Mara looks at me. Her face is raw with fear. "I don't know what I'd do if I had it, and I gave it to her. To my daughter. I just don't know how I'd live with that."

I scoot next to her and put my arm around her shoulder. "But that wouldn't be your fault, Mar. That's just genetics."

My sister shakes her head, crying quietly. Her voice is shredded. "What if my daughter dies of the same thing my mom died of? What if I *made* it happen?"

My eyes are wet, my throat tight. I want to say, *That won't happen.* I want to say, *You're both safe.* But I can't say that. "When you get tested," I say, "then you'll know. We'll both know, and then we can decide what to do next."

Mara covers her face with her hands. "I can't lose you, Lace. I can't. I can't do it again."

"You won't. I'm here, Mar. I'm right here." I rock her gently, smoothing her hair, kissing her forehead. I'm so grateful that she lets me. "I love you, Mar. I'll always be here."

I hold my sister tightly. I never want to let her go.

50.

After a week of torrential rain, Tom and Peter's wedding day dawns cloudless and exactly seventy-two degrees. I'm not above believing Tom has personally arranged for this to happen. Patricia is going to be there, and Eloise, who is visibly annoyed at the news Buntley's own Lacey Whitman made the exclusive guest list. "Tom's the lead investor in Clean Clothes," I reply when she quizzes how I know the couple.

"Oh, yes," she says. "Your *other* job."

"Actually, I'm quitting the app. So I'll be all ready to join the fashion team," I add. "When Patricia makes her decision."

Eloise turns a lovely shade of pale mint green.

Myself, Steph, Vivian, and Vivian's date, Brian, are all driving up together. Brian Wong is an engineer, an old B-school friend who Vivian occasionally solicits for business advice and sex. He shares Vivian's proclivity for efficiency. "I've mapped the route using Google Maps," he says, "because they do the best job comparing their predictions against actual time in traffic in order to fine-tune their algorithms and data sources. If we stop for gas once and keep bathroom breaks to under three-point-five minutes per person in a multistall facility, we should arrive between five thirty and five thirty-three."

"We should stop for snacks," Steph pipes up from the back seat. "I need to eat every two hours."

"You have hypoglycemia?" Brian looks worried, presumably not at her health, just at the addition of another variable.

"No," Steph says. "I just get a bit peckish."

Brian holds up a ziplock bag. "Fruit, candy, bottled water, and gluten-free vegan sandwiches."

Vivian shoots him a look of approval—her version of lust—and overtakes the car in front of us.

"Gross," I mutter to Steph. "At least you're still on Team Spinster."

Steph chokes on the mouthful of Skittles she's just inhaled, coughing. "Sorry," she wheezes. "Wrong pipe." Her cheeks are flushed.

Odd.

* * * *

A suited valet commandeers our Zipcar, directing us to follow a stream of cocktail-attired guests along a rose-petal-strewn path around the back of the estate. I loved my dress when I rented it, but now it feels gaudy; wrong. Fitted black top with a crew neck, strappy back, and full high-low gold skirt that scoops above my knee and falls mid-calf in the back ($415 retail, but thanks to Rent the Runway and an insider's promo code, mine for the weekend for $45). I don't like how my breasts look in it, and I can't put my finger on why: Is the dress too tight? Are they too small? I keep rearranging them with the frustrated air of a harried parent. Vivian looks stunning in a formfitting off-the-shoulder black gown. It shows off her slim frame and looks classy as heck. The look I pulled together for Steph is "lady summer tux": black cigarette pants, fitted white blouse, bright red lipstick. I managed to score her some Stella McCartney red flats, albeit a loan. All in all, very cute and queer.

"Let's take a pic before we get drunk and ruin our makeup." I pull the girls in. We grin at the camera, the textbook definition of Best Friends Forever. *Click*, and then the phone dies. "Shit."

Vivian trains perfectly lined eyes on me. No smile now. "Is Elan coming?"

I take a punch of adrenaline. "No idea." Slicking my lips with gloss, I add, "I assume he was invited."

"I bloody hope not," Steph mutters.

Vivian twists to her. "Why do you care?"

Steph blinks. "Because he's let you both down. Hasn't he?"

Brian taps his smartwatch. "It's five thirty-five. If we want to have one cocktail before the ceremony, consumed at a pace of one sip per—"

"Got it," I say, gesturing at the girls. "*Vamos, chicos.*"

"*Chicos* means boys," Vivian says coolly. She is low-key pissed. Because I'm leaving Clean Clothes? Or because . . . she knows. I've been sidestepping the prospect of seeing Elan, but now that we're here I can't control a mounting feeling of . . . what? Apprehension? Excitement? The idea that I actually want to see him disgusts me. I can still recall the dank stone smell of the dungeon.

Steph loops her arm through mine, jumpy. "There's a *bubble lounge.* I don't even know what that is, but I need to be there!"

We join the guests wending through neat flower beds of pink and red roses to the preceremony party in the "backyard." Which is unlike any backyard I've ever been in. Hundreds of guests mill on a manicured lawn that has an uninterrupted view of the Atlantic, a majestic sweep of glinting blue-green. Inside the huge white tent on the far right of the lawn, a giant black-and-white photograph of the grooms hangs above piles of professionally wrapped gifts. A quartet of musicians in white tuxedos play classical music by the koi pond in front of the house. An empty band stage with a full lighting rig and six-foot speakers is at the far side of the lawn. Gorgeous gay waiters circulate with small, elaborate finger food and crystal glasses of pale champagne. Steph and I pluck one, and take a generous sip.

"Ooh," Steph says. "That's good champagne."

"How do you know what good champagne tastes like? We only ever drink prosecco."

"This is so beautiful," Steph gushes. "Look, there's a petting zoo! Amazing! I bet the meal is going to be ten bloody courses."

"I remember a time not so long ago when you were distinctly against the mainstreaming of gay weddings," I say. "Something about LGBTQ people not needing legitimacy from the straight world."

"No, no." Steph's eyes rove the chichi crowd. "This is *fantastic.*"

"Or an obtuse underlining of our status as sad singletons."

Steph tugs me forward. "Let's mingle."

"With who?"

We only get ten feet into the crowd before discovering the answer to this question.

In a waiter's outfit, offering drinks to a group of old white dudes who are attempting to up their stock by awkwardly flirting with the only Cool Young Person in their social orbit, is Luna.

Steph's tongue unfurls in front of her like a roll of carpet.

"You knew," I say. "You knew she'd be here."

"We've been texting," she says. "Just a little. I didn't want to tell you because I wanted to give you space to reach out to her on your own. But you didn't, so . . ."

"So you figured you'd date my . . . whatever . . . without telling me?"

"You haven't spoken to her since the sex party," Steph says. "You're not still interested, are you? Because I *really* like her."

What can I say? I have no right to be annoyed. "No, go have fun. I'll be here, crying into a shrimp cocktail."

"There's loads of cute people here," Steph says, aggressively side-eyeing Luna.

"Who are all with their plus-ones. The point of bringing you was so we could be washed-up old maids together. Society's castoffs, cautionary tales."

"That doesn't sound very appealing," Steph says. "Shhh, here she comes."

Luna slides in front of us with her tray of champagne. "Hello, ladies."

"Hi," I sigh.

Steph giggles and turns the color of a beet.

"Fancy, huh?" Luna leans close, ice-blue eyes on Steph. "We're serving a 1990 Möet and Chandon Dom Pérignon. Each glass costs, like, seventy dollars."

"I knew it was good champagne!" Steph explodes. "It tastes like fireworks!"

Luna smiles at Steph. Steph smiles at Luna. How best to destroy this unhinged lesbian lovefest? Recount Dr. Ho's description of a mastectomy at the open mike?

"I'm going to charge my phone," I tell two people who couldn't care less, and make my way inside.

* * * *

The enormous kitchen is a bright bustle of waiters restocking trays and a couple of well-dressed women giving a steady string of orders into headsets. I scoot around them, into an empty formal sitting room with a bank of windows overlooking the party. I plug my phone in, feeling a flutter of relief as it starts charging. My lifeline to the outside world, should I need it.

Beyond the windows, the crowd mingles. Peter is black, and so are many of the guests: some from obvious wealth, others more like me: downing champagne in rented gowns, taking two canapés at a time, gawking at the view. Even though the grass is always greener and I would love to have as much green as the Bacons, there's no denying you enjoy the trappings of wealth more when you don't have it.

Or maybe that's the kind of thinking Eloise was talking about. My very own Regina George is standing by the koi pond, shading herself with a delicate paper parasol. She is looking extraordinarily pregnant in a long white dress that clings to her giant tits and belly and butt. I suppose because there's no bride, she chose to ignore the no-white-dress rule. Color me unsurprised. Her Aryan race husband looks like he's been carved out of a loaf of white bread with the personality to match. I dislike him on principle, but shamefully, I'm a little jealous. Of course Eloise gets the husband and the baby and the dream job she's willing to walk away from. I'd be a better mother than her and I cook most of my meals in the microwave. They're standing in a group that includes a very famous Broadway actor, the editor in chief of *Architectural Digest*, and Patricia. Our boss just got back from the Amalfi Coast. She's looking relaxed and refreshed in a floor-sweeping silk-georgette gown swirled with painterly summer florals. Feminine, flattering, and fashion-forward. I should've worn something less . . . something more like that.

Elan isn't here. I know I should feel relieved by this, but part of me feels disappointed. Even though I know seeing him will hurt me, I want to. I don't even know why. I'm mulling this over, alone in the enormous empty sitting room, waiting for my phone to juice up, when I spot a tall young man in a cream linen suit. Dark blond hair. Glasses.

Noam Cooper.

Cooper is *here*.

Why the fuck didn't Steph tell me that Cooper was going to be *here*? I might not have come if she . . .

Oh. That's why.

He's shaking the hands of a cute gay couple, introducing his date, a gorgeous blond thing in a colorful maxi that looks like butterfly wings. Unpolished nails, no makeup. Oh, to be so beautiful that embellishments would actually *take away from it*. Cooper makes a joke and the two men laugh. Butterfly Dress smiles, like she doesn't find it that funny or she just doesn't get it. A small curl of satisfaction: looks like another humorless hookup for Noam Cooper. But my pleasure is short-lived. As the four of them chat in the afternoon light that's spilling like honey, I want to be the one Cooper is touching on the arm, the one sitting next to him during the ceremony. But what used to be simple between us is now complex, and we don't even have a relationship to explain that. Some people just don't fit together. Or perhaps, some people are just no good at relationships. At being loved and loving someone else. The skill of a trend forecaster lies in recognizing pattern. The common thread between the failures of Cooper and Elan and even Luna, is me. I'm not just corrupted by my mother's DNA.

I can no longer pretend that my fuckup father's DNA isn't poisoning me too.

51.

Pick a seat, not a side. We're all family once the knot is tied.

The light is twenty-four karat. Magic hour. Guests take their seats on the folding chairs facing an archway of white roses and the gloriously endless Atlantic. I linger, waiting for Cooper to sit without seeing me. Steph and I end up toward the back and somehow with a maddeningly perfect view of the boy and the way his arm rests on his date's bony shoulders. I try to focus on the celebrant, a woman with the precise elocution of a middle school teacher, but my gaze keeps flitting back to Cooper. Every time it does, an ice cube sears my chest.

Marriage is a kind of forecast, based in the belief that the relationship you have will stay consistent and satisfying enough to weather the inevitable storms. It's a cultural collection delusion: optimistic, yes, romantic, certainly, but ultimately unrealistic. Our attention spans are getting shorter. We demand newness and novelty at an unprecedented rate. It seems impossible we'd find any one person interesting enough for a few years, let alone the length of our life. A soul mate who's also our best friend, tasked with offering comfort and surprise, mystery and complete knowability.

And yet, I want it. I want what Tom and Peter have, both of them bawling as they exchange rings in front of several million of their closest friends. If this whole ordeal has forced me to admit anything to myself, it's that I want love. I want to get married. I think I even want a baby; shit, maybe I want two. I want a full, extraordinary life with someone who challenges me, and laughs with me, and is hungry for adventure and intellectual pursuit and sex. I want a partner, in the most expansive sense of the word. It feels terrifying to admit this, because I might not get it. I have very little control over making it happen; I can't conjure it through sheer will and hard work, like I conjured the rest of my life in New York. But I want it. I want love.

Bang. I jump. White rose petals fill the sky, swirling around the two men, both laughing as they come back down the aisle, husband and husband. We stand and applaud and then, it's over.

"That was so beautiful." Steph's dabbing her eyes, sniffling.

Cooper wipes a tiny tear from his date's cheek and kisses it.

"I'd like to get married," I say, trying it out. "I know it's a bourgeois construct, but I'd like to, one day."

"Well, yeah," Steph says. "Me too."

"Really?"

"Of course. I need a bloody green card."

I smile, grateful for her levity, and we follow the crowd inside.

* * * *

The reception is in a gilded banquet hall the size of a small country. What possible use would this space have when not housing a socialite wedding party: ice-skating rink? Airplane hangar? Twenty circular tables are laden with gold-edged glassware, silverware, and skyward-reaching arrangements of ivory orchids and lilies. From the corner of my eye, I spy Cooper heading toward the back of the hall. I don't think he's seen me. It's so crowded, there's a good chance I could avoid him all night.

Steph, Viv, Brian, and I are all seated at table four, a surprisingly prime spot close to the long head table. My place card indicates that Ms. Lacey Whitman is seated next to Ms. Vivian Chang.

And Mr. Elan Behzadi.

My stomach bombs.

Did I not see him during the ceremony? Or is he planning to arrive after the display of genuine human emotion? I grab a glass of wine, and scoot around the table, subtly raking the guests as everyone filters in. Through the milling crowd and oversize flower arrangements, I see Patricia . . . and Eloise . . . and him. Talking to an older couple I don't know. He's dressed in a crisp white suit that is, unfortunately, extremely classy and rather sexy.

Steph's at my elbow. "Do you want to leave?"

"No, Jesus," I mutter. "I'm not that weak."

"I could kill him." Steph's eyes are burning.

"Steph, be cool," I say. "It's fine. I'm fine."

He's weaving toward the table, all dark eyes and ruling-class confidence. My heart is throbbing painfully. I'm furious with it.

"Hi." He goes to kiss my cheek. I reel back, toss him a *You've got to be fucking kidding me* look. He falters and addresses Steph. "I'm Elan." He extends his hand.

Steph grimaces at it. "Uh, no." She slides into her seat without taking her eyes off us both.

Distress flickers around his face. He gestures at my dress, almost uncertainly. "You look very beautiful."

"You look like a big-game hunter."

His voice turns intense. "Can we talk?"

"We are talking."

"You haven't replied to any of my messages," he says, pleasingly distressed. "I've been trying to get in touch with you for weeks."

"Oh, are we telling each other things we already know?" I say. "Okay: I don't want anything to do with you because you're a selfish prick."

"Lacey, please. I didn't even know if you'd be here. I thought you might be recovering."

I glance at him sharply. "Recovering?"

"After your surgery."

I blink and look away. Steph's still watching us with a hawk's precision. "I didn't go through with it."

From the corner of my eye, I see him exhale. "Can we talk? Please?"

"Don't be ridiculous," I tell him, smiling. "Vivian's coming."

Vivian, Brian, and a handful of strangers find their seats at our table. Wine and a plate of crab cakes materialize. Happily, Elan has been seated next to a venture capitalist's very blond, very chatty wife, who is unable to read social cues. Every time he tries to turn to me, her long pink talons squeeze his arm, forcing him back. Steph is drinking very steadily, staring at Elan in a way that's noticeably weird. Vivian is pinballing between Brian, Steph, Elan, and me, trying to read the situation, charm Elan, and be a good date. I keep up an inane stream of chatter about anything that pops into my head—what *was* Sigourney Weaver's best film? Does anyone actually *like* fermented vegetables? What *should* one name a Doberman?—until one of the chiseled-from-granite groomsmen finally gets to his feet and taps a microphone. "Where do I start with Tom? Tom is handsome, intelligent, char . . . cha . . . Sorry, man, can't read your writing."

The room guffaws. Elan leans to me. I smell musky, expensive soap. My insides twist. He murmurs, "I miss you."

I shut my eyes, trying to quell this delicious cruelty. I cut my gaze at him coldly. "I don't," I say, and join the crowd in a round of applause.

* * * *

In the bathroom, I wipe my underarms with a damp paper towel. Adrenaline has spiked my pulse rate. I can't get it under control.

I miss you.

I stare in the mirror, hearing those words even though I try not to.

I miss you.

The door flies open and two giggly-drunk Australians pour in. ". . . both soooo hot."

"Wish they weren't gay."

"I need a gay husband."

"Ha, me too!"

They fluff up their hair in the mirror. "I hate being single at weddings," one moans.

"I know," the other says. "It was fine when I was twenty-five. Now it just makes me sad."

I reapply my lipstick quietly.

"Everyone says, *Don't compromise, don't compromise,*" the first one says. "But fuck: everyone's flawed. I'm not perfect. I fart in my sleep."

"Everyone farts in their sleep!"

She sighs, serious. "I'm also up to my tits in credit card debt and I've overstayed my visa by five years."

"Well, that is a flaw."

They burst into tipsy cackles.

Elan has followed me to the bathroom. When I open the door, he's pacing at the dark end of the hallway. Apparently fangirls have taught him the art of being obnoxiously persistent. He's at my side. "Five minutes."

I push past him. "We have nothing to say to each other."

"Not true." He grabs my arm.

I jerk it away. "Touch me again, I'll cut your dick off with my butter knife."

Heat radiates between us. My body burns, eager for him. I hate him but for a wild second, I picture pushing him against the wall, my tongue in his mouth, his pants unbuckling.

"Two minutes," he says. "And I'll stop bothering you for the rest of the night. *Please*."

52.

A dimly lit dining room dominated by a polished wood table and two dozen ornate chairs. Elan's licking his lips, pacing. An oil painting of a white-haired man in a military uniform hangs above the table, watching us with haughty dispassion. I stand by the door, affecting the same look as the painting.

"I didn't know if you'd be here," he says. "I hoped, but I wasn't sure."

"A minute fifty," I say.

"Shit, okay. Okay." He stops moving and clears his throat. "I fucked up. I fucked up at the Bushwick party and I fucked up with us. I'm sorry, Lacey. I'm really, really sorry."

I roll my eyes, and make a move to leave.

"Wait, wait. Please, you said two minutes."

I pause. I wasn't really going to leave.

He says, "I am not good at letting people in. It's hard to tell if people like me for me or for what I can do for them. I might be wrong but I always felt like you liked me for me. You really cared about me."

I did. This is true.

He rakes his fingers through his hair. He's shaking. "I've gotten into a pattern of dating unavailable women because I've been scared to commit. I don't trust a lot of people. But I want to stop that." He looks directly at me. "I want a partner. I want to be in love with someone who loves me, and I want to build a future with her. I've been doing a lot of soul-searching and therapy—yes, I'm seeing a therapist, like you suggested—and I really believe I am capable of making that change. I want you, Lacey. We are similar animals, you and I. Please. Please give me another chance."

I am breathing hard through my nostrils, my teeth clenched. "Is that it?"

"Yes," he says. "That's it."

"You are—" I take a step back and try to laugh. My throat is tight. I am roiling with rage, my familiar, trusty anger. Right now, it's not an impediment. It's protection. A weapon. "You're a piece of work."

"What?"

"What did you think was going to happen, Elan? You'd make your little two-minute speech and I'd lift up my skirt and we'd fuck on the table?"

"I—Lacey, I—"

I step forward, my voice rising. "You wanted to break up because I was getting a surgery that could save my life. You told me you didn't want to meet my friends. You fucked me in public at a party and when I said I didn't like it you just left. You left me."

"I'm sorry. They were all mistakes—"

"And now you only want me because you can't have me. God." I laugh sourly. "You're such a cliché."

"I am. You're right. But I mean it."

"You don't."

"I do. Let me prove it. Give me another chance."

"Why?"

"Because I could give you everything you want." His gaze is locked on mine. I couldn't look away if I tried. "I know you, love. I know what you want. You're hungry for life, and I am too. You and me, together. We make sense." He takes a step toward me. "Life isn't perfect. Love stories are rarely perfect. They take effort, and guts." He takes my hand. I can smell him. "But we have *passion*. You can feel it. I can feel it. I feel you in my body and you feel me in yours."

This is not untrue. My heart, my head, my clit are all pulsing, against my will.

"If you can give me another chance, I will give you the world, pet. Starting with this." He puts my hand over his heart. I can feel it beating through his shirt. "It's yours. I mean it."

I don't trust myself to speak. I am furious and bewildered and terrified. I want to slap him and kiss him.

It's everything I wanted to hear. Isn't it?

"You said you thought you were falling in love with me," he

says. "If you were telling the truth, give me the chance to show you I can love you back."

I close my eyes. A carousel of memories: Elan at his runway show, finding me in the crowd. Watching me bite down on a piece of baklava the first time I was in his home. Sitting across from him at Noemi, my legs around him in the limo, toweling his hair as he walked into his bedroom naked the next morning. Kissing him until he groaned. Taking him in my mouth. His dark eyes tracing my body, illuminating it, making it whole. The memory of it sends heat, and my body begs me for contact. But my body does not always know what is best for it. It forgets betrayal; it has no long-term plan.

I can't be with a man who dreams me into being. Who makes me real. I am already whole. Whether my tits are real or not. Whatever it is that Elan thinks he's offering is an illusion, and it always has been.

"No," I say, and I leave the room.

* * * *

The sun has set, the sky deepening into lilac shot through with streaks of fading pink. A new moon rises over the ocean. Strings of white lights circle the lawn, onto which the guests are pouring. Cooper and Butterfly Wings are sitting at a table by themselves looking bored. I about-face. The last thing I want to do is pretend to enjoy meeting Cooper's date. I lurk behind one of the huge speakers near the stage where the band is setting up. Someone clamps on to my arm. Steph. Her lipstick is smeared in a very telling way. "Lace!" She kisses me on the cheek, hard and wet. "Where were you? You mished the speeches!"

"Elan cornered me."

"*What?*" Half her drink splashes to the ground.

I pluck the glass out of her hand and take a sip. "Bastard wants to get back together."

Steph sucks in a gasp. "That *fucker. He's fucked.*"

"I know," I say. "Obviously I said no."

"You can't, Lace, you absolutely *cannot.*" She grabs the glass back off me and finishes it.

"I know," I say again.

"Prick." Her eyes are unfocused, blooming with anger. "Tosser."

"Babe, did you eat dinner? Maybe we should get you some bread."

"He's a *cunt*, Lace, a total *cunt*—"

"Babe, I *know*. I said no." Is she too drunk to understand me? "No more drinkies for you, okay? I'm going to get you a water."

I spin around. Elan is right behind us.

"Lacey," he says, his voice low. "Can we—"

"Cunt!" Steph announces loudly. A handful of party guests turn and stare.

"Not a good time," I mutter, trying to yank Steph away.

Elan glances at the guests, and nods, backing away. He mouths, *Later*. I return it with a glare but his back is turned and he misses it.

Luna is cutting through the crowd toward us. Thank God. Steph lights up. "Hey!" She's all over her, lips at Luna's neck. "You're so *sexy*. I wanna *fuck* you—"

"Oh-kay." Luna grabs Steph as she almost stumbles.

"—In the *pussy*." Steph finishes, grinning proudly.

Luna and I exchange a glance. What to do with drunk Steph? I'd put her in a taxi, but we're all carpooling back to Brooklyn, same way we came up. "I could use a coffee," Luna says to Steph. "Help me find one?"

"Sure," Steph says. "Coffee." She looks at me and laughs. "Coffee," she whispers. "Wink, wink."

"Thank you," I murmur to Luna, who nods as if it's no big deal.

"I got it," she says, hooking her arm around Steph. "Go have fun."

Fun. Outcome seems unlikely.

The crowd gets bigger with every passing minute. I do a lap, cutting through it in a way that suggests I'm on an important mission. I spot Patricia with a handful of Hoffman House clients: the creative director for Apple, the executive vice president of Estée Lauder. If I float by, hopefully she'll reel me in. I'm a few feet away when we lock eyes. Her gaze lights in recognition. She raises a hand as if to wave me into the inner circle. But then, just as quickly, her expression changes. She blinks, her hand moving instead to smooth her hair, her focus back on our clients. I slide by, wondering why she changed her mind.

I head for the bar furthest from the stage, ready for some sad solo drinking. Sitting alone at the end of it is Cooper. No date in sight. His jacket is gone, the sleeves of his shirt rolled up to his forearms, tie loose. In the crazy mess of this overblown night, he is the only calm, quiet thing about it. I steel myself, and approach. "This seat taken?"

He looks up. And smiles. A blazing, beautiful smile. "I was really hoping you'd say hello."

"I was really hoping you'd say that." I slide onto the barstool. "Where's . . ." I mime hair, a dress.

Behind his glasses, his eyes flick to my cheek, then back to my face. "Left. Wasn't feeling well."

A cool rush of relief. "That sounds like the worst lie ever."

"Right? At least give me period pain."

I nod. "A man deserves menstrual cramps when he's being ditched by his insignificant other."

He huffs a laugh. He glances at me sidelong, almost as if he's nervous around me. "How's your night, Lacey?"

"Underwhelming. Steph is blind drunk, and I just got cold-shouldered by my boss and I have no idea why."

Cooper taps his cheek awkwardly. As if to show me something on mine. "You have . . ."

"What?" I touch my cheek. Sticky red on my fingertips.

"Looks like someone kissed you?"

I grab a knife and hold it up to my face. A giant red lipstick mark is smeared all over my right cheek. "*Steph.* Fuck." I dunk a napkin in some water and begin to clean it off, replaying Patricia's look when she saw it. Surprise. Disapproval. Yup, I'm the one with a drunk friend slobbering all over me. Or did she think I'd been hooking up with someone? Even worse.

"It's just lipstick," Cooper says.

"I know," I say. I don't want it to seem like I'm overreacting. But Eloise's words come back to me: *You don't have the pedigree, taste, or composure to be a fashion editor of Hoffman House.* But that is obviously not what's on Cooper's mind. He swivels to face me, and says, very seriously, "Lacey. I'm really sorry how things ended between us."

"Me too. It's okay."

"But it's not, really." He slumps over his drink, like a soldier who's seen too much. "I think about that afternoon on the pier a lot."

"What do you think about?"

"Just . . . a different ending." His eyes on mine again, openly intense. "For us."

Us. I still feel the thrill of this word. I don't want to ask. But I have to. "You're moving to Germany," I say. "Aren't you?"

He closes his eyes and nods. "Next week."

I look straight ahead for a moment and then back at him. Strangely, I feel like laughing. It's all just so . . . sad. Such a mess.

Elan appears at the other end of the bar, gaze roving the crowd. Oh, *hell* no. I am sick of being the source of this idiot's belated epiphany about love, particularly after such god-awful dungeon sex. I slip off my stool. "Want to get out of here?"

Cooper grabs a bottle of champagne from behind the bar. "Where to?"

53.

Moonlight nicks the black ocean silver. We pick our way along the cliff top, salt air turning our skin sticky. The silence between us is not awkward: it is just quiet. I focus on savoring the way our fingers graze when he passes me the bottle.

We find a tuft of seagrass overlooking the water. The dull thunder of the ocean mixes with the sound of the party, wavering on the wind. The water stretches endless. Beneath the surface, another hidden world.

I take a swig of booze. "I didn't do it. The surgery."

"I heard," he says. "Can I ask why not?"

I shrug, not because I don't know but because I don't feel like rehashing his role in my decision. "You know when you're hanging out with people, and you have to leave early? Everyone tells you to stay, but you have to go, so you do a round of goodbyes and hugs and everything. Then, you're at the door, and you glance back, and you want everyone to still be staring after you, waving. But they've all already gone back to their conversation. You're not missed at all." I gaze out at the ocean, the endless, shifting expanse. "That's what makes me feel sad about dying. That after I'm gone and everyone has said goodbye, life just goes on without me."

"You're worried about leaving a legacy?" Cooper asks. "What you'll be remembered for?"

"More like, I'll just miss it. Life. I'll miss being a part of it. I'll miss weddings and the ocean and music and champagne. I'll miss the drama and the gossip and the news and New York. I'll just miss it."

Cooper glances at me sharply. "You haven't . . . found anything?" He gestures vaguely at my breasts.

I laugh, mimicking his somewhat clumsy gesture, and he chuckles too. "No. All clear, for now. It just gets me thinking."

Cooper puts his hand on my shoulder. Warm. Assured. "Lacey. You're not dying."

"We're all dying, Coop. We're all going to die."

His face is somber but beautiful. I'll miss Cooper. I don't even feel nervous when I raise my hand to touch his face. I just want to feel it, beneath my fingertips. I shift closer, so he's able to put his arms around me, his fingers running down my back.

"How did we get this so wrong?" I ask.

"I should have just asked you out. Back in the beginning." He's agitated. "If I wasn't so fucking cautious, maybe . . . Maybe everything would be different." His eyes light hopeful. "We could keep in touch. Try long-distance . . ."

My arms circle his neck. "I fall for you and then you leave?" I shake my head.

He looks surprised. "Love? Really?"

I could bat it back: *I didn't say "love," I said, "fall for."* I don't. "You're pretty lovable."

His mouth drifts closer to mine. I close my eyes. Very faintly over the crashing ocean and the thudding of my heart, I hear, "So are you."

His lips are warm and taste like apricot. It is familiar and it is strange. At first it's slow, even a little timid. I keep bumping his glasses until he pulls back and, with a slightly bashful smile, takes them off. Better. We resume our exploration. How do our lips fit together? What do you like? What are you like? We are still sitting side by side on the grassy cliff top, and it reminds me of high school kisses in the shadows around a bonfire: excited and eager and shy and clumsy. More questions than answers. But slowly, Coop and I find our rhythm. Grow more confident. I feel the sinewy strength of his arms. The warm muscles of his chest. The soft play of the curls on the back of his neck. As every second passes, I have a clearer and clearer picture of him. With Elan, kissing felt like combat: a violent need for his lust, his body, his attention. It hits me almost gently: I am kissing Noam Cooper. And goddamn: it feels *good*.

Something inside of me unlocks, a tentativeness burning away, and in response my body opens. A rush of heat; my desire quickens. I deepen the kiss and he responds, readily, eagerly. We tangle into each other, and now my legs are around him. I pull him on top of me, lowering us to the ground. I laugh and we roll, me on top of him, him on top of me, his weight heavy and delicious. Every kiss more intimate, every touch more assured. His mouth finds my ear and he whispers sweet things into it, words like *beautiful*, words like *perfect*. I close my eyes to keep this, this moment, this blissful second, in my memory forever. Because we don't have forever. He's leaving.

I'm on top of him as I start to pull back, up, away.

He looks like he's been hit by a truck. It takes him a long moment to say anything. "Lacey." He elbows himself up clumsily, fumbling to put his glasses back on. His expression is satisfyingly shell-shocked. "You are . . . wow."

I snuggle under his arm. "You're not so bad yourself."

"No, seriously. You got skills, girl. Mad skills." He brushes a lock of hair out of my eyes, so gently it reminds me of sunlight. "Are you sure you don't want to try it? Us, I mean. I have to come back for conferences every now and then."

"I need someone who won't leave. And I've already had my heart trashed once this year."

"Who trashed your heart?"

"It doesn't matter." Our foreheads touch, fingers spidering together. "Do you remember the day we made pancakes together, you asked me what makes me happy?"

"I do."

"I'm happy now," I say. "Even though it's complicated, I'm happy now."

"I feel the same way," he says, his lips touching mine once more.

"Lacey!" My name, a shout on the wind. It's Luna. Running along the cliff top toward us. "Thank God I found you." She's puffing, red-faced. "It's Steph."

54.

We hurry back to the party.

"She passed out in one of the upstairs bedrooms, but when I went back, she was gone," Luna says. "Viv and I can't find her anywhere."

"She's a bit of a drunk wanderer," I puff back. "Last New Year's she went missing for hours. I found her at the dollar-pizza place."

The house is bordered by cliffs. What if she stumbles, loses her footing? Panic grips me. I shout her name, scan the cliff tops. Nothing. The sound of the party gets louder. The band has started; fun, fizzy dance-pop. The reception is still in full swing.

"Let's just find her and leave," I say. I squeeze Cooper's hand. "Sorry."

"Nothing to be sorry about," he says. "I'll check the parking lot and the front of the house."

We fan out. I edge around the crowded dance floor, searching for a flash of brown skin in a lady tux. Everyone is talking, laughing, shouting over the band. The night is loosening. Little kids race through the adults' legs, knocking over a potted plant. Someone's fedora floats in the koi pond, nibbled by fat orange fish. Two teenagers with hollow cheekbones and flops of hair are voguing with the intensity of a drill sergeant. An old man is sleeping peacefully, his cheek resting in a fat slice of white frosted cake.

Of course. I know where Steph is.

The kitchen is no longer the bustling epicenter it was hours ago. Plates of half-eaten appetizers crowd the counter. I could've sworn she'd be here, inhaling crab cakes and stuffed mushrooms. Stainless steel pots and pans hang like avant-garde decorations above the kitchen island. His reflection appears in a soup ladle, warped and stretched out.

"Not now," I groan.

"Lacey," Elan says, his voice serious and low. "Please. We really need to talk." He puts a hand on my arm.

I shake it off. "Go away. Before someone sees you." I glance behind me.

And see that someone already has.

Vivian is in the kitchen entrance.

For one long moment, we all stand there, frozen. We were talking about business, about something to do with the app. But the truth unfurls over Vivian's face and I know that she knows. My eyes meet Elan's. At least he can take half the assault that's about to happen.

Elan puts his hands into his pockets, and takes a step back.

Don't you fucking dare. Don't you dare back out of this.

But of course, he does, leaving my business partner and me alone in the kitchen.

Her lips are pressed so tight they're white. "Before he joined the board of directors, or after?"

Two party guests barrel in, laughing, drunk, diving for the appetizers. I move closer to her, away from them. "Not now."

"No," she says, her eyes hard as bullets. "Now."

I follow her into a laundry room. Two industrial-size washer-dryers sit silently in the darkness, big enough to fit a body in. The air smells like fabric softener and dryer sheets, the scent so fake and cloying it makes me feel sick. This room is distinctly absent of wedding niceties: it's off the map of this event. We're in no-man's-land.

Vivian speaks through gritted teeth. "When?"

"I want you to know, I never meant for any of it to get this far." I'm speaking quickly, hands raised as if to ward off an attack. "I never meant to lie to you."

"When," she asks, "did it start?"

My heart is racing. I'm sweating.

"For fuck's sake, Lacey, just tell me how long you've been fucking Elan Behzadi!"

I work to steady my voice. "March," I say. "We started sleeping together in March. But it's over now, it's been over for months."

Air drains out of her. She looks at me as if she has no idea who I am.

I babble an explanation, partly timeline, partly excuse: *Thought I'd be judged— Never meant to be serious— To save the company— Fell in love.*

"Hold up," she says. "You're in love with him?"

"I thought I was," I say. "But now I know that the way he treated me isn't the way you treat someone you love."

"How did he— Wait, no, I don't care. I don't want to know." She refocuses on me. "So Elan bailing on Clean Clothes. Is that to do with your relationship?"

"I don't know."

"Lacey," she snaps. "Grow a pair."

"Okay, yes," I say. "I don't know for sure, but yes, probably. But he only got involved because of me, too. I brought him in."

"You should've told me that! That was something I needed to know!" Her body contracts, as if she'd been punched in the stomach. She crumples to her hands and knees.

I rush to her. "Viv!"

She pushes me away. "Last chance," she says hoarsely, her hands planted on the tiles. "That was our last chance. And you fucked it. You fucked it, and you fucked me."

"I'm sorry," I say. I might cry. "Viv, I'm so sorry."

Her words are directed at the floor. "You're rotten, Lacey. You think you're a good person, but you're not."

She's right.

I'm rotten.

My eyes fill with tears.

Vivian inhales deeply and rises to her feet, refusing to take the hand I offer her. She straightens her dress, smooths her hair, and opens the laundry room door.

"Vivian." I trail her. "Wait."

"Why?" She doesn't stop. "We're not friends anymore." She says it like it's a fact.

* * * *

Everything around me is smoking rubble. My life is a bomb site. It's only as I approach the clusters of wedding guests outside, all shouting over the band, dancing, drinking, do I realize I cannot be here. I need to leave. Get back to Brooklyn. How?

I spot Luna in the far corner of the patio, surreptitiously trying to get my attention. I hurry over, careful not to make eye contact with anyone. I'm sure my makeup is a sad smeary disaster.

"I found Steph; kept her in one place with a dozen mini quiches," Luna says. "But we should leave. I have a car."

"Oh, thank God," I moan, resisting the urge to collapse in her arms and have her carry me away, action-hero-style.

Luna blinks at me. "Are you ready to go?"

I can't even answer this question: it's like asking if I like being alive. YES. "Where is she?"

"Here." Luna steps back and points. At an empty chair by the door. "Fuck. She was right here."

I spin around. "She can't have gone far—"

We both see her at the same time. Walking unsteadily up to the koi pond. Peering inside it. Dangerously close to the edge.

Luna and I start moving for her. We haven't even covered half the distance when Steph whips her hand to cover her mouth. As if taking a final bow after a particularly well-received performance, she doubles over at the waist and loudly vomits a dozen mini quiches into the koi pool.

Guests shuffle back, their faces a mix of pity, disgust, and amusement. I lock eyes with Eloise, standing six feet away. On seeing me and making the connection that yes, the puking drunk girl is my friend, her expression settles into: *Of. Course.*

I take Steph's arm. "Come on, babe. Time to go."

Steph takes a step, eyes glassy and unsure. Then she pulls away and vomits into the pond again.

"Good God." It's Eloise, her voice as cold and crisp as a glacier. "Can someone call security?"

I roll my eyes and shoot her a dirty look. "Come on, Steph . . ."

Steph plops down on the ground. "Just a sec."

"She can't stay there." Eloise steps away from her group, addressing me directly. "You both need to leave."

"That's what we're trying to do," I say, wanting her to shut the hell up. Everyone's staring.

"Now," Eloise says, even louder. "This is a *wedding*."

Steph moans softly and places her cheek on the stone edge of the pond, curling into a ball. It's such an accidentally insolent move, so directly defying Queen Eloise, I almost laugh. I look right at Eloise, and shrug. "Guess we're staying here."

I figure Eloise will roll her eyes and stalk off. But to my surprise, it *infuriates* her. An ugly anger I've never seen in her explodes across her face. She strides toward me so fast I think she's going to hit me. Her eyes are burning. "You are being incredibly rude."

I scorch with rage. Everything in me wants to slap her. "Fuck. Off."

"Lacey, leave," she snaps. She raises an arm, pointing at the exit. Her voice is shaking. "I strongly suggest you *leave*."

"No *you* leave." I raise my hands, pretending I'm about to shove her, just to make her flinch. Startled, she takes a full step back. Her heel catches on the edge of the pond. For one amazing second, she wobbles, arms spinning like helicopter blades, before she slowly tips backward and she falls.

A shallow splash. Eloise Cunningham-Bell is on her ass in the koi pond, surrounded by Steph's floating vomit.

There's a full second of silence before she unhinges her jaw and screams, a bloodcurdling, glass-shattering scream. A dozen bodies rush to her assistance. My mind is static with shock, the full horror of what just happened beginning to edge into full consciousness. Dumbly, I look back around at the crowd.

Patricia stands alone on the lawn watching me with grim dispassion. Her arms are folded. One eyebrow is hooked all the way up.

Her expression says everything.

I'm done.

55.

October

New York doesn't have four seasons. It's hot, and then, it's not.
Patricia and I have lunch the first day I underdress for the weather.
Her robust Italian tan is offset by a cream silk suit and black pageboy wig,
but her usual breeziness is absent. We order salad. No wine. The restaurant is still pumping summer AC. It's so cold, my teeth chatter.

I've been dreading this.

Thanks to her enormous ass, Eloise sustained no real injuries from
her fall, apart from the damage to her enormous ego. Naturally, she
parlayed a few bruises into a week off work, spent "convalescing" in
her parents' summer home on Cape Cod. I formally apologized via
email, phone, and then in person when she returned. Not because I felt
she deserved it; I was honestly afraid she'd try to sue me. I was terrified
something might turn up online—nasty gossip or worse still, a clip—
but nothing did. Behind closed doors, the privileged protect their own.

Patricia and I haven't spoken one-on-one since the wedding. I can't
get a read on the fallout: Am I getting fired? Or just punished? In my
most hopeful moments I wonder if, after the dust has settled, she'll
actually find the whole thing darkly amusing and still give me the job.
After all, I didn't actually push Eloise. It was an accident. Sort of.

We slide into our seats and simultaneously unfold our napkins
over our laps, like boxers touching gloves before a fight. "I need to
tell you something," I say, before she can draw breath. "I need to tell
you what's going on with me."

I explain my diagnosis and the choice I've been struggling with all
year. I don't tell her about the list, but I do say that I was motivated to
take control of my sexuality, which led to an affair with Elan Behzadi,

a situation that clearly got out of my control. I'd assumed that Eloise had told Patricia about Elan, or that she'd guessed from the way he was following a junior employee around all night like a lovesick tomcat. From her nonreaction to this part of my tawdry tale, I know one of these options was correct. When I finish, Patricia ticks her head to the side, thinking. I wait, my leg bouncing restlessly underneath the table.

"It's your choice who you share a medical diagnosis with," she says eventually. "But I feel sad you didn't confide in me. About any of this."

This is harder to hear than anger. "I didn't tell that many people." I fiddle with my silverware. "So, am I fired?"

Another excruciating pause. Then: "No. But I definitely cannot give you the fashion editor position. Not just because of what happened at the wedding. Because of what happened with Elan."

Disappointment, cold and wet. And then, surprisingly, a scratch of anger.

"What?" she asks, watching me.

"Honestly? You're punishing me for sex. Which seems archaic and, well, something of a double standard." I'm not convinced the same thing would be happening if I were a man.

"I'm not punishing you for sex," Patricia says. "I'm just choosing not to reward you for concealing a conflict of interest from both of your employers: Vivian Chang and myself. Your relationship with someone like Elan is a setup for pain, but what little power you had to do the right thing, you didn't use it."

Our salads arrive. I pick at mine. No appetite. "Thank you for not firing me," I tell Patricia, not quite able to look her in the eye. "I know you have the grounds. I know I let you down."

"My first husband's sister died of breast cancer," she says. "A girl-friend from high school was just diagnosed with ovarian. Until this country can get its act together, I won't abandon my employees. Even the ones who push pregnant women into koi ponds." There is almost a glimmer of amusement in her eyes.

I was, and am, grateful. Not only because I still have a job, albeit one I don't particularly feel passionate about. Because I need it. Seven weeks after that lunch, on the first afternoon the city is dusted with a suggestion of snow, a mammogram identifies *ductal carcinoma in situ*. "It's not cancer," Dr. Williams, my breast surgeon at NY3C, explains to me. "More like precancer. Cells in your ducts are behaving abnormally and we don't know why."

With no small sense of déjà vu, I reschedule my surgery for the first week of December. It doesn't feel scary or celebratory. It feels inevitable.

* * * *

At first, Cooper and I keep in close contact, texting every day and calling on the weekends. But as time goes by, I realize it's hurting me. I miss him but I have to let him go. He left his furniture when he moved to Berlin, so Steph could sublet a "furnished room," but the things that made it specifically Cooper—the books, the harmonica, the framed photograph of the 1980s New York subway car—are all gone. It makes me sad to go in there now, lost and a little wistful. I scale back our contact and try to focus on what's happening here, in New York, right in front of me.

In a tastefully lit shop front on the Lower East Side, I purchase a handful of sex toys. Colorful silicon that buzzes quietly. A few weeks later, I sit next to a cuteish boy at a book launch and take him home. He's an aspiring stand-up comedian, nervous and grateful. The sex is okay, made better by the vibrating silicon. Afterward we watch *SNL* clips on YouTube and order takeout from Golden Century. A month later, I meet a punky girl called Kat at a fund-raiser for Planned Parenthood and we end up having pretty good sex in her noisy basement apartment in the East Village. Kat's a political nerd. As I reach the limb-quivering, teeth gnashing climax of number six on my bucket list, I unexpectedly lock eyes with Hillary Rodham Clinton, whose framed photograph hangs opposite Kat's bed. When I tell Steph, she laughs so hard she wets herself.

That sex can be this: neither mind-blowing nor deeply disappointing, feels like an odd kind of milestone.

* * * *

Elan formally ends his relationship with Clean Clothes through a tersely worded letter from Tim George. I never hear from him again. Clean Clothes is quietly acquired by a Swedish clothing-retail company. I only get the details of this when I finally convince Vivian to meet me for coffee. She pushes a piece of paper my way. It's a check. For just under six thousand dollars. "Your shares," she says. "What was left of them."

"No." I push it back. "I can't take this. Not after everything that happened."

"Take it. You need it. And you earned it."

I stare at Vivian's small, precise writing.

It's almost the same amount as Elan's commission.

* * * *

And just like that, it's December.

56.

December

"They say I might say some weird shit when I wake up from the anesthesia," I tell Steph, the phone jammed under my ear while I wipe down my kitchen counter for the fiftieth time.

"What kind of weird shit?"

"Unclear. You've seen all those videos of kids after the dentist. I just hope I'm whimsical and amusing and not gross or overtly bitchy."

Steph chuckles. "You sure you don't want us to come with you to the hospital? Or I can leave the missus here and come by myself."

I toss the sponge in the sink. My studio has never been cleaner. I keep trying to tell myself that a recovery staycation will be fun and cozy, but honestly, it's going to be pretty cramped with my sister and, after a few days, Storm. It's a crash pad, not a real home. I only have one coffee mug, one frying pan. From the bed you can see every inch of the apartment except the bathroom. In its current state of violent cleanliness, the studio resembles one of those progressive Scandinavian prison cells.

"I'm good. Mara will be here at six." My buzzer sounds. "Shoot, gotta go. Nude photo shoot lady is here."

"Ooh, lovely," Steph says. "Hope I get to see those, she said, in a nonpervy way. See you tomorrow. Love you."

"Love you too." A new thing we've started doing. I rather like it.

I adjust my kimono in the mirror. Bee recommended this photographer, I don't know her personally. Serena is her name, and I'm just in the process of checking my phone and seeing a message from Serena that starts with *I'm so sorry* when the doorbell rings and Cooper is standing in front of me.

He looks dazed. "Hi."

He's supposed to be in Germany. Shock bounces around my body. "How— What are you doing here?"

He's staring at me. An overnight bag at his feet. "Can I come in?"

Silently, I stand aside. He enters, slowly, looking around. He's never been to my apartment before. My pulse is tapping quickly, my skin awash with heat. I am extremely naked under my kimono. I tighten the sash. "Coop, what the hell are you doing here? Did something happen with the job?"

"I . . . had to come back for a conference. Last-minute. Just for today."

I can't believe he's here, *here*, in my apartment.

"I'm flying back tonight." Wild eyes lock on mine. "Come with me."

"*What?*"

"I know this is crazy, and sudden, and *crazy*, but I was sitting in the hotel bar drinking some wine and there were these two Germans next to me talking about toy poodles. You know, the dogs?"

"Poodles? Cooper, what the hell are you—"

"And it was just so funny"—he's pacing, babbling—"the way they were saying *toy poodle* in their German accent was just so funny and they had Alfredo pasta on the menu, which I know you like, and—" He exhales hard, and looks right at me. "It just suddenly hit me how much I wanted you there. With me. All the time. As my girlfriend."

I goldfish my mouth a few times. "But . . . you live in Berlin."

He grabs my hands, eyes wide behind his glasses. "Come with me. They've put me up in a huge apartment and are paying me a stupid amount of money."

"Coop, I *can't*." I pull my hands away. "My surgery."

"Get it there." He steps closer again. "I'll take time off to look after you. All the time you need, I'll be there."

"You can't, you just started a new job!"

"Well, we'll figure something out!"

I don't step away. Of course I can't, I absolutely can't . . . can I? I want to travel. I want to see the world.

And, I want Cooper. "My stuff—my apartment—"

"The company will ship all my partner's things. I'll pay for you to break your lease. I don't care about the money." He cups my face with both hands. I've never been this close to someone radiating so much serious, directed, devoted energy. "I want to be with you and I don't care how much that scares me. It doesn't scare me anymore. I feel so alive when I'm with you, like I could do anything, go anywhere. I want to make you happy. I want to make you pancakes. I want to make your life amazing. You inspire me." His gaze is deep, soft, and unflinching. "You're the one for me, Lacey Whitman. You always have been."

I stare back at him, stunned. I feel like I've just discovered a secret world under my bed. None of this feels real. And while the possibility of Coop's declaration being a colorful presurgery delusion is exceptionally strong, I know it's not.

Cooper is here. And he wants me to go to Germany with him. He wants . . . me. "I don't speak German."

"Everyone speaks English!"

"But my job—"

"You don't even like your job. You could get work there easily. I know people."

"Steph, Mara—"

"They can come visit!"

"Cooper!" I spin away, laughing deliriously. "I can't go to Germany with you!"

He follows me. "Call me crazy, but I think you can. I think you're thinking about it. I think you want to."

"Stop thinking. I can't." I look at him. Really see him. Scruffy hair. Good heart. "I care about you, Coop. Even though this year was nutso, I do, I care about you, a lot. But I care about me more."

"Meaning?"

"Meaning tomorrow morning my sister is taking me to the hospital, where a very nice surgeon will be removing every inch of breast tissue from my body so I don't get cancer and die. And that's more important to me than anything anyone could possibly offer." I put my hands on his chest. His heart is jackhammering underneath his T-shirt. "I gotta save my own life, Coop. You get that, right?"

He deflates, his entire body contracting. "Yeah." He blinks and rubs his eyes, as if just coming back into himself. "Sorry if this seems insensitive or insane. It all just came out."

"I'm glad it did." I slide my arms up around his neck. I'm smiling. "As far as grand gestures go, that was quite impressive."

He takes a long moment to study my face. "You're so beautiful, Lacey. I almost forgot how beautiful you are."

I don't say, "No, I'm not!" I don't say, "Just good lighting." I just feel it: his kindness. His love for me.

His hands slide to the small of my back. I feel the warmth of his skin through my robe. "Should I quit my job? And stay?"

"No," I twist my fingers into his hair. "If it's meant to be, we'll work it out. There's always next year."

"And the year after that"—his mouth moves toward mine—"and the year after that"—closer still—"and the year after that."

I smile as he kisses me. I could be thinking about so many things. How I feel when he walks out that door. What's happening tomorrow. But all I feel is his mouth on mine, his body pressed to my chest, his hands sliding to cup the curve of my waist. It's a sweet kiss, but it has weight. It's a kiss that says, *You mean something to me.* It's a kiss that says, *I hope this isn't the end for us.*

But it might be. Because I made the choice I had to make.

My kimono slides open. In a way that seems languid rather than tentative, he slowly slides his hands inside my gown. His fingertips skim my stomach, summoning a scatter of goose bumps up my arm. "You're so soft," he whispers.

I draw in a breath as his hands find my breasts. Cupping them, weighing them, feeling every inch of them. His eyes are heavy with desire, looking down at my chest to wonder at me. His thumbs run over both nipples, quick, almost playful. A shiver of pleasure. Then he pinches them, slowly, deliciously slowly. The sensation shoots down my spine, all the way to my clit.

This is the last night I'll feel this.

We break apart. His pupils are dilated, his breath ragged. "Should I go?"

I shake my head. "Stay. Just for tonight."

It's sex unlike I've ever had before. More tender than fucking, less serious than making love, more loving than a hookup. I don't feel shy about telling him what I want, what I like. I close my eyes and focus on my breasts, on the sensation of having them stroked and nibbled and squeezed. An altar, soon to be artifact. We take our time, both explorers with the same luxurious mission: to discover this glorious body we're lucky enough to be in bed with. We pause to talk and laugh and tease. I stay in the moment. I savor every bite. When I arch my back as he slides inside me, it's not a show. It's not for him. It's for me. It's how I feel. I don't feel sad when it's over. I don't feel happy. As Cooper's breathing deepens into sleep beside me, I feel alive: conscious and very present of being in existence, on this day, this week, this year. In New York City, on a continent of planet Earth.

The screen of my phone reflects my body back at me, my skin shimmering pale.

My breasts look beautiful.

I look beautiful.

I take one photo. One photo to complete the nude photo shoot, number two on my bucket list: the list that caused so much drama. And heartache. And fun. And sex. And . . . everything else.

Through my window, a suggestion of gray.

A new day is dawning.

Part Three

57.

Hospitals are a different country. Passing through the sliding glass doors is a border crossing into a world where hope and despair are mediated by people in pale blue scrubs with patient smiles. I've been afraid of this: returning to the scene of the crime that took my mother's life. But it's not as bad as I anticipate. In fact, it's almost underwhelming. It's oddly ordinary. After all, I'm here under vastly different circumstances.

I'm not dying.

After signing in, I change into disposable underwear and a robe, and wait for the doctor squad. My skin smells like the sickly disinfectant I was instructed to wash with this morning. Not my smell. It makes all this seem even more . . . weird. I'm reminded of the original meaning of the word (one of the few things I remember from high school English)—having the power to control destiny.

I FaceTime Bee. She answers from a darkened bedroom, sleepy. "Babe."

"Babe."

"Today's the day, huh?"

"Yup."

She sits up. A pink eye mask with *Fuck off* in cursive script is pushed into her blond hair. "You got this. You so got this. Is your sister there?"

"Getting coffee." I frown, realizing something. "Wait, where are you? That's not your bedroom."

"Shhh." Bee giggles, putting her finger to her lips. "You'll wake—uh—him." A whisper. "Shit, I forgot his name. I picked him up at that open mic night."

"You did it?" I wasn't sure if she'd go through with her plan to sing a few cabaret songs at a local bar.

"Oh, I did it. I brought the house down, honey! They want me back. Regular slot."

"That's amazing!"

A muffled groan, out of frame. A man's voice, "What time is it?"

"Shut the fuck up," she tells him. "It's my friend; I'm talking to my friend." Then to me, grinning but sincere. "You'll be fine. I believe in you. I can't wait to see your new titties."

I warm with the feeling of her support. It's wonderful and strange how tragedy brings you such unlikely bedfellows. Bee and I would most likely never have become close in our ordinary lives. But I feel certain that we are, as the forums say, BFFs: breast friends forever. And for that, I am beyond thankful. Silver lining, indeed. "See you on the other side."

Mara returns with her coffee. None for me till after it's all over. She smooths stray strands of hair into my hair net. "How are you feeling?"

Afraid. Determined. Strong, sad. "Ready," I say. "I feel ready."

She takes my hand in hers. It is dry and calloused, nails bitten to the quick. It feels like home.

Dr. Williams and Dr. Ho greet us warmly. I'd seen both of them a week ago for my last check-in, the same day I'd come into the hospital for presurgical testing: checking of my heart rate, blood test, a pregnancy test. Now they're in scrubs, asking if I have any final questions.

"How much will it hurt?" I ask.

"Everyone's pain thresholds are different," Dr. Williams says. "But you'll have plenty of medication to manage the pain."

"Right," I say. "But how much will it hurt?"

"Don't worry, Lace," Mara says. "You're going to be doped up till New Year's."

"And I'll also have my meds, right?" I'm making a joke, but apprehension gnaws at me. This is happening. This is real. I'm anxious and low-key terrified. And I'm grateful. Grateful that these smart, kind doctors are able to help me feel powerful in a situation that renders me powerless. I want to express this, but all I can say is, "Thank you."

Dr. Ho smiles. "Ready?"

I don't realize I'm holding my breasts until I'm wheeled into the OR and guided to the table. It's brighter than a CVS at midnight, and freezing.

My nipples are hard and sensitive and I don't want to think about how they'll feel when I wake up. Everyone around me is busy, moving in a ballet of checklists and coordinated movement. No chitchat now, just a clear sense of order. Some of the women on the forums described being given a mild sedative before this point, something that made you feel like you've "had a few glasses of wine," but I am stone-cold sober. I wish someone had bonked me on the head as soon as I came into the hospital. I don't want to be conscious for any of this.

I won't be for much longer.

IV in my arm. The friendly anesthesiologist makes small talk about God knows what.

The lights above me are so bright. Everyone is smiling.

And now . . . I'm floating; delicious sunshine, warm summer days. I'm counting down from ten.

Nine.

Eight.

Se—seven . . .

* * * *

Me and my mother, who is actually Meryl Streep, are bra shopping in a giant department store. The only bras I can find are the wrong size and crazy colors: neon yellow, lime green. "But where are they?" I keep saying, wading through the endless, mismatched racks. "Where are my boobs?"

"Here," Meryl/Mom says. She holds out Mara's photo album.

Relief. I take it.

In the change room, I pull aside a curtain. Donald Trump is already in there, trying on my bras. He looks embarrassed and covers his chest. His hands are very, very small. Rage, like a freight train. "I hate you!" I yell. "*I hate President Trump!*"

Someone tries to soothe me, as I continue to scream at him.

* * * *

Can't see. Black gauze over my eyes. Through slivers of vision, a nurses' station. A window. I moan.

An underwater voice I don't recognize. "You're fine, honey. You're good."

I'm being dragged under by something as powerful as the ocean. Opening my eyes, a Herculean feat. "Mom?"

Someone near me. "You want some ginger ale, baby?"

It's only after I throw it up that I realize I'm thirsty and that I was drinking something and I'm nauseous. Jumbled time. Someone's wiping my mouth saying, "It's okay, baby. It's all okay."

I mumble something like, "Feel . . . fucked . . ." and then the ocean envelops me.

* * * *

The next time I wake up, I actually wake up. I'm in a low-lit hospital bed in a hospital room. Key word: *hospital.* To my left, an empty bed, to my right, an older Hispanic woman is snoring lightly. Dark outside. An elephant on my chest, planet-size pressure caving it in. My back muscles are screaming. I'm wrapped up like a freakin' mummy.

Mara is slumped in a chair at the end of my bed. When I try to move, her head snaps up. Her face is so familiar, it's like looking in the mirror. It almost brings me to tears.

"Hey, there you are." She's by my side, face flooded with relief. "Welcome back."

My croaked greeting sounds like something you'd steer clear of in a swamp.

"Ready for this?" A plastic cup of water.

I gulp it down. "What time is it?"

"About seven. Luna and Steph just stepped out to get coffee." She skims my cheek with her finger. "How are you feeling, sweet girl?"

IV in my arm. My chest is strapped in bandages, a compression bra, tubes everywhere. It doesn't feel like my body. It doesn't feel like anything. "How did it go?"

"Perfectly," Mara says. "They were done early. Something to do with you being young. Everything as it should be."

Not really. It's just everything as it is.

She slips out to tell a nurse I'm awake as Steph and Luna come in holding a cardboard tray of coffees. Their faces bloom when they see me. "She lives!"

My friends. I am happy to see them but also anxious. I am fundamentally incapable of entertaining them.

"How are you?" Steph's breath smells like espresso.

"Peachy." I try for a smile but it ends up a grimace.

"For the record, you definitely said some crazy shit earlier." Steph giggles. "Yelling at all those nurses about Trump. Classic."

"What?" That wasn't a dream? "What'd I say?"

"Nothing," Luna says, giving Steph a quick glance. "Don't worry about it. Don't worry about anything. You don't even have to talk right now."

Mara comes back with a nurse. I try to focus on her (easy) questions and (simple) instructions. I don't want to forget anything or fuck anything up. But then I see that Mara, Steph, and Luna are all listening too.

* * * *

The nurses inspect what's underneath all the bandages. I don't have the energy or desire to see the results yet.

My thick beige compression bra is strapless, circling my body like a bandeau with a Velcro opening in the front. It's as sturdy, unfashionable, and uncompromising as a Dickensian governess. Beneath it, an expert swaddle of bandages. Two drains snake from the stitches in my skin, attached to a belt I wear around my midsection. Every time I move, they swish and pull. They're gross: I hate them after day one.

I also hate being in the hospital. There's no quiet. Machines are constantly beeping. Every time I start to fall asleep someone comes in to check on me. I react badly to one of the pain meds and throw it up into a silver pan held by a nurse, a friendly nurse, but a stranger who I don't know. The gravity of what just happened sinks in heavily. I don't have any regrets, I'm happy I did what I did, but this part of the process is harder than I thought. Every minute feels like an hour. I just want to go home, but I am woozy and thickheaded. Drugged. When the cleaning lady knocks over a framed photo of Mara and Storm, I react as if she'd just informed me she'd had them both killed. "Noooo!" I cry, hysterical. "*Noooo!*"

I stay two nights. My ticket home? Proof I can use the bathroom on my own. It's not easy, but I am desperate to leave. The woman next to me calls out to someone named José in her sleep. I feel sad for her: José, whoever he is, must be far away. My sister doesn't leave my side.

Getting to Mara's beat-up old Jetta is one of the most painful experiences of my life. Even after a huge shot of Demerol and two Percocets, my chest feels like someone took to it with a kitchen knife. I put a pillow over my chest and hold the seat belt strap in front of me. We take back roads, avoiding the freeway. I'm still groggy, not entirely with it, which is why it's only when we're at the front door of the loft in Astoria that I realize we're not at my studio in Williamsburg. "No," I wheeze to Mara as she opens the front door. "I don't live here anymore."

The loft is clean. Magazines stacked, blankets folded. Pale winter sunlight sparkles through spotless glass. A banner strung above the sofa: *Welcome Home, Lacey!* In smaller writing: *We Luv You and Yr New Boobies.*

"Hi!" It's Steph, wiping her hands on a pink apron that reads *Vagatarian* in looping script. "Welcome!"

Fresh flowers on the coffee table. Food is cooking, something warm and savory.

"Mara and I figured you might like your old room back for a few weeks," Steph says. "We split the rent to keep it for the month. That way Mara can stay at yours with Storm."

"We can take shifts looking after you," Mara says, dropping my hospital bag on the floor. "We just thought it'd be more comfortable than your place, which is so, you know: spatially challenged."

Stacks of pillows and wet wipes. A sippy cup. The La-Z-Boy, the remotes. It's all set up. For me.

I think I'm going to cry.

"Or not," Steph says, alarmed. "Up to you, we can definitely go back to plan A—"

"No, no." I'm welling up. "This is— You guys are—" Tears stream down my cheeks. "Sorry, it's all the meds. I'm just very touched," I announce, and promptly start weeping in earnest.

Steph and Mara surround me for an awkward three-way hug/shoulder pat that leaves a foot of air around my chest.

"Come on," Steph says. "Let's get you settled."

I hobble over clean wooden floorboards. I don't think they've ever been mopped before.

"Hope it won't be weird for you to sleep in Coop's bed," Steph says.

She doesn't know yet. I give a lopsided little laugh. "We're sort of past that. I'll tell you later."

The futon is neatly made, piled with the pillows I'll need to sleep sitting upright. More flowers on the desk. And a small leather trunk.

"He sent you something," Steph gestures to it. "A present. Said you'd understand."

I pop the trunk open. Inside, seven leather-bound books. On top of them, a note.

Let the adventure begin.
—NC

Naturally, Cooper has sent me the entire series of Harry Potter.

For the first time since I regained consciousness, I smile.

58.

Back scratchers. Wedge pillows. Button-down men's flannel shirts. Bendy straws. Thank God for bendy straws. One of my new secret weapons when it comes to life postmastectomy.

In the immediate days after my breasts volunteered as tribute, I am a mess. Not the hot kind. The mess kind. I feel like I've been hit by a bus. It hurts to take a deep breath. I sleep a lot. I cry a little. I try to read Harry Potter, but even that is too much for my foggy brain. I can watch TV, but only when the people onscreen have the IQ of a mango. My body is the aftermath of a bloody battle, still in the hysterical *What in God's name have you done?!* phase. I try to whisper this is all for its own good, that it was done with love and care, *I swear* . . . but my body is having none of that. Moving, in any way, is beyond awful. The pain is like nothing I've ever experienced before: cruel, quick, deep pain. Life revolves around my med schedule. I have a prescribed bottle of one hundred Percocet next to the microwave. I feel like Mick Jagger.

Steph empties the two drains that collect the pale pink postsurgery fluid (my body is used to hydrating tissue that's no longer there). It's supposed to get lighter and less over time. She keeps a log with the diligence of a cop on a stakeout: *Saturday, December 9, 12:35 p.m., left side 20 ml, right side 22 ml. Target remains grouchy and a little stinky.*

I can't shower until they remove the drains. My sister bathes me with giant wet wipes like a giant baby. After I go through an entire can of dry shampoo, she offers to wash my hair in the tub. This operation resembles an elephant being airlifted. But once I'm settled, head over the edge of the old bathtub, and my sister starts pouring warm water over my scalp, I start to relax. Mara massages shampoo that smells like oranges into my greasy hair. No sound except for the squeak-squish of her fingers. I close my eyes. I love how close she is to me. How gentle she's being. I wish she could do this for me every week.

A little sniffle. "Mar?" I look up. "What's wrong?"

She wipes her nose with the top of her shoulder. "Nothing. Just having some feelings."

"About what?"

She pauses for a long moment. When she speaks her voice is tender. "About you." Her fingers continue to dig into my scalp slowly.

I nestle closer to my sister and let her take care of me.

* * * *

Finally, I'm ready to see them. My foobs, the nickname the forums give to fake boobs. I wait until Mara, Steph, and Luna are all home. In front of Steph's bedroom mirror, we remove the compression bra and carefully unwrap the gauze. Part of me is hoping for a Christmas miracle, two perfect breasts, no scars, even better than the original with 100 percent sensation. But what I see almost makes me gag. My entire chest is swollen and bruised, a lurid paint palette of yellow, pink, and purple. Nothing like Luna's perfect rack at all. I try not to panic and instead make a joke. "I look like I've been in a fight. A vicious boob fight."

"That'll all go down eventually," Luna says, examining my chest. "Both your scars look great."

"Really?" I ask her. "Are you sure?"

She nods, authoritative. "You'll barely be able to see them once the sutures dissolve."

"It's not as bad as I thought it'd be," says Mara, frowning critically. "The shape looks good. I mean, they're not totally the same. But still, not bad."

"Are they wonky?" I turn forty-five degrees. I don't feel at all self-conscious of the girls examining my foobs. They don't yet feel like a part of me. "I think they're wonky."

"I don't think so," says Steph. "Honestly, Lace, I reckon you've got a couple of cracking foobs on your hands."

They're still too sore to investigate with my fingers. But maybe, hopefully, Steph's right.

* * * *

Cooper texts me every single day. Sometimes it's short and funny, sometimes long and introspective. Sometimes it's pictures—his office in the city, his new apartment in Kreuzberg—or a poem, or a link to something that made him think of me. He's liking his new job and he's loving Berlin. Every time his name appears on my phone, my chest glows warm. It's a brief, bright respite from the slow, heavy pain. But my brain, or maybe my heart, isn't working well enough to reply with the same frequency. I thank him for the books and tell him I miss him, but that's about it. Somehow, I know he doesn't mind that he doesn't hear from me every day. Somehow, I know he's willing to wait for me.

* * * *

Vivian visits. She brings a stack of salads from Sweetgreen, giving us a break from Steph's cheese-and-carb-focused culinary creations. In my nest of pillows and blankets and low, cozy light, her black leather pants and wing-tipped eyeliner are strikingly out of place. But I don't mind. It reminds me there is another life out there, waiting for me.

It's a short visit: I have the staying power of a newborn baby and things are still a bit strained between us. But as she's about to leave, she swivels back. "I just found out my cousin-in-law is BRCA positive."

"Shit," I say, the meds rendering me exceptionally eloquent.

"Crazy, right?" Viv shrugs. "I just thought, when you're ready, you could talk to her."

"Sure," I say. "Of course."

"She's really young. Twenty, I think. My mom says she's freaking out." Viv shoulders her bag. "I think it'd be good for her to meet other people who've gone through the same thing."

"Definitely," I say, thinking of Luna and Bee and all those endless hours on the forums. "It really helped me."

* * * *

Later, I'm mulling this over as I aimlessly scroll through Instagram. Perfect avocado toast, sunsets over city skylines, #makeupfree selfies from girls with flawless skin. My own feed is just as carefully curated: a perfect s'more in front of a crackling fire, a lovely stack of old books. I haven't posted since the surgery. I linger on my picture from Tom and Peter's wedding. Viv, Steph, and me, all grinning, bathed in afternoon light. Best friends forever without a care in the world. Ha.

Over the last few days, I've been sending Bee a steady stream of selfies. I find one from the day of my surgery. I'm in my disposable gown, hair in a paper net. I'm making a peace sign with a goofy face. I type:

> Four days ago, I chose to have a PDM, which all the hip kids know means #preventativedoublemastectomy because I'm #BRCA1 positive (Google it, nerds). I'm smiling because I knew when I woke up, I would FINALLY be free from the fear of getting breast cancer like my mom, the disease that ended her life at 31. But really, I was scared. I spent a lot of this year hiding that fear from the world and it made me feel pretty isolated. If you're a BRCA1 babe, YOU'RE NOT ALONE. #Foobs #savingmyowndamnlife.

I tag the New York Cancer Care Center and a few of the support organizations whose forums I lurk on. I post it. Five minutes later, I'm fast asleep.

* * * *

Mara is there when I wake up. We idle away the morning keeping up with Kardashians and their perfect, perfect butts. It's not until Steph gets home from the library midafternoon and she tells me she *loved* my post and how *proud* of me she is that it comes back to me hazily.

"Oh yeah," I yawn. "Vague recollection of that."

She drops her bag on the floor. "You haven't seen it?"

I have eighty new followers. Even more comments. *Go, girl! We're with you!* and *How are you feeling? I'm about to go through the same thing!* and *Hi from Tokyo, also BRCA1, also lost my mom.*

DMs from college friends. Texts from work friends. Emails from clients. An outpouring of surprise, curiosity, and support.

I stare at Steph, my mouth hanging open.

She could burst from pride. "I just think it's *so great,*" she says, plopping down next to me. "That you're reaching out to your *community.*"

Community? I scroll through the comments: women's stories of the same diagnosis, the same course of action. The same losses. "I suppose I am part of a community." My gaze lands on the last comment, left just six minutes ago. *BRCA1 in Ohio. Scared/alone/confused. Thanks for your post.*

That was me. Scared and alone and confused.

And just like that, Lacey Whitman is back on Instagram. But with a brand-new policy.

Radical honesty.

* * * *

Steph sets up a meal delivery spreadsheet for my friends to donate meals. This is New York—no one's about to bake a casserole—but hitting the buy button on Seamless, that's what New Yorkers are good at. Now that I've come out of the BRCA closet, so to speak, I don't care who knows. Bee sends lasagna and a bottle of vodka. Ash sends buckeyes and buffalo wings. Camila and Cam send sushi. Patricia sends everything off the menu at Le Coucou. And I keep posting.

I post a picture from my hospital bed when I managed a shaky thumbs-up for Bee, even with all my tubes and bandages and med haze.

I post a video of me walking for the first time after my surgery, shuffling like an old lady in my baggy hospital gown.

I post about how breast cancer is the most common form of cancer for women, and how important it is for every woman to know her body and her family history, and to get early screenings.

In the past, I just posted pictures with one-line captions or emojis. But now I find myself writing paragraphs about how I'm feeling and what I'm going through. I don't sugarcoat anything. If I catch myself slipping into bad 'Gram habits (e.g., Describing my recovery as "the perfect chance to rewatch the *Godfather* trilogy"), I stop myself and tell the truth—(a) I do not have the attention span for nine hours of complex cinema, and (b) I've never seen a single *Godfather* movie to begin with. And every time I do, I get so much positive feedback and a flood of followers connecting with me. Okay, so there are some nut-jobs posting their basement wankfest comments and a few misguided friends raving about how "lucky" I am to get new boobs (er, no—it was an amputation I didn't want to have), but for the most part: I'm feeling the love.

I knew I could get through this with Mara and Steph in my corner. But connecting with this community of "previvor" women from literally all around the world is truly astounding. Powerful. Meaningful.

It just feels so, so good.

* * * *

A couple of days before Christmas, I head back to NY3C to finally get the drains out. It's a significant step in my recovery. Once removed, I can shower on my own and am a lot more mobile. I'm still nowhere close to normal. I get tired quickly and I'm prone to feeling randomly sad. I still have to sleep on my back, which takes some getting used to. Ordinarily I'd never sleep in a bra but now I can't imagine sleeping without it—it helps me feel like the implants aren't sitting on the exterior of my chest but are moving deeper to become part of my own body. I can't pull a door open on my own, I have to use my shoulder or feet to shove it open. When I walk around the neighborhood, I hold my arm in front of my chest like a shield or a crazy person.

But, my foobs are healing. I have more freedom of movement. I don't have to second-guess every time I lift my arms. The day I reach up to grab a packet of tea from a high shelf without thinking is a certifiable victory. And my attention span is increasing. As the city decks itself in boughs of holly (fa-la-la-la-la), I crack open a story about a boy wizard.

At first I tell myself I'm just trying to kill time: the winter nights are long and dark, especially for someone under house arrest. But as the year crawls to a snowy, slushy end, I find myself returning to Hogwarts again and again. Not just because the story has literally zero to do with preventive surgeries. Wrapped in his old wool blanket, drinking hot chocolate out of his Cal Bears mug, I feel close to the boy whose old room I'm sleeping in. On New Year's Eve, when I insist everyone go out without me, I get to the part where (spoiler alert!) Dumbledore dies. I'm weeping, and it's not just the meds.

My father must've been devastated when Mom died. I don't remember this—his grief, how overwhelmed he must've felt at losing his wife and suddenly being tasked with raising two daughters on his own. For the first time, I feel a profound, aching sorrow for Dad, and what he went through, all those years ago.

I open Cooper's message thread and type *Dumbledore* 🙁.

Minutes later, a reply.

Giving you a virtual hug. I miss you, Lace.

I write back.

Me too.

59.

April

J udy-Ann McMallow's office still smells like a hot cinnamon bun. The last time I was here, over one year ago, it felt like the walls were closing in on me. Now, it is Mara who has that look on her face as we sit across from the genetic counselor, awaiting Mara's results.

My sister decided to get tested for the BRCA1 gene mutation three weeks before her thirty-first birthday. Originally, she didn't want to see a genetic counselor. After an hour of passionate negotiation, I convinced her to meet with Judy-Ann to talk through both possible outcomes, and then take the test with her: what I should've done in the first place. She insisted on going alone, so I waited for her in the café next door. When she met me afterward, she looked pale. I could tell she'd been crying. But she didn't look broken. She looked resolute. "I'm glad I did it," was all she said. "Now we wait and see."

It's not her own health she's most worried about.

It's Storm's.

I've been thinking a lot about family these past few months. What we pass down and what gets passed down to us. The gifts we're given and the cycles we work to break. It wasn't until I had my mastectomy that I realized how much anger I was carrying. Anger directed at my father, but also at my mother. I was angry they'd left me, one purposefully, one not. I was angry at the ways I was like them: in my genetic makeup and in my personality. I was angry because I felt vulnerable. I was scared. Scared of being alone. Being abandoned. Being left behind in a city like New York. And while that fear has not magically evaporated, recognizing it and looking it in the face has helped dissipate it. I don't feel as scared anymore. I feel more sure of myself as an individual. I am the child of two complicated people but I am my own person. I have agency. I feel sure of my friends. I feel sure of my community. I feel sure of my sister, sitting beside me, holding my hand with an iron grip.

"Whatever happens," I say, "I'm here for you. We'll get through this, okay?"

I was feeling strong this morning, confident that Mara would be negative. But as we sit in the waiting room, tension fills my body. My chest—a site of many strange phantom pains these past few months—is a new kind of tight.

I'm more than just scared for her. I'm terrified. I know what this knowledge brings. I know what it puts you through.

My diagnosis was out of the blue. The anxiety about hers has been building for weeks.

Mara is breathing shallowly. I can feel her heartbeat. She's sitting ramrod straight. Every muscle is tense. I'd always associated this posture with my sister's anger: I thought it meant she was mad. Now I see, she's just scared.

Judy-Ann sits across from us. She has a large white envelope in her hands. We watch her pull a single sheet of paper out. She looks up at us, speaking in her calm counselor voice. "I have your test result here." Her tone is neutral: neither celebratory nor watchful.

Mara lets out a small whimper.

I break out in a sweat. My teeth are chattering. I clench my jaw.

Please don't let her have it. Please, please, please.

Judy-Ann clears her throat. "Mara, you have tested negative for the BRCA1 gene mutation."

My sister lets out a strangled cry. Her entire body collapses forward. "Oh my God," she moans. "Oh, thank God."

Hot tears spill down my cheeks. I'm shaking. "Are you sure?" I demand. "Are you absolutely sure?"

"Yes, I'm sure." Judy-Anne smiles. "A completely clear test."

My sister starts sobbing, her face buried in her hands. "I don't have it. She doesn't have it. She doesn't have it."

"That's right," Judy-Ann says. "There's no way you could have passed this down to your daughter."

"She's safe," Mara weeps. "She's safe. My baby's safe."

I'm crying now, my arms around my sister. I can't quite feel where my breasts touch her: that part of my chest is numb now. But I feel everything else. "You're safe too, Mar! You're safe too."

"I'm safe," Mara says, her body shaking with sobs. "I'm safe and she's safe and so are you. Oh, thank God. Thank God."

We sit there together, crying and holding each other.

My sister is safe. And she is here, with me.

60.

June

In the Luxembourg Gardens, Parisians sits on mint-green metal chairs facing the beds of red and yellow tulips. The manicured grass lawns are dotted with hundreds of sunbathers in barely-there bikinis. The park was built in 1612, the biggest in Paris, and like everything in this city, is beautiful and romantic and utterly dreamy on a summer's afternoon. I've been coming here most days with a *café au lait* and *pain au chocolat*, to sit in the fragrant, dappled sunlight and watch the world go by.

Beyond the grand limestone buildings and twinkling Eiffel Tower, Paris is full of delightful eccentricity. Like the tiny elevators that only fit two people or the fact you get a baguette as a side with everything, even burgers. In the supermarket, the cashiers sit on stools and they have an entire aisle devoted solely to yogurt. Cops on Rollerblades whiz past rows of tiny cars packed bumper-to-bumper on narrow streets. Everything opens after midday and closes after midnight. Everyone smokes, even the chic mothers pushing frilly strollers. Everyone downs daily double espressos, including me, drunk side by side with the office workers crowded at the café counter. Yesterday, I listened to someone play a piano in the subway (the Métro de Paris) for half an hour. In the morning, the cool air smells like butter and freshly baked bread. By the afternoon, it's sweat and camembert.

Paris is sophisticated and sensual. Or perhaps, that's what it brings out in me.

The sun is warm on my skin. I'm wearing sunscreen but no foundation: I see freckles when I look in the mirror now. I close my eyes and inhale slowly, trying to still my heartbeat. Usually, I bring a book or magazine to read in the Jardin du Luxembourg. But today, I'm jittery. I can't drink my coffee.

I'm excited.

I'm waiting.

I've been here for a week on my own. A week of strolls along the Seine and getting lost in the Louvre and taking in the afternoon with a cheese plate and a chilled kir, like the locals drink. But today my solo adventure ends.

He's coming to meet me.

We promised to do summer in Paris together, after all.

"Are you sure?" Steph had asked, watching me pack with obvious concern. "It's a long way to go, if things don't work out."

"I'm sure," I'd replied. "One thousand percent."

It was always going to be him. Everyone in the world could see that.

And there he is. Right on time.

The sight of him, so effortlessly sexy in a white T-shirt and wire-rimmed glasses, makes me want to laugh out loud. I want to throw myself on him, devour him whole. But I don't need to rush this. I almost want to see how long I can last before I need to kiss him.

"*Hallo*," I call as he approaches. "*Schön dich hier zu sehen.*"

Cooper laughs, and it is such a beautiful sound, I want to hear it every day. "You're learning German. Of course you are. I bet you'll pick it up really quickly."

"Why do you think that?"

"Because you're smart," he says. "You're really clever; it'll be easy for you."

We stare at each other, amazed idiotic grins on our faces. I start laughing. I'm just so happy.

He pulls me close, wrapping my arms around his torso. He feels strong and solid, like he always does. My nose on his T-shirt, I breathe in his scent. I want every part of us to be touching, always. "How'd I get so lucky?" he murmurs, running his fingers through my hair. "To meet a woman who's smart and beautiful and crazy enough to move to Germany with me."

I can't wait anymore. I pull his mouth to mine, and we kiss. It's hungry and passionate and very, very French. It's been so long since I've seen him, been able to touch him. And now, I get to see him and touch him every day. Because yes, I'm moving to Germany with Noam Cooper. It is the single most daring thing I have ever done, and that includes everything on my bucket list, and the reason for it. But I don't feel afraid. I feel alive.

I'm leaving a lot behind. I'm leaving Steph and Mara and Storm and Bee. I'm leaving New York, my tiny studio snapped up within hours of being back on the market. I'm leaving my job and I don't have another one. I don't know what I'll do for work in Berlin, and that is the most un–Lacey Whitman thing about all this. It wasn't an easy decision. I'm nervous about being in a new city with no support system outside one person. But I have faith. In Cooper. In us. And most importantly, in myself. I used to see the future as something I could master, through hard work and sacrifice. Now, I don't have as many expectations. I'm curious about the future. A little apprehensive, but open to whatever happens.

Cooper's fingers graze the side of my foob. I can't really feel the sensation of his fingertips on my breasts anymore. But I feel a lot more than I used to. My body and my heart are both wide-awake.

On the back of my hotel door, a dress is hanging. Black stretch jersey with a plunging neckline all the way to my torso. It's the last thing on my bucket list: my boobs-on-parade dress, the sexiest thing I have ever owned. When I tried it on this morning, in anticipation of the decadent Michelin-starred dinner date I'm taking Cooper on later tonight, I noticed a few inches of pale pink scar circling under either breast. But I don't care that you can see the scars, or that I'm a few pounds heavier than I was this time last year.

My body feels like a triumph to me.

My scars are beautiful. They're just another part of me.

We break apart. Everything in me is on fire.

Cooper grins, an open and easy grin. "I love you."

"Whoa." I take a step back.

His grin broadens, completely unfazed. "Does that scare you?"

I think about it. "No," I say. "I love you. I think."

He laughs. "You think?"

"I'm pretty sure. It's a distinct possibility."

His voice is low, almost a tease. "Let me convince you." He kisses me again. This time, it's slower. Gentler. As if I'm the only woman in the world. Because that's what I feel like right now, standing here in the Luxembourg Gardens, with all my worldly possessions waiting for me in a foreign country I've never even been to. I am confident and brave. My body is mine to enjoy.

I feel like a woman.

We break apart. Sunlight slants across our skin, turning us golden.

I smile at my boyfriend. "I'm hungry," I say. "Let's go find something to eat."

Arm in arm, we move forward into the afternoon, in search of our next great adventure.

Acknowledgments

While reading a novel is a private experience, writing one is very much a collaboration. Here are the fine folk who helped dream this book into being.

I'm so very grateful to my powerhouse editor, Emily Bestler of Emily Bestler Books, for taking a chance on my "sexy mastectomy" novel. Huge thanks to everyone at Atria/Simon & Schuster, especially the lovely Lara Jones, superstar publicists Stephanie Mendoza and Alison Hinchcliffe, and cover genius Kelly Blair.

I'm lucky to have the best agent in the biz, Allison Hunter at Janklow & Nesbit, whose diehard enthusiasm for this novel started with an email entitled OH MY GOD IT'S SO GOOD and only grew from there. Thanks also to Clare Mao for thoughtful notes/spreadsheets/Instagram-ming. To the fantastic Chelsea Lindman for getting the ball rolling. To Stefanie Diaz for foreign rights.

Sarah Cypher, will you always be my freelance editor and never leave me?! Collaborating on our third book together has been, as always, an absolute dream. Your ability to see the big picture and break it down for me in a way that's understandable and achievable is something I am so, so grateful for. Ready for the next one?

Thanks to Jason Richman at UTA, and his right-hand man, Sam Reynolds. Always so fun to have an excuse to come to Beverly Hills and pretend to be fancy!

I'm thrilled to have the chance to work once again with the irrepressible Crystal Patriarche and co. at BookSparks. Thank you for being so firmly on Team Georgia and spreading the word about my work far and wide.

I am not at risk for hereditary cancer, nor have I had a preventive surgery. I was only able to bring Lacey's story to life through the generosity and openness of those in the previvor and breast cancer community. It was an honor to enter this world, and be shown around by so many extraordinary individuals. Thank you to everyone who spoke with me and shared their experience. First up, my badass BRCA babes: Caitlin Brodnick, Cara Scharf, Grace Talusan, and Tina Moya Zotovich, who all shared stories of their preventative mastectomies, patiently answered my endless questions, and gave important feedback on early drafts. Thanks to Sue Friedman and Karen Singer at FORCE for trusting me enough to let me in. Dr. Andy Salzberg explained one-step mastectomies. Angela Arnold and Mary Freivogel introduced me to the world of genetic counselors. Dr. Neil Collier weighed in on the medical stuff.

Thanks to Anneke Jong for schooling me on start-ups and answering "just one more question." *So* fun to connect with Ellen Sideri and Lindsey Smecker at ESP Trendlab. I knew nothing about trend forecasting when I started this book, but you ladies soon changed that!

Cheers to Nora Wilkinson for an insightful early read.

I created the outline for this book at Ragdale, in Lake Forest, Illinois, and worked on the drafts at the New York Writers Room: both essential spaces for authors. I adore my extended writing fam: thank you to all my fellow scribes who are so quick to cheer me on or commiserate, whatever the twisty turns the life of the writer calls for. #Bookstagram crew: #blessed every time I'm a #currentread. Many kisses for my sweet pals in Brooklyn (especially Noz/JT/Foxy/Big D/ Iz), and my friends in LA and Sydney. Big thanks to the loyal Generation Women community, especially Jessica Paugh and Camila Salazar, for helping create my dream storytelling night.

Lindsay Ratowsky, the last book was dedicated to you, and even though this one isn't, it kind of is, in that everything I do is dedicated to you. Sweet girl, I love you infinitely. Thank you for being my girlfriend, my best friend, my first reader, and my everything else. You delight me every single day; I'm so lucky to be yours. Also, hi, Chris, Craig, Justin, Erika, and all the Ratowsky fam. Love you guys!

Thanks to my family: Mum, Dad, Will, Louise, and adorable Evie. The hardest thing about living in New York is being far away from you. I feel lucky that we have such a loving, peaceful, fun family.

This book is dedicated to my dear friend, Nick "Nicki-Pee" Salzberg. A lover and a fighter, Nick passed away from complications related to T-cell lymphoma in January 2017. Nick was a part of the first family I made independent of my own, in Sydney, around the turn of the millennium. With his black eyeliner and razor-sharp tongue, Nick was a central part of every house party, every protest, every creative pursuit. He was political, funny, and fearless. The last time I saw Nick was at my Sydney book launch for *The Regulars* in August 2016. He had just started his fourth cycle of chemo and was very fragile, but he came, in a red scarf and blond wig, and sat in the second row. In the Q and A after the reading, he asked, with a shy, sweet smile, a question about the importance of queer visibility in my fiction. Nick taught me many things, but what resonates with me is his queerness, which felt unique and unapologetic. He was no cookie-cutter gay boy, as I doubt exists anywhere. To know Nick was to know someone grappling with the world, but not his sense of self. Nicki will always remind me to seek difference, in myself and in those around me. I love you, darling boy. You will always be with me.